Walking the Stones of Time

Walking the Stones of Time

Oswald Brown

Copyright © 2014 by Oswald Brown.
Cover Illustration by Gil Balbuena Jr.

Library of Congress Control Number:		2014915890
ISBN:	Hardcover	978-1-4990-6909-9
	Softcover	978-1-4990-6910-5
	eBook	978-1-4990-6911-2

All rights reserved. No part of this book may be reproduced or transmitted in any form or by any means, electronic or mechanical, including photocopying, recording, or by any information storage and retrieval system, without permission in writing from the copyright owner.

This is a work of fiction. Names, characters, places and incidents either are the product of the author's imagination or are used fictitiously, and any resemblance to any actual persons, living or dead, events, or locales is entirely coincidental.

Any people depicted in stock imagery provided by Thinkstock are models, and such images are being used for illustrative purposes only.
Certain stock imagery © Thinkstock.

This book was printed in the United States of America.

Rev. date: 09/22/2014

To order additional copies of this book, contact:
Xlibris LLC
1-888-795-4274
www.Xlibris.com
Orders@Xlibris.com
650802

Contents

Prologue		11
Chapter 1		13
Chapter 2	Pender's Adventure to Slave Island	19
Chapter 3	Pender Meets Mari and Zari	25
Chapter 4	Kain's Treachery	30
Chapter 5	Zalenda	41
Chapter 6	Rahana	66
Chapter 7	Pender and Zalenda Find Kain and Deal with Abbi	83
Chapter 8	Becca	96
Chapter 9	The Mission to the Warrior Women Tribe	101
Chapter 10	The Missions to the Cave People and the Great Forest People	109
Chapter 11	The Destruction of the Barge	125
Chapter 12	The Plan to Rescue Castor	129
Chapter 13	Castor Lifts the Doan Stone	136
Chapter 14	The New Chief of the Tribe	155
Chapter 15	The Teams Go Out on Their Missions	167
Chapter 16	Rahana's Revenge	180
Chapter 17	Remi's Treachery Revealed	188
Chapter 18	The Mole Discovered and Punished	193
Chapter 19	The Team to Warn the Tribes of Tamor's Plan	196
Chapter 20	The Breakup With Zalenda, the Queen in Waiting	208
Chapter 21	Gena and Lacey Join the Team	212

Chapter 22	The Bitterness of the Bile of the Soul	221
Chapter 23	The Mission to Rescue Rona	226
Chapter 24	Remi's Treachery Punished	231
Chapter 25	Cymon and Zalenda Switch Sides	236
Chapter 26	The Destruction of the Barge	242
Chapter 27	The View from the Top	245
Chapter 28	Becca Is Wounded on Her Mission Home	248
Chapter 29	Zalenda's Return and Reconciliation	256
Chapter 30	The Dogs Bring Victory out of Disaster	263
Chapter 31	The Great Storm	266
Chapter 32	The Journey to the Palace and Establishing the New Order	283
Chapter 33	Pender and the Lost World	293
Chapter 34	The Valley of the Flies	310
Chapter 35	Zalenda's Search for Pender	322
Chapter 36	The Plan to Free Carla	333
Chapter 37	The Missions in the Lost World	344
Chapter 38	Zalenda's Journey to Find Pender in the Lost World	354
Chapter 39	The Mission against the Baldheads	359
Chapter 40	The Journey Home	376
Chapter 41	Rici and Raymond—the Prelude to War	382
Chapter 42	The Search and Apprehension of Rici	387
Chapter 43	Raymond's Army and the Coming Storm	393
Chapter 44	The Tribes Prepare for the Coming War	403
Chapter 45	The Day of the Burning Rock	405

The People of the Lost World

The hero Pender of the Island People
The heroine Zalenda of the Warrior Women

The family

Castor, the Great Chief of the Island and Settlement People, Pender's father
Brid, Castor's wife, and Pender's mother
Lay, Castor's second wife
Kain, Pender's older brother
Cisi, Pender's oldest sister
Ester, Pender's second sister who is two years older than him.
Abbi, Pender's uncle on his mother's side
Brini, Pender's friend and mentor
Seth, Pender's uncle on his mother's side
Rici, Pender's cousin, Seth's son
Tina, Pender's cousin

The Team

Pender, the leader
Zalenda, coleader and love of his life, a Warrior Woman
Mari and Zari from the Treetop People
Rahana from the Cave People
Becca from the Water People
Rona, Pipa, Morag, Nena, Ester, and Tina from the Island and Settlement People
Mini and Marta from the M People
Lilly, Lara, Nanci, Ena from the Mystic People
Lena, a displaced person
Elecia from the Nuit Tribe
Carla, the mystic woman from the Mystic People

The Family Tribes

The Island and Settlement People
The Treetop People of the Great Forest
The Cave People
The Water People
The Warrior Women Tribe (The People of the Plains)
The Nuit Tribe (the redheads)
The Auit People (nomadic)
The M People
The Mystic People
The Bald-Headed People
The North Winds Tribe

The Slave Traders and Scoundrels

Tamor, chief of the Nuit Tribe
Somer, Benic, and Rolf, slave traders
Bisram, slave trader
Taaker, slave trader
Raymond, transporter of the slave trade
Dayton, chief of the Water People

The Traitors

Abbi, Pender's uncle
Castor, Pender's father
Kain, Pender's brother
Rici, Pender's cousin
Seth, Pender's uncle
Remi, Rona's brother
Cymon, former team member
Aron, Bart, Caleb, Josh, former team members

Other Characters

Tomi, the old merchant
Bobi, the merchant hired to find Pender
Mac from the Nuit Tribe
Marsha, Rahana's older sister
Zarena, Lena's baby
Merca, chief of the M People
Eram, the wall artist and chief person among the Mystic People

The Dogs

Tarag, Toto, Rollo

Prologue

This is a fantasy of time that might have been long before recorded history was written, of a people who existed and left their signs of being here not only on the strange standing stones we pass daily without seeing them but also in the customs and the way they lived. As they lived, we live, trying to avoid some of the same scourges of society such as human trafficking and the enslavement of the unfortunates in our world.

It is a love story of an awkward young man and an equally awkward young woman, who, despite their lack of social skills, forged a love that was stronger than all of their inadequacies. A love that was immediate, romantic, and compelling, even overcoming the torture of her soul.

It is a story of treachery overcome by the most unlikely means by the resolve, courage, and fidelity of one man and twenty young women, the team, against overwhelming odds. Indeed it is the story of the perfidy of men and the fidelity of women.

Today in our own time, we learn almost every day of young girls being kidnapped to satisfy the appetites of the human traffickers of our modern world, sold as slaves into the sex trade's ferocious needs and appetites for younger and younger girls. Even now in our somewhat enlightened world, organizations exist to prevent the sale of young six-year-old girls, being sold to work in the sweatshops of some Eastern manufacturers so that unscrupulous merchants can enjoy greater profits. I cannot wield Rahana's club. Is the pen mightier than the club? Perfidy or fidelity? That is the question this story is asking you.

Chapter 1

The sun had risen early that morning. It had for the past four weeks, which was unusual for that time of year. In fact everything was most unusual. A drought that had brought with it the lowest levels of water in the lakes and hill dams in centuries had changed dramatically the character of the countryside. The rivers that fed them were mere dribbles of their normal rushing, gushing, glorious selves, and the fields were producing late harvests never experienced in living memory. Absolutely no rain! Day after day of blue skies from morning till night, with just the occasional wisp of cloud floating over the majestic hills. The ice cream trucks played their bells on every street, long into the evenings. Unusual! I say it was unusual.

I dressed in a hurry. I wanted to experience this new day, in this new world of home that I had left so long ago. I looked out of the window to see the hills. The view was spectacular; the hills were truly alive with color. The brilliant morning light streamed down producing a kaleidoscope of green ferns, yellow broom, and purple heather establishing its dominance and gave the glorious shape and outline of the hills against an azure blue sky. This is what I had come home to see. However, as I watched a lone black cloud drifted across the face of the hills from the east, would that change this unusual day? It seemed to stop in its track and for a moment. The perfect day seemed in jeopardy. I put on a light rain jacket at the front door where the rain was falling without too much enthusiasm. I wondered whether I should risk my new running shoes on the dirty roads, but just then the rain stopped, and I was off on an adventure I would remember forever.

The front gate closed behind me, and I remembered to put the slip bolt in place. This was according to my sister's strict instruction—to keep her border collie from doing his escape protocol and to protect her next-door neighbor's chickens. This task completed, I picked up the long walking stick I had purchased the day before and took the old wagon road in the direction of the Nature Park that contained the old dam. When I was a boy, it had been illegal to fish or bathe in the water of the dam; but of course, this had not applied to us. Any opportunity for adventure, which included the chance to explore the island near the point where the old lake and the dam met, was a challenge that could not be ignored by young boys and girls. So it was often, with or without our swimming gear, I led them many times in these illegal activities. But today my interest was piqued for a different reason. I had read in the local paper that the dam was at its lowest level ever and that soon people would be able to walk to the island. This was most unusual.

As I reached the bridge over the wagon road, a very surprised driver of an old dirty van gave me the horn and passed me in a shower of dust and dirt. I supposed he was not in the habit of seeing people on the road this early in the morning. When he disappeared in the morning air, I noticed on the back of the van that he was the local veterinarian. I mused within that I almost got killed so that he could save an animal. Still, the day was young, and I was alive to enjoy it. I stopped at the top of the hill to view the river and the farms beyond. Little had changed here in the fifty years since I had run these roads and fields. I unwrapped my camera and spent some time clicking away, thrilled with the changes in what had been a planting of saplings trees, now mighty oaks. I continued on with my walk climbing the hundred steps up to the dam head. What I saw when I stepped onto the dam wall was worse than I had anticipated. The normal expanse of the water was only clear fifty yards from the wall, a drop in a bucket, compared to what it had been. The rest of the basin that had contained the wide spacious lake formed millenniums ago was like a swamp on one side of the island and a sandy mud mixture on the other. The new part that had been dug by hand a century ago, to drive the local brewers and woolen mills, had drained down past the depth markers, leaving perhaps three to four feet of water. If I was going to walk to the island, the only way possible, it seemed, was to transverse miles of mud and muck.

Skirting the shore of the lake was very pleasant because the established nature trail followed its wandering ways. The sun was brighter now, and the larks were singing high above the water. It was just an idyllic situation. On the steep hill fields to the east, farmers were gathering the last of their wheat and corn harvests. To the west, in a still vibrant green field, I could hear the bawling of a cow in great distress. I gazed at all this beauty and observed in the corner of the field an old gray van. Now it was clear to me—this was why the vet was in such a hurry; his patient was in great pain and needed immediate attention As I walked, I replayed in my mind the number of times I had illegally swam to the island from the opposite shore, a much shorter distance than I was now planning. But even from here I could see the insurmountable difficulties that would be involved because of the slough. I was right on top of the ridge that ran from the moor down through the depths of the dam before I recovered from my reverie. The water here was dirty, brackish, and full of decaying vegetation. I looked for a possible way through and was not too successful. Every time I took a step, I sank up to the middle of my calf, and it was only with great effort I managed to pull myself out of the quagmire. I retraced my steps back to the ridge and was about to give up in frustration and disappointment. I was extremely thankful that I had the presence of mind to bring my long walking stick, for without it, I would never have been able to escape the swamp. The next operation was to free myself from the clinging mud. I scraped it off the best I could with a piece of wood from my legs, socks, and shoes, and then washed them off with the dirty water. It was while I was bending low over the water I noticed what appeared to be flat stones just under the water level, four to five feet apart, following the line of the ridge. I took my stick and tested what lay between the stones and found to my great surprise that the rock of the ridge seemed to have been cut down by some ancient stone workers to create columns topped with stepping stones. Each stone was carved from this very hard ridge rock, which had stood the test of time, water, weather, and wear. The stones, which were just visible, appeared to have been well traveled, worn more in the center than the outsides, indicating that the travelers had intimate knowledge of their presence. I made up my mind I would follow in their footsteps. I was excited at the prospect of discovering something that had existed here in the old lake perhaps from ancient times, now only made visible by this drastic drought.

The sun was now reaching its zenith, and the air was warm with absolutely no breeze to carry away the sounds of a normal day in the country. The voices of the people working in the fields rang out as they laughed and joked while they tried to dodge the midges. From the moor a way back behind me, the birds rose to celebrate in song, each adding its own peculiar sound to the choir. From everywhere around the basin of the lake that day, nature's intent was to be heard—the bees around me, the crows high up in the great oaks on the island, sheep and lambs in the fields. Away to my right, a clucking cockerel with his little party of admiring hens and, of course, the bawling cow. It was just a very pleasant cacophony of sound unlike the roar of the highway traffic I had experienced these last few days. This had its own peace.

I sat down on the ridge rock to consider how best to walk the stones. The mile or so to the island would be a slow onerous journey, and I could only see a path of stepping stones for about the first fifty yards. I decided my long walking stick could be of value for balance, so I disposed of my other nonessentials on a nice slate six feet back from the water's edge. These would be safe here till I returned.

I slung my camera over my shoulder and placed my sun hat over my already sweating head and took my first step out onto the swamp. After making five steps of about four feet each, I realized that the stones were quite smooth on my bare feet. But balance was essential because one slip and I would be in that deep slough of putrid decaying water plants and mud. Each step therefore was taken with great care, and I moved only to the next one when I was sure of its location and direction. I soon got into a cadence, step locate, step locate, and rest. At each rest I tested with my stick to see if I was still walking along the underwater ridge. I was more and more convinced that this had been constructed by workers from an ancient past and not the dam diggers. I was now almost halfway to the island, and it was here I faced my first anomaly. The forward direction of the stones stopped. One pathway seemed to go in the direction of the east of the island and the other to the west of the island. At the junction, about two stones ahead, I could see a larger white stone, which stood out in contrast to all of the others because they were made of the red ridge rock. Now I had to make a decision, east or west. I made my decision; I would take the eastern pathway away from the dam side because it appeared that the island was easier accessed from the long point, which seemed to run down on a nice low slope to the merse. Whether that decision affected what happened next, I will never know. I placed my left foot on the stone with extreme care. It suddenly moved, and I was caught completely off guard; something was terribly wrong. The stone moved again. I had both feet firmly planted in place when the stone began to turn, and I turned with it. Spinning at an ever-increasing speed like some crazy theme park ride, I was not enjoying the ride. Everything had changed in the batting of an eyelid, and my world changed with it, down, down, down. I was losing consciousness, but the spiral never seemed to be completed. I screamed loud and long, but no one heard. Suddenly the world stopped revolving, and I was in a world away back in time. It was unbearably cold. The green fields with the cattle grazing were gone; the laughter of the young people in the fields, gone; the choir of birds, gone; the bawling cow in its extreme pain, gone; everything I knew from a few moments ago, gone. In its place I saw a bare landscape of rocks wild and desolate. I thought for a few moments that perhaps I had landed on the moon. But the moor was the same, however; it took up the whole area where the beautiful verdant fields had been. I turned on the stone, and I saw the island. I could not understand it, but I could not deny it; there was the island, completely bereft of its beautiful oak trees, nothing but a barren piece of reddish rock with a much-transformed lake lapping at its shores.

I shuddered with the cold and stood transfixed when I saw what appeared to be smoke rising from a dome like rock in the middle where I knew the ruin of an old monastery had been. I was conscious of a mist rising, obliterating everything from view, the lake, the island, the moor; all were gone in this all-encompassing mist, and I was suspended in the mists of time.

I was no longer in my own time. I was in a long ago time, among the old people, the old people who must have had an existence here, the old people who had lived here but who had no history because they had no one to tell it. They had been lost from time, for millennia, leaving little or no trace of having been here. Was that why the stone had brought me back through the tunnels of time, to see what might have been? The story of families and tribes, people who left indelible marks on their environment that we were too blind to see. I now knew my destiny and why the stone had brought me here, out of my time into theirs—could this be their stories?

Chapter 2

Pender's Adventure to Slave Island

The screaming stopped.

Pender tried hard to concentrate as he moved in and out of consciousness. When the screaming started again, he could not tell whether the screaming was coming from deep inside him or from someone else. He blacked out feeling pain like he had never felt before, but this relief was only temporary because the screaming started again, this time from far, far away.

Then he remembered everything.

That day had started like any other day. Pender was working in the brewhouse as he usually did at this time of year, mashing down the corn, barley, and hops in boiling water into a liquid slurry to start the fermentation process. The mashing and stirring would usually take the whole day, and his hands were sore, red, and rough; even wearing leather pads made little difference. It was mindless work that had to be done, as the people depended on this production for their beer, mead, and ale. He had been doing this for six years since he was twelve; it was heavy work because the mashing tools were heavy made for grown men. They were made out of white oak so it would not flavor the produce. It was unusual to mix the grains, but the small fields where they grew had been raided by a much-smaller family tribe just a few weeks back that had been nearing starvation. With starvation being the motivating factor, they had raided the family tribe of Castor the Great, Pender's father, knowing full well that retribution would be swift and terrible. They had wasted no time in tearing down their own poor buildings of turf and wood branches and fleeing the area, leaving the sick to die and their servant girls to mercies of others or the slavers, most likely the latter. Castor had become chief through the normal methods for his tribe. Every candidate had to be able to lift the Great Doan Stone, which stood in the middle of the island. Castor was a giant of a man, head and shoulders over everyone in the tribe. When challenged for the chiefdom, he simply walked up to the stone, grabbed it by the handholds, and easily lifted the stone and carried it a distance equal to its height, this being according to the rules of the old people. This feat alone gave him absolute control of the tribe, and he ruled it with a strong hand; he was no man to be trifled with.

Pender, as his father's son, had little or no privileges in the scheme of things in the family tribe; he was assigned day after day to mix the mash. This day he was oblivious to anything as he scraped the mix out of its stone container. He had been told the story over and over again from Brini, the old man who was his mentor in the brew outhouse. Thanks to Brini's penchants for storytelling, Pender knew the history of the tribe and how they were all related to the people on the other shore, who were uncles, aunts, brothers, and sisters, and how they all owed allegiance to Castor. Even the implements they used were a wonder to Brini, how everything they had was made, and made so long ago before he was born. In particular he was proud of the big mixing basin that they used in nearly every aspect of the brew. He would rhyme off the dimension three sticks deep, four sticks wide, and quarter stick walls. He was equally proud of his knowledge that it had been chiseled out by hand using long flint tools. But Pender was not really interested in these old things today, although he did listen with great courtesy and attention. His real interest today was to complete the mash process and leave the now-liquid brew to ferment. This involved counting black pebbles, one for each day, from a clay container that was full into an empty one, thus counting of the time to absolute fermentation. When the second one was filled, the brew would be strained through cloth bags until all the sediment was removed. It would then be poured into skins, and the counting process was employed again, this time with white pebbles. Finally, it was moved along a hanging bar in an enclosed area, newly filled skins on one side more mature on the other. When the pebbles told them it was time, they were moved to where it was deemed to be fit for consumption, and these were definitely consumed.

Pender had been on pins and needles since last evening. Abbi, his uncle on his mother's side, came back from the Slave Port on the Big River with orders from Castor that Pender was to accompany Brini back to Slave Island; they were to take two skins of mead each. The business of buying and selling slaves must have been going well for such a request to be made, as it was only yesterday that Pender had supplied them with four skins of the best they had, four very potent brews.

It was easy to get off the island on the moor side because that side of the lake was frozen over, not so the opposite side nearest the land settlement. That neck of water was open all year round because of the hot springs, which at different times would affect the island crossing and the temperature on the island, especially inside the building where the floor was always warm. Much to the chagrin of the people in the settlement, they had to ply back and forth all year pulling supplies across on a wooden raft, and it was pulling! The raft was attached to an endless cord made of plaited leather strips covered with animal fat. When he was ten, Pender had spent the whole summer pulling on that cord; his hands were sore just at the memory of it.

Today he had none of these worries; he was off on a great adventure. Brini rode the little garron horse with the four skins attached, and Pender trotted along side, excited and in wonder at all that he saw. They went over the moor rather than take the river route because it was easier on the little horse. The river route would have taken them to Slave Island faster, but it was a beautiful day, sunny and very cool, so they conspired to enjoy their outing away from the brew room. Once they were off the moor, they were able to travel faster because the path to Slave Island was well worn by the unfortunates who had lost their freedom and were on their way to be sold as slaves.

Slave Island was not what Pender had anticipated. The island was just a flat slab of mud in the center of the Big River; a wooden bridge connected it to the main land. A wooden palisade reared up from the muddy banks of the island, and it seemed to run the full length and breadth of it. There was not a space that was not packed with human beings. The fence was at least three to four times the height of a normal person, and the fencing slats were so close together that you could barely see the faces of those on the inside. From the elevated position where they were, Pender could see over the fence and look into the faces of the unfortunate prisoners who would soon be on the selling block.

One tall young girl with blonde hair stood out among the crowd. She was amazingly calm, surveying the scene with clear blue eyes that did not appear to be in fear of her fate. She was dressed in a leather skirt and tunic with a wide belt that contained a pouch, where it was obvious that a weapon had been. Her legs were long and slim; the leather legging tied with leather laces and the wooden soled sandal seemed to accentuate her height. She was the most beautiful girl he had ever seen. He made up his mind there and then, this would be his mission in life—no matter how long it would take and where it would take him, he would free this young woman from slavery.

He asked Brini, "Why is she here and where did she come from?" His answer was not what Pender had expected.

"She is a dangerous one that comes from a tribe of Warrior Women who do the fighting and where the men stay at home and work the fields. Keep away from her—you could die in your sleep." Pender could not believe that such a beautiful creature could be what Brini was describing. It was probably just another of his stories, he thought, but he kept his opinion to himself and resolved to keep his mission no matter what it would cost.

"Come let us seek out the slave master and find your father and your brother before the day is through. Wait here with the horse till I come back," Brini ordered. Pender was happy to comply, for it meant he had more time to look at the girl. He reckoned that she would be seventeen or eighteen stones; this was how he had been taught to count his own age, one stone for each year or every four seasons, but not all tribes counted the same way. He wondered if she would notice a boy like him. Cisi, his older sister, would be the same age as this girl, and she just ignored him. Just then the girl looked his way and smiled. It lit up her whole face. That smile meant he was lost forever; he could no more forget her now than he could his mother. He was her slave forever. He took one of the skins from the bag round the horse's neck and threw it over the fence away from her so that all of the prisoners ran after it, all fighting for a drink. What he did next brought him a huge reward—he took his own container of water and honeyed cider and threw it at her feet. Gracefully moving to pick it up, she never let her eyes leave his face; he was captivated entirely by her. She took the skin and drank deeply, the liquid spilling over and running down her face. She carelessly wiped it off with her sleeve, the whole time keeping her eyes in contact with Pender's. Two guards approached her, grabbing her by the arm. She never flinched; instead she placed her hand on her heart and signed it to him. She still kept her eyes on him as she was led away; he was overcome with grief.

It was obvious when the normally placid Brini returned that he had great reason to be upset. His first clue was that he had Tarag and Toto, his father's two very large wolf hounds, trailing reluctantly behind him. His father never went anywhere without them; they were his constant companions. Then he noticed that he was carrying Castor's big leather bag over his shoulder; this could not be good. "Where is my father and brother?" Pender asked, finding it difficult to keep the tremor out of his voice. The look on Brini's face was one filled with sadness and foreboding; this was not a story he wanted to tell.

"We must get back to the island and the settlement immediately. Your brother, Kain, and his cohorts have betrayed your father and sold him to the slavers. I know it sounds to you impossible, but they got your father so drunk last night that it was easy for them to overcome him. They beat him with their clubs until he was unconscious and stripped him of the Doan Stone, the symbol of his authority. Now Kain wears it and claims now to be the chief of our family tribe. Castor never could handle drinking too much. Once as a young man it almost cost him his life when he and his friends raped a young woman, but Castor was too drunk to do that. They will pour their strongest brews down his throat to keep him servile till they can sell him. A strong man like Castor will go to the highest bidder, and there will be no lack of potential buyers. We must accept the fact that your father is lost to us for the present.

When we get back to the island, we will try to reason with Kain. I think I know what this is all about. Kain has been angry with your father since he took Lay as his second wife, even though it was Kain who bought her from the Nuits. Your uncle Abbi and I tried to tell your father that this was a bad idea, but Castor was stubborn and insisted he had the right as undisputed chief to take whomever he pleased to be his wife. Kain has never forgotten, and now there will be real trouble, because in exchange for your father, Kain got access to the inner circles of the slave traders.

Pender went and fetched the horse from where it had been grazing. It was most upset at being disturbed because this late in the day it was normally safe in his stall. Despite its lack of cooperation, Pender led it back so that Brini could mount for the journey. "We cannot return the way we came," Brini said, "because it will be dark soon, and it looks like we could get snow. Besides, Kain will be on the lookout for us coming across the ice, where we would be at his mercy. I hope Abbi has gotten to the settlement safely. There is no love between him and your brother, and I fear things could go badly there. In the meantime, we will make our way up the river, but only as far as the Great Forest. The Tree People will give us shelter for the night.

Pender replied, "I thought the Tree People lived among the treetops and never came down? Are they not the Broken People? Why would they trust us?"

Brini shook his head trying to keep his displeasure out of his voice. "No, Pender, that is not the case. The Broken People is only a bad name people have given them. They are good people who have been dispossessed of their families or tribal land. They come from many places and find shelter and support in the forest among the trees, but that does not make them bad or dangerous people. Yes, they do live in the treetops, and some never leave or come down, but that is to escape the forest animals and to hide from the slavers. You will see this for yourself tonight. We will be well treated, and we will be safe and secure." They stopped talking to concentrate on the rough going, Tarag leading the way and Toto bringing up the rear. Every so often Tarag would stop and sniff the air, a deep growl rumbling up from his throat, but whatever was there it decided not to show and slunk off into the woods.

Chapter 3

Pender Meets Mari and Zari

It was obvious that Brini had been here before because he knew all the paths to take and went directly to a large oak tree that appeared to be very, very old. Pender guessed it would take ten men with hands outstretched to circle its girth, but its secret seemed to be on the side away from the path. Brini dismounted and went directly there. Pender followed him, curious to see what would unfold next in this adventure. Brini rapped three times on the bark of the tree and waited for a few moments. To Pender's amazement, a door opened in the tree to reveal that this great oak was hollow inside, and two men emerged from it and greeted Brini like an old friend. They talked together for some time in a language that Pender did not know at first, but as he grew used to their cadence, he began to understand the general gist of the conversation. It was arranged that they could stay there for the night, but they would accept the horse for payment; it certainly would augment their food supplies, for this was going to be a hard winter. In due course, the horse was led away, but the matter of the dogs seemed to be the stumbling block. The matter was solved, however, when Tarag took off into the night followed by Toto; they would find their own meal and place of rest. So it was that the travelers were led into the tree and climbed up very steep steps cut into the wood. Pender had little time to examine his surroundings, until they had to stop at a junction with a large branch; here they were high above the forest standing on a platform. Soon in the darkness, Pender heard a strange sound, a rasping sound, and there before them was a movable platform supported by four very stout leather ropes. He was very carefully moving onto it, taking care to show no fear; after all he was Castor the Great's son. The sensation of being lifted up speedily into the air took him by surprise, and as he got used to it, he wished it was daylight, what wonders would he have beheld. The lift bumped to a halt, and Pender soon saw the means of his upward journey. Four well-muscled young men had been pulling on the ropes. Even in this cold, they were stripped to the waist, and even their leather skirts were covered with sweat. They smiled at him in welcome, waving their twice-covered leather-gloved hands in greeting. But Pender could not return their eager-eyed interest because he was being ushered along a wooden roadway that wound from tree to tree high up in the forest roof. After they had walked some distance, Pender was led to an enclosed area where fine weaved birch branches formed the walls of a living room. This was how all huts and homes were constructed even on the ground; smaller branches were then woven over the top, and leaves or turf were added to it, making it waterproof. The door was also made of the same materials, and it opened to reveal a very comfortable sleeping area with two bed cots in each corner. As Pender moved into the room, he was conscious of three pair of eyes focused on him. In one corner, a young woman sat with a young child on her knee, the infant was obviously asleep. The other two cots were occupied by a boy and a girl about the same age as Pender. The young woman pointed to herself and said, "Mari." She opened her hand and smiled at him to indicate his name.

Pender told her his name and then introduced himself to the boy, who rather sullenly said, "Ari," then turned on his side, facing the wall, and settled down for the night.

The girl looked at him with interest and placed her hand on her chest and said, "Zari," all the while twisting her plaits round her head into a crown. When it would not stay in place, she gave up in disgust. She signaled to Pender to take the empty cot, and when he sat down, she joined him and proceeded to take off his jerkin and then his leather boots. She examined their quality, running her hand over the fine leather, and then intently unlaced his undershirt and pulled it over his head. Without saying a word, she disappeared from the room and returned with a wooden basin with water and a towel. She applied some kind of salve to his body and proceeded to wash him all over and dry him with the towel. She went into the corner and produced a rough woolen shirt and put it on him. Pender stood embarrassed; he looked at Mari, who smiled her encouragement, so he endured Zari's ministrations, hoping they would end soon. Apparently this was part of Zari's work to make visitors to the treetop welcome because as soon as she was satisfied with her accomplishments, she took off again and came back later with a wooden goblet containing bark tea and rough-grained bread. Pender wolfed it down and enjoyed the hot tea. He had eaten early that morning, but he had shared his bread with the dogs, so he was ravenous. He began to warm to this young woman who had been so kind to him. Mari gave the baby to Zari, who immediately took it away somewhere for the night. She then blew out the candle and settled down to sleep. Pender lay on the cot and tried to replay in his mind the happenings of this day that had changed his life so drastically. But each time he thought he had answers, fear for tomorrow invaded his mind and confused the issues anew. At last he drifted off into a troubled sleep.

During the night he was conscious that he was naked and someone equally naked was hugging him. They were lying like two spoons. He was so comfortable that he raised no objections. He knew he was not dreaming because he could feel and hear her breath in his ear. He realized it was Zari, and he was not about to waken her; this felt too good. He wondered if they would be staying another night.

That, however, was not to be. When he awoke from his sleep, Zari was already gone, as were the others. His clothes were cleaned from the dust of yesterday and laid in a neat little pile with a carrying flask with cider and honey. Oat bread and cheese were carefully wrapped and laid beside his clothes; on top was a little white flower. He liked this Zari. He had just finished dressing when two young men came to guide him to the exit. He put Zari's supplies into the pouch at his waist and the flower on his jerkin lapel then followed his guides out onto the treetop walkways.

The two young men told him they would not be leaving the way they had come because bad people had come looking for them in the night, but the dogs had frightened them away. This was confirmed when he met up with Brini, who got down to business right away. He gave no clue to where he had spent the night, or asked Pender about his. Pender was relieved not to be cross-examined like he would have been by Abbi, so his secret about the night spent in Zari's arms was safe. Brini had concluded after his talks with their hosts that they should not follow the river road back to the settlement. Instead they would take the longer circular route around the moor so they would get to the settlement and see if there was any new information on where Kain and his bunch of thugs were. Tarag went ahead as he was trained to do—to give warning of any possible traps that might be set up—while Toto covered their trail, as she was trained to do. With these two on duty, woe to anyone who might seek to impede their progress.

Pender was aware that Brini was tired—the stress and the walk were playing havoc with his aging frame—but he would not hear of stopping to rest. It was late afternoon before they stumbled into the settlement from the rear gate. The guards recognized them and immediately gave them entrance. Brini collapsed and had to be carried into his cousin's hut, where a large group of men and women had gathered. After Brini had recovered, they waited quietly for him to speak. He told them what had transpired at Slave Island and how he had been duped by Kain to go and get more skins of mead, thus leaving Kain a free hand. In the meantime, he and his gang had betrayed Castor and sold him to the slavers. He blamed himself for being so blind to his nephew's real purposes, and now he must pay the price for that folly.

Abbi spoke not of blame but of the betrayal that was Kain's, and how he had gained entrance to the settlement yesterday and immediately proclaimed himself to be the new chief. He told them Castor had been kidnapped by a large group of slavers and they had been powerless to stop them because they had no weapons. The settlement group wanted to go to the island immediately while it was dark and take Kain and his thugs and punish them for their shameless lies and betrayal of their chief. But Brini thought the situation could be better handled if he and Abbi went to the island and reasoned with Kain so the situation would be calmed down. In the meantime, three people should be sent with armed guards to Slave Island to see if Castor could be bought back. The discussion went on for some time before the decision was made that

Brini, Abbi, and Pender should go to the island using the floating ferry. The feeling was if Pender went, it was unlikely that Kain would do him harm. They chose three men to represent them and gave them the power to offer up to one-half of their winters food supply for Castor's ransom.

Pender went down to the landing to make arrangements for the crossing. It was normal to have six men to man the ropes to pull the platform over to the island. The dogs had followed Pender, and he was glad of their company as he sat in the cold waiting for Brini and Abbi to come. He was not sure that the reception they would get would be conducive to reasoned discussion that his two adult friends hoped it would be. He had been a witness many times to the violent fits of temper that Kain showed when he did not get his own way.

Chapter 4

Kain's Treachery

As the time passed, his mind went to the island that had been his home for almost eighteen years. It really was a work of nature; his forefathers had built the stone structure, but nature had provided its foundation and its unique shape. Sometime in the ancient past, a volcano had gushed its lava around when there was no lake. The movement of the earth since and countless numbers of landslides obliterated the evidence of its early beginnings. Now all that was left was the circular crater and wall of up to eight feet, which was the major part of the building. For a wandering tribe of nomads who were looking for a place to settle, it was ideal. The location of the island could provide for them shelter, safety, and isolation. It had a never-ending supply of water that require no long-distance carrying, and the heated waters of the geyser that sprang up from deep under the lake basin meant they had year-round access to the island. The fact that they could control this accessibility when they wanted made this site an ideal place to settle. The hundred-foot diameter floor area that was shaped by the crater housed the whole family. Over time many rooms were constructed. The low pole roof dome gave little resistance to the winds that blew over the island, and light came from portholes in the walls. The wood and stone were readily available on the island, and as the building proceeded, space was provided for other work areas; it had become a well-built refuge. But Pender knew only what was in Brini's memory. He waited impatiently for his two friends to arrive, his mind filled with foreboding.

It was another hour before Brini and Abbi came with the men who would pull on the cables to send the ferry platform over to the island. There was absolutely no conversation on the way. Pender was used to this lack of being informed of their intentions in normal circumstances; after all, he was only a boy, but these were not normal circumstances. When the ferry ground to a halt, Pender jumped off and secured it to the moorings. Abbi whispered in his ear, "Take the dogs, keep them quiet, and go to the back entrance through the brew room. Move two skins of the newest brews to the finishing line." Pender did not question these unusual instructions and went quickly to obey.

The dogs were keen to be fed and went straight to the outhouse, where the leftover food scraps were kept for them. They made no sound as they went, which was unusual for them; it was as if they were part of the silence conspiracy. Pender walked down the ramp from the ground level to the brew room and let himself in. He was not prepared for what it contained. Nearly all of the young serving girls were huddled in a corner tied hand and foot, with cloth gags in their mouths. He signaled to them to remain quiet; the last thing he wanted was for them to panic and alert those in the main hall. It was difficult to get around them to his workstation without tripping over the bodies that were crammed into this small space. First of all, he moved the skins, and as he did so, the purpose of it became clear to him. Then he picked up his flint cutting tool and began freeing the prisoners. Quietly he told the youngest girls to go up the ramp to their outside living quarters, put on warm clothes, and to assemble at the ferry ramp. Everything must be done without panic and in complete silence; any sound made could result in them being brought back as prisoners. They were to go to the ferry signal, the settlement, and cross in the darkness. To avoid confusion, he put one of the older girls in charge and instructed her to tell the men there what had occurred and any other news she might have. This left him with a crew of four girls who were his age. He asked them why they had been tied up and what had happened yesterday after Kain and his cronies had come home. The information was just as Pender had expected. Kain had arrived in a blazing drunken rage, angered by his family tribe's refusal to accept him as their chief. He had lost all control, kicking and beating anyone who got in his way. Without his control, his followers had gone on a rampage. First, they had rounded up all the men and boys, beat them unconscious, and had thrown them in the pigpens. The older women had been selected to serve them, after they had been stripped and raped, and they had not been heard from since. One of their attackers had told them that younger girls were to be sold to the slavers because virgins brought a higher price. They believed that this was not an idle threat and were therefore ready to do anything they could to avoid this fate.

Pender took a few moments to digest this information and tried to think what Abbi would do in these circumstances. The first problem was he really did not know these girls because he was not allowed to socialize with anyone except Abbi and Brini. The second problem was he had to get help to the men locked in the pigpens and get them to the ferry before daylight.

The girls were quite talkative in telling Pender their names, how long they had been working in the kitchens, and their family connections in the settlement. It made him more determined to save them from Kain's thugs; they were family, and family was everything. He tried to impress on the girls that no one inside must know that they were free, if his plan was going to work. He selected Rona, the youngest girl, to leave from the back entrance to alert the ferrymen that they would need more help from the settlement to form relief teams so they could operate all night. She would be responsible to go with the first group on the ferry to organize the women of the settlement so that the injured men would have their wounds attended to as soon as possible. They would need salves, clothes, and vinegar to bandage and treat wounds, and they should send to the mystic; she would know how to set broken bones. When this was done, it would be her task then to inform the elders of what the situation was here. Pipa, the next youngest girl, was to keep the ferrymen informed when another group of men was ready to leave and to make sure they maintained silence throughout. For Pipa's safety, she was to take Tarag with her; he would not allow anything to happen to her. The dogs adore the girls because they fed them tidbits from the kitchen and saw that their daily feedings were done on time. Toto was made to follow Tarag; they were normally inseparable, but Pender told her to stay, as she was needed to protect the transfer of the wounded men and boys to the ferry. The two older girls, Morag and Nena, would go and free the men from the pigpens. They would need hardwood staves to break open the doors and flint knives to cut the bonds. He had chosen them for this rescue because he knew them to be stronger than the younger girls, as he had often seen them lifting very heavy bags of corn on their backs. They should organize the men into groups of four, two wounded with two relatively fit men. Morag was to take as much food as she could carry from the kitchen and a skin of cider, since the men would need some type of sustenance. Nena would carry the staves and the flint knives to cut the men free from their bonds and any clothes she could find to temporarily bind their wounds. She was to return to the house and quietly creep upstairs and hide near the service wall where she could hear the conversations from the main room. Pender believed he might need an independent witness to his meeting with his brother, for Kain had a habit of lying. Nena understood how dangerous this assignment could be if she was discovered, but she wanted to do it, knowing that later any information she might gather could prove to be vital. The girls went out just as one of the thugs who tied them up came into the brewhouse demanding more beer.

Pender moved immediately to get the skins. He was glad of Abbi's instructions about moving the newest and unfermented brew to the outline. Anyone who drank this stuff would not be standing on their feet for long. Abbi had hoped that these scoundrels would be too drunk to notice the difference, since they had been drinking steadily from the day before. No sooner had he given the skins to Kain's friend than it was opened, and the drunk was drinking from it in great gulps, the excess running down his unkempt beard. Abbi's plan was working better than Pender thought it would—one down four to go.

Pender now moved into the main hall to confront his brother. He was trembling inside, but he did not want it to show. He need not have worried Kain was not there, but he could hear him shouting from his mother's room. Pender moved cautiously to the door of his mother's room and stood quietly, observing Kain's demeanor. Brid, his mother, who was quite sick, was lying on her couch remonstrating with Kain, who was leaning possessively on Lay, his father's second wife. Lay was white faced and appear to have been beaten into submission; she was naked from the waist up, and her normal beautiful red hair was in disarray. She wept silently. Kain went and stood over his mother, posing in a dominating stance. Brid looked up at him coolly, facing him as if he were a troublesome child who needed to be scolded for bad behavior. This was not the reception Kain had planned. He wanted his mother to receive him in a manner he thought he was befitting to the new chief of the tribe. Pender moved cautiously forward to hear her reply. "You are not the chief, your father is. You cannot lift the stone, and you have no right to wear the Doan Stone. You do not have the ability or the wisdom, and you have shown this in your treatment of Lay, your father's wife. Go and grow up and gain the respect of the tribe then someday you may be considered somewhat fit to succeed your father." Brid said this, waving her hand dismissively.

"How dare you dismiss me like this. I tell you my father is dead. I saw it with my own eyes. Ask any of my friends. They will tell you that this is true. My father wronged me. He took Lay from me. I bought her from the red-haired people, the Nuits, and brought her here to be my wife, and he took her for himself. How can you not see his fault?" Kain shouted his anger growing as he spoke.

When Brid spoke again, her voice was cold. "You had every right to buy yourself a wife, but only when the price you paid was with things that you owned, not with things you stole from the tribe. The tribe spoke on it and disallowed your claim. You should have been punished and banished from all future association. But your father pleaded on your behalf, repaid the stolen property, and healed the affront suffered by the Nuits by taking Lay as his second wife. He should have had you flogged, but he spared you that. Why are you here? If your father has been taken and killed as you claim, why are you not out seeking his killers and revenging his death? Are you a coward as well as a thief?" As she spoke, she slowly rose to her feet, standing unsteadily before Kain looking into his eyes. She saw fear and loathing; she guessed what was coming but did not flinch. She saw Pender at the door, and her standing up was an attempt to distract Kain. She did not want Pender to witness what would follow. Kain's anger was apoplectic; his face went from red to crimson, his eyes were wild and full of hate, and his speech was indiscriminate, garbled words, oaths, and cursing. It was as if he was speaking in a foreign language. Suddenly he lashed out with his fist and smashed Brid in the face. She was dead before she hit the floor. Pender stood transfixed for a moment then launched himself at Kain.

Kain turned to Pender with a sneer on his face. "What's wrong, little brother, someone stolen your tongue so you cannot address the new chief of the tribe with some deference! Kneel before me now!" He forced Pender down on his knees before him. Lay rushed in to intervene, but Kain cuffed her with the back of his hand and knocked her to the floor. She lay there bleeding and unconscious.

Pender looked Kain in the face and said, "You are no brother of mine. You are a monster. You betrayed our father and sold him as a slave. You lied to the tribal elders and murdered my mother. You will never be the chief of this tribe. Everyone will know that you are nothing but a drunken liar."

Kain kneed Pender in the face as he knelt before him, knocking him backward, then he picked him up with one hand and Lay with the other, and dragged them into the hall. His five cronies were all in different stages of inebriation lounging on the floor around an open fire. They had poked a hole through the roof lattices to let the smoke escape into the cold winter air. Castor would have cleaned the floor with them for such foolishness, but Kain did not seem to mind. "Here take her and use her," he said, throwing Lay on the floor beside them. They stripped the rest of her clothes off then started a fight to see who was to be first. Lay was oblivious to this, still unconscious from the blow Kain had struck to her head. Pender was glad that she would never know the indignities that they would cause her.

Throwing Pender against the wall, Kain pointed to the two most apparently drunk of his cohorts. "Take this one and hang him with the other two, he knows too much." The two stumbled to do his bidding, but Pender suddenly came back at them off the wall and punched one in the nose with such force that he broke it; the man yelled in pain. Pender kicked the other in the groin, and he fell to his knees. The unfermented brew had been working on them, and they simultaneously threw up falling to the floor, clutching their stomachs in obvious pain.

Kain commanded the others to leave Lay and to do his bidding—hang Pender. But they immediately suffered the same fate as their companions rolling over on the floor holding their considerable bellies. Even with his terrible fate already prescribed for him, Pender felt quite elated that Kain's power was now drastically reduced. Kain picked up the empty skins from the floor and sniffed them suspiciously. He roared with anger when he realized how they had been duped. He ran at Pender, kicking the fire over as he went, sending pieces of flaming firewood all over the floor, which he ignored; his attention was absolutely centered on the cause of his wrath. The last thing that Pender saw when he looked up was his two sisters, Cisi, his older sister by four years, beautiful, serene loving, the keeper of the animals; and Ester, two years his senior, the only one trusted by her father to dress him and bring him his food. Both of them had a passionate dislike for Kain, and they had observed everything that he had done. Kain stopped in his tracks. He realized his problems were bigger than he thought. He threw Pender down and ran after his sisters. The girls screamed, screams that could be heard all over the island—they had to be stopped. He caught them on the stairs, and before they could react, he had them. First, he stripped them of their outer clothes and tore them into strips, which he used to gag and bind them. "Little sisters, you are like your little brother Pender here, you know too much, he will hang, you will die outside in the cold of the night," then he slapped them until they were senseless.

 Kain knew he had to act quickly. He picked up the hardwood spikes he had planned to use to hang Pender above the outside door on an old wooden lintel; this wouldn't kill him, but the cold would. The girls would have similar fate; dressed only in their underwear, they would soon succumb to the cold and die before anyone came to help. First, he took Pender outside. He grinned in satisfaction when he saw the snow falling with large flakes like they had come from plucked chickens. "Good-bye, little brother, now you know who has all the power, me! Look, there are your two best friends hanging in the old oak tree. Once there was two, now you make it three." Then he took Pender, hit him on the head with the wooden mallet, lifted him up, and drove the wooden spikes through the shoulders of his leather jacket and left him dandling in the cold. He dragged the girls outside and threw them against the wall. There was already a snowdrift there, so he placed them in it. Within the hour they would be covered and dead. Kain's business on the island was finished. In fact, anywhere his family might be or go, people would hear of his treachery, just as his mother had predicted. But it was all their fault; if only they had accepted him as chief, things could have been different.

He went back inside and got his outer wear, checked to see if any of his friends were alive, but there did not appear to be any visible signs of life. He looked around once to see if there was anything that could later be used against him; he would blame everything on his dead comrades. He left in the worst of the snow, making his way over the ice knowing that his tracks would be covered and no one could follow him.

Nena observed everything from the gallery where she had gone according to the instructions she had received from Pender. Now she carefully made her way downstairs, checking as she went to make sure Kain had left completely. First, she went into Brid's room and found that she was indeed dead. She lifted her up on her couch and covered her with her bedclothes. Nena then went looking for Lay and found her completely nude, lying in a pool of blood, surrounded by her attackers. It was obvious they had died violent deaths at their own hands, being so drunk that they could not discern that the unfermented brew was not so silently killing them. One of the bodies was on fire because of the way Kain had carelessly kicked the fire over in his hurry to get to Pender. She ran and got a basin of water and put the fire out. Then she collected the scattered firewood and replaced it in the makeshift hearth. Kain's hope that the fire would destroy all the evidence against him was thwarted. She then dragged Lay's body back into Brid's room and covered her up, but she could not move the bodies of the men; they were too heavy for her. She then ventured out the front door. What she saw finally unhinged her. Nena had managed to keep her emotions bottle up inside because she was committed to the task at hand, but she could no longer keep things under control. When she saw the bodies of Abbi and Brini hanging in the old oak tree, she screamed and screamed and screamed.

Her screaming finally brought Pender back to some semblance of consciousness. He actually felt the snow on his face as it fell harder and harder. He opened his eyes and was conscious for the first time that he was not alone. Abbi was hanging by the neck opposite him, and if his would-be hangmen had made a good job of it, he would have been dead. But they were so drunk the knot they had tied only made him uncomfortable. Not so with Brini—his face was contorted in death; the beating he had received from Kain had killed him, not the hanging. Pender was trying to concentrate, wondering how he was going to get free before the cold would take him when there was aloud crack. The weight of the snow and the two bodies were too much for the old tree. With a loud groan and a swoosh, the branch detached itself from the tree trunk, and the two bodies hurdled down into the snow.

The major part of the branch hit the door lintel above Pender's head, dislodging the wooden pins that held him suspended above the ground. He fell into the snowdrift beside his sisters, but he was unable to move because of the cold, and his hands and feet were bound by leather cords.

The loud crack finally broke Nena's state of immobility. She ran toward Pender and pulled him out of the snowdrift. She found that he was breathing but could not move because of the bindings on his hands and feet. As time was against him, she ran inside to retrieve a flint knife and came out in a hurry to free him. It was difficult to cut through the leather, but she discovered if she used a sawing motion, the task was easier. Finally, she had him free and soon had him in beside the fire. She went and brought the girls in one at a time, as it was necessary to carry them in on her back. She put them beside the fire and covered them with as many covers as she could find. Abbi staggered in under his own strength but collapsed at the fire. Nena undid the leather rope from his neck so that he was able to breathe. She then left them to go and get honeyed cider to heat at the fire, and as they drank it, they slowly regained some semblance of comfort. Soon they were all asleep safe and free from the events of this tragic day. Nena was exhausted, overcome with grief for her friends who had died, and haunted with what she had witnessed, but grateful that Pender had trusted her and she had found the strength to respond. She watched over them as they slept, and when she was sure all was well, she lay down beside Cisi and fell fast asleep.

In the morning, they all awoke to the smell of more hot honeyed cider and cheese bread, which they gratefully accepted. Nena had awakened earlier from a fitful night, caught between the need to check on her patients and a very troubled sleep. It actually was relief to be up and involved in her daily work. After she had prepared the food, she went and got clothes for the girls and prepared water for them to bathe with. The exposure to the winter elements that they had all suffered had caused skin problems, so she had searched for salve and found it in Brid's room. Abbi's face and hands were the worst, though he tried to make light of it, but he was so grateful for her ministrations. After they had all hugged Nena and thanked her for everything she had done, they could not stop talking about the happenings of the day before. They then decided to get the story straight so when Abbi met with the elders, these extraordinary details could be rehearsed in all truth.

First of all, Nena wanted them to know of the very detailed way that Pender had organized not only the freeing of all the young women but also his plan for how the rescue was accomplished. She detailed the work done by Rona and Pipa in organizing the men at the ferry and the care for the wounded men. Next, she outlined the escape plan that she and Morag had taken part in and then the insight Pender had shown to make sure she would witness everything that had occurred. She also declared that everything would have been a disaster without Pender's input.

Abbi talked of how he and Brini had hoped to reason with Kain, to turn him aside from his folly, but how foreign that idea was to his plan, especially when he realized that Brini knew everything about his treachery. They had agreed going in that they should not reveal this, but because of the anger and disrespect that Kain had shown both for the elders and his family, that this was the only way to bring him back to his senses. That idea had obviously failed and led to them both being hanged, and now Brini was dead and Kain was a fugitive. He congratulated the young women for their courage in the face of such acts of rage, rape, and murder, but he wanted to know if any of the serving women had been found. Cisi said she had seen Kain's friends carrying their naked bodies out through the back area and burning their clothes before the snow came. This news was received with silence and sadness. After a long pause in the conversation, Abbi said, "Kain must be found and held accountable. He would talk to the elders and discuss how best this may be done."

Pender talked about his journey to Slave Island and what he had observed there. He said that he could not comment on what had gone on between the slave traders and Brini, only what had been reported already to the elders—that Kain had sold his father in an act of supreme treachery. He had not seen his father in the slave compound, but that did not mean he was already sold; he could have been lodged in a different area. The question he wanted answered was "Why did the thugs die when they drank the unfermented beer when it should only have made them very sick?"

Abbi replied that "this was Brini's master plan, when all else failed. When he visited the Tree People, he was able to get a very potent tree bark poison. He had ordered Pender to move the newest batch of brew to a place on the line where he could introduce the poison into it so its taste would be disguised by the beer. He had already poisoned the brews that Pender moved. The intention was that Kain and all of his friends would die this way. The plan had worked well, except Kain had not partaken of the killing brew. The rest we have all experienced."

Later that day, they made the journey to the settlement to make their report, but none of them could rest easy because the bodies had to be removed for burial. It was the saddest of times, times they could not forget. The screaming that had sounded from so far away, eerie, high pitched, echoing down the canyons of time from a time so far in the future. How could anyone one know that walking on stones could produce such a sound? Pender could not, but he heard it, and it had kept him alive.

Chapter 5

Zalenda

Zalenda watched the young man outside the compound. He had done her a great kindness by giving her his water for absolutely no reason. She took the water container and hung it on her belt and decided this was something that had to be—she was a warrior. From her earliest recollections, she had been trained for this life. Girls and young women were chosen especially for their body type, height, and ability to be trained. She had heard all the stories of how in the earlier days the tribe had moved from place to place, and every time they became established, they would lose all their possessions to stronger tribes. The males of the tribe were small of stature, weak, and incapable of holding and defending any place that they had settled in. When they had cultivated crops and land, stronger tribes would come along and take away all the fruits of their labor and lead their people into slavery.

Then along came a queen. She came to succeed to the position of authority when her husband was killed a in skirmish and there was no one to replace him. She was a very impressive woman, tall, strong, and intelligent. Her blonde hair and blue eyes and perfect body made her a source of great attraction. She was dedicated to developing a strong system of defense by creating the perfect woman warrior. She quickly established a standard of height, fitness, toughness, and ability to kill opponents with or without weapons. The standard of height was her own. She stood naked while the men who worked in stone captured her likeness. Forever that would be the reference point for all women warriors, and only those were trained to fight for the tribe from early childhood. Those who did not meet the standard were

not cast away; they were trained as guards and lived high up on the hills to give early warnings of impending attacks. Soon the tribe became feared among its neighbors for the intensity by which the women warriors fought, and even the biggest of tribes thought twice about making any kind of threat against them.

Zalenda was such a warrior. She had excelled in every area of her training and was trusted by those in authority to take on hazardous missions. Although the first queen was long dead, her standards remained, and Zalenda was absolutely committed to them. It was that commitment that landed her on Slave Island. Her mission was to protect three men who were entrusted with the task to go to the island and bargain for the release of the son of the new queen. The price of his release was Zalenda. When she realized the treachery that had been practiced against her, she killed two of the three men belonging to her tribe and two of the guards sent to imprison her. She only succumbed when she was hit from behind by the reinforcement guards who were called in to take her. It was this that Pender had witnessed when the two guards had grabbed her and taken her away. As she was being led away, she looked back one more time at the young man who had given her water and his container that now hung on her belt.

She was not troubled by the snow. The cold had little effect on her, as part of her training as a young girl had been to stand for a whole night with little clothes on tied to a tree. The guards, however, were charged with keeping her safe until the sale was made, and they relished what they might be allowed to do to her at that time. She was led in into a hut with about eight other prisoners and thrown down in corner beside the biggest man she had ever seen.

He paid little attention to her, but when the guards closed the door, he turned and asked her where she had gotten the pouch she was wearing at her waist. She was surprised that a man would talk to her, especially such a beautiful specimen; she was used to being ignored and ignoring men. "This is very precious to me," she said. "I was just given this by a young man who was standing outside the palisade. He distracted the prisoners by throwing a skin of beer into a corner so that

I could be alone to receive his water container with cider and honey in it. He is so beautiful and kind. I think I will love him forever."

"That boy is my son. I am Castor, the chief of my tribe. I am here because of the treachery of his older brother." They talked then about how their tribes had fared and what they might accomplish together. Castor was enchanted by Zalenda, so they discussed how they might escape. Castor suggested that it would be better if Zalenda escaped first, as he was bound hand and foot. He would find a way to distract the guards and help get her over the fence. Zalenda showed him a flint knife she had secreted on her person. She was so slim that the guards had thought that impossible and had not bothered to search her.

The guards came around to silence the prisoners. Castor and Zalenda pretended to be asleep, but Zalenda wanted to know more about Pender; she now knew his name, and her thirst for information about him was endless. Castor told her all about him, his sisters, his mother, his family, and he confirmed for her that he was the person she had thought him to be. As he talked, Zalenda drifted off to sleep, dreaming for the first time about a boy who had stolen her heart by one unmitigated act of kindness and his loving reception of her heart when she threw it to him. As Pender had resolved to free her, she resolved to free herself for him. Castor watched her sleep and said quietly to himself, "Come, my daughter, sleep well," and he drew her to him so that she would sleep in the security of his arms. He knew that the guards had designs on her because outside that was a constant topic of conversation. Now that she had a connection to his son, he would make sure nothing happened to her. Even bound as he was, they were afraid of him.

Castor wakened as the guards came through the door at first light. They were grumbling because the snow was still falling, and this meant they would have to carry all the food inside. They were lazy and balked at anything that would cause them any work. Castor filed this away in his mind; it might be useful in an escape plan. Zalenda wakened and was embarrassed at how she had been sleeping. No man had been allowed to touch her, let alone embrace her in this way. In a battle, of course, things were different when any man grabbed her in an unseemly way; they were killed. Bearing children was not an option for a Warrior Woman. Castor noticed the way she pulled away from him and explained his actions were for her protection while she slept, and he would continue to do so as he would protect his own daughters. "Is that because I love your son?" she asked with a tremor in her voice.

"Especially that, and because we cannot allow any daughter of mine to be sold to some greedy foreigner, now could I?" She smiled at this and was secretly pleased, but acted a pouty face, which made him laugh. Castor realized that was something he had not done for some time. They were good for each other in these circumstances. The guards came with a flat piece of wood board with a slurry of something splashed on it, a small piece of cheese, and an even smaller piece of rough corn bread. They both ate this not-delicious meal, and when they were doing so, Castor thought of another use for these flat boards that had nothing to do with food. He made a show of carrying them over to place them in the discarded pile, but instead he hid them in his tunic. Zalenda looked at him with obvious questions in her eyes. Castor put his fingers to his lips and signaled he would explain later when the guards were gone.

They had just settled down again when the guards returned. The order was that it was time for the prisoners to line up for their daily outing to the palisade. Two of them approached Zalenda, leering at her and laughing that they would soon get her and no one could mistake their intentions. She was moving out in two days' time—the buyer was coming to pick her up—and they made as if they were about to grope her, but Castor intervened. The glare he gave them frightened them off. They had no illusions what would happen to them if he wanted to attack them, even with his hands bound.

The snow had stopped, so the prisoners who had their hands free were moving the snow from inside the compound with long wood poles and bark blades held in place with hardwood pegs. It was a long process, as the bark kept falling off; this gave Castor time to survey the weaknesses of their prison. The snow was pushed around, and about three-quarters of the compound was visible, the ground hard and frozen. The piles of snow that remained were pushed against the palisade fence. It was impossible for the prisoners to throw the snow over the fence because of its height. There was only one man who could throw anything over that fence, and that was Castor. He measured himself casually in his mind standing on the snow, throwing Zalenda over the top. Then he calculated the distance she would fall onto the snow and ice outside the fence; she might break bones if this means of escape were used, but it might be used as a valuable divergence. The snow clearing was pushing its way out the gate and across the bridge from the compound on the island to the mainland. Castor, with his feet free while this process lasted, pretended to be bored by the whole thing and backed his way ahead of the snow clearers' pack. It was then he discovered the way out for Zalenda—halfway along the bridge on the west side was an opening in the fence. The gate for it was not pin hinged like all other doors in the place, so there were no leather straps to hack through, which would take too much time. This section of the fence was made to slide into sockets and held in place by its own weight. It normally would require a team of men to lift it up even a little. No one man could possibly lift it up on his own, except the man who could lift the Doan Stone and carry it the length of its height.

That night Castor rehearsed his plan with Zalenda, but she did not want to leave without him. He pointed out time was not on their side—she must leave tomorrow, or she would be handed over to her new master. His plan was to wait till it was dark the next night, when all the prisoners were asleep. She would use her flint knife to cut him free, and then they would quietly go to the bridge and he would lift the movable fence section enough to let her go under it. The meal boards he had borrowed that morning when she got out were to be tied to her feet with the remaining leather ties from his bonds. This would prevent her from having to plow her way through the deep snow. She was to walk on top of the snow and not the ice, as the crunching sound of the ice might alert the night guards. Her journey was to be made while going west till she came to the winding river and then up this river till she came to Great Forest. Here she must find a place to hide till morning. In the morning she was to find the largest oak tree in the forest and approach it from the river. At this point directly opposite, she would find a hole near the bottom of the tree; in it she would find a shiny black stone. This was her way into the Tree People: she had to knock three times, pause, twice more, pause, then once more; this was his secret signal. After a small length of time, a door would open in the tree, and the person who came out would ask her business. She was to say Castor the

Great had sent her so that she might get shelter from the slave traders. She was to stay there till it was safe to leave.

The next day passed slowly. They rehearsed every part of the plan, going over it again and again. Zalenda said she needed some kind of weapon to defend herself from animals or any guard who might be alert enough at the time. Caster suggested one of the wooden poles that they were using to clear the snow. She thought it might be a bit long, but it would do. They found one that had been discarded because a part had broken off.

That night they slipped it through the fence. Castor was counting on the guards to be their normal lazy selves, so he expected it to be there when Zalenda needed it.

As evening approached, Zalenda began to feel guilty that they had a plan to have her escape, but they had not discussed how Castor would get away from the slave station. He would only say that at present, she was the priority, as her timeline for sale was known, his was not. Besides, he wanted to bring these people down and put an end to the slave trade. He could only do this from the inside. He would let himself be sold, and when his buyer was found, he would then systematically dismantle the whole business. Zalenda could not keep the tears back from her eyes; trained as she was to resist all human emotions, this man's greatness was not only in great physical power but also in his great humanity. No one in her tribe would sacrifice as much as he was prepared to do to help others. It left her completely drained of everything she had been taught. She would be his disciple and would adopt his way of thinking. "Will I ever see you again?" she asked.

"You say you love my son. I think that it is entirely possible that we will see each other again," he replied. "Promise me that when you see him, you will tell him everything about what has happened to me and what I intend to do. If you are lucky enough to meet my family, tell them that I love them."

That night when darkness came and everyone in the hut was asleep, Zalenda cut the straps from Castor's hands and feet, and picked up the ties with the wooden flats and made ready to leave. Castor covered his hands with old rags and gave Zalenda a hug, and she hugged him back. Silently they left the hut, stopping for a few minutes to get their eyes accustomed to the dark and to check where the guards were. The noise from one of the huts suggested they were gambling with stones, so there was not going to be any trouble from them. Their footsteps on the bridge sounded too loud, but no one called for them to stop. When they reached the section in the fence, it looked much larger now that they were here. Castor bent down and placed his hand on the cross rails of the fence gate and lifted the gate upward; it moved slowly. He adjusted his stance and lifted it upward more till it was well clear of the ground. Soon she was able to lie down and slip under the fence, and she was free. She heard the fence quietly close down again as she was tying the wooden plates to her feet. Zalenda picked up the hardwood pole, and she was off walking over the snow.

The night was cold and dark, and she hoped this would deter anyone who might have witnessed her leaving from sounding an alarm. Along the Big River banks, the snow had been blowing into the river; therefore, it was not as deep and easier to move along at a good speed. Periodically she stopped to check to see if anyone was following her. After two hours of sliding across the snow, she came to the winding river where she turned inland. So far everything had gone according to Castor's plan. As he had warned her, the going would get harder here; the banks were steeper here, and this caused her to lose her forward motion and slither down to the water's edge. It was at that moment that she saw the wolf. She had been so intent at keeping her feet that she slid into a tree, and when she stopped to take her bearings, he was following her but higher up the bank. She grabbed her pole and positioned herself with her back to the tree, ready to fend him off when she saw the rest of the pack coming at her from the opposite direction. Her warrior training came to her aid immediately. She jumped upward and caught a branch of the tree and quickly scaled up through its branches, kicking off the snowboards as she went. The tree was deciduous, its leaves long gone, and its branches were stripped and weak; she had to transfer her weight to another tree. On the other side of the river was a very large strong coniferous with one of its branches bridging the river. The branch beneath her creaked as she launched herself at that very inviting branch and caught it with both hands then went hand over hand across the river into the confines of her new home for the night. It was ideal; she could see the ground for a long way out to the Big River, but no one could see her. The wolf pack thus thwarted took off to look for easier prey. Zalenda settled down on a large branch that was more than strong enough to take her weight, but first, she removed the belt from her waist and tied it round her feet and the branch so she would not fall from her perch. She had been in similar circumstances many times when scouting enemy troops' movements, so she was comfortable with her position. Before she drifted off to sleep, she thought about what her life would have been had she not met Castor, but her last thought as usual was of the shy young man she loved whose name was Pender.

The morning came early for Zalenda. She thought she heard voices in the distance, so she quickly climbed down from her tree, replaced her belt, broke some ice, and washed her face and hands in the frozen water. She had nothing to dry them with, so she blew on her hands to get a little circulation going and then wiped her face. Her hair, as was the case with all Warrior Women, was tightly plaited and was normally worn down her back. Today she chose to cover it with her leather tunic because she didn't want to be so easily recognized. Three possible groups might be after her: the guards from the slave station, her own tribe whose queen had been prepared to give her in exchange in order to redeem her son and who would now order her capture and certain death—such was the penalty for defying a queen of the Warrior Women—then there was always the present fear for any traveler, that she might be captured by roving gangs who would then sell her back to the slave station. She decided to travel down low on the ice so she would not be as visible. She retrieved her pole and wooden sliders, tied them on, and was off on her search for the Tree People.

After two hours of hard sliding, she was actually sweating and tired and still some distance from the Great Forest. A friendly tree would be nice right now, she thought, and she could see such a friend just a little further along near a bend in the river. As she reached the tree, something inside warned her to hide her pole and sliders in the snow. This done, she climbed the tree and hid under its branches and pine needles. No sooner was she in position than a group of men about twenty strong appeared on the opposite bank on the way down to the river to fill their water bottles and allow their dogs to drink.

Zalenda thanked her internal warning system for the wisdom to bury her pole and sliders. The problem was now her movements in the snow might lead them to her hiding place. She need not have worried—the dogs had been leashed and having just been released were running all over the place; one even lifted his leg against her tree so her tracks were completely obliterated.

The men sat down and rested for a while, so she was able to listen to their conversations. It turned out that her queen, rather than send her troop of Warrior Women after Zalenda, had bought this gang of slavers to track her down and kill her. Zalenda now knew she could never return home. Before, there might have been a chance to explain why she had to escape, but the queen's behavior now ruled out any such explanation. Soon the men got bored with the inaction, and when the leader called them to prepare to move, they called the dogs in and leashed them and were on their way.

Zalenda waited until she could hear the sound of the gang recede into the distance and then left her hiding place. She picked up her pole and her sliders and moved as quietly as possible, stopping every so often to check for any warning signs that she might be in danger. The journey to the Great Forest took longer than she had anticipated. The winter sun was beginning its evening descent for night when she found the big oak tree described by Castor. She quickly found the stone in the hole in the tree, and she tapped out the signal. As she waited for the signal to be recognized, she felt very exposed. After some time had elapsed, suddenly and without warning, a door opened in the tree, and a young man asked her why she was here and what was her business. She told him Castor the Great had sent her here for help, he had helped her escape from Slave Island, but he had not escaped at this time. He told her to follow him as they climbed up inside the tree. If Castor had not prewarned her, she would not have believed it. Soon he indicated to her to wait for a few minutes while he went ahead to arrange for her reception.

As she waited for him to return, Zalenda took stock of her surroundings. She was amazed at how clean everything looked and found it difficult to take in that she was so high up of the ground in a forest of trees. The platform she stood on was better constructed and showed better workmanship than anything that might have been made in her home tribe or on any of her travels. The woven walls of lightweight branches that were interweaved by smaller and finer branches until there was not one remaining space for the wind and weather to blow through were not only lightweight but also structurally sound. The roof was arched and made with the same materials and covered with bark that seemed to be sewn in place with long strips of leather.

While she was examining the genius of the workmanship, she noticed that light came in from roof lights made from semitransparent skin. The only thing she could think of that could do this and be able to cast of rain and snow had to be made from what looked like the intestines of some rather large animal. She was about to touch it when her guide returned. "Don't touch it please. If you touch it, it loses its tension, and then it is no good." Zalenda hastily withdrew he hand; she did not want to get off on the wrong side of things. "Don't worry," he said laughingly, "you would not be the first to try to understand how it's done. It is a wonder, isn't it? Come, I will take you to your quarters for the night."

Zalenda followed him a long a corridor over countless trees. She was in awe of it all. He stopped at a junction and pointed to a door. "In there they will look after you," he said blithely and went on his way. She opened the door and found herself in a nice comfortable room. The occupants looked at her with grave suspicious faces. They had heard of Warrior Women before but never had come into contact with one. This person confirmed everything they had been told. Many awkward moments passed by until the youngest of the two women in the room came forward and pointed to herself and said, "Zari."

With the tension in the room now broken, the young woman approached and said, "Mari." Zalenda smiled at them. They were immediately captivated with her. They had never witnessed anyone like her, so tall, so blue eyed, so slim, so blonde, so perfect; they were already entranced by her.

She moved toward them and pointed to her chest and said, "Zalenda."

They repeated in chorus, "Zalenda,"—and smiled—"Zalenda." So were sealed the beginning of a great friendships. Zari was the first to spring into action. She left quickly to go and get water and salves so that her new friend would be clean and refreshed. Mari came forward, smiling as she came. Her part in receiving women visitors was always for her an unpleasant chore, but this service she was about to perform would be a pleasure for her as well as Zalenda. First of all, she removed her leather belt and tunic and then the high boots. She undid the leather leggings and stripped them off. Next, she undid the glorious blonde hair, reaching up as high as she could to unfasten it from a wooden clasp. She then undid each plait and let the blonde mass of hair fall down to her new friend's waist. Zalenda was now totally nude. The door opened, and Zari returned, gazed at Zalenda for a few seconds, then went right to work, bathing her from top to bottom, drying off, and rubbing salve over all her body. Mari brought a stool for Zalenda to sit on, who, the truth be told, was so tired with the happenings of her day, collapsed rather than sat down. Zari and Mari both took handfuls of her hair and proceed to wash every strand. Then they produced wooden combs and combed out these beautiful tresses. Finally, they went to a cupboard and found night attire that was too short, but they put it on her anyway. Zari disappeared again, this time coming back with bread and cheese and a large wooden goblet of honey cider. Zalenda ate and drank with great relish. This was her first meal of the day. All the time Zari held her hand, while Mari put her arm around Zalenda and helped her drink from the goblet. Zalenda tried to speak her thanks, but her friends guided her to the same cot that Pender had slept on, so it was fitting that her last thought that day was that she loved him.

Next morning Mari and Zari were up early and went to work in the food kitchens. Every item of food they used had to be brought up from the forest floor. This was the weak link of the tree fort's defense because the lifts could only be in use if there was no danger from roving bands. Although they always had emergency food supplies, in times of a full assault, these had to be used sparingly. The men here had been farmworkers from poor broken tribes and families. They were a mix of broken people with no land and no means of support; only the forest gave them some sense of security. They were not men trained to defend themselves, and their guards and lookouts were the same—they had no skills to read the forest, but they could outlast bands on the ground particularly in the winter. This was why all hands were at work today to get food from secret underground stores, where they could keep wild boar and deer carcasses. Other foods were kept frozen in rough wooden containers of corn, bean, oats, and wild fruits and vegetables. These were the main essentials that made up the diet of the Tree People, and today was the supply day, and everyone must work.

Zalenda awoke from the longest sleep she had in months, no pressure to perform, no danger to overcome, no mission to complete, and for the first time since she qualified as a woman warrior, she had a sense of peace. She looked around to see where her new friends were and discovered food had been left for her and her leather tunic, pants, and leggings had been scrubbed clean and laid in order; this was all too much. She took off her borrowed night attire and quickly donned her clothes. She noted that her hair was free, and she felt wonderful. After she had eaten, she tried to put things together in her mind, what had really happened last night. She remembered her reception at the tree and the amazing discoveries of her passage then being shown into the room and meeting two young women. Trying as hard as she could, she could not remember their names, she had been out on her feet! How did she get so clean? Then it all came back to her, all their ministrations, they had seen her naked! She felt totally embarrassed. What must they think of her? How would she be able to face them? As she was mulling over these things in her mind, the door opened, and in they came completely exhausted from pulling load after load of supplies up to the kitchens. They immediately stripped of their working clothes and collapsed naked on their cots, completely oblivious of her embarrassment. Mari stood after she had rested for a few minutes. Zari followed and picked up some wet clothes and salve they had brought in with them. "Come and help me, Zalenda," Zari said expectantly.

Zalenda approached hesitantly. Mari noticed her reticence. "You haven't done this before?" she inquired. "It's all right. Take a cloth and wipe all the pine needles off me. When you work up here, it's part of the territory—they are very uncomfortable."

Zalenda wiped gently at first. Zari said, "No, no, harder than that, or else it will take all night, and we have a lot of questions to ask you and even more things to discuss." After that, Zalenda worked hard, and soon there was pile of pine needles on the floor, a testament to her work.

Mari turned round to face her and said, "Now rub the salve in. Just forget it's a naked body you're working on." Soon they were finished, and the whole process was repeated on Zari, and then they put on their nightgowns.

When the girls were comfortable, they plied Zalenda with questions. First of all, they wanted to know about her life as woman warrior—how did she become one and what was it like? Zalenda explained to them that the likelihood of her remaining with her tribe as warrior was very slight, if not entirely impossible. She told them how all the young women in the tribe were measured at aged eight for height, weight, and body type then fed diets of fish, herbs, and certain wild vegetables and fruits. Each year they were measured against an ideal that the queen had established. They were trained to be self-sufficient and in every aspect of being able to kill. Often, as young girls, they were left out all night in the winter with very little clothes to teach them how to control their minds and bodies in extreme conditions. As they grew older, they were treated with certain herbs so that they would not have their monthly menstruation, as this could be a great distraction for a warrior. A stone statue of the first Great Queen was the model they must comply with in every aspect. The perfect candidate would be the same height as the statue, slim to the extreme, strong tested by rituals, small breasted, and exhibit great determination, and they were absolutely forbidden to have any type of contact with men.

Mari wanted to know how she came to the Tree People and why when she had all those skills. Zalenda told them about her present queen's treachery in sending her to be sold as a slave in return for the freedom of the queen's son.

She then described what it was like in the slave camp, how she fell in love with a young boy called Pender. Indeed it was Castor the Great, his father, who planned and executed her escape, while he remained in the camp. She told them why he must remain in the camp and what he was prepared to do to end the trade in slaves. It was Castor who had given her the directions and the correct signal to gain entrance to the Tree People, and that had been a fortunate situation because she now knew that her queen had hired people to track her down and kill her. The fact that she was here safe and sound, she owed to Castor; she owed her whole life to Castor, and she would dedicate it in helping him in his mission.

Zari was so excited she could hardly speak. "Listen, Zalenda, we had a visitor some weeks back, and you will never believe this, he slept in the same cot as you slept in last night, his name was Pender, isn't that amazing! He is a beautiful young man, so well mannered, so shy with us."

Mari chimed in especially, "When you stripped him naked in front me and washed him all over, poor thing he didn't know what to do or where to look."

"It's my job to provide that service to all our visitors no matter who it is, just as we did last night for Zalenda," replied Zari.

"You didn't need to enjoy it so much," said Mari with a smirk on her face.

"Wait a minute," said Zalenda, "you had my Pender here! Come, ladies, tell me more." The conversation went all night. Everything that happened on that occasion was rehearsed in its fullest detail. Only then was Zalenda satisfied, and again as she drifted off to sleep; her last thoughts were of how she loved someone she had not yet met.

In the morning the three young women were wakened by urgent knocking on the door. Mari went to see what the problem was. She conversed with someone for sometime then turned to her friends and said, "We are wanted in the meeting place. Hurry and get ready. It's important." They were ready in minutes and left, Mari leading the way, Zari and Zalenda following behind.

The meeting place was a much larger room at a four-way junction. Already there were at least fifty people gathered together, and all waited in silence. From among a group of older men, the speaker came forward; the gravity of the situation showed on his face. "We have been encroached upon by a person whom we received as being in danger of his life, but apparently he was sent in by an unscrupulous group of people searching for a young woman whom they have been charged to kill. We believe that young woman is present with us." Questions came fast and furious from the gathering. Who brought him in? Where is he now? How can we protect ourselves? Why is she here? The man looked around at them. "This man has betrayed our trust at present. He is isolated in a tree, but we believe he is waiting to guide the gang here. At present we have no plan to get to him."

Zalenda stepped forward. "I am the person they have come to kill. On my way here yesterday, I was fortunate enough to evade capture. But I did hear a discussion they were having on what they would do to me before they killed me—none of it was good. However, I can tell you that they are not really to be feared. They are not good at scouting, nor are they good soldiers. I was right among them up a tree, and they were completely unaware of my presence—such carelessness in a war band of would-be soldiers is unforgivable. This traitor is up a tree. I will bring him to you tomorrow at this time if you will allow me to do this for you."

The speaker turned to Zalenda. "Young woman, that is an exceptional offer, but how do we know that you are the person Castor the Great referred to us? As far as we know, you might be part of this plot."

Zalenda coolly looked back at the speaker. "Sir, there is one way that your dilemma can be solved. Give me the longest-braided leather rope and enough to make a harness and allow these young women here to come with me to be my witnesses, and I will deliver on my promise. What do you have to lose? Without me will you have this traitor in custody tomorrow. Think well on that."

"You make a good point. Now withdraw while we debate this matter further. We will give you our verdict soon." The speaker turned to the group of men, while everyone filed out of the room.

Mari and Zari found Zalenda and were overcome with doubt. "Why did you offer us for this kind of thing? We are not trained warriors. We would not know the first thing to do."

Zalenda smiled at them. "I would not risk you two for anything in this world. You will be completely safe. All I ask is that you witness from afar when I bring this man in."

While they were talking, a messenger came from the committee to tell them that Zalenda could undertake her mission and the things she needed would be put at her disposal. The girls were excited. Zalenda asked them to calm down. She listed things that needed to be done right away. Mari was to find the guide and to get him to take her to the nearest point where the man was holed up in the tree, and she must be able to find that way later when Zalenda was ready to go. Zari had to go and get the rope and harness and bring them to the room. The last thing they were to do was to come back and to go to bed; they would be needed during the night.

Early that evening Zalenda went with Mari to reconnoiter the situation, and as she went, she memorized each turn, the sounds of her feet on the wooden walkway, because in the dark things would look different. Every detail was brought into mental focus; she was alive in every aspect of the word. She was in fact like a finely honed tool, sharp and ready for the work at hand. When they approached the area, Zalenda signed to Mari not to speak because in these woods, even the slightest sound could be magnified, and she did not want her quarry to know she was on the job. Zalenda stood for some time again, committing to memory every nuance of the scene; she noted the position of every branch of the tree. It was easy to find his hiding place. She noted that he had earlier relieved himself and left the evidence for her sharp eyes to see. Marks in the snow-covered branches indicated he was lying along a branch with a leg on either side. All this she quickly processed, and a plan was formulated. One of the largest trees she had ever seen towered over his tree, with multiple points of intersection. This was going to be easier than she thought.

With her reconnaissance finished, she indicated with her hand it was time to leave, and they headed back to the room. The girls were still very anxious of the part they were to play in the apprehension of this traitor, but Zalenda tried to comfort them by saying, "All you have to do when I have captured him is to go and tell the young men to come and guide me to the big oak and give me entrance. Now go to sleep, as we will be up when it is still very dark. Sleep with your clothes on."

When Zalenda awoke them, they were very sleepy; she, on the other hand, was ready and alert. She herded them to the observation point and had warned them before they left that they were there as witnesses so that they would be able to give a truthful account to their elders. The second purpose for their being there was to raise the alarm should anything go wrong. One would do this, and the other would remain to give her help getting back into the forest home.

With their hearts in their throats, they watched Zalenda wrap the rope and the harness round herself and launch herself up the great tree in front of them and pull herself along a stout branch. Moments later she was lost to their sight, as she was completely immersed by the snow-covered branches.

Zalenda silently and carefully moved down the big pine tree, being especially deliberate in placing her feet each time on each branch nearest to the trunk. She was guided in her quest by the loud snoring of her target; one quick shot to the neck, and he was unconscious. In this state, it was very easy for her to get the harness over his head and tie it in place. She then tied the leather rope to the harness and made it secure. When she was satisfied with the situation, she then made her way along one of the bigger intersecting branches of the tree that was her original point of access and secured the end of the rope. She pulled on the rope until the unconscious man was free of the pine, and then he was gently lowered to the ground. Once she had freed the end of the rope, she climbed down to the ground and tied him securely to the tree with the rope. She signaled to the girls all was well and to go and get the young men.

After what seemed like ages, two very tired young men approached, not sure what they would find. It was obvious to Zalenda that they were afraid to handle the man, although he was still unconscious and well tied up. It was left to her to pull him to his feet and half carry him. After a few steps, even to them it became obvious that this was not going to work. She made them overcome their fear and carry the man one at his shoulders and one at his feet. Soon they were back inside the tree fort. The man was placed still tied up in a secure place. Zalenda went to the room, tired with her exertions, and found her two friends in ecstasy. They were so proud of her and what she had accomplished. "None of the men could have done this," they told her. "We want to be on your team always."

After they had all slept soundly, they were called for the meeting with the elders. The man had regained consciousness in the meantime, and when they joined the group, he was sobbing bitterly. The person who had disbelieved who Zalenda was yesterday now regarded her with respect. It was he who seemed to be the main spokesman for the group.

"We are very much impressed with what you have done on our behalf. You told us what you would do and when you would do it, and you have delivered exactly what you promised."

Zalenda was very composed and did not immediately answer; she waited for him to continue. "Why did you not kill him? He is a traitor. He pretended to be in need. We gave him refuge, he partook of our hospitality, and then proceeded to betray us. You knew this, so I ask again, why did you not kill him?" His friends sounded their agreement, and others cheered. Zalenda waited till everyone was quiet, and they all looked expectantly at her.

"First of all, sir, you have answered your own question, I told you what I would do, and I have done it. That did not contain any promise on my behalf to kill this prisoner. He has not betrayed me. In fact, he has not wronged me in any way. The wrong he has done was against you and your people, therefore, his judgment is in the hands of this assembly. I will take my leave of you now while in it is in their hands."

As she left, Mari and Zari made to follow her. Zalenda held up her hand. "You must stay here as my witnesses, and you have my permission to answer on my behalf. I trust you with my life. Please stay," and the appeal was in her eyes.

Zalenda went straight to their room. By now she had the treetop walkway memorized, and the first thing she did was strip off all her clothes. Zari earlier in the morning had brought water and salve for her to wash with, but she had been too tired to take advantage of it. Her muscles were sore with the effort and the weight of lowering the prisoner to the ground, and somehow dead pine needles had fallen down inside her tunic, making her itch all over. She washed herself and scrubbed the pine needles of every part of her body and the inside of her clothes. When the salve was applied, she began to feel more comfortable and went to lie down on her cot, when the two girls returned. "Hey! That is my job," Zari teased. "Stand up till I see that is done properly.

Zalenda stood up and spun around like a top. "For your approval, missy." Both girls laughed so much that they collapsed on the cot Zalenda had just vacated.

Mari looked at her naked body critically. "How did one who is so slim and so light overcome a full-grown man and then on her own tie him up and lower him down from a high tree? Everyone wants to know."

Zalenda looked down to the floor and said quietly, "I was trained from when I was a very young girl to be what I am, a woman warrior, and I was never allowed to be anything else. I can never be a normal woman, have babies. I can love but never be loved. Look at my breasts—at my age still not developed, and I have never known what it is like to have a monthly flux like normal women. My queen turned me and others like me into a sexless thing to be used at her convenience, to defend our tribe because the men were farmers not soldiers. Now she would like to dispense with me and is trying to have me killed. I can never go back to my own people."

Mari and Zari came to her and wrapped their arms around her; they were weeping. "We are your family now. Wherever you choose to go, we will go with you. If you want to go and find Pender, we will go with you. We will be your true friends on any mission or on any journey that you have to make."

Mari said, "I have no purpose left here, I was raped by one of the men here. He was never judged for what he did to me, and every day I must see his leering face. I was pregnant and delivered a beautiful baby. A month ago they came and took the baby and sold her to another tribe. That is what they do to illegitimate children here—it broke my heart. I have no reason to stay here."

Zari then spoke up. "When I am another two years older, I will be taken and given to a man in this treetop community, whether I love him or not. I will give up one type of servitude for another. I have only that future to look forward to. I will follow you wherever you go."

Zalenda looked thoughtful. "All right, let us see what the elders here have decided what to do with their prisoner. We will go and have an audience with them and then make an intelligent decision on whether we leave right away or wait here over the winter."

They talked long into the night about what the future might hold for them and at last drifted off to sleep. Zalenda worried in her own mind whether she should go and find Pender. She loved him, but would he love her? And even if he loved her, would he want a wife that may not be able to have children? Whatever happened, she would love him unconditionally forever. This decision having been made, she fell into a deep sleep.

In the morning the girls were ready early to meet with the elders. The spokesperson on this occasion was not known to Zalenda; however, he appeared to have full knowledge of the circumstances. First, he informed them that the assembly had rule on the fate of the prisoner. Since they have a no-killing policy, even although he had betrayed their trust, they could not sentence him to death. He would be made to work cleaning and disposing of the human waste of all the Tree People. He would work during the day tied to his guard and would be secured at night with no room to move, and this was life sentence.

The prisoner had volunteered the information that he had divulged to his coconspirators—the code to gain access to the main entrance to this treetop bastion of safety. He then was to distract the young men on duty, while the others gained access, and they were to hold it till the rest of the slavers came. He then turned to Zalenda. "The elders have already expressed how much they were impressed with your work in capturing the traitor, and since we have no warriors among our people, they ask if you would consider protecting us against this new threat."

Zalenda waited till the full meaning of what she was being asked to do was understood by all, and when it looked like the loud discussion among those who had just come into the room was going on too long, the spokesman called for silence. "Sir, I know how evil these men are. As I told you before, I was their prisoner about to be sold as a slave, and I have no wish to see anyone here suffer that fate. I believe I can help you against these vicious men. However, I have some conditions that must be met. First of all, I will need the help of these two young ladies that are here with me. Then there are some supplies we will need, warm winter wear and food for at least three days." As she was speaking, Zalenda was watching the faces of the two young men who had assisted in carrying back the traitor. But the face of spokesman revealed even more. Her suspicions were heightened when he turned and signaled to them, and they left the room immediately.

The meeting was soon brought to an end, and it was agreed that the supplies would be given so that the new mission could be started the next day.

Zalenda told the girls to wait till everyone was gone. Mari was to lead the way back to the room but to be very vigilante; Zari was to stay close, and she would back them up. The girls wondered why she was being so concerned and asked her what the problem was. Zalenda said the whole thing was a setup—there never was any danger from the outside; it is from the inside. I noticed in my surveillance the other day that there were no tracks in the snow anywhere near the tree. How then did he get up the tree?—the same way I did. Who helped him?—the young men who pretended to be helping us. They had hoped to take me down when I was carrying him, but when I pretended weakness and made them carry him, they could not refuse, so they had to change plans. Now we must go back to the meeting room and finish this business. When we go into the room, stay behind me and stand with your backs to the wall."

When they entered the room, they found today's speaker, the two young men, and the traitor standing in deep conversation to the point where they did not know they had company; this is what Zalenda had hoped for.

"Gentlemen, I am not surprised to see you together, all of you traitors. Perhaps you have been discussing my demise, so I thought I would save you the trouble of coming to find me, I am here. Which one of you has taken my queen's money to kill me?"

The speaker looked up and said, "Kill her! We will never have a better chance."

The two young men rushed her keen to make a good impression. The first one was out of control. She kicked him in the groin, and as he was going down, she kicked his head; he was already dead. His brave friend slowed to a halt, fear in his eyes, and was turning ready to run when she hit him in the back. He went down with a whimper blood gurgling from his throat. The traitor approached slower than the others, a large club in his hand, which he kept swinging from side to side in an effort to make her back up. "You should have killed me when you had the chance, girly, but it's too late now." Zalenda circled to her right and noticed this was his strongest side. "This is true, but then I would not have found out who is the real traitor here—you, I expected—the other two were bought, but this one, that is the real treachery."

The speaker, his face red with rage, screamed, "Kill her! Kill her! We can sell the other two, just kill her." The club swung just over her head, and the effort he had put into it carried him past her, which left his left side exposed. She kicked him in the left leg, and something broke. He staggered and fell. Zalenda allowed him to stagger onto his feet. He lifted the club weakly and managed to poke her in the chest; it was forceful enough to make her cough. He tried to follow up, hoping now he had hit her that it would be enough to make her back away. Instead, she moved in like a flash and chopped his neck with her left hand. He would never laugh again. When she stopped, three dead bodies lay on the floor. The speaker looked aghast, his world had collapsed—he was about to be revealed as a crooked dealing liar, the true traitor. He bent to pick up the club from the floor, but Mari beat him to it. As he bent down, she brought it up, smashing him in the face. He staggered back, his nose broken and his face covered with blood.

People began to file into the room. They were alerted by the noise and the speaker's scream. Someone sent for the elders. When they came in, there was an unnatural quiet; people were barely breathing. Zari stood forward and told the whole story, how the speaker had contracted with another tribe to kill Zalenda and in the process sell them as slaves, and it would not have stopped there. She was about to continue when the elders rushed forward and beat the speaker with the club. They were so infuriated that each one took the club and smashed him in the head. He was dead long before they finished. "Take away the bodies and throw them down for the animals. We have received a lesson this day, let it be remembered forever. We will convene tomorrow to speak on these things," the head elder commanded, his breathing affected by his exertions.

Zari could not contain herself; her nervous energy overflowed as she recounted again and again everything that had happened. She replayed every kick, every stroke that Zalenda had made, even falling down and playing dead like the traitors. She pantomimed Mari picking up the club and breaking the speaker's nose. Then like some great sage, she acted out the story she had told before the whole company with flourishing hands and breathless gestures. Zalenda and Mari laughed and laughed until they were sore. The tension was broken, and when they saw the mock hurt look on her face, they collapsed in further convulsions of mirth. Any bond that had existed before between them was cemented now forever. The happenings of the day had shown how much they were prepared to sacrifice for each other.

The next morning they were called to appear before the elders again. They washed and did each other's hair; this was becoming a norm for the start of their day. While they were doing this, Zari noticed there was a large bruise on Zalenda's chest right between her breasts, where she had been hit by the club. Mari was visibly upset when she saw it. "This is bad. Let me go and get the special salve we got from the mystic woman to treat this. Zari, don't let her put on her clothes till I come back."

Zari examined the bruising critically. "Your physical activities are over for a little while, my dearest one. Why did you not tell us you had sustained this injury?"

Zalenda coughed and coughed again. When she stopped, she was quite breathless. "I was quite careless. I allowed him to get up. When he was doing this, I let my attention wander to the speaker. It could have cost me my life, one careless moment."

Mari came back just as Zalenda finished speaking. "We also are responsible we allowed you to face these men on your own. You were wonderful, but as we are friends for life, you must teach us how to protect ourselves and each other." When she had finished applying the salve, she bandaged quite tightly Zalenda's chest and helped her carefully into her leather tunic. The meeting was under way when they got there; one of the elders was speaking.

"We have been far too complacent trusting our tree fort would protect us, and it does. But if there is any lesson we must learn, it is this—it does not prevent us from being infiltrated. Our policy of accepting those in need and under attack from the slavers must be reconsidered to make sure they are genuine and not like those we have been fortunate to escape from without any lasting damage to our security. For this we can thank these three young people who have just arrived." He pointed to the girls, and everyone stood up and cheered them.

Another elder took the floor. He was the one who attacked the speaker first with the club. "I am not proud of what I did yesterday. I helped kill a man whom I trusted, whom I admired, who I thought was beyond suspicion, one who was loyal and true to this community. I was wrong. I believe we must not only change our policy in the acceptance of strangers but also train our people to be more watchful. They must be able to read the signs of approaching groups and individuals before they are on us so we can prepare ourselves for every eventuality."

The elder who struck the last blow at the speaker's head asked, "Where is there such a person among us who has these skills that we might learn?" This was greeted with silence.

Mari broke the silence. When she stood up, it seemed that everyone in the room exhaled at the same time. "Sirs, people of the treetop community, I know of such a person, one who is here today, one who has been with us these past five days. I speak of the young woman who last night delivered us from a very present danger. She is expertly trained in every aspect of defense and is more than capable of instilling into our young people the skills needed to give us early warning of approaching danger."

All eyes in the room were focused on Zalenda. When she did not answer, an elder who had not yet spoken asked the question that was on everyone's mind. "Is the young lady interested in spending the needed time here to help us with this problem?"

Zari replied, "Sir, the young woman you are referring to, her name is Zalenda. She was injured in the action in this room last night. I have been deputized to speak on her behalf. It was her intention to ask if she could stay here until the winter is gone. Now because of this injury, it is expedient that she does. This would give her the time to do the training that is required. At the end of this period, she and Mari and I will take our leave together, for we have another mission we are likely to be involved in."

The elders conferred for a few minutes then declared this was a good solution, but they would be sorry to see them leave this community. As people were leaving, several young women came forward and said they would like to serve their people training to be the fort's lookouts. Mari took their names and promised to contact them in two days' time, as it was necessary to allow Zalenda's injury to heal. That night the girls talked about the training that would be given, who would do it and when it would begin. But they also talked about the future, and number one on their agenda was to find Pender and then go and help Castor to get rid of the slavers. Zalenda's recurring dream to be with Pender took over her sleep.

Chapter 6

Rahana

Rahana looked out of the bottom cave. It was early in the morning, and her people were still asleep deep inside the hill. They only used the bottom cave in the winter because a shelf of rock immediately above it guided the snow down either side, leaving the front of the cave nice and clear. Sometime in the distant past, a landslide had swept down the hill, removing the earth cover, leaving the hillside completely denuded; only the black-blue volcanic rock remained. On a day like this, it was dangerous to try and climb up the slope, as the worn rock covered with ice and heavy snow could move at any time and cause an avalanche.

Rahana, however, had no intention of going up the slope. In her sixteen years, she had carried full-grown sheep and lambs up to the beautiful flat fertile fields that topped these majestic hills. She knew every nook and cranny, every step that could lead to disaster; for her it had become the safe highway to peace and indescribable beauty. Today while everyone else slept, she had put on her warmest sheepskin jacket and picked her steps down the slope. The heavy coat of mutton grease kept her moccasins from becoming uncomfortable and water logged, and her sheepskin leggings kept out the cold from the rest of her body. Her destination was the wide valley. This valley was six miles wide and fifteen miles long. Of course, these dimensions would have been meant little to Rahana; she only came here to appreciate its flatness with no slopes to climb every day—what a wonderful place to live. Centuries from now it would be, when it was safe for people to live in peace and security. But in Rahana's day, to live there for any family tribe or people would have been suicidal. It was indefensible; they would have been under constant attack from murderous bands. This was the reason that the original members of her tribe, when they came across the three caves, decided that this was good place to settle. Each of the caves went deep into the hillside, and where easy to defend, the bottom cave had the added advantage of having black rock that broke easily and burned with a deep red heat.

Once this wonder fire was started, they did not require to look for firewood as long as it was kept burning all night. The only disadvantage was the black soot that came off the fire and the rock; it coated everything, even people's skin. They soon became known as the Black People. Rahana hated that name, and she made sure she washed it off every day; for this she was mocked daily especially by the young men and her older sister, Marsha. She really didn't care; she had made up her mind when she was old enough she would leave this place. She had seen the world from the top of the hills and could not wait to see the lands beyond the rivers.

As she sat on a huge rock overlooking the valley, she watched every movement of the crows and the golden eagles. She saw a wolf pack hunting down by the small river where a stag had gathered his hinds. The older animals would be sacrificed in favor of the young. As she watched the life-and-death drama played out, she contemplated what her own life would be. If she stayed here in two years, the council would demand that she accept the position as a second wife to an older man on the council. Her mother had gone that way; she had lived in misery until the man died, all this because they were deemed lower-class people because their father was not on the council.

What Rahana lived for every year was the time before the spring lambing, when they moved up to the top cave and she had to carry the sheep on her back up the hill for the lambing season. The old rams were troublesome, but once they were on her back and smelled the scent of the sheep, they quickly settled down. The journey up the hill would have been dangerous enough without the added problem of carrying a full-grown sheep had it not been for the fact that sometime in the past someone had cut steps into the hillside. Once she found this ladder up the hill to her heaven, the view from the top was all the incentive she needed. The people wondered how this small person could take such a load day in and day out tirelessly up and down the hillside and never ask for relief. When the last sheep was up and in place, her job then was to notify the chief shepherd of anyone who was approaching the hilltop from the northern side of the hill. At this point, the plateau at the hilltop sloped gently down to a wide moor, and beyond was a mighty mountain range; it was a very impressive scene. The shepherds care little for it; their job was to increase the lamb yield from the year before, and they worked hard for this outcome. Their reward was the freedom they were allowed to take liberty with the young women who worked with them. Most of the young women welcomed this attention, as it was not allowed at other times in the year. Rahana resisted this vehemently; she had the reputation as hands-off. She would not only have fought them off—rape was not allowed—but also have reported them to the chief shepherd.

Today as she sat and watched the valley, her attention was caught by a scene she had often witnessed—a great eagle was attacking a young goat that was trapped in a hawthorn bush. Out of nowhere, she saw a young man and two large dogs trying to save the goat. They managed to free the goat, and it ran quickly away up the hill into some bushes. What happened next was difficult to take in—the dogs were exuberantly jumping up and down and knocked their young master backward down the hillside. He went head over heels several times down the hill until he came to rest on the edge of a cliff caught by the collar of his leather jacket. Rahana was up and on her way carefully picking her steps amid the snow and ice. When she arrived at the cliff edge, she immediately realized the dangers of the situation—the young man was unconscious, his jacket was holding, but the dogs were trying to get to him. She ordered the dogs off; they eyed her up but appeared to decide that she was here to help. Reluctantly they lay down nearby. Next, she dug footholds into the ice right though to the rock then placed her toes in the footholds and stretched out till she had her arms round his chest. She had to get him back into a conscious state so she kissed his ears and then bit them sharply; it had her desired effect. He started to mumble and then began to realize his predicament. He was hanging over a cliff with about one-hundred-foot drop.

Rahana asked his name.

He said, "I am Pender of the Island People."

She said, "I am Rahana of the Cave People. Between us, Pender, we are going to get you out of this situation. First of all, can you see how secure this tree is in the rocks?" It took Pender a few minutes to get used to his situation. At first, he felt giddy with the height, but as he got acclimatized to it, he carefully turned his body and was able to determine that the tree was definitely well anchored. He looked down and saw his feet were just an inch or so above the trunk of the tree.

"Rahana, if we had a small rope, I could get down on the tree."

She said, "Unfortunately, Pender, we do not have a rope, but I have an idea. I am going to give you my hair plaits—they are long and thick—you must use them as a rope. When I give the word, I will undo your jacket from the tree. As I am doing this, you must pull on my hair, and I will stress back against the rock."

Pender was about to object when she put her plaits in his hand and said, "Now!" He felt his jacket collar being undone, and then she was stressing backward and the plaits tighten. He thought her pain must be excruciating then he felt his feet on the tree. "Keep holding my hair," she ordered, "and turn round and face the cliff." It took some time for the feeling to return to his legs, and Rahana understood this. Her hair felt it was being detached from her skull, but still she held on. Pender felt the strength in his legs return and gingerly turned round and found that his head and shoulders where above the cliff. "Let us rest for a while till we recover our strength."

Pender gasped, "You must be in great pain."

"Let's not think about that just now. We must get you up from there," Rahana replied. "Have you any ideas?"

After they had rested for a while and felt more like continuing, Pender said, "Take my jacket, and I will tie the sleeves under my arms, give the dogs the body, and tell them to pull, and I will put my arms under yours and yours under mine. When I get off the tree, I will climb over your body. I apologize in advance for the pain I am going to cause you."

Rahana said, "Never mind that now. Let's just do it." Pender called Tarag and Toto over and commanded them to pull on the ends of the leather coat. It took the dogs just a minute to get the idea, and they gradually backed up the ice-covered slope, pulling Pender up as they went. When his knees were over the edge, he climbed over Rahana's prone body to relative safety. The dogs kept pulling on the coat until he was clear of her then he ordered the dogs to sit.

Nervous exhaustion overcame them both. Rahana turned round and hugged Pender, and they lay like that for some time. She realized it was the first time she hugged anyone, and it felt good. When they had overcome the stress of what they had just done, it was time to move from this precarious position to safer ground. Pender now felt the cold and had to retrieve his torn jacket from the dogs and put it on. Rahana carefully stood up, and she led the way. She told Pender to take great care in following her footsteps till they had crossed the ice and snow. Pender took his time until they got to Rahana's rock. There they rested the dogs with them.

Rahana waited till she and Pender had completely recovered from their ordeal before she asked who he was and why he was there. He wanted to know who she was and why did she put herself at such great risk on his behalf. They decided he should go first.

"My name is Pender. I am the second son of Castor the Great, chief of the Island People. We are a family tribe of about four hundred people, most of whom live in a settlement at the side of a lake. Many generations ago when the tribe was small and was being hunted from place to place, they came to the lake and saw the island as being the perfect place to put down roots. We have been there since. Why am I here? My older brother tried to take over as chief of the tribe and committed many despicable deeds, for which he is sought by our elders to bring him to justice. We heard that he had been seen in this area, but like many other rumors, I found it to be false. The rest you now know."

"As I told you, my name is Rahana. I belong to a family tribe known as the Cave People. We get this name because there are three caves we live in. At this time of year, we live in the bottom cave because it has a black rock in it we can break down and burn. It gives off wonderful heat. In the high days of summer, we move to the top cave. So the weather dictates which cave we live in. The caves go deep into the hillside. Water is readily available, and the caves are easily defended. For a small tribe of one hundred people, they are quite comfortable. As a people, we are smaller in stature than most tribes, and we tend to have darker skin. My skin is darker than most, and the young men taunt me by calling me blackie, a name I hate. They use me to carry sheep from the center cave up to the pasture in time for the lambing—it is a difficult task. The young women who go up to help watch the sheep behave abominably, my sister among them. In the caves that behavior is punished, but up in the pasture anything goes. I will not be associated with that type of behavior, so I am mocked. Today I was up early to come to this rock. I often come here to look over the valley and wish I could get away from this place. I was contemplating what my life is going to be like when I saw you rescue the little kid goat. Most men I know would have ignored it, but you had compassion for it, and I thought to myself this is a person I would like know.

"It was then I saw you fall, and I knew I had to do something to help. I had this urge inside me that I cannot explain, to do everything in my power so that you would continue to live. I am not good at socializing with people and definitely not with young men. If I have said anything to embarrass you, please forgive my inexperience."

Pender said quietly to Rahana, "I to have a problem in dealing with people. As the son of Castor the Great, I was not allowed to socialize with anyone except my uncle and his friend. Until recent happenings in our family, I had never spoken to anyone other than my sisters. You saved my life. How could I be possibly be embarrassed with anything you said when all I want to give you is my everlasting gratitude?"

"Come, if I don't take you and feed you now, you might die of starvation, and that would be truly embarrassing. Follow me up over the ice and snow, but we had better leave the dogs here. We are shepherds, and strange dogs will not be popular with my people."

Pender ordered the dogs to stay at the rock.

On the way up to the first-level cave, Rahana stopped and whispered to Pender, "Pretend we are stopping for a rest. When we get to the cave, a large group of my people will surround you. Let me do the talking. I will tell them you have difficulty with our accent. Let me warn you of a man who often comes here, his name is Bisram. You will recognize him quite easily because he will be the only fat person there. He comes here to trade for mutton, lamb, and sheepskins, but he is a bad man. He masquerades as jolly person, but all the time, he is soliciting information, which he sells to any interested parties. Some believe he buys young girls, uses them, and then sells them to the slave traders. He is a dispiteous man."

Just as Rahana had predicted, when they got to the mouth of the cave, there was a group of about twenty men lounging around, and women were running to serve them. They bombarded Pender with questions, which he appeared not to understand. Rahana told them he was a traveler who had lost his way and she had offered to help. She did not stop to explain and casually linked her arm through Pender's, guiding him deeper into the cave. While Pender's eyes adjusted to the gloom, Rahana sat him at a table and brought food and a drink then sat down beside him. Forty pairs of eyes bored into her; this was not according to their custom. She should have introduced him to the elders first then the rest in order. She knew full well what she was doing and was prepared for what would come. That morning at the rock had changed her forever.

The head elder stood up. "Young woman, you have transgressed our tribal customs and courtesies, and for that you will be punished. Bisram here has asked for you. He shall have you and this young man to sell where he will."

Rahana didn't even stand up. She turned to Pender and said in a very low voice, "Call up the dogs." Then she addressed the seated company. "This young man is the son of Castor the Great, a very large tribe that we really do not want to offend or go to war with. He already knows the reputation of your friend Bisram here and is not impressed."

Bisram sneered, "Young woman, I will have you, and when I am finished with you, I will sell you as a slave and young Pender here with you. Oh yes, I know him and his family. I also know why he is here. You see, I have business with his brother, Kain."

Pender did not say a word. He stood up and whistled. Two minutes later, the wolf hounds bounded into the cave. Bisram screamed in terror. He was absolutely terrified from dogs; Rahana had known this. "Now,

Bisram, tell me exactly where my brother is, or the dogs will eat your liver." Pointing to the dogs, he said, "Up, up," and the dogs jumped up on the table. The people sitting at the table scattered in all directions, but Bisram was transfixed and he could not move.

"Your brother, it is said, has gone to seek refuge with the Water People. In return, he has offered his services as a warrior."

"Thank you for that information," Pender replied. "Now you will tell these good people here why you are here and what business you have with the slave traders—the truth mind, sir. Tarag, take him by the throat."

Bisram wept as he related that the real reason he was there was to find out when the shepherds were going to move up to the hill pasture. While they were engaged in this, he was to inform the slave traders, who would attack and have everyone at their mercy.

Pender spoke to the elder. "I will make allowance for your behavior because this man has fooled you, but it was not hard. You take your authority too far, and because of this, you placed your whole tribe in danger. As punishment for your foolish behavior, I would suggest to this company that you be removed from your position. I also suggest that those who make the decision should replace you with someone more circumspect as to whom you allow into your confidences. The slave traders employ men like him to get to know your business and men like my brother to enslave your people. Do not treat them as friends—they are your enemies. This man must be punished. I will leave you all to make that decision. Now Rahana and I will take our leave, and anyone who follows us, the wolf hounds will eat."

As they were leaving, a young woman stopped them and thanked them for what they had done. She had been given to Bisram as well and would have had to suffer the same fate as he had promised Rahana. She questioned Rahana about leaving her sisters, what she should tell them. "Just tell them what you witnessed here—that will be enough."

A commotion from the inside made them pause. Bisram was being frog marched out, and the people were shouting, "Over the cliff with him. Let the wild animals eat his flesh."

Rahana said to Pender, "I feel no sorrow for him."

"You were magnificent in there. You spoke so confidently. I thought you had gone too far when you criticized the elder, but I saw all the heads nodding in agreement. It looks like something good will come out of it. I hope the girls will be treated better."

"You were pretty good in there yourself. I knew when the elder spoke, I had to get you out of there. Are you ready to leave?"

"I will pick up some food for the journey and a sheepskin jacket for you—your leather one is badly torn. By the way, where are we going?"

"We are going home to my family, back to the island, where we will rest for a few days then we will go and look for my brother."

"What will they say when they see me?"

"What do you mean?"

"In case you haven't noticed, I am very small and black."

"I didn't notice it when you were holding me from falling over that cliff with the hair of your head, and should anyone of my friends notice it, they will have me to deal with. Let's get on our way. We have a long way to go, and we will have to find somewhere safe to rest tonight. Tarag will lead the way, and Toto will have our backs. Don't worry, they are very good at what they do—they were well trained by my father."

They walked for the rest of the day descending the treacherous hillslopes, but down in the valley, the snow was pretty well gone, and there were only small parts where the going was tough. As they went, Pender told Rahana the whole story of why he was hunting his brother for betraying his father and murdering his mother. That night they slept under a hawthorn bush. The dogs were excited because the last tenant had been a wild boar. They found dried ferns to make a bed, and Pender lay down, and Rahana lay on top of him with a dog on either side. They were quite warm, and soon they were fast asleep. In the morning Rahana was quite embarrassed when they awoke to find she was cuddled into Pender, arms around him cheek to cheek. Pender passed it off as reaction to the cold of the night. But Rahana felt she had to make him understand that though she liked him very much, she had no romantic feelings for him and never had for anyone, and she was sixteen!

Then Pender told her about Zalenda and how he loved her but had never even met her, only that one incident, and he was not quite eighteen yet. They laughed and decided they could be best friends. It was time to move on, and after they had eaten their meager breakfast and fed the scraps to the dogs, they cleaned off the dried ferns from their clothes and started their trek for home. In the valley the morning here was different, no bone-chilling winds; instead it was warm, and the light gave a brightness to every color. This was even better than she had imagined. The air was cleaner and easier to breathe; she felt reborn.

By midafternoon they reached the settlement, and straight away Pender asked for a meeting with some of the men and Abbi. He took Rahana into the meeting with him and gave a report on where Kain was said to be with the Water People. He introduced his new friend Rahana and gave a full account on how she saved his life. Soon everyone in the settlement heard what she had done to the point where she was applauded everywhere she went. People stopped to tell her how much she was appreciated, and they hoped she would stay.

When the business of reporting to the meeting was concluded, Pender was impatient to return to the island, but not before he had received very clear instructions for his next mission. It was to collect information on where Kain actually was living and under what circumstances without endangering himself or his companions.

Rahana was very attentive as Pender explained to her how they would pass over to the island and what they would find there, as things had normalized since the earlier troubles with his brother. At the ferry, Rahana was mystified, excited, and scared; mystified how the ferry worked, excited to be going on it, and scared because she was afraid of the water in case she fell in. The young men at the ferry were interested in Rahana. Like the people in the settlement, they had never seen a black person before. They wondered at her height and were enchanted with her beauty but were too shy to speak to her. Rahana, however, was not at all shy. Through speaking to the settlement people, she had quickly picked up the cadence of their speech; so the whole trip over, she chatted to them about their work and what would happen if they fell into the water. She was disappointed when the trip across the water was over so quickly; this indeed was a very exciting new life. As they were leaving the ferry dock, one of the young men told Pender that three beautiful young women had arrived the evening before looking for him.

Pender assumed that the strangers must have news of the whereabouts of Kain and hurried in to meet them, while Rahana lagged behind, eyes wide open in wonder at all she saw of her new home.

To his great surprise, his visitors were the center of attraction in the main room. His sisters, Cisi and Ester, were hosting a gathering of young women, Morag, Nena, Pipa, and Rona, but the guests of honor had their backs to him and were so busy chatting that they had not noticed his arrival. Zari noticed him first and rushed to meet him. She was busy hugging him when Mari pushed her out of the way and threw herself at Pender. Zalenda stood back looking in awe at what her friends were doing to Pender. Pender hugged them back, but his eyes were on Zalenda.

It was at that point that Rahana made her entrance. She surveyed the gathering and noticed the embarrassment of the situation—two girls all over Pender. One whom she recognized from his description must be the girl whom he loved and had never met. She immediately took control of this dilemma, walking into the center of the group, thus becoming the new center of attraction. She announced, "I am Rahana of the Cave People. Yes, I am black skinned like most of my people and small in stature for my age, and I have come to live with you if you will accept me. I would love to tell you how I met Pender and how we are special friends, as I can detect that you all are, but first, I must tell you that there is one person here whom Pender loves desperately yet he has never met, and now I know she loves him."

She pulled Pender by the hand toward Zalenda. Mari and Zari caught on to what was about to happen, and they pushed Zalenda toward Pender. Rahana said, "Pender, this Zalenda."

And Zari said, "Zalenda, this is Pender." For a few moments, they stood and looked at each other, oblivious to anyone else but uncertain what to do next.

Cisi broke the silence. "Kiss her, brother, you're supposed to kiss her." After an embarrassed silence, he did, and everyone cheered. Zalenda did not want him to let go, so she held him as close as she could, but after some time with everyone talking at once, she pulled him over to where Rahana quietly stood.

Still holding Pender's hand, she bent down and picked Rahana up. Everyone fell silent. Zalenda said to them all, but especially to Rahana, "This is my sister. Anyone who rejects her rejects me. Anyone who accepts me must also accept her. Anyone who loves me must love her. Anyone who hurts her I will hurt in return." Then with tears running down her cheeks, she kissed Rahana then she took her by the hand to all in the group and said, "This is my sister Rahana. Love her as you would Pender and me, and we will love you forever in return."

In the morning, Cisi and Ester had arranged for the breakfast to be served in the main hall so that it was easier to keep the group together for the meeting with Abbi to plan for the upcoming missions. Abbi had given up hope of trying to get a consensus among the men for a plan to catch Kain and free Castor, and even less chance of freeing up some of the young men to take part in any kind of mission.

After breakfast was finished, Pender reported on his unsuccessful mission to find Kain and his experience with the Cave People and how once again the slavers were using inside information to plan their operations. He showed how agents for the slavers cooperated with two elders of these tribes to commit the ultimate treachery to make slaves of their own people. Mari supported Pender's statement by telling how three people from the tree community, two young men and an elder, were betraying their own people to an agent and how they all would have ended up slaves had it not been for Zalenda. She then told them how Zalenda had dealt with the traitors and then devised a plan to train young women as the eyes and ears of the forest so that tribe would be better informed of the movements of the slavers.

Rahana was not used to speaking in front of people and being listened to, but her earlier experience with this group had given her great confidence. "I have told you already that I belonged to the Cave People. My work there was mostly involved with carrying sheep up the hills to pasture. This was considered the lowest of the lowest form of work. An agent called Bisram inveigled his way into our tribe and arranged with our main elder to betray us. I was to be taken by Bisram to be used as he saw fit, and this would have happened if Pender and his dogs had not intervened. I believe that every tribe must be warned of the tactics that the slavers are now using and follow the plan that Zalenda has already put in place among the Treetop People.

Abbi had listened to the conversations with great interest and suggested an unofficial plan should be in place for each tribe, but that it should not be talked about outside of this group. He had already tried to have a discussion with his own elders around these issues but found them most unwilling to relinquish any of their perceived authority surrounding tribal safety issues.

"In the face of this foolishness, it would be a complete waste of time to suggest any plan that would involve taking young men away from their daily occupation to guard against a danger that was not seen to be prevalent. I agree with our new friend Rahana that an unofficial group of young women trained in Zalenda's methods should be the eyes and ears of our tribe to prevent infiltration from outside."

Zalenda looked around at her friends and just for a moment let Pender's hand go and said, "If it is not possible to alert our leaders to this new danger, then we must give our young women the skills to know where danger lurks. They must learn the language of the crows, the chatter of the birds, the sudden upward flight of flock of feeding starlings, and why the forest becomes strangely quiet. They must learn to read the faces not only of travelers looking for rest also but of people they have trusted all their lives. It is a lonely occupation if you are in it alone, but we have been alerted to the problems, and we do have each other. Mari and Zari have become very adept in these skills and are imparting them to the young women in their tribe. The people of the forest will not be caught a second time unprepared. I suggest that we ask them to stay here to train our young women. Perhaps Nena and Cisi can come up with a reasonable excuse for them to remain here for the next four or five weeks. I must leave, and it will break my heart to be without the person I love most in this world. I made a vow that I would follow the trail to Castor the Great and assist him to destroy Slave Island and all it stands for, and not only there but also wherever else they operate.

"Castor protected me from the guards on the island and made it possible for me to escape. He told me about the young man I loved even before I had met him. I owe Castor my life and my love. I will not be untrue to my vow. I will leave on my own to search and to observe and will return in two weeks—that is thirteen days, fourteen nights. With the information I gather, we will make a plan to set Castor free so that he might lead us to destroy Slave Island and all those involved in this treacherous, despicable trade."

Pender took Zalenda's hand again and looked into her eyes and said, "I cannot think what it will feel like to be without you now, but this vow you have made is worthy of you, and therefore you must go, and my heart will go with you. You go for my father. I must go for my brother."

Before the meeting broke up, Abbi told them he must leave before the elders became suspicious, but not before they had decided that Mari and Zari would stay to learn how to make mead and ale, but also to train Ester, Morag, Pipa, and Rona. Nena and Cisi would be the leaders because they already had legitimate business in the settlement looking after supplies for the whole tribe. Nena would request the elders look into acquiring sheep for the settlement, as they were a good source of food and winter clothing. Rahana would take charge of the sheep in the settlement and would also learn to make mead, beer, and ale on the island. Cisi would continue to be in charge of everything on the island. Pender would continue to report to the elders, as usual, on his progress to track down Kain.

When Abbi had left, Pender quietly told the group not to confide in his uncle; although he hated this group of elders, he also was one of them. Pender also believed that the elders were not interested in ransoming his father because they were enjoying the prestige the position gave them. He already knew they had sent him at least twice on information they said they had gathered on where Kain lived, and it was nothing but lies. He now had what might be called reliable information, and he would continue to hunt him down with the help of the dogs.

Pender would leave at the same time as Zalenda and return just before she came back. Before they left to go and bathe in the hot springs, he took Nena aside and asked her to keep her eyes on Abbi—he already knew too much—and if any of the girls entered into a relationship with any of the young men.

In the afternoon, Cisi took the young people to the hot springs, and of course, Pender was not invited. Rahana held back as the girls stripped off all their clothes and jumped into the hot spring water. She was amazed at how completely uninhibited they were with each other, cavorting and laughing in obvious delight.

Zalenda was in the middle enjoying the freedom to laugh and enjoy these moments, naked in these beautiful waters. When she noticed Rahana fully clothed, standing, looking quite miserable, she vaulted out of the water and came to where Rahana was standing. She said, "Come, sister, we must play. The water is delightful, and who knows when we will have such an opportunity again?"

Rahana replied, "I have never been in water in my life, and I am afraid. No one has ever seen me naked. I am black, and you are all so beautifully white, and you are the most beautiful."

"Rahana, you must never say anything like that again. You are the reason today that I am happy, but for you I would be in despair—you saved my lovely Pender. For that I will love you forever, but not for that alone—I love you for being you. I have taken you as my sister, and I will guard and protect you in all circumstances, especially today while we play in the water. Come, let me help you take off your clothes, and I will help you into the water." Rahana stood transfixed as Zalenda very gently took off her clothes and led her to the water. Once in the water, she took her into the middle one step at a time, never for a moment taking her eyes of her frightened friend's face. The girls seemed to know that this was a special experience for Rahana, and they all came quietly to her side to encourage her. Soon she was able to relax a little, and Zalenda walked her around the pool a few times till she was ready to walk on her own. Then she picked handfuls of water and let it run down over her body. She sat down in the water like the rest of the girls and luxuriated in the hot water. This was so much better than anything she had experienced before—and she was naked!—with her new beautiful friend, not self-conscious, not afraid, accepted for who she was; her rock had led her aright.

Nena came with cloth towels they had traded for skins of ale and beer from a passing trader. Each one was given one, and Rahana was about to dry herself when Morag came and asked her to dry her body. The towels were so lovely and soft, and Morag insisted she dry her everywhere. When she was finished, Morag took her towel and proceeded to rub quite vigorously over all of Rahana's body. She then produced a small woven basket with honey wax and rubbed it all over Rahana; then she did the same for Morag. Rahana looked around and saw that all of the girls were similarly engaged. She thought within herself, *I want to stay here forever.* But the experience was not over yet. They all dried each other's hair and washed their hands in a very light oily substance and rubbed into each other's scalps. Then she was asked if she wanted one braid or two, and Cisi and Ester did all their hair dressing with flowers and shells. The day ended with a beautiful meal in the hall prepared by Cisi and Ester. Then they all sat down and enjoyed each other's company; tomorrow's problems forgotten for now.

Zalenda and Pender were up early in the morning and sat in each other's embrace for a long time, each of them unwilling to break the silence. Knowing the dangers they faced made this time together even more precious. Pender broke the silence. "Zalenda, now that I found you, I do not ever want to leave you, but circumstances have evolved to keep us apart."

"What do you propose, for I feel the same way?" she said, turning her head until they were face-to-face and looking to his eyes.

"I have grave suspicions about my uncle Abbi. He never looks me in the eye, and he spends too much time at the settlement—this he never did before. I believe he craves the position of temporary chief while my father's position is still uncertain. I think that although my brother tried to hang him, he would gladly send me into Kain's trap. I propose we pick up our supplies and cross to the settlement now. You will make sure you are not seen by circling around it, and I will make sure I am seen by going through it with the dogs. We will meet at the ridge on the hillside and climb into the trees so we can watch the road—the dogs will be quiet. Should there be men sent to warn Kain, my suspicions will have been proven true. Then I will accompany you on your mission to keep your vow and bring my father back. I can deal with my uncle and Kain later."

Zalenda smiled and said, "From the first time I saw you in that compound, I knew that I loved you, and I also knew if I ever got out, I would seek you out and that you would be in my heart forever. Although I had never met your family before, I love the girls and your father, but like you, I watched your uncle and his statements. While we were discussing, our plans rang strangely untrue, especially when he insisted that we should not involve the young men. Most men would have seen this as the first line of defense. Your plan is good, especially the part where we go together."

Chapter 7

Pender and Zalenda Find Kain and Deal with Abbi

When they were ready to leave, Zalenda went and found Nena and told her they were leaving according to plan. Then she went and found Rahana and hugged her and told her that they would be back soon.

Pender went and picked up the vial of tree bark poison and a skin of beer; Abbi's plan might be needed again. They crossed over in the ferry and had to pull the ropes themselves, but this meant that no one knew that Zalenda had crossed with him.

Pender took the dogs and made his way through the center of the settlement, making sure he was noticed by stopping and speaking to some of his relations. He noticed that there was action around the meeting place, which was unusual for it being so early in the morning. His interest was further piqued when he saw Abbi come out with a wooden goblet in his hand—that might indicate that they had been meeting all night. He signaled a greeting to his uncle then carried on out of the settlement without looking back. After walking for a mile or so, he let the dogs run ahead. It was a beautiful morning, the sun was just climbing over the hills, and the birds were in song; spring was in the air. As he approached a grove of mature trees, he saw that Zalenda was already there. She had watched him from the distance, her keen eyes scanning the horizon to see if he was being followed. They embraced each other, kissing very tenderly as if they had been apart for a long time, not just for two hours, but they were still reluctant to release each other.

She reported that she had not detected anything suspicious and was confident that no one had noticed her. Pender told her about the meeting place being in use this early in the morning and seeing Abbi there with a goblet in his hand as if he had been drinking for some time. Pender believed that this in itself was not suspicious, but it was definitely behavior out of the ordinary for Abbi to drink so early in the morning.

They decided that she would take up a position in a tree near the center of the grove so she could scope in all directions. He would go further up the hillslope to a point where the bracken was very thick. There he would have an uninterrupted view of the road coming from the east. As both dogs were trained to be quiet while on watch, they would share them; Tarag going with Pender, and Toto, who was preferred by Zalenda, would remain with her. They would only communicate through the dogs. If Tarag came, she would know something was up, and the same would hold true if she would send Toto.

He reminded her that if the need should arise, the dogs should be ordered to kill. They kissed again and went to their posts.

Two uneventful hours had passed when Zalenda saw Abbi riding on a small horse making for her position. Two other people walked along the path well behind him. Zalenda slipped down from her position and sent Toto off to Pender, only to find Tarag coming toward her. She ordered Tarag into a hawthorn bush where it was impossible to see him because it contained lots of dead undergrowth around it. She then slipped up into the tree, taking great care not to disturb any of the branches so that even a careful observer would not see her movements. She chose branches that would give her good support and cover, but not so high up that she wouldn't hear conversation on the ground.

Pender, having been warned by Toto's arrival, was about to change positions when he saw Kain riding from the opposite direction down the next valley. He knew then he was being set up. They had been wise to have taken the precautions they had planned. Pender could see the track that Kain was on would intersect with the grove of trees where Zalenda was in position. He decided that he would watch and wait and see what would transpire.

Abbi arrived first, dismounted, and tied his horse to the tree Zalenda was hiding in. He took from his saddle pouch a skin of beer and drank deeply then sat below the tree to rest. The two other men arrived but did not come any further; they stayed on the perimeter as if on guard. Sometime later a big man arrived also on a horse. He just dropped the reins and let the horse wander.

"You don't trust me, Uncle?" Kain said, gesturing to the two men on guard.

"Should I, nephew, considering what you did to me the last time we met?—hanged me, as I remember, and old Brini as well in that old oak tree, then murdered my sister and left my nieces to die in the snow, and now you ask my help to get your hands on your younger brother. Trust you, I think not."

"I was drunk, and my men were stupid," replied Kain, "and my family would not accept me as their chief. They were just as much responsible as I was. All they had to do was accept me, and everything would have been all right"

"You were completely out of control. They knew you were responsible for selling Castor to the slavers, and because of your impatience to be chief and your nefarious deeds, you never will be chief."

"Then why are we here, Uncle? You sent the message to me. I did not contact you."

"Listen carefully to me, Kain, I have a proposition for you. We have been too long without a chief. Castor is still alive, and my nephew very foolishly let me in on his plans on how he intends to keep the tribes from the slavers and to rescue Castor with group of girls. He is very intelligent, and the women with him are as well, so don't make the mistake of underestimating him—he is no fool. My proposition is this—if you give up your claim to be the chief in my favor, I will deliver Pender to you. Things are changing among the elders. With me at the helm, I can make it possible for you to succeed me."

"How do you propose to give him to me, Uncle? If he is so smart, perhaps he already suspects you."

"Well, it is like this, Kain, when you have a formidable opponent, you concentrate on their greatest weakness. Your brother is in love with a very beautiful, talented young lady—you will like her. We take his woman, and he will do anything to save her. That's when you get him and her as well. All you have to do is let me be chief."

"I am interested, but I have to know when you intend to move against him, and, yes, I could use the woman's distraction. It's very lonely living up in your old summer hide. I cannot wait to get back home."

"It will be soon, but you cannot come back until I am firmly established as chief."

"Then our business here is finished, Uncle. You must be off if we are to avert suspicion, and I must go back to the hill. A word of advice, Uncle—don't bring these two to a fight," he said, pointing to Abbi's companions, "you will lose."

Pender watched Kain leave on his horse and then carefully made his way back to Zalenda's hiding place. She was already on the ground playing with the two dogs. As she heard him coming, she looked up and said, "Come, my love, I have much to tell you. I heard every word of your uncle and your brother's conversation. Such perfidy is beyond words." They sat down and shared some of the food they had brought with the dogs, and she related everything that she had heard. She held him close while he tried to make sense of his family's faithlessness and treachery.

"I could forgive my uncle for his disloyalty to me, but to seek to use you for his own ambitions is beyond my comprehension."

"He has proved your suspicions to be correct. What we did based on these today has forewarned us. We now must move immediately to reduce our danger. We must deal with them one at a time."

Pender was lost in thought as he tried to take Zalenda's words in. "We now know that Kain is on his own. We know where he is, and he does not know that we have that information. It would make sense to deal with him first. We have enough supplies to last another three days. What do you think?"

Zalenda smiled back at him. "Do you know our thoughts are more and more in sync? Sometimes you say exactly what I am thinking. Where is this hide that he spoke about?"

"The hide is just that, an old wooden structure that travelers used when sheltering from storms, Kain would not have known about it.

He must have learned about it from Abbi. Abbi has been feeding me misinformation to keep me away from Kain. He did not want me to meet up with him because it did not suit his plans."

"If we are going to take Kain out, and I presume he is not going to leave on his horse and go traveling anytime soon, we had better do it tonight. Later when it is dark, there could be some moonlight, and we will need this to travel on the hill." Zalenda spoke without emotion; she was already in her mission persona.

Pender was in that mood now. "We must go now up this hill while there is light so that we will come down on him from above. The dogs will lead us if there is no moonlight. We do not have any kind of weapons, and he is a big strong man. How do you propose to subdue him?"

"Big strong men get careless when faced with young women. I will deal with him. You must keep out of the way, but be ready to send in the dogs when I tell you."

They quickly packed up their supplies that they had hidden in the fork of a large tree. "From now on, we cannot talk because sound travels in these conditions, so we can only sign when you want to stop or change direction." Zalenda signed with her hand to show what she meant.

They climbed steadily for about an hour, Tarag in the lead and Toto bringing up the rear. Pender signed that they should move over to the west side, and after a short time, they were on the slope down to the valley. Kain made it very easy for them to locate him. He had kindled a fire and was obviously very drunk, singing at the top of his voice. The hair on the hounds stood up, making them look more like wolfs than dogs; they were ready. Zalenda held up her hand and listened carefully to make sure that Kain was on his own. Then they moved to the far side of the hide so that Kain would have to look through the fire as they approached.

"Is that you, Kain?" Zalenda asked in a very soft voice.

Kain stood up and said, "Why, it's my little brother and his whore come to visit me."

"No, Kain, we have come to kill you. You see, I was in the tree above you when you met Abbi today. You two were so good to tell us all your plans, and you were so keen to carry them out that we thought we should come tonight. Was that not nice of us?"

Kain let out a roar that echoed up and down the valley. He launched himself forward until he towered over Zalenda. "Now you, little whore, I will show you who is going to die." He staggered forward, his arms swinging, attempting to punch her on the body to bring her down, but where he punched, she wasn't there. She was coolly wearing him down. He stopped for a moment to catch his breath; this was part of her strategy. As he bent over gasping for air, she darted in and kicked him in the head. He was caught completely off guard. She caught him again with a kick to the front of the leg. He buckled and went down.

It was then that Pender ordered the dogs in saying, "Kill, kill." They tore his throat out, and he was dead. Pender did not feel a thing. This was the brother who had murdered his mother.

It took the two dogs and the two of them to drag Kain's body to the edge of the valley and push it over into a clump of bushes where the crows and the vultures would find it. Zalenda watched his impassive face as they did it. "What are you thinking about? I cannot believe that you can do this to your brother."

"I saw this man drag the bodies of my mother and Lay, my father's second wife, and throw my sisters out in the snow to die. He beat me and hung me from the lintel of the door, and he had his men hang Brini and Abbi because they would not accept him as chief. He was evil incarnate, not my brother."

Zalenda asked, "Why then would Abbi collude with Kain to bring us down? It doesn't make sense."

"It does when you factor in unbridled ambition. He used to be an enemy of Kain, but you heard what he planned for us. We will deal with him tomorrow," Pender said sorrowfully. "That will be more difficult for me. As well as being my mother's brother, he was also my friend."

That night they kept the fire burning and lay quietly together, the dogs on either side; it was not a comfortable situation, but as their minds slowly dealt with the day's happenings, they slowly drifted off to sleep.

Pender wakened early in the morning before the sun was up and spent time watching Zalenda sleeping. He thought about what would have happened had Kain hit her with a punch, like the one that killed his mother. He realized that he would never be able to live without her. She had lived with danger all her life; he was new to it. Now they must share everything that the future held because of their love. As he was thinking about what it would be like to lose her, she turned over in her sleep and stretched out her hand to touch him, and he was not there. She was awakened immediately in a state of absolute panic. She saw him sitting, watching her. "Never do that again," she scolded him. "I thought I had lost you. You must promise me that we will wake together every morning." The dogs looked at them, wondering what was going on. She cuddled Toto to her, and their world was back in balance.

As soon as the sun was up, they were on their way. "We must find where Kain put his horse. We do not want it to be caught by a pack of wolves or cougars. Besides, I cannot wait to see you ride it home."

"You might be surprised by this, but I have never ridden a horse in my life. I was five, four in your way of counting—why do all of the tribes have different ways of counting ages? It is very confusing, is it not?—when I was measured against the queen's standard. We were never allowed to walk or ride. We had to run everywhere. If we were found walking, we were beaten."

Pender laughed at her. "I promise never to beat you. You can crawl, walk, run, or ride, as long as you are coming to me, not away from me."

"Young man, you have a way with words. Oh, look! There is the horse. Quick, let's catch him before he runs away."

"It's all right. He is tethered. Now we will see how you look on a horse," Pender teased. "This I am going to enjoy. Turn and face the horse. When I lift you up, put your right leg over his back and hold on to his mane."

After several attempts, they were both in tears with laughter. "Young man, I perceive you are having way too much fun at the expense of my bum."

"That is the second 'young man,' and we had only traveled thirty steps. What are you trying to do—dazzle me with your aged wisdom?" Pender exclaimed with laughter.

"No, I am trying to dazzle you with my bum. Now get me up on this horse." Finally, after many more attempts, she was up on the horse. The laughter and fun helped to release the tension that had built up from the previous night. Now they were relaxed and ready for their next meeting with the elders at the settlement.

Pender led the horse down the valley slope on to the valley floor. Zalenda kept sliding forward onto the horse's neck until she learned to squeeze with her knees and hold on to his mane. "Well, how do I look now, your greatness?"

"Like the princess you are," Pender replied.

"Well, let's hope the elders will be as easily impressed."

"How could they fail to be?—you had the great wisdom to pick me." The pleasant banter continued until they were in sight of the settlement.

"What is your plan for this confrontation?" Now they had to get serious.

"It will depend who is there. Just follow my lead."

When they got to the settlement, they stabled the horse and went directly to the elders' meeting. Abbi was speaking and looked surprised to see them, probably thinking they were still out on the wild goose chase he had arranged for them. He was trying to convince the elders that as Castor's brother-in-law, he was the best choice as temporary chief so that important decisions could be made for the day-to-day running of the settlement. The elders wanted to have an open discussion with the people on that matter, when Pender asked to speak.

"I have information you will need before you allow this matter to go before the people." The speaker for the elders said that he was too young to have any wisdom on this issue. But Pender did not allow him to finish. "Kain is dead. My dogs killed him on my orders." Silent shock filled the meeting. "It is well known among you what kind of man my brother was. He killed three people, my mother among them, and there would have been more if one of our young women had not carried out my instructions. I would now be dead.

"But let me give you some even more important information. Early yesterday, my lovely lady here and I went to look for Kain. We had been supplied with false information as to where he was hiding. This information came from members of this committee. I suspected that this was the case, so we laid a trap. My very experienced lady climbed a tree in a grove just north of here. I hid in the hill high enough to see in all directions. Imagine my surprise when I saw Kain coming down the next valley to meet with someone in the grove. My lady will now tell you what she saw and heard while up the tree."

Zalenda stood up and looked directly at Abbi. He knew then he never would be chief and tried to rise and leave. But Pender moved across the floor and forced him to sit down. "Members of this elders' group, it is with great sadness I make this report. We were suspicious of Abbi's trustworthiness before we went, but because he is Pender's uncle, we hoped we were wrong.

"We found out we were right. Abbi, with two young men as guards from this settlement, arrived for a meeting with Kain. What is of great interest to you today is that Abbi was there to make a deal with Kain. Kain was to withdraw any claim he had in being your chief in favor of Abbi, who, when he was established in that position, would work on Kain's behalf to have him brought back into favor. In return, Kain was to be given information to trap Pender and myself, and we were to be his to do what he wanted with." Zalenda sat down, and there were gasps of fury and indignation from all around.

Pender stood again and continued to address the meeting. "As that discussion was going on, Kain gave away the information that he was living in the old hide up on the hill. Abbi knew this along and was prepared to have me murdered by Kain and Zalenda used as his whore. I cannot tell you how it feels to be so badly betrayed by a man I have looked up to all my life, a man whom I would have died for—this is the horror of betrayal. We went last night when it was dark and found Kain drunk as usual. He tried to kill Zalenda, but he was no match for her skills and training. When he went down, I ordered the dogs to kill him. They tore his throat out, and we dumped his body for the vultures. This was a fit ending for a man who defiled young women, sold my father to the slavers, murdered at least four people, and caused the deaths of many others. For this I showed him no mercy. You, as elders of this family tribe, must decide what you will do with my uncle. His betrayal is yours as well."

He stood up and took Zalenda's hand, and they left the meeting together.

When they got to the island, they conveyed all that had happened in the last two days to the girls. They were horrified when they learned of Abbi's betrayal. Pender said from now on they must all sleep in the same room with the dogs on guard till they knew if Abbi had any secret support in the committee or in the settlement.

Zalenda said that because they had slept out last night on the hill, she needed to go and bathe in the hot springs, and she wanted Pender to go with her. Pender was not sure if it was proper for them to bathe together. He was shy at the best of times, and he remembered how embarrassed he was when Zari stripped him and washed him in the forest treetops. He was just getting used to kissing and cuddling Zalenda, and he really liked that, but being naked in the springs with her was just too much too quick; besides, if she saw him nude, she might not like him. When he tried to tell her, she just turned and walked away. She did not turn up to eat that night, and when he got up in the morning, she had already gone with Mari and Zari back to the Forest People. She did not even leave a message! He knew then he would never see her again. He resolved that he would never fall in love again with a beautiful woman, but he knew within himself that he would love her forever.

While he was trying to find consolation in what they had accomplished together, a message came from the elders that he was required at the settlement. On the way over in the ferry, he asked the men on the ropes what time the ladies had left. They said it must have been early, and they probably had to pull themselves over. Pender knew then that she had deliberately avoided him. At the meeting, everyone seemed to know that she had left him; there was a lot of whispering in the audience and knowing looks being exchanged. The speaker told him Abbi had requested a meeting with him in the next room. He was very suspicious of this not knowing what Abbi might have planned.

When he went in, however, he found Abbi bound hand and foot and suddenly looking very old. "I will not attempt to apologize for my actions, Pender, but I have some important information for you. I know you will not trust me, I have given you little reason lately to do so. The first thing and most important to you is that a boat or barge will be coming up the Big River at the time of the new moon to take the slaves down to be sold in the market at the river mouth. If you are going to make an attempt to rescue Castor, make it soon. The second is that there are men, I believe at least three, presently with the Water People who plan to attack all the smaller tribes and take as tribute as many of these people as they can to be sold as slaves. The Water People are unaware of these men's intentions. The Cave People must be also warned as well as the Forest People. You must go as soon as possible. Do not trust anyone, even people in our settlement, and do not tell anyone where you are going. When you come back, I probably will not be here. Be true to yourself. I know you are the only person who can do this. Do not be afraid. Go and get the one you love. You need each other. A love like yours is a rock to build the rest of your life on. I forgot this and let blind ambition take away the people and the things I loved. Now go and be great like your father, but remember he almost ruined his life as well. He as a young man fell into bad company and got drunk with his friends Somer and Raymond, and they raped a young woman. Your grandfather soon sorted him out. Keep away from evil companions and do not start to drink like he did—it could have ruined his life. You are a better man."

Pender left the settlement and went back to the island. He had to see Cisi and Nena to tell them what had transpired. He wished Zalenda was here to talk about what Abbi had said, but as things were, he would have to handle these things on his own. Nena and Cisi already knew why Zalenda had left and were very sad that it had happened. "You just do not know enough about young women," Cisi said, "Zalenda, in her mind, was trying to pay you the ultimate compliment. In her tribe, that is a sign that you are bound forever. She could not see that your inexperience with girls and your natural shyness and social awkwardness with women and our tribal customs prevented you from attending on her. It is the wish of all of us here that your relationship can be repaired. You have two very loving friends in Mari and Zari who understand and will work on Zalenda to bring you two back together."

"Now let's talk about the situation that has come up and what we can do to help." Pender explained what the interview with Abbi was about and why he had to leave immediately and what supplies he would need. His first priority was to alert the smaller tribes. Then they had to have a plan in place to rescue their father from Slave Island before the new moon. He would need Zalenda's help for that mission; she had made a vow to do this, and he felt despite their problems she would keep it. "Now there is something you must do here, Nena. Abbi suspects that there are people in the settlement who are in league with the slavers. Somehow we must devise a method of watching those coming to and leaving on a regular basis. If we can identify who they are and where they are going, that would be helpful in setting a trap. Be exceedingly careful that they do not suspect that they are being watched. We do not want to put the girls in danger. Now I must go and warn the tribes."

Pender collected his supplies and the sheepskin coat he had been given by Rahana. She would have loved to have gone with him, but since part of his mission was to go to the Cave People, he did not want to put her in a difficult situation. He would take Kain's horse so he could travel faster and his dogs for protection along the way. His plan was to go round the lake and over the moor. This would bring him to a point that would overlook the Crannog on the big lake in the lower hill region. This was an artificial island built over many years, fortified and protected against roving bands and warring tribes, built mostly of large wooden platforms supported by stiltlike wooden tree trunks driven into the lake bottom. The walls were sturdy vertical round smaller trees with the joints mudded against the wind and rain. The roofs were supported by wooden trusses planked and covered with turf. Angled staked wooden fencing provided the defense against being boarded from the lake, and four wooden bridges gave access to the land. These had removable ramps that were taken up at night. At present they were all down, and people were moving along them as would be expected on a normal day.

Pender stationed himself where he could see people coming and going from all sides. He tethered the horse in a low-lying area where it would not be seen from the lake. Toto stayed with the horse, and Tarag lay down beside Pender to commence their lonely vigil. The night was cooler as the daytime temperature fell. He was thankful for the sheepskin coat and was quite comfortable, but as his mind strayed, he wished he had Zalenda beside him.

In the morning he was very careful in his movement so that he would not attract attention. It was late in the afternoon before anything interesting happened. He had watched a young woman in the morning taking eight goats to pasture on the main land. From his vantage point, he saw two men with red hair cross the bridge in the direction of the young woman—the Nuits, he thought to himself, working with the slavers. He had a premonition of what was going to happen next. He called to the dogs and was off running, keeping well back from the edge of the hill so no one would see him coming. When he got to the pasture where the young woman was, the two men had her down on the ground with most of her clothes stripped from her. Without hesitation, he kicked the one standing around, laughing at her distress in the middle of the back, bringing him down where the dogs savaged him. The one who was about to mount her rolled over in surprise, only to receive a kick in the head. Pender made the dogs stay back while he helped the young woman recover her senses and put her clothes on. Then he told Tarag to take the man who was still on the ground by the throat. "Now, sir, I want to know how many of you are in the Crannog. Tell me the truth or you die right now. See how your friend died? That is what will happen to you." The man sobbed that there was only one more of the Nuits in a meeting right now with the elders of the Water People to decide how many people they were prepared to give up to the slavers in exchange for being left alone in safety. "Now you dispiteous piece of trash, your fate is in the hands of this young woman whom you were prepared to rape and dishonor. What should we do with him, young lady."

She said, "Make sure he cannot do this again to anyone else."

Pender said to the dogs, "Kill, kill," and they did.

Chapter 8

Becca

The girl sobbed uncontrollably. Pender allowed her to recover before he asked her, "What is your name?"

She answered, "My name is Becca. I am the second daughter of the second wife of Dayton, the chief of the Water People."

"Listen, Becca, I am Pender, the son of Castor the Great. I am here to help your people, defend themselves against the slavers. We must get into the meeting right away. How can we do this?"

Becca said they will have people watching at the entrances. "We will have to swim out and come up behind them." Pender said that he was not a good swimmer. "That will be all right. I will help you all the way. Take your clothes off, and I will get your clothes before we go in to the meeting. Hide them here beside mine." Before he could think about it, he was in the water swimming naked with Becca, holding him as he swam. Several times he thought that he was going to go under. But she pulled him to the surface and kept him afloat till he could breathe and recover. They came to an underwater platform that they had to swim under. She took him straight down till he felt his lungs would burst, but she was swimming confidently underwater and brought him up the other side. As they surfaced, he was about to gasp out to let his lungs fill up, when she covered his mouth with her hand and put her finger to her lips to indicate that he must be quiet. She was quite unconcerned that they were both naked. She rubbed him down with her hands because he was frozen cold and shivering. She seemed to be oblivious to the cold and signaled to him to stay there while she went up a small ladder. He had plenty opportunity to see a woman absolutely naked. Becca came back fully dressed with clothes for him, and he quickly dressed. They were surprised to find the dogs had followed them, even swimming underwater to the platform. The dogs shook themselves vigorously and followed them up the ladder. Pender found himself in a small room with piles of supplies. So that is how they resupplied their stock, underwater! He had been trying to figure out how they would do that if they were under attack. Becca led Pender along a corridor into a meeting room that was full of people. A redheaded man was speaking.

Becca took Pender up to the front. A buzz of whispered conversations filled the place. The Nuit was saying the cost of doing business with him was fifty slaves. Pender ordered the dogs forward. He said, "I am Pender, the son of Castor the Great, chief of the Island People. I am here to tell you that your fellow Nuits are lying on the mainland with their throats torn out. The new price I demand is your head on a pole, to let the tribes see what happens to scum like you and those who support you. I came here to inform these good hardworking people not to give any hospitality to anyone, but especially to people who have red hair. I will be meeting with members of other tribes to give them the same message. I have not been able at this time to assert if the whole Nuit Tribe is involved or just people like this man who have gone rogue. This young woman here is a heroine. She was about to be raped by this man's fellows when I heard her cry for help. They will never threaten another woman again. She brought me here at considerable risk to herself, and I am beholden to her for her help. She is a remarkable young woman. Now let us find out what information this treacherous snake of a person can give us."

"Young man, you do not know who you are talking to. I am Taaker of the Nuits, and I have great power with the slave traders, and I can take you down anytime. I will tell you nothing."

"Sir, I beg to differ. You will be very pleased to tell me everything I want to know. Tarag, take him by the throat." Tarag took him down and held him by the throat, squeezing just enough to send Taaker into parallactic shock of real fear. "Now, sir, tell me how many agents do you have working for the slavers."

"I do not know, and I cannot tell you."

"Tarag, do it." The dog started to tighten his grip. "Toto, do it." Toto came forward and caught the man by the groin. "Now squeeze." The man convulsed in agony.

"Stop! Stop! I will tell you everything. In the next few days, we will send agents to every tribe. They will find a way in by promising help. Then they will pressure the leaders to give up their people for slaves. Our chief, Tamor of the Nuits, made this pact with Raymond and Somer, the head slavers. Our instructions come from the top. When this gets out, your life will not be worth living."

"Thank you for your help, sir, however, there is one thing you have not told us—who among the people here helped you?" As he asked this question, four men tried to get up and leave. "Are these the men?" Taaker nodded meekly. "Ladies and gentlemen, the plot has been made clear. I leave you to take whatever action you deem necessary. Remember these four men were prepared to sell you," pointing to Taaker. "If he is despicable, and he is, I ask, what are they? These men and many more like them are the reason I must take Becca with me. I cannot protect her here because she has helped me identify their agents. There are those who will be sent to try to kill her if she remains. We will give her time to say her good-bye and pick up her belongings, but we must leave here tonight because I have other tribes to warn of these dangerous people."

Becca came and whispered to him that there was no one whom she needed to talk to, for she was ready to leave now. "But my goats," she said imploringly.

Pender nodded and said, "Becca would appreciate if someone would go and pick up her goats before nightfall." As they made their way out, the chief of the tribe stopped them and said that he wanted to thank them for what they had done. They had saved many people from slavery, and he was announcing that the agent would be drowned immediately and the four traitors would be punished according to their customs. "Now," he said, "it would be most unfitting if I did not give them an invitation to come back at anytime to partake of the tribe's hospitality." The people stood and cheered and stamped their feet in appreciation.

When they were on the way to pick up the horse, Becca asked, "Where am I going?"

Pender laughed and said, "You have picked a fine time to ask. First, I must take you back to my home among the Island People, where you will be safe. My sisters and their friends are helping me in a mission to destroy the slave trade, but their agents were faceless men till we unveiled them today as those of the Nuit Tribe. You have been an invaluable source of help and courage, first of all, for getting me there. I would never even have thought of using the water as a way in and would have drowned had I tried. At one point near the platform, I was sure I was going to die, but you pulled me to safety. My mission succeeded today because of you, and I cannot thank you enough."

"Keep going, I love all this praise, but do remember that I was about to be raped. My worst nightmare was about to be played out. When I needed a hero, you were the one. Right now I would have been a broken person, but instead I am on my way to a new life. All because you ran to my aid—how special is that?—but keep heaping on the praise, I like it. However, it was a good thing we were there for each other, was it not?"

They got the horse from the little valley he had been left in, and now being quite expert at lifting young women up onto a horse, they left quickly. The dogs took up their usual positions, and it was getting gray dark before they reached the ferry. Pender had taken a circuitous route past the settlement, and as he hoped, they had to pull themselves over to the island. It was difficult to get the horse on and off the platform, but they discovered if they held his head up, he settled down. The dogs took off in a hurry to get to the kitchen to see what scraps were left for them.

In the main hall, the rest of the group were having their evening meal when Pender and Becca arrived. He did not introduce Becca right away, telling his sisters they were famished and needed food. After they had eaten, he introduced Becca and told them in detail about the mission and the significant part Becca had played in its success. He described in detail how they had obtained the information that the Nuits were now big players in the slave trade and were sending agents into all the tribes to pressure the elders and chiefs to give them a quota of their people as slaves. He explained that they had now very clear evidence that this was a concerted effort by the Tamor of the Nuits, Raymond the Transporter, and Somer, the head of the Slavers, to take as many people into slavery as they could. They discussed their plans for the next two days. Nena, Morag, and Pipa were to continue to keep their eyes on the settlement. Now that they had a definite description of their quarry, it should be easier to identify any agent who would be trying to infiltrate the system. When they found one, he should be dealt with right away by men whom they found it possible to trust. Pender told them he would leave early in the morning to go and warn the Cave People and the Warrior Tribe of the plot by the Nuits and the slavers. He asked Rahana whether she wanted to go with him to the Cave People, but she said she had no wish to go there, but if he wanted, she was prepared to go with him to the Warrior Tribe. It was then decided that they would go there first, and then he would go to the Cave People the next day. Rona, Cisi, and Ester would continue to get supplies ready for each of the mission, because within the next five days, they must free Castor before the slave barge came up the river.

The girls had arranged to go to the hot springs to bathe, and they invited Becca; they wanted so much to wash and work with her beautiful red hair, and of course, she was delighted to be included. Pender brooded about what had happened the last time they had bathed in these same springs and what it had cost him. But a bigger source of worry was what would happen when he had to go the Tree People within the next three days.

Chapter 9

The Mission to the Warrior Women Tribe

Pender and Rahana were up early to eat. While Becca walked the horse to get him ready for the journey, the dogs were feeding in the kitchen, and Nena was preparing her team ready for their mission. They crossed to the settlement without incident. Becca calmed the horse and fed him some oats. Pender took the same route as the day before, but he need not have worried—no one was moving this early. They turned east down the valley and arrived at the territory of the Warrior Tribe.

Rahana produced more oats from her pouch for the horse, and he kept nudging her for more. When she would give him no more, he turned his attention to the luscious green grass of the wide valley. The spring came early here. There were no hills or mountains to keep the air cool. Rahana removed her coat and lay down on it; she was sore from the hard ride. Pender looked around for cover, but there was none. He could see three very large rocks one visible to the southwest, one in the middle that ramped up from the valley, and the nearest one sticking up between a river and the hills to the north side. The only available cover was some very large trees at the bottom of the rock. He decided to follow the riverbed that wove its way around the rock, which was the only chance they had of getting there unobserved, and it would also be a good place to tether the horse. Rahana rubbed her legs and her rear and stood up, smiling. "I would have asked you to do it, but I know you have a problem," she teased.

"Now, now, I might have made a special case for you. You did that so prettily, I may have been tempted," he teased back.

"What is your plan for getting access to the queen and her senior ladies? What are we looking for, and how do we proceed?" she said, getting serious.

"According to Zalenda, there is a deep divide between the men and the women in the tribe. The women are tall and statuesque, beautiful, and are highly trained from childhood in all aspects of self-defense and war. We really do not want to get into a fight with them. The men are short and broad. They have a history of running away from a fight, and the women treat them as cowards. The men do all the work in the fields, in the home, and even make all the garments for the women. Only certain men are chosen for breeding, and only really special ones are allowed to service the queen. No one is allowed to know who their parents are, and anyone breaking this code is punished. However, Zalenda knew of one anomaly on that rule. Apparently, the present queen has a son who got into trouble with the Slavers—they took him. It was then the queen arranged for Zalenda to be taken in exchange. We know from this incident that we cannot trust her word.

"My plan is to approach the men working in the fields to find out if they have seen anyone visiting the tribe who has red hair. If an agent has infiltrated the inner circle of the tribe, we must unmask him and anyone working with him from the tribe, just as we did with Bisram, so you must have the dogs under control. If no one from the Nuits is there, we just make sure they are warned of the potential danger they present, and if that is the case, we can return home."

They made their way down to follow the river to their new vantage point, moving carefully and quietly, trying not to upset any wildlife that would give away their presence. Once they had gained the cover of the trees, they tied up the horse and fed him. Pender surveyed the new situation. He could see men working in a field some distance away, and there did not appear to be any of the women guards in sight. "Let's go and talk to the men and see if we can get any useful information. You can turn on the charm."

"Do you want to be hanged by nightfall?" Rahana laughed. "You remember my specialty is carrying sheep on my back up a hill."

"Thanks for reminding me. That might come in useful before the day is over."

They approached two men, and Pender asked them if they had seen anything unusual today. The men kept their heads down and continued with the work they were doing. Pender tried again but got no response. "What are you going to plant here?" Rahana asked. The men stopped and looked up, astonished.

"You're a woman and you're short like us and you are black skinned."

"Yes, all that is true. My name is Rahana of the Cave People. All our people have black skin. We come from a faraway land, I am told. I looked after sheep for my tribe." Men from other parts came to see why these men had stopped work, and they were equally fascinated with this very different young woman who talked to them as if they were equals. Soon they were telling her their names, what they did, and why they were there. One of them, whose name was Davi, asked if he could touch her skin. She said yes but only if he answered her questions. He agreed that this would be all right. Rahana leaned forward so he could touch her cheek, but he shook his head. She then offered him her hand, which he very gently touched. Others wanted the same privilege, so she shook hands with them all. She then asked Davi if he had seen any men recently visiting the tribe who had red hair.

"Yes," he replied. "Three men with red hair came yesterday to meet our queen."

Rahana invited all the men near so they could hear what she was about to say. "I want all of you to know why we have come. These red-haired men are bad people. They are agents for the slave traders. They will pretend to protect your queen from the slavers, but the price she must pay is perhaps all of you in this field to be given up to the slavers. You will be sold as slaves. We cannot allow that, so we would like your help to get into the meeting with your queen."

Davi said, "We will all go with you, and we will recruit the women warriors as well. We are not allowed to talk to them under normal conditions, but we will stand together. Even the young women hate this queen. Jona, go quickly and find out where the meeting is being held. The rest of you, stay here and pretend to work. I will go and tell the young women what we are about to do and why it is necessary."

Pender and Rahana continued in the field. He said to her, "That was very well done. Let's hope the Nuits are not alerted. I will get the dogs. We may have to apply pressure to get the truth."

Davi and Jona were soon back and reported all was in order, but they had to go now. Pender and Rahana were led through a labyrinth of rooms and into the back of a large meeting place. The young women filed in, and the men came in after and stood in a group.

The queen stood up and screamed, "What is the meaning of this intrusion into my presence? I will have you all whipped."

Davi answered, "You will whip no one today, Lady." He signaled to Pender to come forward and take the floor.

"Queen of the Warrior Tribe, let me introduce myself. I am Pender, the son of Castor the Great, chief of the Island People. The purpose of our being here is to unmask in your presence these treacherous individuals who are here with one purpose only—and that is to take as many of the Warrior Tribe as you will give them as slaves. You people should know that the Nuit Tribe has entered into inglorious pact with Raymond and Somer, the heads of the slaver who sell children, girls, boys, women, and men for their own personal gain." He turned to the people in the group and said, "Do you want to see this here?"

"No, no, no," they shouted.

Pender whispered to Rahana, "I think it is time to try the dogs." He whistled for the dogs, and they came bounding in and sat down quietly.

The Queen looked at Pender coolly. "Young man, you have made claims you cannot support."

Pender walked forward and pointed to the senior of the Nuits then said to Tarag, "By the throat and hold." To everyone's amazement, the dog leaped up and caught the man by the throat. "Now, sir, you can die right now or later, but one of you will tell these people what you have planned for them."

He said, "Never! Never!"

Pender called up Toto and said, "Now, Toto, now." Toto grabbed the man's groin and bit hard. The man screamed but said nothing. "Tarag, squeeze now." The man was choking and could not speak. Out of the corner of his eye, Pender saw one of the Nuits in an agony of despair.

"Wait, wait, please wait, that man is my father. I will tell you everything."

Rahana asked, "Who sent you, why are you here, and who else is a traitor to these people?"

"We were sent by our chief and the heads of the slavers to bargain with the queen to get as many people from this tribe to sell as slaves. The slavers are particularly interested in the women warriors here because virgins sell at a very high price. We have only dealt with the queen."

Rahana said to the group and the senior Warrior Women who were in attendance, "The Nuits are here on orders from their chief and have acted for personal gain. They must not leave here to alert their friends. You judge them according to your laws. Your queen was prepared to betray you all. Can you allow her to continue? You must deal with her now while the danger from outside is prevalent."

Pender said, "We have dealt with this problem here today, but the danger is not past. I have been advising the other tribes to establish lookout patrols and have constant guards around the perimeter of their territories to be wary of any visitor with red hair. We must leave you now, for we have other tribes to warn. I thank you, men and women, for standing up together today and making our task easier." Their leaving was delayed because everyone wanted to thank them. Rahana gave Davi a kiss.

Pender told Rahana that it was time to leave, as they had a long ride before nightfall. The young women warriors in training and a number of men from the field walked with them to the horse. They were all excited because the news from the senior women was that the queen was deposed and a more moderate person would soon be queen.

Rahana mounted up, and they said their final good-byes, the dogs in their normal positions, while their new friends waited till they were out of sight. Rahana was completely alive with joy, exhilaration, and effervescence. She could hardly sit still on the horse. "I think we made a big difference there. Your soberness personified. Be happy. I would dance if I was not on this horse."

"Yes, I think that was our most successful day yet," Pender replied, ignoring her jibe. "You were magnificent. Without you, it would not have ended like that. You, the sister of sobriety, kissed a strange man!

I asked you to charm them—they all loved you! I think I am going to make you our ambassador."

She almost collapsed of the horse, laughing. "What, a diminutive black woman an ambassador? That would go over big with the Cave People."

"How did you know if you picked the older man the son would give in?"

"Zalenda taught me to read faces, and this time it paid off, but without the dogs, it would not have worked."

"Who taught the dogs to do that? They are so gentle yet so fierce."

"My father had great patience. He taught them everything. See how without command they take up our protection? When we travel, they are invaluable to any journey we take."

"Pender, I think I would like to go with you to the Cave People tomorrow, would that be all right?"

"I was hoping you would change your mind. Let's get home. It is awkward carrying on a conversation on a horse."

It was late before they got to the island. They could not get the horse to go on to the ferry platform, so Rahana had to cross over with Pender pulling on the ropes. Becca came back with Rahana, and she calmed the horse down. Soon they were on their way. Becca saw to the horse, and Pender and Rahana went with the dogs to get something to eat.

The rest of the group showed up to hear the news of what had transpired at the Warrior Women Tribe. Pender let Rahana make the report. They could not believe the newfound confidence they saw in her. It was left to Pender to tell them how she charmed the men and even gave one of them a parting kiss. The girls teased her endlessly, but she gave back as much as they gave her. It could have been a perfect end to a perfect day, but it was not to be. Nena said she had learned that the slavers had brought the barge for moving the slaves from Slave Island three days earlier than it had been anticipated.

In the light of this new information, Pender said they would have to move up their plans to free Castor or find a way to delay the movement of the barge. It meant that they must visit the Cave People and the Forest People on successive days and do their scouting of the circumstances at Slave Island the next day. He would take both Becca and Rahana with him for the next three days. "Could the supplies be available in the morning?" Cisi said she could supply them for three days, but Nena would have to get the girls at the settlement to work with her to resupply the stocks on the island. Nena pointed out that would mean only two girls would be on watch. Ester offered to work the night to get everything ready for the morning and then take over for one of the girls on watch. This was seen as the best solution. Everyone went off to bed with plenty to think about. The next three days would be critical to their plans.

Pender asked if there was anything suspicious to report from the settlement. Morag reported that two men met with the elders briefly the day before, but they were there to talk about sheep. She had found a place to hide under the floor of the meeting room, which she could access from the palisade fence around the settlement. She had a position on the watchtower so she could watch who was coming or going. Her cover story was that she worked for the mystic woman delivering her potions and had to watch for deliveries. The nice thing about it was she was actually working doing this, so no one was suspicious.

Pipa reported that during the last two days, there had been a lot of discussions going on with two elders and some of Abbi's friends and relatives. She had posed as relative on her mother's side to be in on the discussion, but they were only were trying to dispose of Abbi's belongings.

Pender thanked them both for their good work and asked if they needed anything to continue. They both said they were excited to be involved in the plan and felt they could keep it up till the emergency was over.

The girls left for their time in the hot springs, and Pender turned his mind to the problem of how to delay the barge from leaving with the slaves. First of all, there was the time constraint. The new moon was in seven days. If the slavers were going three days early, he had to get at the barge. It must be done in such a way that they could distract the guards and be able to rescue Castor. Who could he trust to be on his team? Who had the skills and ability? Then there was the visit to the Cave People and the forest community. The dogs could only be used for journey protection. He wished Zalenda was here to help him.

In the morning, none of these things had been resolved in his mind. But he had resolved not dwell on them until the work at hand was done and he had made a thorough inspection of where the barge was tied up and studied the Slave Island defense system.

Rahana and Becca were all ready and waiting with the supplies, the dogs and the horse ready to be under way. They crossed to the settlement and skirted around it and made their way north over the wide valley. At the winding river, they found it was easy to ford because there had been so little rain. Becca and Rahana were riding the horse with the supplies, so they followed Tarag over to the other bank. It was a good place to rest, as they were protected from view by the high riverbank. Pender, walking a little behind, caught up to them, with Toto trailing as was usual some distance in the rear. After they had eaten, Rahana showed Becca exactly where they were heading and explained to her how they would be received. Pender felt it would be better if he did the initial report, explaining that they had received information that the Nuits were ready to aid the slave traders in an attack on their tribe. Depending how this was received, Becca would report on how they had planned to do this with her tribe and how it was avoided. Rahana would report on her experience yesterday with the Warrior Women Tribe.

Then Pender would tell them how and when the attack was to be made and how it could be defended against. The horse and the dogs were fed and ready to go, and as they made to carry on over to the opposite bank, they came to a sudden halt. They saw, away to their left just visible on the horizon, the unmistakable signs of a large company heading in their direction.

Chapter 10

The Missions to the Cave People and the Great Forest People

"Quick, Rahana, ride as fast as you can. Take Tarag with you and get to your tribe as quickly as possible. Tell them of what is heading their way and who it might be. Becca, put all of our supplies on the horse. You and I must run, walk, whatever to get there quickly as possible. Rahana, we will meet you at the rock."

Pender and Becca ran, walked, and ran again until they reached the rock. Tarag and Rahana were already there, but the horse was nowhere to be seen. Rahana reported, "I have alerted the Cave People, and they are already evacuating the bottom and middle caves. Some of the young men are carrying more heavy stones up to the top cave. The women and children have been moved into the deepest part of the cave, and the rest of the women are making hot coals to fling at the intruders."

Pender said, "We will stay here to observe how well they are organized and how many there are as they advance. We will vacate our position, and you can carry any information we gain up to the defenders. The Nuits may have stone slings, so tell your people to take great care in how they move."

Becca had been thinking about the situation. "Pender, if I went now with the dogs and went further up the river, I could swim the river and come up behind them and cause havoc by sending the dogs in at their heels."

"Becca, that is great thinking, but you are putting yourself in grave danger. I did not anticipate this. I would rather keep you with me here safe."

"Oh, yes, I see what you mean, here, right in front of an invading army—how safe can that be? I promise if I get into trouble, I will swim underwater all the way to the lake."

Rahana supported Becca. "If I could swim, I would rather be where the action is."

"OK, you two, enough. Now let's make trouble for the slavers."

The Nuits advanced without any seeming plan of action and stopped just short of the rock. They were laughing and joking about how many women they were going to have. Just before they were ready to advance again, Rahana gave the signal, and heavy boulders came rolling down the steepest part of the slope; it wiped out the first three lines. Just then Becca sent the dogs in. Some men had turned to run, but the dogs were told to kill, and they did. The rest of the Nuits and slavers were milling around, standing together in a tight group for protection against the dogs. Rahana held up her hand, and a rain of blazing coal rained down on the depleted force of slavers. Those who could ran. Their commander screamed at them to stand until Tarag jumped up and took him down.

Pender and Rahana ran down the slope to stop any further killing because they wanted some left alive to extract information on what other intentions the slavers might have for the other tribes. Pender asked who had thought of the burning coals as a weapon because it was key to finishing off the resistance. One of the women said they suggested throwing the coal, but they had no idea how it could be done. When Rahana came to us, she suggested using the wooden paddles we normally used to carry fire into the back of the cave at night. The young men picked up the coals and threw the paddles and the coals together. Rahana told them to wait on her signal so that it would have the greatest effect. Now we will have to go and pick up what is left of the paddles, for we need them for firewood.

Pender brought the two girls to the front so the people could show their appreciation. They cheered them for a long time. The girls were embarrassed. But Pender's motive was to show the Tribe's elders how valuable these young women could be if given the opportunity. He said he was glad they had got there just in time to provide warning and to assist in the defense of the people, but now they had to leave immediately to go and warn another tribe. The senior elder came to the front and said, "Young man, this is the second time we have had to thank you, but this time it is even more special. Who knows how many of our people would have been led away today as slaves? We are so proud to know you and your friends who have the interests of other tribes at heart to be so involved in such a way to save them from this kind of danger. We are so proud of our own young woman here, Rahana. What you have made her into is a lesson for us all. Go now with our very best wishes for your journey and for the missions you have undertaken. Cave People, look and be proud you have known this day our saviors."

When they left, they were sore being hugged but happy with what had transpired. "I think that went very well," Rahana said, climbing up behind Becca. "Now let's hope we don't get fire rained on us on our next mission."

Pender looked pensive for a few moments before he replied, "The slaver prisoners had no information about any other attacks that might be pending, I wish Tarag had not killed their commander. He was the only one who might have been able to give us intelligence on where they might strike next. But on the other hand, at the time, he was trying to rally his troops, no telling what would have happened had he been able to do so."

Becca said, "Look on the bright side, we have taken a whole army of their soldiers out of play. That means we have a lot less to worry about. Let's talk about our next mission. Where are we going, and what is it we have to accomplish?"

"Yes, that was something special, was it not? The Cave People will be our best supporters and publicists. Other tribes will hear and take steps to arrange for their own defense. By the way, you two were absolutely magnificent throughout the whole affair. You adapted to every situation and were inventive. Rahana, that thing with the wooden paddles was great! And, Becca, you had the foresight to get the dogs behind them—that was excellent!"

"That is good, but not good enough. We expect you to be our slave and serve us night and day, especially in the hot springs. We expect you to pamper us with all the best salves and body perfumes, hand applied!" The two of them giggle and giggled, so there was no use talking of serious things until it had all subsided.

They had traveled more than half the way to the Great Forest, and the horse needed to rest. Pender stressed that they could not stay in the open because they could not risk being seen. The girls dismounted, and they decided to walk to a small bush covered hillock near the river. The dogs wanted to be off hunting, but Pender brought them back. As they neared the bushes, they discovered they were already inhabited by an old man who was quite ill and starving. Becca was the first to get there with the horse, and while she tethered it, she collected some food and water. Rahana was at first afraid to go near him because she thought that he might be a leper. Becca was feeding him bread with cheese and cider from a flask when Pender returned from checking the area to see if they had been observed. He waited till Becca had finished her ministrations to the old fellow who seemed to be in such bad condition. They found he had been badly beaten and had problems standing up; it appeared that he had broken ribs. The first thing they had to do was to wash his wounds and bind his ribs. The two young women did this all the while assuring him he would not be left to die here.

Once he realized that they meant him no harm, he opened up to them and told them he was a traveler who sold flint goods, knives, hooks, and other small implements. He had visited a tribe of red-haired men and women with whom he had been doing business for years. This time they had taken all his goods and thrown him in a pound with about a dozen other people, mostly women. This morning they had walked them all from their tribe's land and were on their way to Slave Island. When he could not keep up the pace, they had set—they beat him with clubs and threw him in the bushes.

Pender asked him if he knew why they were in a hurry. The old man said he had heard them say they had another job to pull off before the barge left. Pender asked how many of them there were in the gang. He said four men and one woman. Pender told the girls that they should pack up quickly, as they had some people to save. He asked the old man what his name was, and he said it was Thomi. Pender asked Thomi if he thought he could ride on a horse to the Great Forest. Thomi answered it will be hard and sore for him, but that it would be better than being dead, "so do not tarry on my behalf. I will bear anything to see these people get their just desserts. So they were off, this time they walked, Becca leading the horse with the old man perched uncomfortably but safely on its back. Pender led with Tarag, and Rahana in the rear with Toto. They were almost at the forest when Pender signaled them to stop. He put his finger to his lips, so they knew to be quiet. He came back to them to tell them he had seen smoke rising just ahead, which meant his quarry had stopped for the night. He asked the girls if they had brought any flint knife; they shook their heads. Thomi said he had one hidden in his jerkin. They had to get him of the horse, so they very carefully lifted him down, and he produced the knife. As he took the knife, Pender remarked that he had never seen such a tool before. Thomi said it was specially made for cutting leather ropes. Pender told them to keep undercover because he was taking the dogs with him.

Pender need not have worried about being heard or seen because like in the case of Kain, his quarry were already drunk and being entertained by a naked woman who was dancing for them. They kept time with her moves, clapping and shouting obscene remarks. Their prisoners were tied hand and foot lying in a corner. The women were weeping, and the men were cursing. Every so often one of the Nuits went and kicked the prisoners and ordered them to be quiet.

Pender kept to the shadows till he reached the area where the prisoners were and used Thomi's knife to cut their bonds. One at a time he free them and took them out into the darkness where he told them to remain quiet till he had dealt with their captors. This done, he took the dogs with him and walked into the center where the naked woman was still dancing. He told her to put on her clothes, as the prisoners were now free and he wanted to talk with her. She picked up a club and ran at him. Tarag took her down, and she fell into the fire. The four Nuits in different degrees of drunkenness struggled to their feet. Toto took one, and Tarag the other; soon there was only two left. "Now," Pender said to the other two, "who sent you, where are you going, and when is the barge leaving?"

One of them sneered at him and said, "What you have done is stupid. We are expecting an army with a whole load of people from the caves to be here soon. Then you will die, and these dogs as well."

Pender ordered the dogs to take them one by the throat and the other by the groin. Then he called them to hold. "I am sorry to disappoint you, but your so-called army is no more. None of them were left alive. The Cave People were warned of their coming and rolled boulders down the hillslopes, and as I said, they will not be coming to your rescue. Now whoever answers my questions might see tomorrow. Toto, bite now." The man screamed in pain but said nothing, "Tarag, kill! Toto, kill!" and it was all over. Pender had noticed that the woman was injured but still alive. "Now if you tell me what I want to know, the people might spare you if I tell them that you helped me." He stood above her and called Tarag and Toto over.

She said, "No more, no more please. I am a Nuit, as you can tell by the color of my hair. Many of us are ashamed of what our tribe is doing, but to refuse our chief means certain death not only for me but also for my children. I have three little girls. To keep them safe, I became the team whore. The answer to your question is our chief sends people he steals from other tribes to the slave traders, but they want more and more. He pays men, bad men, who are cast out from their own tribes to attack weaker tribes. This is what happened today. We were taking them to the barge. It leaves in three days."

Pender thanked her for her information and asked her if she could walk with him back to his camp so that his friends could attend to her wounds. As they were talking, she had put on her clothes. She asked Pender, "What is your name, young man?"

"I am Pender, the second son of Castor the Great, and today my business is to rescue people from every tribe who are taken prisoners and to prevent them being sold as slaves."

"If you would allow me, I would like to help you in that undertaking. I cannot go back to my tribe, as it would go badly for me if I did it right now. I know that my sisters will look after my children until I can find my way back into the tribe—that will take some time. I have been on the inside and know how they work. I think I could help get today's captives back to their tribes."

"Elecia, I will think about what you have said, but it is critical that we get back to my friends and get these unfortunate people fed and ready to move, so let us go quickly."

When they returned, Rahana and Becca scolded him for being away so long without contacting them. He introduced them to Elecia and explained what had happened. They quickly bandaged Elecia's wounds and moved to their new camp. Elecia got the fire going, and Pender brought the captives back from where they had been hiding. Elecia found the Nuits food supplies and soon had everybody fed. Pender spent some time with the captives finding out where they came from and trying to determine if they were capable of finding their own way home. Once they were rested and fed, Becca and Elecia had dressed their bruises and wounds. The men and women all felt they were capable of going home if there was no fear of them running into more Nuits.

Elecia informed Pender quietly that there was little fear of that because the Nuits had committed all of their force in the attack on the Cave People. She assured him she was speaking the truth and offered to go with them. If the Nuits found her, she was most certainly going to die, so she had nothing to gain in playing a double game.

It was arranged that in the morning, Elecia would divide the plentiful food supply equally among the freed people so that no one person would carry more weight than his fellow traveler. They would take Thomi with them to their home, and Elecia would be their guide, since they had been blindfolded and bound on the way there. They set two men and two women as watches, and they all settled down for the night.

In the morning after they had eaten a good meal provided by Elecia, they were ready to go. They came and thanked Pender for what he had done. Thomi was almost in tears when he said good-bye to Becca and Rahana. He said he would adopt them as granddaughters. Becca joked that the arrangements were being made as he spoke. They all laughed and moved out on the road. Becca brought up the horse and loaded the supplies, and the girls mounted for the short ride to the Great Forest.

As they approached the great oak, Pender began to wonder how Zalenda would receive him, and he did not know how he would respond. Rahana read his dilemma in his face. She whispered, "Don't worry, she still loves you. She has to learn who you are and what your standards are, as you do of hers. It will be all right. Just be your beautiful self."

He grinned. "You read me that well?"

"All the time, so I know all your secrets."

He laughed. "Remind me to spank you later, young lady. You are too disrespectful."

"I wished it was later."

"Can I never have the last word?"

"Now what would be the point in that?" They laughed, and the tension was broken again.

They were on their way up the lift inside the forest fort, and Rahana and Becca were lost in wonder at what they were seeing. They were guided along the walkway to meet Zari and Mari. After all the hugging and kissing were done and the introductions were complete, they got down to business. Mari reported that the training program was going so well that the young women involved were quite capable now of carrying on unsupervised. Zari said that there had been no sign of the Nuits in or around the forest; in fact, everything was going very smoothly. They had weekly meetings with the elders, which was a great step forward. Zalenda was at present out in a tree somewhere keeping watch near the palisade on Slave Island.

Rahana told them about the attack at the caves of the Cave People and how the Nuits forces were completely wiped out. Then Pender told them of the essential parts that were played by Rahana and Becca and how on the way here they had rescued fourteen people destined for the slave barge. Becca and Rahana were busy filling in the details when the door opened, and Zalenda came in.

At first she didn't notice the visitors and was saying, "I have been up that tree all night, and I am no nearer to finding a way of stopping that barge from moving." Her voice trailed away into silence. She looked but did not see him.

Everyone in the room recognized the importance of these moments. Rahana broke the awkwardness associated with the two estranged lovers, "Zalenda, my dearest sister," she said, moving forward, putting her arms around her. Zalenda stood silent and unresponsive. Rahana pretended not to notice. "Come and meet our new friend Becca. She is from the Water People, and we have been doing great things these last weeks. Come over here, and we will tell you all about it." She guided her over to the bed, where she sat down. Zalenda appeared to be in a trance.

Pender realized it would be better if he was not there. He had dreaded this meeting, and it had all gone terribly wrong so far. He said to Mari, "Come and show me how your training program is progressing." Mari, recognizing this as an escape mechanism, followed him out of the room. In the silence that followed, no one chose to speak. Even the normally talkative Rahana was suddenly struck dumb.

Zalenda finally vented her pent-up emotions. She almost screamed. "How could he do this to me?—come here without any warning, let me walk in, and there he is. Does he not realize he broke my heart? What am I to do? He is here, he is here!" She broke down sobbing. "I cannot do this, no, I cannot."

Zari and Rahana ran to her and held her while she cried. Becca was beside herself. *Why is she like this? He loves her, he loves her, what is wrong?* and she ran out of the room to find Pender. When Zalenda finally became quiet, she hung on to the girls and tearfully apologized, "I didn't mean for you to see me like that. You must think I cannot control my emotions, but it was just that I had no warning."

"Sister, sister," Rahana sobbed, "you must not break your heart like this, no, no, do not apologize, do not. He loves you, I am telling you, he loves you. Please! Please! Let me bring him to you. I know he loves you. One night we had to sleep out in the open. In his sleep he kept calling for you. Do not despair, I tell you he loves you."

Becca and Mari returned, each leading Pender by a hand. They brought him to where Zalenda sat. They forced him down onto his knees before her and said, "Now tell her."

Pender kept his eyes on the floor and spoke so low that they could not hear him. Mari, Zari, Rahana, and Becca all said as one voice, "Louder so we all can hear."

Pender now looked up at Zalenda. "Zalenda, I love you, and I always will. I am sorry for the misunderstanding. What you asked me to do in your tribe meant we were bound for life. I only learned that afterward from Cisi. I was stupid and immature, fearing when you saw me naked you would not like me. I am used to our tribal customs—that you only bathe together with your loved one when the chief of the tribe gives his permission, as an excuse. I have regretted that decision ever since. Please do not walk away from me ever again."

The girls held their breath, waiting expectantly for Zalenda's reply. Zalenda knelt down beside Pender and looked in his eyes. "Pender, I love you, I need you, I cannot live without you. These last days I have felt as if I was dead, and I do not like that feeling. I was shattered when you would not bathe with me, but it was my fault for not telling you what it meant to me. There is no circumstance or situation where I would not love you. I am ready to be bound to you right now. Please we need a cord to bind our hands together."

Rahana came forward, untying her long plaits. "We do not have leather straps here, would these do?"

Zalenda kissed her. "Sweet sister, you will be part of us forever." Mari came and tied Rahana's long plaits around both their wrists and hands. Zalenda said, "Pender, I bind myself to you forever."

Pender said, "I love you, and these beautiful tresses are symbols of my heart bound to yours forever."

The girls wept and held on to their kneeling friends, kissing and hugging them. "This so precious," said Becca, the tears running down her face. "I am so happy."

"Then why are you crying?" asked Zari.

"Why are you, Zari?" Becca said.

"I think we are all crying because we are so happy."

That night they all slept together. They pulled the three cots out to the center of the room, Pender and Zalenda in the middle and the rest on either side. Rahana and Becca were telling stories how they knew Pender loved Zalenda in spite of everything. Zari and Mari said that was not news—they knew that all the time.

In the morning after they had washed and eaten, it was time to get down to business. "First, we must deal with the barge to delay and distract the slave traders," Zalenda said. She had spent a considerable time studying the situation and could see no possible way to do that. Pender asked if she had noted the times of high tide and low tide or when the tide came in and out.

She said not specifically; she had been more interested in timing the guards' movement and finding out where Castor was being held. There is one important thing she had noted that was not visible when the snow covered everything—there is a sewage tunnel that starts just inside the fence and runs for about sixty paces under it to the river. The sewage only seems to be cleared out in the morning.

"Anyone have ideas based on what we have heard?" Rahana asked. "At this point, do we know how big the sewage channel is? Could I fit into it? I am the smallest person here."

Pender said, "I see where you are going with this. We must get a message to my father, and this could be a way in. Zalenda, do you have any knowledge of the habits of the night guards? Do you think this has any merit?"

"I think that this has exciting possibilities. I suggest Rahana and I go out tonight so she can see for herself if this is something that is in the realm of these possibilities. Then we can make a workable plan for the next night to make contact with Castor."

"Mari and Zari, I would like you to watch tonight and tomorrow in the tree that Zalenda has been using. We need to know when high and low tides are and how strong they might be. We also need information on the guard movement—this is crucial to my plan."

"Becca and I will go tonight and check out the area where the barge is tethered. We will note how far it is out on the river and where the smaller craft are tied up. My proposal is to cause as much trouble as possible for the slavers and to distract them from our main mission, and that is to free my father. If the situation is favorable, tomorrow night Becca and I will swim out underwater to the barge and cut the rope on the barge that ties it to the land. I will use the large flint knife I got from Thomi to do this. We will throw all the oars and paddles into the river and swim back, hoping the tide will carry it away downriver. While we are doing that, Mari and Zari will destroy any of the small craft they would use to pursue the barge by untying them and letting them drift with the tide. They will then wait for Becca and me to return. I have brought two skins of beer and some tree bark poison, which we will leave for the guards. Rahana, if she can get through the sewage tunnel, will free my father and the slaves. Then together they will lift up the section of the palisade that was used to free Zalenda, and everyone should be free. Zalenda will be there with Tarag to kill any guards who do not take the poison. We cannot afford to take prisoners. Becca and I will be tired and cold, so it will be left to Mari and Zari to make their way carefully to the prisoner exit point and guide them to safety toward the Great Forest."

"This is my plan—it is very ambitious. It is a lot to handle for the six of us. There are many dangers, but I believe if our intelligence gathering is good tonight, then we have a fair chance of success." Zari wanted a list of all the supplies that they might need—food, clothes especially that would be suitable for Pender and Becca to use for swimming because the water would be very cold.

Zalenda suggested that Rahana would need old clothes to go into the sewer and good flint knives to cut the prisoners free. Mari said she would attend to the clothing and have everything ready before she left tonight. Zalenda suggested everyone should wear dark clothes so they would be less conspicuous in the shadows. "We should get to sleep now, for the next two days and nights will be busy and tiring."

Rahana teased her, "And of course, dear sister, that would have nothing to do with the fact that you will be cuddling into my boss, wouldn't it?"

Pender replied for everyone, "Who would like to see this cheeky little person put over my knee and soundly smacked on the bottom? I have threatened her before, but she keeps getting more and more cheeky." Becca lassoed Rahana and placed her on Pender's knee. Then they all took turns at giving little pats on the rump.

When they finished, she quipped, "I was looking forward to something more than little pats. I can see I will have to give you all lessons how exactly it is done." They all had a good laugh, and everyone relaxed, and in spite of the tension-filled days to come, they all slept soundly, six people in one embrace.

They were wakened in the morning by one of the young women from the watch group who had news about some unexpected action on the fringe of the forest. The girls on night duty had noticed people walking down the river in the direction of Slave Island. Zalenda and Pender dressed quickly. They decided in the light of this news that they had better find out what this meant in case it would impede their plans. This rest of the team would continue to prepare for the various parts they would be playing in tonight's mission. Zalenda took Pender to the tree where she had captured the spy because it was the point nearest to the trail that these people were taking.

They were quickly on the ground and following the tracks of the travelers down the winding river. At the tree where she had encountered the wolf pack, Zalenda stopped and signaled to Pender that she was going up because she wanted to check to see if they had stopped.

She was no sooner up in place than Pender saw two men walking toward him with their heads down watching how they were placing their feet as the slope there was quite steep. This had saved him from discovery, so he backed carefully into some undergrowth were he knelt and was obscured from the line of their sight. The men rested on some rocks almost opposite from his position on the other side of the river.

They were discussing some momentous move, but Pender could not hear because of the noise of the river. He was about to change positions when Zalenda dropped from a tree on the other side, right on top of the men. He was just about to ask himself, *How did she do it?* when she chopped one man down on the neck and kicked the other in the back. They were quickly subdued. Pender crossed the river to help, but it was all over, and Zalenda was asking questions. The men, taken completely by surprise, were having a difficult time concentrating. So she asked them again, "Why are you here? And what big move are you talking about, and where are your friends going?"

The one who was rubbing his neck looked at her and spat at her, saying, "And why would I be telling you that, bitch?" She hit him again on the other side of the head, and he would never spit again. The other man, seeing what had just happened, begged Pender not to let her hurt him; he would tell them everything he knew.

"We were sent to guide a large group of prisoners taken from the surrounding tribes down to Slave Island so that they can be transported as slaves on a barge to their new owners. The barge is to leave in four days' time. They were supposed to leave tonight on the high tide, but something has slowed them up, so they will take the next suitable tide. We were sent to hurry them along and guide them by the fastest route.

The people you saw were recruited to help ferry the prisoners to the barge."

Pender asked him why he had taken this job. He said his name was Cymon, and he belonged to the North Wind Tribe, whose territory was many days' walk from here. He left because there had been a plague among them and many people had died; his whole family were gone. He was starving, and the slavers gave him food in exchange for his work. He had not beaten or killed anyone, nor would he do so willingly.

Zalenda said to him, "Who is this man?" pointing to the body of his companion.

"He was the brother of the chief slaver, Tamor, and like his brother, he was a nasty piece of work. He would beat and rape even the youngest girls, and his brother allowed him to do it. I am glad he is dead."

"Here is our problem, Cymon, we are here to stop the slavers. That large group of people that they were expecting is not late. They are safe in their own homes, and that army of soldiers that was sent to take them will not come back because they are all dead. Now, Cymon, you saw me kill this despicable piece of trash, and in your own words, he deserved it. Now what do I do with you?—because you could easily betray us, but I have no desire to kill you. What do you suggest that I do?"

"I would suggest that you allow me to change sides. If you keep me with you, then you would be certain that I cannot betray you, and if I worked for you, perhaps I would prove to be useful."

Pender thought that might be a good option because they needed inside information. Zalenda agreed, but she warned Cymon that if he let them down in any way, she would kill him without even a second thought and feed him to the wolf pack that roamed these woods. "Now your first job for your new masters is to take this body and hide it in the undergrowth so it will not be seen from the pathway."

Instead of following the river down to the Great River, they used a path that Cymon showed them that took half the time. They came to Slave Island from the back, up over a hill that was covered with trees, which offered excellent cover. They could see the barge tied up near the center of the Great River. It was roped back and front, one to the post land side and the other to a rough rock that acted as an anchor. Pender reckoned it would take an hour each to cut through them with his large flint knife. He could see that with the normal river current, it moved the barge around. This was good for even without a high tide flowing out. It would be carried about a day's walk to the next winding turn, where it would probably run aground. With Becca's help, he could easily swim to the other side of the barge. He saw that the slavers had conveniently left ropes hanging over the side where the smaller craft were tied. They would have no problems boarding. "Do you swim, Cymon?" Pender asked.

"Yes, I am a good swimmer. We have a big lake up in North Winds."

"Do you think you could swim to that barge out there in the dark in cold, cold water?"

"If the reason is good, I am sure I can."

"That is good because that is what you will be doing tonight."

Zalenda asked him if he had been in the slave compound. "Yes, I worked there sweeping up, cleaning out the huts, looking after the sewage, and feeding the prisoners."

"How often is the sewage tunnel used in a day?" she asked.

"Once in the morning then we let water run through it in the afternoon to keep it clean. There is a small burn that runs underneath the stockade that we block to guide the water into the sewer."

"If we wanted to gain access to the stockade and the prisoners' quarters, could we do it through the sewer?"

"If the person was small enough and strong to lift the cover at the stockade side, yes—both of these things are possible."

They watched the guards move some people around the compound. Then Pender began to feel exposed, so he said it was time to return and updated the rest of the team. The journey back to the Great Forest was uneventful. Cymon carried the food supplies, while Zalenda and Pender discussed what they had seen and some changes that would be necessary to their plans. Pender thought it would be best if they went that night to cut the barge loose.

The arrangement would be that Cymon, Becca, Zalenda, Pender, and the two dogs would leave just before it was dark, Zalenda would stay on guard while the others swam to the ship. When the barge was freed, Cymon would stay on board to steer it as far away as possible down the river. He then would swim back to the north shore and find his way back to the tribal lands of the North Winds People. This was his request, and Pender and Zalenda agreed that this would solve the problem on how far the barge would have gone following the tide.

Mari would make sure that he would have enough food supplies and clothing for his journey. Everything would be triple-wrapped to keep it dry during the swim. They rested till later in the evening the freeing of Castor could well depend on this night.

Chapter 11

The Destruction of the Barge

It was almost midnight before they got to the vantage point for the shortest possible swim to the barge. They stripped off their clothes and donned the black suits Mari and Zari had provided for them. Becca complained hers were much too big. She went into the water and disappeared, having chosen to swim underwater as far as possible. Tarag wanted to join them, but Zalenda order him back; he might be needed to guard the return of the swimmers. She picked up the clothes and retreated a safe distance to cover where she could keep an eye on the swimmers and the compound.

Becca arrived first and swung herself aboard and went immediately to the forward hawser and went to work cutting at the leather strips, making sure she kept down out of sight in case there was a guard watching. Cymon and Pender arrived simultaneously. They climbed up the mooring ropes for the small craft and carefully vaulted over the sides, making as little noise as possible. Cymon's task was to detach the front hawser. He examined how it was attached to the barge and concluded the quickest way was to cut it. He started hacking away with the big flint knife and found it was not going to be as difficult as was thought. He crawled along to the stern to make his report because it was important that both ends were released at the same time.

Pender had taken over the cutting from Becca. She was deep underwater, checking to see if there were any other ropes that were not visible from this side of the barge. She did this by swimming the full length underwater, checking by touch, because the water was very murky, and of course, it was after midnight. She returned to report to Pender that the barge was attached as they had thought just front and back. Pender was already halfway through. They had decided to cut the front first and then a few moments later the back. Becca had gone to the middle to try and signal when the front one was cut. All of a sudden, the barge lurched forward. The strength of the current pulled the last vestiges of the ropes apart, and they were moving forward slowly but picking up speed. Cymon came quickly to where Becca and Pender were finishing cutting the rope. He hugged the two of them and said good-bye.

Pender and Becca were off balance and thrown over the side holding the ropes then they hit the water together. Pender disappeared under its current. Becca went under and came back up. The barge was passing her quickly, so she had to swim hard to keep from being drawn under in its wake. Becca saw Pender was in trouble. By the time she got to where he had been, he had disappeared. She dove down into the murky waters and swam around in every increasing circles but could not find him. She was about to give up and move to different area when her hand touched something. She reached out and caught hold of his hair, and with all her strength, she pulled him to her and kicked with her legs for the surface. As they surfaced, she saw the barge was now well away from its mooring moving quickly on the tide. She held Pender to her, trying to swim for him and keep him afloat. She pushed hard on his back as she had been taught to try to get the water out of him. The only hope now was to get him to the shore, so she swam with all her might till she felt the muddy bottom of the shore. She was all in when she felt Zalenda and the dogs pull them out of the water.

Zalenda carried Pender up to the safe place and laid him down. She pounded on his chest till he sputtered and gasped and threw up. She drew him to her and held him while he slowly regained full consciousness. "Where is Becca?" he gasped.

"I am right here, Pender, right here."

"How did we do?" he asked.

"Look for yourself," Zalenda said, holding him till he saw the barge disappear into the night.

"Everything went according to plan until you forgot which way was up," said Becca, now fully recovered and putting on her dry clothes. "Let's get him changed and out of here," Becca said, reaching to pull off his wet clothes. "In years to come, you will dream of this, young man, two beautiful women in a hurry to get you undressed." When he was naked, she rubbed him vigorously and dried him with an old piece of rag. Zalenda stood looking but doing nothing. "Here, finish him off while I get his stuff, after all he is your man." Pender stood meekly and allowed Zalenda to dry him off. She was concerned at how cold he was and tried to shelter him from the rising wind. Becca came back with his clothes, and they quickly moved to get him dressed. She was concerned at his lack of response. Even with his clothes on, he felt cold and clammy. She took of her sheepskin jacket and put it on him, hoping that as they walked, the warmth would revive him. They half carried and half walked him up the hill. Tarag seemed to sense all was not well with his master. He kept running ahead then back again to lick Pender's hands.

The journey was not without mishap. Becca was tiring rapidly and was exhausted with the tension and stress of the mission. As they walked the river path, she slipped and went down heavily. This seemed to energize Pender. With Zalenda, he got to Becca just as she was about to slip into the river. They pulled her up and saw a nasty gash on her knee. Zalenda cleaned and bandaged the wound and, with the dogs at their heels, pulled her back up to the path. Pender, feeling more normal now, took off the sheepskin jacket and put it on Becca. With the aid of a stout tree branch and a dog on either side, she managed to limp home to the forest fort. Zalenda went and got the rest of the girls to help Becca up to the room, but she was very tired, so they left her to sleep. Pender and Zalenda lay down and slept till morning.

It was midday before they wakened to the exciting news from Mari and Zari, who had been up early at their vantage point, that Slave Island was in turmoil. The missing barge was indeed the kind of distraction that Pender had hoped it would be. They reported that a large group of guards was being assembled with food and equipment. Tamor, the chief, was shouting and screaming at all his people, beating and kicking anyone who got in his way. He was dressed for traveling, so it looked like he was taking charge of the search himself. Zari said she had left one of her trainees in the tree to watch and make a further report as the day progressed. Rahana went with Becca to help her get washed and to dress her wound. Zalenda and Pender had already told the team of Becca's incredible bravery in putting herself at risk to save Pender from drowning.

Rahana was exceptionally gentle with her as she washed off the dirt and river mud from her body. It was difficult to tell if the bruising on her back and ribs had been caused by the fall or by the buffing she had received in the river. Becca was so sore, she did not want to talk about it. Rahana was not used to being rebuffed by anyone in this team, but she continued rubbing salve on her back and side till Becca said softly, "That is enough, my love. I appreciate your care. Please do not be disappointed with me. Last night was a near thing. When the barge broke free, I was taken by surprise. While the men were cutting the ropes, I was finishing throwing the barge oars in the river. The barge lurched to the side, Cymon came to hug me, I was still off balance, and I fell backward hitting my back on the side. Then I was in the river still holding the small mooring rope. I went under, and I don't think I missed one of the oars I had just thrown overboard.

"I surfaced to tell Pender I was all right, but I could not find him. Like me, he was caught off balance. He had been talking to Cymon one moment, the next he was in the river—he went straight under. He almost drowned. Fortunately, I found him and got him out. As I said it was a near thing. I need time to recover. I am sore and very tired. Please be patient with me."

Chapter 12

The Plan to Rescue Castor

Rahana after that was very quiet. She finished dressing Becca and then dressed the wound on her knee. "I will have to report that you are out of commission for any missions for the foreseeable future." There was no reply; Becca was already a sleep.

Rahana found the team assembled. They were discussing tonight's mission. Pender asked her how Becca was feeling. Rahana told them she was very tired, bruised all over, and her knee would take time to heal; she would be unavailable for any type of mission.

Zari had reported that the observer she had in position had indicated that the search party for the barge had left later than was their intention. It appeared as if the chief wanted to leave right away, but nothing seemed to go right for him. His shouting and cursing seemed to hinder the progress, not make the men work faster. The young woman said it looked like they had left eight guards; she had seen nothing of the prisoners.

Pender said it was absolutely necessary for the mission to free Castor to be undertaken that night. They would never get a chance like this again. Everyone involved must wear dark clothes. Rahana would lead the dogs through the sewer and lift open the access if she could. Zalenda, Zari, and Pender would scale the palisade fence from the riverside using ropes. Zalenda would deal with the guards, making sure she kept one alive for information. Zari would go and lift the sewer cover if it proved difficult for Rahana to move. The dogs would be free to attack the guards as needed.

Everyone would need knives to cut the prisoners free. Once they were free, they would assemble at the lift section of the fence and help Castor lift the fence to freedom. Food from the slavers' store would be issued to the prisoners, and they would be guided toward the winding river to be as far away from the slavers as possible. When everything was completed, a means would be found to burn the huts and the palisade down. This would hopefully be the end of Slave Island.

Later that evening, the group assembled at Mari's lookout point. She was to remain there in case anyone needed urgent help; otherwise, she would watch till she saw the prisoners were free. Then she would assist in food distribution and guidance to move the prisoners out as soon as possible. Pender waited till he saw two guards stick their heads out of a hut where it appeared they had gone to eat. They promptly returned to their food. Zalenda said from her experience as a prisoner, this was typical of the nonchalant attitude the guards had to their duties.

It was time to move into position very quietly and carefully, placing every footstep in place because now was not the time to slip or have an accident. Zalenda had drilled them on this approach. In her mantra, preparation was everything, and they had one opportunity to get this right, and it was right now. They were in position. Pender made the sign, and Rahana disappeared into the sewer with the dogs. He gave her time to get under the fence before Zari threw her rope over the fence and climbed over, dropping quietly onto the wooden floor. Zalenda signed Pender to go, while she watched in case the guard stuck his head out again. When all three were inside, Zari went in search of the sewer cover. She located it just inside the fence. She lifted it up just as Rahana popped her head through. "Special delivery," she whispered, and the dogs were through, ready for action.

Pender and Zalenda went to each side of the door of the hut and listened. They heard nothing but the normal sounds of men eating. Zalenda gave the prearranged signal, and Rahana and the dogs moved forward to a position where they would intercept the other guards, who, by the sounds coming from the main hall, were gambling.

Zari went in search of the huts where the prisoners were. She found them lying tied hand and foot. She told them she was there to set them free but that they must be quiet at all times—to make a sound would alert the guards, and they would be prisoners forever.

Zalenda counted down from three with her fingers and then sauntered into the hut. Pender followed. "Gentlemen, sorry to interrupt your meal, but I have something for you." The two guards looked up from their meal, choking on their food. One stood trying to recover his guard persona. "What the . . ." but he never finished his sentence. Zalenda moved so quickly, she caught him on the front of the throat; food spewed from his mouth. She chopped down with great force on his neck, and he crumpled almost in slow motion to the floor.

The other guard reached for a long thick club, partially tripping over his friend's body as he moved to get clear shot at Zalenda. The trip was fatal. As he swung, she moved away, the club bouncing harmlessly to the floor. He cursed and tried to throw a platter at her to distract her, and as he did so, he rushed at her. She sidestepped him, and he ran headfirst into Pender.

They both went down. Zalenda turned and kicked him in the back. He tried to hold on to Pender, to pull himself up as they struggled on the floor. The man was bigger than Pender, but Pender prevailed. He turned the man around just for a moment, allowing Zalenda to kick him in the face. He was about to scream, but Pender grabbed him with both hands over his mouth to prevent him alerting the rest of the guards. Zalenda kicked again, and the man was dead. "I thought we were going to keep one alive," Pender said ruefully.

"Maybe the next one," Zalenda said with a tight smile. "Just let's say we both kept him quiet—that was important."

Zari had cut free ten of the twenty-five men in the hut, when she approached a very big man. He asked her who had sent her, and she replied that she was part of a team who were dedicated to freeing all the prisoners and especially Castor the Great. He said, "I am Castor." She worked feverishly slicing through his many bindings, and he leaned on her as she helped him to his feet. While she was working, she told him that Rahana was outside with the dogs and that Zalenda and Pender were dealing with the two on-duty guards, but there could be at least another four guards that they knew of who needed to be dealt with. They would need his help. She went on with her work, while Castor went and explained the situation to the prisoners.

Then he quietly went outside to help. What he saw made him slow in his tracks. Three of the guards were holding Rahana. She was struggling and kicking out at them. Tarag was attacking one guard who was on the ground, his knee torn to shreds. Toto was engaged with two other guards who were deathly afraid of her, but they had long pointed shafts with flint heads that kept her at bay.

As he emerged into the open, Zalenda and Pender came from the other door. Zalenda went into action immediately. She rendered one guard who was holding Rahana useless. She kicked him so hard on the back of his leg that everyone heard it crack. As he fell, he pulled everyone down with him. Tarag went in to kill. He tore out the throat of the fallen guard and savaged the arm of the guard who had his arm round Rahana's throat. She kicked back at the guard and was free. He made to run, but Pender was in his way. He lunged at Pender and did not see Castor till it was too late; one punch from Castor and he was down. The two with the lances saw their friends dead or nearly so and gave up the fight and begged for mercy.

Pender set the two dogs to guard them, while Zalenda attended to Rahana's wounds, which were very superficial, but that did not stop her from hugging and kissing her. Pender went to his father and embraced him. Together they interrogated the two guards and learned where all the food supplies were kept. They also gave them the wood slot keys of all the huts and entrance gates. Pender sent the freed prisoners to free all the rest, and others to bring the food supplies into the compound. The two guards told them they also had a wooden marked board that listed all the prisoners and their tribal connections, and if they allowed them to go free, they would help in every possible way. Pender asked them to go and get fire starters, as it was their intention when they left to burn the place down.

A further sign of their cooperation was in the information they provided regarding the intended return of the slave traders and the whereabouts of the eight horses that were left for them in case of an emergency.

Mari arrived down from her observation post into the compound in the middle of a frantic scene, people hurrying about in frantic haste. She stood and watched for a few moments before she realized it was an organized frantic, and that was good—better than the news she was about to give them, which was not good.

Pender and Zalenda were talking to a tall, broad, handsome stranger whom she could not keep her eyes away from even when she tried to look away. *This must be Castor, Pender's father,* she thought, but he had noticed her approaching and his eyes were on her. No one had ever looked at Mari like that, and she was self-conscious. Pender had been explaining some of their plans, but no one was listening. He turned to introduce Mari, saying this is another member of our team, but again no one noticed. The atmosphere was electric, time was suspended, and the two looked at each other in amazed silence. Pender tried again, this time Zalenda came and kissed him full on the mouth, effectively silencing him. She whispered in his ear, "Even in desperate circumstances, love can strike and lives are changed forever."

Rahana broke the spell, coming to Pender with the news. "We have more food than we need. What will we do with it?" Her voice broke off in embarrassed silence. As she realized, something life searching, life changing, here in these chaotic minutes, was happening to one of her best friends, and she thought, *Please, please let him love her back.*

Mari realized she must move, although she wanted these moments to last forever. She could not forget the danger that was fast approaching. She managed to garble out the words, "Pender, we have to get out of here now."

The climate changed immediately. Zari came from one of the huts to join them as Mari gave her report. "Late last night while I was on watch, Cymon staggered into my little camp. He was worn out and badly injured. He told me he had taken the barge down to the widest part of the river. The tides were high, and he could no longer keep it on course. The tides, the wind, and the rain were at their very worst. The barge kept swinging around with every new directional change the elements brought. Finally, it crashed into a really large rock and began breaking up. In the ensuing destruction, Cymon was thrown against the side of the barge and broke his left arm. Then the tide changed again, this time throwing him out into the water. He could not swim, but fortune smiled on him—a piece of the barge came past. He caught hold of it with his good arm and rode it downriver till the swirling tide threw him onto the north shore of the river. He collapsed where he was and slept till morning. In the morning, he was glad we had the foresight to triple-wrap his food. After he had eaten, he found a branch and made a splint binding it to his arm with his food wrappers. He was on his way home when the path he was using cut down low into a small riverbed. He was having a drink when he heard voices. He decided in his present state caution was the best part of valor, so he cautiously crawled into a position where he could see but not be seen. What he saw sent shivers up his spine. His late boss, Tamor, the chief of Slave Island, and about sixty men were camped in the next valley. He recognized Somer, the head of the slave trade business, and his men, as he had been present in the compound many times when they visited to pick up slaves. They were discussing the loss of the barge and putting it down to a freak of nature and the strength of the tides at this season. They did not realize it had been lost to good planning and two men and a young woman. Their next discussion had him really worried. They were waiting on another barge, which was due in the next two days to take the chief and some of his men back to Slave Island. The slaves there would be sent to market. The only thing they had to set was the price."

Cymon walked all day and all night to get back and warn Pender about what he had seen and heard. He was so tired that he could hardly speak to Mari, whose hiding place he would never have discovered if she had not been on watch.

Pender and his team held a quick meeting and decided to get everyone out by tonight. Castor got all of the people together and told them the news.

Rahana and Zari were to move them out ten at a time with their food. They had six horses available, and there were two pregnant women, so they would have one each. The other four would be used to carry the extra stores. They must leave by the west island gate and walk all night until they came to the winding river. At that point, they could stop to eat. They must not stay in the area. The men would be armed with clubs and long spears in case of problems along the way. If they did not want to be back in Slave Island, they must walk every day into the night and be watchful, and even more important, they must not allow the red-haired Nuits to inveigle themselves into their groups no matter what help they promised.

The prisoners responded even better than Pender had thought possible. The sun was still above the horizon when the last group left. The two surviving guards had indicated that they wanted to stay and work with Castor. The fires were set, and soon Slave Island was blazing. The team leading the horses left to pick up Cymon for the journey to the settlement and home. Mari suggested she should stay and keep an eye on the slavers, but Castor would not hear of it. However, he did agree that all family tribes in this area should be warned of what was happening and to be on guard. He would select trusted men from his own tribe to do this.

Chapter 13

Castor Lifts the Doan Stone

Castor's return to the settlement caused great concern among the elders. They had been working on the assumption that he would never return. In the meantime, each of them had been advancing their own agendas to profit their own family interests. When he walked into the meeting, their cleverly hatched plans went up in smoke. They were shaken to the core, and they were looking for somewhere to run and hide, but there was none.

He looked round the room and then at each one in turn. "I am Castor the Great, and I will wear the Doan Stone again. I know you are greatly disappointed at that. You hoped I would never find out that you had no intention of paying the ransom that was demanded for my release. In fact, you were prepared to negotiate with my treacherous son to let my brother-in-law succeed me. Not only that you provided my son, Pender, with false information as to where Kain was to be found, thus putting his life in danger. I know everything about your ambitions and what and who you were prepared to deal with to accomplish them, no matter who in the tribe might suffer because of your detestable desires. I should revoke your positions as elders—that would be just and deserved, but that would only lead to even deeper festering animosities. So I will retain you for the present, with the warning that you will be watched carefully. I am appointing four young women to this group as full members. Do not despise their youth, do not despise their council, do not despise their sex, and any one of you or any group of you who do, I will feed to my dogs. Go and do what you were appointed to do—serve, serve the people, serve the family tribe of the settlement and island as men of honor."

It was well after midnight before Castor and Mari made the crossing to the island. This was the first time they had been alone, although Castor had requested that she stay with him, when the others had left earlier for the island. Mari waited for Castor to break the silence, so she pretended to be interested in the platform and the long leather cords he was pulling on, which soon brought them to the landing. The dogs bounded toward them, barking excitedly, welcoming their master and Mari with whom they had often stood guard. Tarag was aggressively jumping up on Mari. When Castor intervened, he spoke sharply to him. "Don't do that to my lady, Tarag."

"Your lady?" Mari inquired.

"Yes, my lady. I suspect that you already know how I feel about you, and I suspect that I know how you feel about me, which is precisely the reason I requested you stay with me at the settlement, my lady." Mari blushed. Her personal experience with men had never contained expressions of love, having been raped by a drunk man two years past. Now she wondered what he would say if he knew, but tell him she must. He noticed her reticence but trusted the look in her eyes. "Will you allow me to kiss you good night before we meet the rest of my family?" He leaned in and kissed her, and she kissed back. "We will talk about this tomorrow. Now let me show you to your room."

Cisi and Ester had waited patiently for their father to arrive back from the settlement. They were excited at the prospect of seeing their father again. It was something they had never expected to see. They wanted to tell of the many sorrows they had borne, the treachery of their brother, and the murders he had ordered or committed—the loss of their mother and Lay, who had been like an older sister to them; Brini and Abbi, who had been their mentors; and all because of Kain's ruthless ambition. They also wanted to tell of him of how proud they were of their younger brother, how time after time he had acted with wisdom and courage, in defending his mother and Lay, in organizing the rescue and relief of the island, which almost cost them all their lives, and his maturity at taking on mission after mission, the ultimate of which was the destruction of Slave Island and bringing his father back to them.

They waited until after midnight and were about to give up when they saw their father with the dogs and a young woman. He was talking quite earnestly to her then he leaned down and kissed her, and she appeared to kiss him back. Cisi was about to interrupt them when Ester pulled her away into the shadows. "What's going on?" Cisi whispered.

"I don't know, but now is not the time to find out," Ester replied, "tomorrow is. Let's go," and she pulled Cisi away, and then they watched Castor take Mari to a room and get her settled and then go to his own room.

They went to their room that they had shared since they were children. Cisi wanted to speculate as what it all meant. Ester feared within herself what it meant but did not want to voice the obvious. She tried to sleep but was haunted in her dreams by what they had witnessed.

The morning came too early for them, but the rest of the group were in the hall eating breakfast prepared by Nena and Cymon, who despite his injuries seemed to like working with her. Zalenda and Pender were in a deep discussion about how they should react to the information brought to them by Cymon.

Becca, Rahana, and Zari were teasing each other as to who had the sorest bottom with the ride home. They were about to ask Pender to umpire who had the reddest bum, when Castor appeared. All conversation came to a halt, while everyone tried to appear as natural as possible, but looking at each other with questioning eyes, where is Mari?

Cisi and Ester came to the hall door and signaled to Zari to come. Zari was loath to leave her companions with the question unanswered, but she went anyway to see what the sisters wanted. They were most insistent that she tell them everything, why her father was kissing a young woman when their mother and his second wife were so recently dead. Zari could only tell them what she had observed before the destruction of the compound and that their father had requested Mari to stay with him while he addressed the elders.

Castor asked Rahana if she would mind going to waken Mari, who had spent the night in the guest room, and since they had not eaten anything at the settlement, she would be very hungry.

Cisi and Ester came to the table. They made a show of embracing their father but then remained aloof from the conversation. Pender and Zalenda noticed the stress involved and tried to head off the coming storm. Zalenda whispered to Pender, and he made an announcement that there would be a family meeting right after lunch then immediately after there would be a team meeting to gather information on exactly where the slave traders were in light of the information supplied by Cymon.

Pender led Cisi and Ester into their mother's old room. He asked them what they wanted to know. They were about to answer when Castor and Mari came in. Cisi said, "This is a family meeting, why is she here?"

Castor answered, "She is here because I asked her to come. This young woman has given me the reason to want to live again. When Zari cut me free, all I wanted to do was to kill, to kill and kill again anyone who had anything to do with the slave business. I only wanted to get home and take my revenge on the elders, who had connived together to keep me in prison and plotted with Abbi to set up Kain in my place, the traitor son who murdered my wife and Lay, my second wife, and murdered my old friend Brini and would have hung his own brother and caused the death of his own sisters. When Pender told me these things as we stood in the compound waiting to set all the prisoners free, my soul died within me, that I should have raised a son like Kain was bitter bile to my being. Then this beautiful lady walked in to bring Pender news. She looked not only into my eyes but also into my soul. What happened to time, I really don't know. I no longer yearned for death but for life. I will work not to kill nor to take revenge, but to repair all the damage that has been done to our family and tribe, and I will work with others to bring the slave business to an end. My dear girls, I know how this must sound to you. Please do not blame Mari."

He was about to go on, but Cisi put her hands over his mouth, while Ester took Mari and kissed her then Cisi hugged them both. "This is a family meeting. I am glad she is here," Ester said, and the girls kissed and embraced their father.

Castor said he had to leave the meeting to go to the settlement, as he intended to convene a full meeting of the family tribe that afternoon, and he had some issues he still needed to deal with. He told them of the changes he was making to the management of the elders. He had already announced that four young women were being added to represent the rights of young women who currently were under the heel of some very dominating men. The announcement he would make today was that Morag, Nena, Pipa, and Rona would be installed and that they would have immediate access to him at all times should the elders proved to be uncooperative. "Their unwavering courage in the evacuation of the women and young men from the danger they were in on the island and organization of their care at the settlement was exceptional and must be recognized by all of us.

"I will demonstrate to all the settlement and island people alike that a new age has arrived in our thinking in which every person must be seen to be essential to our collective betterment. To this end, I will do something that no chief has never done before. Two days from now, I will call the whole tribe together here and lift the Doan Stone for a second time.

"Those who oppose these changes will be invited to state them publicly and given the opportunity to challenge them by lifting the stone. If they fail to do this publicly and work to undermine these changes, they will be punished according to our law—complete banishment for them and their immediate family from our family tribe."

The meeting that followed was difficult to control because everyone wanted to talk about what Castor had said and the changes he had announced. Eventually and with great patience, Pender got them back on track. Cymon was called on to repeat what he had heard and saw of the slave traders and the local group. He estimated there might have been between both groups at least sixty men. According to their plan, a new barge would be available to them the day after tomorrow. There would be great pressure put on the Nuits to restock the freed prisoners, so every local family tribe would be in danger. Pender pointed out the Nuits will resort to force to get people for their purposes. He saw two things that now were essential. First, tonight he and Zalenda would leave to observe the arrival of the barge and the slave traders. From Mari's hiding place, they would attempt to gain information as to where and how they would strike. A team would be required to shadow them so that an early warning system could be put in place. Another team would then be required to pass that warning on so that tribes would be forewarned and could put a defense in place. It was arranged that Zari would take over the winding river watch with her trained team from the Great Forest, but at the slightest indication of danger, they were to withdraw to safer cover. This was to be for information gathering only. Nena had pointed out that neither Cymon nor Becca had recovered sufficiently to be available for any fieldwork. This left Rahana and Mari. Cisi objected to Mari going because she did not want her to be placed in danger, and she was sure that her father would object anyway.

When Ester realized that the mission involved riding from tribe to tribe to warn them of impending danger, she volunteered immediately; she loved riding.

Pender and Zalenda left with their supplies right after the meeting. They picked up two horses at the settlement and took the eastern route around the lake and over the moor. This was to allow them to see the Big River from high up on the hill. They hoped to see if the barge was on its way. As they reached the crest of the hill, they had to quickly reverse and find cover. The horses were tethered in a little bower of trees with low branches that completely hid them from sight. Zalenda crawled forward in the heather to a vantage point where she could see both the river and the sloping moor that ran downward almost to the river. Pender finished with the horses and brought some food from the pack and crawled on all fours and lay down beside her, kissing the back of her neck. She rolled over so she could kiss him back, and for a few moments, the mission was forgotten.

When the world came back to them, they looked over the heather that grew in great abundance on the moor and saw two Nuit men beating a woman. Pender thought he recognized her, but he was not quite sure. He was about to say to Zalenda, when Zalenda jumped into action. The men were so intent on what they were doing that they did not notice Zalenda until it was too late. She hit the nearest one on the back of the neck. He fell to the side, and she kicked him in the ribs. He went down coughing his lungs up and spitting blood. His accomplice swung the canelike branch he was using to beat the woman at Zalenda. He missed, and she took the cane out of his hands, reversed it, and thrust with it at his throat. It speared him through, and he fell, his tongue lolling out of his mouth as he hit the ground. He tried to plead for mercy, but the words could not be spoken. He saw the kick coming and knew it was death.

Pender picked up the woman; it was Elecia. She could not speak. Her face was battered, her ribs were broken, and her legs had been beaten with the cane. It looked like she was beyond help. Pender carried her into the shelter of the trees and gently laid her down. She whispered, "You rescued me again, my dear friend. Thank you for being here." She closed her eyes, and he thought she had died, but then he noticed she was breathing with great difficulty.

Pender went to see if it were possible to gain information from her other assailant. However, Zalenda was equal to that task; she had him sitting up, wiping the blood from his face and questioning him. "Why were you beating this woman?" she asked. He made as if he was about to refuse to answer, so she took the stick and pushed into his ribs. He screamed in pain, but he shook his head. She pushed again, this time putting her full weight into it. Only then did he signal with his hand for her to stop.

He whispered, his words coming in great gulping breaths, "The bitch would not tell us were that bastard Pender could be found."

"She actually did very well for you. See, I am here. I am Pender, the son of Castor the Great, and I can assure you I am no bastard. But I must ask you now, why were you looking for me?"

"We have a spy in his tribe who says he has a big army that met and defeated our army when we were there to take all of the Cave People for slaves. They also say he killed all the guards at Slave Island, freed all our slaves, and burned the place down."

"Who was it that sent you?" asked Zalenda, again holding the stick in readiness.

"It was the big guy and his two sons," he gulped again.

"Do you mean the chief of Slave Island?" Pender asked.

"No, I told you the big guy!"

"You mean the man who owns the barge and transports the slaves?" Zalenda's questioning voice held more menace now.

"No, no, the big guy, Somer is his name. He and his two sons, Rolf and Benic, they control everything to do with the slave trade. They know all the traders and transporters—it's big, big business!"

"How does he know me?" Pender asked again.

"Somer used to be a childhood friend of Castor the Great. His son, Kain, and Rolf were best friends for a while—that is where we got the inside information." He was about to say something more when he coughed up more blood and became very still and died.

Pender and Zalenda carried the bodies of the two dead men into the bushes where the wild animals would find them, but not the vultures or the ravens; they did not want to attract attention to this place. They cleaned up the site of the attack then went back to where the horses were hidden. Elecia had recovered a little bit. When they arrived, she was sitting up trying to clean herself off. Pender introduced her to Zalenda and asked her what she was doing here, why she had not gone home. She explained that her own people did not want her and did not trust her. One night she found she had been sold back to the slavers.

She told them that she had left in the middle of the night and was traveling toward the Great Forest when she stopped to rest. The two thugs caught up with her. They thought that she knew where Pender might be, and they would have beaten her to death to find out.

Zalenda was busy feeding her and cleaning of some of the blood from her wounds. Then she fixed her beautiful red hair and tidied her clothing. When she had made Elecia more comfortable, Elecia asked Pender, "Can I come with you please? I have nowhere to go."

"We certainly would not leave you here, but we may have to leave you for a little while. We were on our way to gather some much-needed information on how the slavers are progressing. However, you can look after our supplies and tend to the horses while we are gone. Would that be all right?" Elecia said that would be fine as long as she knew there was somewhere for her to go to where she would be useful, but in the meantime, she would rest for the journey home.

Zalenda and Pender moved carefully over the ridge, keeping low so they would not be visible from lower down on the shoreline of the Big River. They could see quite clearly a big barge moving slowly up the river, the rowers working hard against the tide. They moved quickly now, as the path was well traveled, and were soon in place at Mari's hide. It was true the fires had left nothing. Slave Island was destroyed. It would take time and money to rebuild it. Their plan had worked well.

They could see a small contingent of slavers examining the ruins of their compound. The men were keeping well clear of the man standing in the middle, who, even from this distance, was quite visibly upset, swinging his arms around, stamping his feet, and kicking out at anything that got in his way. He obviously was Tamor, the chief of Slave Island.

From the left, a much-larger contingent of men was on the move. Pender realized that Cymon's estimation was correct. There were easily sixty to seventy men in this group. Pender counted by tens as he had been taught by Abbi and marked then on the ground with a stick. There were two separate groups. The first seemed to be controlled by a very large man sitting on an even larger horse. Pender thought that this was the man Cymon had recognized as the slave transporter, Raymond. It was his barge they had destroyed.

The second group was even larger; three men were in the middle riding among marching men. Pender thought to himself, this is the big guy, Somer, a friend of his father's, and his sons, Rolf and Benic, friends of his brother, Kain. Now he knew whom and what he was up against.

They watched the meeting of the groups with great interest. The big guy pointed to the other two, gesticulating with both hands, and then to the approaching barge. He turned around and left the two standing looking at each other in dismay. The big man on the big horse was even more vocal. Pender and Zalenda could hear him cursing and shouting. He was blaming everything on the chief of Slave Island. He had lost him his barge and his cargo of slaves. He had better get them all back or there would be severe penalties to pay.

On the way back to pick up Elecia and the horses, Pender and Zalenda discussed the temporary dissolution of the terrible trilogy. Pender saw it as a good thing. "Temporary as it might prove to be because, one, they now knew what they were up against; two, the split may have made them easier to deal with; and, three, as a united enemy, their total strength was away beyond our team's resources and capabilities." Zalenda agreed with this rationale but wondered if they were being played. It was obvious that the big guy knew Castor and Kain, and had Kain become the chief of the Island People, it may have been a way of establishing a confederation of slavers. She felt that from now on they would have to be even more selective in whom they trusted for information. She saw a clear line from Kain to Abbi to whom? Were the successes they had enjoyed real or allowed to happen? Were their plans too easy to read? Were they being watched as carefully as they were watching them?

"Do we need to proceed differently? Our missions have all been well planned and well executed. We have been successful, but is the similarity of our methods also our weakness?"

The successes, the battle at the caves, the destruction of the barge, the freeing of the slaves, and burning down the slave compound could not be questioned. They had seen the effect it had on the slaver's hierarchy.

They agreed that before they sat down with Castor and the team, they would analyze every past mission, who was involved, who provided the information, its execution, and the results. They agreed to reexamine the new people, Cymon, Elecia, and the four girls added to the elders, and every family attached to the elders.

Elecia was still asleep when they returned to pick up the horses. Zalenda carefully woke her in case she screamed in her dreams because sound traveled a long way on the moors. She looked up at Zalenda and then at Pender and said, "You are so fortunate to be in love and have each other. It is so obvious to everyone. It's the way you look at each other like something very precious."

"Then you won't mind then if I do this," Zalenda said, kissing Pender full on the lips then on every part of his face.

"I am jealous of that kind of love. I have never loved anyone in my life. As a child, I was taken away from my mother, so I never knew a mother's love. I was just the child who had to be fed sometimes, kicked around the rest, to clean up the dung animals and people dropped. I was still a child when I was first raped and beaten for not knowing how to please a man, and that has been my story ever since. I have had three children—who fathered them, I do not know. My sisters are not my sisters in the real sense of the word. I have no allegiance to my tribe. If I went back, they would kill me. Please take me home with you. I will serve you in any way to take down the people who have no other purpose in life other than to enslave good hardworking people for their own profit. I will never betray you. I will never divulge to anyone your plans or information you may share with me. I will be your trusted friend and worker. At any assignment you may give me, I will do it to the best of my ability."

Pender said to Zalenda, "You are more precious to me than life itself, but we have made a disciple with one kiss. Can I have a hundred more?"

They laughed, and Zalenda said, "Here is our answer. Elecia, get up on this horse. We are going home." Pender helped them both up on the horse, and Zalenda put her arms around Elecia to hold her in place because of her injuries.

Elecia said, "Now I feel safe, and I am going home."

The journey across the moor was uneventful, but when they got to the landing for the island, Pipa was there. She said she had urgent news for them but did not want to discuss it in front of the ferrymen.

That evening Pender assembled the team to give a report on what they had observed on their trip to Mari's hide and to introduce Elecia so she could describe what she had learned. Pipa's report would wait till Castor and Mari joined them.

Zalenda told them how they had witnessed the breakup of the infamous trilogy and how this gave them a little breathing room, but there was danger that lurked in being complacent, so they must at all times be on guard.

Elecia was introduced by Pender, who gave them her background and how he came to know her. Elecia told them of how she had been rescued twice by Pender, how she was beaten and raped by her captors, and how she had been able to give them information, but this would not be revealed at this time until it had been evaluated.

Ester had not returned from putting the tribes on notice. She had taken Rona with her to witness their reception, from the elders of these tribes. Nena reported that Cymon and Becca were improving rapidly and would soon be available for service.

Pender told them that everyone must be on guard tomorrow, when the whole settlement would be here to witness Castor lifting the Doan Stone and the subsequent challenge to the tribe. They were to make sure that no one gained entry to the building, especially people they did not know. He and Zalenda, Mari, and Cisi would have to witness the challenge. Nena would make sure that they had someone to cover the three entrances. Cymon and Becca should stay with Nena throughout, and any unauthorized entrance was to be reported to Nena immediately. They had their evening meal and would meet again tomorrow after the people had left.

Pipa came to Pender and Zalenda after the meeting and said she had to talk to them in private; it was really important. They went to the center of the hall where no one could come near without revealing that they had an interest in the conversation nor could they hear from anywhere in the hall.

Pipa said yesterday she was on watch when she noticed a stranger coming into the settlement. Because Rona was away with Ester, she had to cover it herself. She said the stranger was hanging around near the hall where the elders held their meetings, so she decided to get into the hall where she would not be seen but could hear. The hall had a false ceiling, so she decided that it would be her hiding place. She got in when no one was around and crawled through the ceiling till she was above the meeting place. Time passed, and she was getting uncomfortable and was about to give up when the head elder came into the room with one of the young men who worked on the ferry as rope puller. A few moments later, the stranger came in. He introduced himself as Somer's man, and he had come to do the job. The elder knew exactly what he meant. It turned out he came at the elder's invitation to kill Castor at tomorrow's challenge. When Castor bent down to pick up the Doan Stone, this man was to put a knife in his back and kill him in front of the tribe to demonstrate the power of this elder. The young man was to wait at the ferry until Rolf came, and he was to bring him directly to the ceremony where he would declare himself the new chief. He would take a large hammer that the elder would supply him with and break up the Doan Stone. He would then designate the elder to rule in his place. Pender was to be pointed out to Rolf, who would kill him and take Cisi as his woman.

Pender and Zalenda could hardly believe what they were hearing. This young woman had put herself into such danger to get them this information; now they had to act on it. They decided not to tell anyone of the plot. Pipa would identify the killer for Zalenda, who would deal with him as Castor was lifting the stone. Then they would unmask the elder. The two dogs would be on hand to deal with any emergency. When Rolf came, he would be introduced to Pender in the presence of Castor and Cisi, while Pipa rehearsed for him his treachery at the invitation of the elder. The young traitor would die in front of the tribe, being torn apart by the dogs. Rolf would be forced to pick him up and lay him at the feet of the elder. Each of the elders would be given a club to strike the elder till he was dead. Rolf would be held till Castor and the new elders dealt with him. That was the plan. Would it work?—they had no way of knowing. Would the elder go through with it?—they had to wait and see. They could not cancel the challenge because according to the tribal custom, any cancellation would lead to the forfeiture of the chiefdom, and Castor would not allow that to happen. Pender knew his father would be angry that he was not informed, but at this stage, the less people that knew, the more chance it had of success. Pipa had to stay on the island that night for her safety and had to sleep in the same room with Nena, who knew better than ask questions.

Pender and Zalenda went to their room but did not sleep for some time, as they rehearsed every move they would make at the ceremony. When they were satisfied with their plans, they kissed and kissed until they fell asleep.

The people started to arrive early for the midmorning ceremony. The custom was that the stone had to be lifted when the sun was at its height in the sky. Pipa stayed near the reception area until she identified the would-be killer to Zalenda, who then made it her business to stand behind him in the crowded space in front of the stone. Rahana had the two dogs with her, and her only instruction was to have the dogs in the area near the head elder.

Castor greeted the people of the tribe amiably because he was confident of his ability to lift the Doan Stone. Pipa noticed the elder had a sneering smile on his face, so he was going through with his deadly plan. The crowd was in a festive mood, and they surged forward to get a better look at the ceremony.

Pender saw that this was going to be awkward for Zalenda, so instead of letting the caller make the announcement, he asked the crowd to be quiet, as he wanted to recognize some important people. Castor looked at him in dismay for going outside the normal custom. Pender asked the killer to step forward and be recognized as an important visitor here by special invitation of the elder. The elder's smile got even bigger; things were going his way. Zalenda moved forward behind the killer; now she had room to operate. Pender signaled to the caller to make the announcement of the challenge, and Castor went forward and said, "I, Castor the Great, chief of the island and the settlement family tribe, take up this challenge to lift the Doan Stone a distance equal to its height, as is the custom of our people, to reestablish my status as chief."

As he bent to lift the stone, the killer went for his knife; but to his surprise, his arm would not move. Zalenda had broken it with a chopping motion of her left foot. The people cheered as Castor lifted the stone and walked with it to its new station. He turned in horror to see Zalenda holding the visitor on the ground with his own knife at his throat.

Pender called for quiet as the crowd saw the drama that was unfolding in front of them. At his signal, Rahana came forward, yet mystified to the part she was about to play. "People of this tribe, you are about to witness the unmasking of an act of treachery. This predation was to be practiced against your chief by the man who lies on the ground in front of you, a hired killer—hired by that man there to kill your chief while he was in the act of lifting the Doan Stone." The crowd was left in no doubt to whom he was referring as the elder almost collapsed with fright. Pender called the dogs to bring him forward. They caught him by the arms and dragged him in front of Castor. There was a commotion in the crowd as someone was trying to get away. Pipa identified the young man from the ferry and Rolf to Pender.

Zalenda moved in and kicked Rolf in the groin, while the dogs caught the young traitor. The people in the tribe were going crazy with anger especially when Pender told them that Rolf, the son of Somer, friend of his brother, Kain, had colluded with this elder not only to have Castor killed but to have Pender killed as well. Their intention was that today Rolf would assume the title of chief, and he would take Cisi as his reward.

"We discovered this plot late last night but could not forewarn anyone, as we did not have any proof that this elder had any intention of carrying out this dastardly act against my family. The proof, you see here." Pender went and stood beside Zalenda, Rahana, and Pipa, leaving the floor open for his father.

Castor quieted the crowd. "People of this island and of this settlement, I am like you. I can hardly believe what my eyes have seen and my ears have heard. My son was right in not mentioning this awful cowardly treacherous act that was concocted by these four people here to be performed on this special day. I would not have believed it! But you and I see the undeniable truth there," pointing to the four criminals. "These four young people, my son and these three young women, have served us well today. What a calamity it would have been for us all not for today only but for the rest of your lives. What do we do with them?"

The crowd shouted, "Kill them, kill them!"

"We could do that, and it would spoil this beautiful day of celebration. Look at all the great things for you to eat and the fun that is planned. Let us put these people away from us, bind them hand and foot, gag them so they cannot talk, put them in our darkest cellar, and allow their consciences to talk to them. Then tomorrow we will all convene here to coolly exercise our justice on them. The celebration will now continue. Please be happy for our freedom today!" Castor replied, looking directly at the four, without making any eye contact with his son.

Castor ignored Pender and his friends for the rest of the day, and they all noticed it. Cisi and Mari stayed with her father supposedly entertaining all of his family and friends. Rahana, Becca, and Elecia served their group from the lavishly spread tables of food and brought it to a grassy knoll, just beyond the new position of the Doan Stone. As they ate, conversation was sparse. It was left to Becca as usual to break the dearth of friendly chatter.

"Well, I think that was not very well appreciated. You would think the way everyone is avoiding us, we were the traitors. What is next—bound hand and feet, gagged, and the darkest cellar?"

Nena interjected, "Don't be silly, Bec. Castor could not afford to have Pender outshine him on this day. We should just have left the hired killer do his job. He might have missed, who knows!" she said sarcastically.

"Why were we kept in the dark about the plot? Have we not proved ourselves trustworthy? I had no idea why I was there with the dogs," Rahana complained.

Pipa spoke up, which was very unlike Pipa. "After our meeting last night, you all left very quickly. It had been a long day, and like you, I was tired. Rona was away with Ester, and I was covering the watch on my own. I noticed a stranger hanging around the elder's place. To get information, I got in a position above them and observed the stranger arrive. I heard the elder give the stranger his instructions of how and when he wanted Castor killed. The plan then was that Rolf, the son of Somer, would kill Pender and take over the chief's place. He would break the Doan Stone with a big hammer that the elder would give him so the stone could never be used again. The elder would be allowed to rule for Rolf, and Cisi was to be taken as his woman."

Her embarrassment at speaking before the group was palpable. Her words came quickly and quietly. She let her voice drop off at the end, and no one was sure she was finished. She was nervous, and there were tears in her eyes.

No one spoke. She was about to get up and run out, when Zari came and wrapped her arms around her. "Our precious one, you have saved us all. Without your integrity, intelligence, and intense devotion to your duty, this day would have been a disaster, Castor and Pender would be dead, and all of us here would have been fodder for the slavers."

Everyone applauded and said Zari has spoken the truth. Cymon asked the question that was in every one's mind, "What do we do next?"

"I think that is not our dilemma, it is Castor's."

Pender spoke for the first time. "Is Ester and Rona back?" he asked.

"Yes, over there. Look, beside the table,"—they looked all in, "poor dears," Zari replied.

"Rahana, could you please find Morag and bring her here as well? We have a lot on our plates, and it is not food. We must be prepared for every eventuality, and I want us all here for safety." He did not elaborate, and they did not ask.

Rahana came back with the three girls. They were still wolfing down their food. "We are famished," said Ester.

"We have been riding all day. My bum is sore," said Rona.

"We will look after that later in the hot springs," Becca threatened. Pender asked them to move quietly away and not to attract attention and to meet in the hall for an impromptu meeting later in the evening, as the ladies would want to go to the hot springs after all the visitors had left.

"Cymon, I have a special job for you. I want you to go down the hall, down the ramp. The very last door at the end, there you will find our supposed-to-be-bound prisoners gambling, if I am not mistaken. Take this skin of beer to them and tell them it comes from Castor. In one hour, take this one here. I am sure they will enjoy it."

The nine women came back from the springs in good fettle. Zalenda came to Pender and kissed his ears and asked him if he was ready for what was the inevitable showdown with his father. Cymon came in and told him the medication had worked. Just before midnight, Castor came storming in, his eyes blazing with anger. "What were you thinking about today with that display of showmanship?" Mari and Cisi came in and went and sat down with the rest of the women. He noticed but went on. "You forced me to imprison the son of an old friend for some mistaken notion you have of treachery here in my own tribe. I should have you all beaten and sent to the slavers."

Pender finished for him, "The ultimate betrayal, Father?"

"Let me tell you what will happen. I will banish you all from this tribe, and you two will regret the decision you have made today," he said, pointing threateningly toward Cisi and Mari. "Rolf will take you directly to Somer then we will see how smart you all are."

"Father, the only way we will be going to see Somer will be with an army of all the tribes behind our backs, and he will run like the coward he is. Whose side would you be on? Rolf will not be able to help you today, Father! He and his three friends are dead! See, I think you have lost the respect of the tribe, and that is really not nice. You told your friends in front of the whole tribe that they were to be taken, bound, gagged, and placed in the darkest room. Would you believe their insolence? They were put in a nice room here, fed, and were gambling until an hour ago when the nice beer you sent them was poisoned, and they are dead!

"Now how will you explain that to your good friend Somer and his killer son Benic? Do you think they will believe your stories? I would not. Now let me tell you what is going to happen. In a very short time, you will become breathless. It so happens that the last brew you drank had Abbi's secret mix. You see, we began to suspect that some of our missions went too well. Even good planning and excellent execution could not account for the good fortune we had. We did surprise you with the destruction of the barge, but only eight drunken guards at the compound. They just had to get you out for the exchange of all the inside information you were giving them.

"We were certain our next mission would fail and we would all be taken. I even told you how we gathered information. You were about to use it—that was a mistake. You see, on our last mission out to check on the falling apart of your gang, which is yours and Somers, we had to kill two of your leading spies. They were looking to kill me, but Zalenda and I had not told anyone the route we were taking, except you. The other thing was even more stupid—you were in that place for months and you never lost weight. How was that even possible? Even Zalenda lost weight."

Castor began to breathe erratically. "Ha-ha! The stone, the stone, you can never be chief, you cannot lift the stone."

"Sorry, Father, you thought you were running the show. Your value to Somer now is limited. They did intend to kill you. Rolf did expect to succeed you. Your elder friend brought a big hammer to smash the stone. Someone has knocked big chunks off it, and as such, it can no longer be used as the standard. They had thought of everything, or almost everything, when I would not allow them to kill you in front of the tribe. They went to their secondary plan to get you drunk like they did before and take you for a slave. But your friend, the elder, wanted to make sure you die tonight, so guess what, it was he who poisoned your last drink, not me, but because he was afraid you might taste it first, he gave you a smaller dose—that is why I believe you are still with us. I am sorry to tell you that from tomorrow, Cisi will succeed you as chief. I believe she will do a great job, don't you?"

Chapter 14

The New Chief of the Tribe

Castor was apoplectic, his arms swung all over the place, and although he was dying slowly, his eyes blazed with anger. Zalenda asked him when they were in the compound together if he meant any of the things he said. He calmed down and wept, "Yes, that was the true me, but I allowed Somer to talk to me about his big plans. At first, none of you were to be hurt, but the incident with the barge and the burning of Slave Island then the freeing of all the slaves. I had to be seen to go along with it to make you trust me, but Somer was angry because of what you cost him and how you made him look weak."

Cisi and Ester came to him and took his hands. Cisi spoke first, tears running down her face. She said, "Until this moment, I have loved you, but you would have given me to Rolf, a man I loathed. I am glad my mother did not see this day. You are a despicable person. Kain was ready to let our bodies freeze to death. You have frozen our hearts."

Mari came forward just before he died and said, "I looked into your soul and saw nothing. I could not love you, and I am not about to weep for you. Everything that has happened to you today you have justly deserved." These were the last words Castor the Great heard then he was dead.

Pender said, "We have a great deal to be thankful for. Our team is still complete, and we are safe for the present. Tomorrow I will announce the deaths of the prisoners and the poisoning of Castor the Great by the elder and the succession of Castor by his oldest daughter,

Cisi, as chief. This means we will have to get a home in the settlement for you. I suggest that if you may need assistances in the short term, you should use Morag and Rona until you develop your own team.

"The rest of our team, this is your home. Now go and enjoy your home this night. It has been an eventful day."

Zalenda and Pender went to the hot springs instead of going immediately to bed. They could hardly believe it was just days ago they had started to suspect that the person responsible for aiding the slavers was not just the elder but someone nearer to the top. Pender had mused at the time, *My brother, my uncle, my father, a family of treachery*, but not expecting it to be true. Zalenda could see the direction of his thinking and tried to distract him with her embraces. There was nothing to spoil the mood. The moon was at its zenith high in the early morning sky, silver bright. Everything had that eerily silent presence that happens in the magic of the time before dawn.

This was the first time they had ever bathed together, and Pender was now aware of its special significance to Zalenda. He had been very nervous when she had removed his clothes. To keep himself from shouting "stop!" he kept his eyes focused or her face. She then very gently removed the last vestige of his manhood pride till he was completely naked. Then with beautiful lithe grace, she entered the welcoming waters of the springs and received him in her arms. For the first time they were naked together in the waters.

She took a handful of water and rubbed it on his face. She felt the fuzz of the beginning of facial hair. "Oh, my sweet love, you are growing a beard," and she kissed him as if it were some joyful celebration. "I must see if, oh there is, there is hair growing right down here!" He immediately started to respond to her tantalizing touch. It was the first time anything this intimate had happened between them, and he was embarrassed, but she pressed her naked body against his, and that sense of embarrassment turned into an unrecognizable source of urgency. He wanted it to stop, but at the same time he didn't want it to stop. He was kissing her back with the same urgent want. They had never gone this far before! Their kissing had always been beautiful and sweet, kisses that tasted like honey. Now their lips and tongues were hungry, searching deep inside their being. He never wanted it to end, but end it did. Zalenda had never done anything like this before either; although her body was responding to his sense of urgent need, she was uncertain of what the next move should be. As a Warrior Woman, sexual touching was not allowed, yet she was feeling this delicious swelling between her legs that transmitted a need that was older than life its self. That unpracticed need was driving the both of them on. She wanted to take pleasure in this new shared intimacy.

Just then the girls arrived. They could not sleep after this day and the evening's happenings. They were emotionally drained and needed the restorative healing of the springs. They had no idea what they had just disturbed. But this was big; the breach between them was healed. They all jumped into the water and hugged and hugged Zalenda and Pender. Now instead of his beautiful naked Zalenda who was pressed so close to him he could hardly breathe, he was being hugged by the naked members of his team. For them this was big, but so was his embarrassment.

Spent and overtired they all crawled into bed, but none of them could find sleep. The sense of accomplishment they had enjoyed in the destruction of Slave Island had disappeared in a web of treachery. The stillness of the night and the healing of the springs, however, brought the magic of sleep.

Zalenda wanted more, so the kissing started again, and now being completely naked in bed for the first time, it was easy to pull him on top of her. But the magic of the moment was gone; worn and weary, they both fell asleep comfortably in each other's arms.

The morning came for all of them too soon. The whole team was on duty and was expected to be present at the settlement for the announcement of Castor's death by poisoning and the naming of Cisi as his successor. Pender would provide the details of the deaths of the would-be murderers and the trail of treachery that involved his own family. They would have to discuss the return of Rolf's body to his family and how that was to be accomplished. An investigation of the elder's family must be undertaken to see if they had any involvement in his ambitions and schemes.

They crossed in two groups. Pender's group went first. Zalenda was being teased by Becca and Rahana, who kept cooing like turtledoves whenever she approached them. She abruptly took the wind out of their sails by asking them whether they should allow Pender to grow a beard like his father.

"Definitely not," said Rahana.

"We want him to be neat and refined. Castor's beard was strong but unruly and untidy. We don't want our Pender to look like that," Becca said. "Not like the men in most tribes whose beards were never trimmed or washed. Pender is handsome, quite beautiful, in fact. His beard should complement his face, neatly trimmed to his jawline."

Zari chimed in, "That is right. I can picture him with shoulder-length hair, shining, well kept. We must look after that too. He is so good looking."

Becca chirped again, "I am prepared to be on the keep-Pender-beautiful team, as long as I also get to beautify his nether hair."

"I am afraid not, Becca. I have already selected that privilege and prerogative for myself, and it is a nonshareable item." Zalenda laughed. "However, there are some duties I am prepared to share."

"What would these entail—anything interesting?" Becca kept up the chatter.

"Yes," said Zalenda, "washing his undergarments." They all laughed and made faces at Becca, who decided to retreat.

The humor all vanished when they entered the hall where the people had all gathered for Castor's acceptance speech, for that was the custom. The people looked on with interest when Pender, Cisi, and Ester went to the front where Cisi made the announcement of her father's death. There was the collective drawing in of breath, people looking at one another in shock and amazement.

Pender asked them to hold their questions till the team had given all the information they had of the events leading up to his father's death. "This team or group of people I am about to introduce to you, some you know, because they are your daughters, and some you will be meeting for the first time. He introduced each of his friends and told where they came from and the circumstances that brought them together. He explained the history of how he had become involved with working to stop the slavers and how they had helped the Treetop People of the Great Forest, the Cave People, the Water People, and the Warrior Women Tribe.

Finally he spoke about how two men and one young woman who had frustrated the whole machine of the slave traders by destroying their barge, and at the same time with other members of the team, they had killed the guards of the compound, set all the prisoners free, and burned down Slave Island. "In doing this, we have made many enemies among the slavers and some in this family tribe. It became necessary to form a group of watchers to watch the coming and going of strangers among the tribes and to gather information about their activities. The young woman who will speak to you now is one of our watchers. I want you to listen carefully to what she has to say, because it will better explain to you the things that happened yesterday and how they led to the death of my father."

Pipa came forward. She was shaking with fear and trepidation at having to speak in front of her own family and friends. To make it easier on her, Pender had arranged that he would ask her the questions and she would answer. "Pipa, you are one of four people selected to watch our tribe—is that correct?"

"Yes, that is correct. Some months back you approached Morag, Nena, Rona, and myself to watch any suspicious strangers who visited the settlement. These turned out to be dangerous people whose only interest in our tribe was to supply information to the slave traders in the likelihood of getting, by nefarious means, people of our tribe as slaves."

"Were you on watch here three days ago?" Pender asked, trying to slow her Down; she was speaking so quickly, she was getting breathless.

"Yes, I was, and because Rona was away on a special mission, I had to be on duty all day and into the night."

"What was special about your watch at that time?"

"It was quite late in the day when I observed a stranger come into the settlement. No one appeared to ask him why he was here and what his business was, so I followed him and heard him ask where he could find our elder. I was suspicious and decided to get into a position where I would be able to observe them and listen to their conversation."

"Where did you go to do this?"

"I went upstairs and crawled into a position right there." She pointed to a position right over her head.

"Who was at that meeting, and what did you hear?"

"Our elder and the stranger were the only people present. They were discussing how and when the stranger was to kill Castor. This man was to wait till Castor was in the act of lifting the stone, when he was utterly defenseless. Then he was to murder him by plunging a long flint-tipped knife into his back."

"To kill Castor. Then that was the only reason for him being here?"

"No. When Castor was dead, the man was to take a large clublike hammer to break big pieces of the stone so it could no longer be used as the standard test for selecting the chief of our tribe."

"Was there to be any other involvement by others in this treacherous deed?"

"Yes, one of the young men from the ferry station was to wait till he saw a man named Rolf, the son of Somer, Castor's childhood friend, who was to be brought to the center with the sole purpose of killing you, to avenge for your actions in preventing them from selling the slaves imprisoned on Slave Island. He then would proclaim himself as chief, and since there was no standard left to substantiate his claim, he would take Cisi as his wife."

"What would have been the elder's role in this new governance?"

"He was to be Rolf's subchief solely in charge of everything in the tribe. He would make all the decisions. The young women of the team were to be handed over to Rolf to be used at his will and then sold as slaves."

"When did you make this report to me?"

"I made this report to you at midnight before the celebration of the lifting of the stone."

"People of the Settlement and Island Tribe, you have heard Pipa give you a very comprehensive answer as to why we acted yesterday the way we did when my father lifted the Doan Stone. Have you any further questions you would like to ask Pipa before we continue? Please direct your questions to me, Pender, the son of Castor the Great."

"Yes," said one of the past members of the elders' group that Castor had removed. "Why did you not report this to the proper authorities instead of taking this on yourself? Who are you to act in the way you did?"

"Good question, sir. The first reason is that my father had removed you and your fellow elders from your position because he did not trust you and suspected you were involved with the same treachery as Kain and Abbi. Perhaps you could tell these people why they should trust you."

The people turned round looking expectantly at him, but he said nothing.

Pender went on, "The second reason that we waited was we were not certain that the elder would go through with this plan, so we waited till the stranger drew his knife before Zalenda here"—pointing to her—"went into action. The rest you know. She put down the stranger, and she could easily have killed him, but she did not because it was not part of our job to pronounce judgment—that was left to my father. You were all witnesses to the unmasking of the elder's plans and what the end result was to have been. I would have been dead, and Rolf would have been addressing you today. You called for their deaths, but my father allowed them to live. Like you I wondered why, so I went last evening to find where the prisoners were. I found them not bound as my father had prescribed, but free, eating, and gambling and having a great time.

"The final treachery was played out before my eyes. Castor the Great, my father, was no better than my brother, Kain, or my uncle Abbi. He was the ultimate traitor. He had been working with Somer all the time! My friends and I had discovered some anomalies that at the time we could not understand, for he did work with us to free the slaves, but that was just a cover. Late last night he went to visit his friends who had intended to kill him on Somer's orders, for he was of no further use to him, so he had to be removed. He had a friendly drink with them prepared for him by the elder. It contained a slow-working poison. This elder hated him so much that he was determined to kill him. Unfortunately for them, as they drank to the success of their plan, they themselves were drinking from a skin of beer Abbi had prepared that contained a lethal bark poison. Last night they died, and we watched our father die. Cisi and Ester held his hand. He had time to ask for forgiveness but chose not to, so he died unrepentant of the evil deeds he had done to us, his family.

"Cisi, by the order of succession, is now the chief of the Island and Settlement People. Since the elder had the Doan Stone partially destroyed, it no longer is the standard, so there is no impediment to her claim.

"People of the Settlement and Island People, here is your chief!"

The people cheered and cheered. They came and kissed her, the men kissing her hand, promising to be faithful to her, kneeling before her in the obligation of fidelity. They crowded around Pender and his team, thanking them for their service and faithfulness to their cause. Pipa was embarrassed at the attention she received. Her family and friends were so surprised at her abilities and told her how proud they were of her. All of the team was feted with joy and everyone joined in the celebrations.

Pender then announced that the induction of Cisi as chief would be held on the island at noon the next day, and everyone was welcome.

The team would meet in the afternoon. Like two nights before, there was much to do and little time to do it.

The most immediate item on the list was to organize the induction of Cisi as the new chief and the celebrations afterward. That type of organization normally lay as the responsibilities of the elders. There was no appointed elders' group, as Castor had removed the old ones and had not appointed new ones. He had, however, made it clear that Morag, Nena, Pipa, and Rona were to be on his new committee. It was agreed that they would take over that role, and everyone on the team would be under their supervision to make sure it was a success. This would be the first impression of Cisi's rule as chief, and it had to be good.

The meeting the next day would decide on Castor's burial and those of the elder and the young ferryman. Then a decision would be required to be made on how to contact Somer about the death of Rolf and what to do with his body.

Nena took over the organization of preparing the food with the help of the girls. Cymon and Pender would get it all over from the settlement and organize extra help for the ferry. Morag, Pipa, and Rona would set up the food at the island, and Ester would get her sister dressed for the occasion. Zalenda, Mari, and Zari would be on watch in case of any intrusions from outside. They agreed that Pender should conduct the investiture and that it should be simple and short. Cisi would then appoint her new organization to run the settlement and their dealings with the other tribes. Security would be a major issue in the light of recent history, and a new and separate team would be formed to keep the tribe safe. The rest of the day was taken up with everyone carrying out their assignments.

The ceremony went on the next day without any problems. It was simple, quick, and fast. The young women were beautiful. Rahana and Mari did their hair in long plaits that were gathered up on the heads like crowns. Nena found them all dresses that fitted, so they all looked like princesses. Cisi, of course, was the center of attraction; she looked like a queen. Everyone had a very enjoyable time. Elecia in particular seemed to enjoy serving the food, smiling and talking pleasantly to everyone she came in contact with. She told Pender it was like finally being home.

Zalenda, for the first time since Pender had met her, laid aside her leathers. Mari had taken great care of her blonde crown and dressed her in long flowing blue gown; in his words, she was simply magnificent.

The meeting that afternoon was surprising, to say the least. Cisi was not expected to be there, but she turned up with some of the elders that Castor had removed from office. Pender wondered what that meant; he was soon to find out.

Cisi took over the meeting and right away startled her friends who had always supported her. First of all, she said as chief, she intended to act like one. She had already reinstated the former group of elders but would dismiss the young women Castor had added to their number. She would take responsibility for all aspects of the tribe, and that would include security. She did not want the young women on watch because that made the elders and others uncomfortable. Pender's group would have no legitimate standing in the tribe, and she would not guarantee any support for their actions. She would take charge for the burial arrangements for the three bodies on the island and contact Somer to see what he wanted to do about Rolf's body.

Pender addressed his new chief, "Sister, you have grown horns since this morning. It is obvious you have been in contact with these men before this and deliberately hid this from me. It appears as if I must add your name to our family's roll of shame, but fear not as soon as this meeting concludes, our team will say good-bye, and we will never return to this island again. However, be sure of this—if you form any kind of alliance with the slave traders, we will do our best to bring you down with them. Beware of Somer. He will want you for his son, Benic, so he can get what he has intended all along—this tribe to add to his slave trade."

Ester spoke up. "My dear sister, the faithful one, the good one,"—she let the sarcasm drip from her voice—"how quickly you forget who saved your treacherous little life and has worked to make you chief almost at the cost of his own life, and you, you who did not have the courage to leave the island, would threaten us who did to put you where you are. Don't ever call me sister again."

Mari, who had been Cisi's friend, said, "I am glad I am leaving. I did not know the other night when you cried, I held a viper in my arms."

When the meeting was finished, as each one left, they moved to the front, looked Cisi in the eyes, and then left. Ester and Pender were the last to leave. As they left, some of the elders sneered and snickered. Cisi turned on them like a raging bear. "Do not ever do that again in the presence of my family or I will string you up. None of you are worthy of scraping the mud of any of these people's shoes, and if I find anyone spreading false gossip about them, be sure I will cut their tongues out of their heads. You are under a new chief, and you will do exactly what you are told and when you are to do it. Now go and think about what I have said and make sure you really want to be an elder. This settlement has been poorly run for years. This is not a men's club run for the interests of a few to make them rich. You will be working for me to make this place safe, secure, and prosperous. Now leave. I will see you all in the hall at noon tomorrow. Do not be late." Cisi sat and brooded and considered what she had done. She had not meant to drive away her friends—she needed them—but at the same time, she did not want always to be in Pender's shadow.

She got up and went into the main hall where they were all gathering their personal belongings. The chatter stopped immediately, and everyone looked away. Ester emerged from a side room to see what had happened. "What do you want?" she asked.

"I want to speak to you and Pender please. I don't want to make any more mistakes."

"You have already made more than can be repaired with me," Ester said, ice in her voice.

Zalenda came in just then and took Cisi by the hand and pulled her into her room. "Now what was all that about this morning? Tell me now so I can heal this putrefying sore that has developed since you became chief."

Cisi told her she wanted to be a real chief, not to play at it so everything would stay the same. She could not do that and be seen to exist only in Pender's shadow. "I know he only wants to help, but that is not what the elders will see. They will see him ruling the tribe through me. That is why I tried to make them see that I will be making all the decisions and no one else. In doing it, I overstated my case. I don't want to lose my family and friends, I need them. Please, can you do anything?"

Rahana popped her head in to see what was going on. Zalenda asked her to go and get Pender and the rest of the team and bring them here.

Zalenda took over the meeting and explained what she had just heard from Cisi. "You mean to say that we do not need to leave here?" Elecia said. Cisi nodded. "Good. I like it here. I am unpacking."

"Wait, hold on till we get this straight. As long as we leave you to be the real chief, your words, making all the decisions, with no interference from us whatsoever, and only when you make a request for help from us would we be involved with settlement affairs. Otherwise, you would like us to stay here and make it our center of operations so that you can still have your family and friends with you. Is that what you want?" Zalenda said, looking round the room and fixing her eyes on Pender.

Pender went to Ester and brought her over to Zalenda. "Now tell her," Pender said to Ester. "Go on tell her what you said to me just now."

"Cisi, I love you, and I never wanted to leave here—it is my home. I was hurt, and I spoke in anger. Please forgive me."

"Now I have something to say. I accused you of being in the same league as my father. I said it knowing full well that it was not true. I said it to return some of the hurt that I felt when you spoke before the elders. We will keep any limitations you will place on us when we are here. We will strive to make our leaving and arriving with the minimum of distractions for the people at the settlement. Only when we are invited to attend any social gatherings will we stay for any time there. I also must say, sister, I love you."

This said, Pender bent down and kissed Cisi. She hugged him and said, "I love you to, my brother."

Becca shouted to all who would hear, "Everybody, unpack then into the hot springs." She didn't bother to unpack.

After the ladies had visited the hot springs, they continued their discussion on the how each family tribe had developed differently. They compared social behaviors, different methods of calculating a person's age, differences in counting days in the year, differences in controlling population growth and in even doing simple business deals, and the differences in how the sexes coexisted in certain areas. Becca could not understand why in this tribe men did not bathe with women, whereas in her own tribe, the Water People, everyone from babies, boys, girls, single women, single men, mums and dads, and grandparents all played in the lake together. Nena said, "Someday that will change and all the tribes will be united, and we have to start the change now."

Chapter 15

The Teams Go Out on Their Missions

The first item on the agenda was to establish a system or a new way of dealing with the problem of the slavers. Now that they were disorganized, how would they respond? Zalenda believed that the success they had achieved so far could largely be attributed to their ability to gather intelligence. She proposed three teams: the first to watch Somer, which would be the most difficult and would require an experienced team; the second to keep tabs on the transporter, this would require a fast-moving team; and the third to watch any new developments at Slave Island, this team could contain the team's new watchers.

It was decided that Pender, Zalenda, Rahana, and Pipa would form team one to track down and observe Somer's interests in this area only. For the present, they would only work in a defensive way and try and leave no trails back to this team.

It was necessary for team two be good riders, to follow from a distance. In this case, Nena, Cymon, Ester, and Becca were designated to keep the team informed on what was happening on the river.

As Mari and Zari already had a hide in a good position, they would share these duties with Rona and Morag. For protection they would take the dogs.

The horses would be picked up at the settlement, as they were part of the island's farm animals and sheep herds; no special permission would be required to use them. Elecia would stay and look after the supplies, a service she loved to provide. As this was being discussed, she arrived with refreshments.

Each team would leave in the morning and use a different exit route, being careful not to attract attention. Pipa and Ester, knowing the area, would bring the horses for their team. They were all to return on the evening of the third day and report their findings if indeed there was anything to report. Zalenda again reinforced the need to be careful and not attract attention on their travels, to avoid travelers if possible, and to make sure each morning campsite was left pristine. It was important that they not get into conflict if it could possibly be avoided because she had not been able to train them all in unarmed combat; they would have to submit to that later.

Pender's team waited till Pipa led the five horses into place in a covered shed on the edge of the settlement. They lifted their supplies on the pack horse and mounted up and rode quietly away. The route they would take would be long and arduous, so there would be the need for frequent stops. Pender led the way with Pipa and Rahana in the middle, and Zalenda covering the rear. The morning air was cool, necessitating the need for them wearing their sheepskin jackets. As they went, they took irregular stops in case they were being followed. Each time, Zalenda would leave them in a covered spot, retrace their steps carefully, and surveyed their trail. It was while she was doing this that she became aware of birds rising off the moor away to the left of her position. She kept looking in that direction and soon saw what looked like five horsemen coming across their path. She waited to make sure that this was indeed the case then retraced her steps to the hide. She quietly told the team of her discovery, so they readied themselves for possible action.

They could not lead the horses away without being discovered, so they decided to wait and watch the developments as they happened. The horsemen were in no hurry, and it was cold hugging the ground; it appeared that this was going to take some time and patience. It was Pipa who heard sounds coming from the other side, and she signaled with her hand to Zalenda, but Pender held up his hand showing two fingers. He could see riders coming from the right some distance ahead.

They waited while Zalenda crawled forward to a new position into a large gorse bush, where she could see both approaching parties at the same time. She motioned to Pipa to join her. When Pipa got into position, Zalenda drew on the ground where she thought the two groups were heading. There appeared to be a hollow forward to their left, where she could hear ducks and water hens. They would need water for their horses, so that was their likely destination. Pipa was to wait here till she was certain, and she would know when she saw the wild birds take to the air. Zalenda was moving forward to broom and gorse bushes near the hollow. When Zalenda was set, Pipa was to report back to the others and wait for Zalenda to come back. Pipa was really beginning to feel the cold up here high on the moor. The wind was strong, when suddenly the air was full of squawking birds. That was the sign she was waiting for, so she carefully reversed her direction and went back to the others to give them Zalenda's message.

Pender saw her coming and had a nice warm sheepskin for her to wrap up in as she explained Zalenda's instructions. Rahana brought her a drink of spiced honey and cider, which she carefully cradled in her frozen hands.

In the meantime, Zalenda was witnessing the meeting of the two groups. The two riders she had seen before, but could not remember where or when. The other group, she discerned that four of them were lackeys. The other two were much more interesting; one was obviously Somer, and the other from the descriptions she had heard must be Benic. The lackeys were kindling a fire, while Somer and Benic sat in padded wooden chairs brought with them for their every comfort. The other two were busy attending to their horses. Zalenda was meticulous in moving so as not to disturb anything; even the sound of a small branch breaking might cause alarm out here on the moor. When she was sure she could not be seen from the hollow, she got back quickly to Pender and the others. She told them what she had observed and who she believed the people were. For identification purposes, it would be better for Pipa and Pender to come forward with her. Rahana brought her something to eat, and she brought warmer clothes for all of them, as this could be along night in the cold.

Rahana went back to feed the horses and make sure they were adequately covered and everything was cleaned up then they were ready to move forward.

The fire was blazing, and the men had already started to drink and they were quite noisy shouting at each other over the fire. Benic, in particular, seemed to be angry about even being there. He did not seem to enjoy the cold. It was easy then for the team to get near, to hear and see without being seen. The two horsemen were soon identified by Pipa as being friends of Abbi and the now-dead elder. Somer wanted to know why Rolf was not here and where were his slaves and women. The two men told him that nothing had gone as planned; Castor was dead but not according to the plan. The plot had been discovered, and Rolf and his killer friend were prisoners, as was the elder and his helper, but the elder had managed to poison Castor somehow and he was definitely dead. The woman whom Rolf was going to take to make his claim legitimate was now the chief.

Somer's response was immediately irrational, shouting and cursing at the pitch of his voice, dancing with rage, punching and kicking at his drinking men, then slumping down suddenly into his chair as if he had a stroke.

Benic's reaction to his father's collapse was noteworthy; instead of hurrying to his father's side, he laughed and laughed, rolling his fat body from side to side. "I told you, I told you, but you would not listen to me! Oh no, Rolfie boy knew better, he would do it his way, and there would be no problems. There would be only the minimum of deaths, plenty young women for me, and he would get the chief bitch. Ha! See what that got him. I hope he is dead. I wanted to take our whole army and take what we wanted and destroy the place, burn it down, but that takes guts, you have made us look weak with your 'be nice, be nice.' Look at you, an old fool, if there ever was one." He spat at his father's feet and walked away, snorting like some great beast.

"Now," said Zalenda, "we will never get a better chance. Let us take Benic out!" She walked forward down the lip of the hill into the firelight. She pointed to the six men. "Stay where you are and you will not get hurt." One got up and charged her from the side; it was a mistake. In his drunken state, she easily avoided him. One kick broke his leg, the other his neck. He rolled over dead. Another, seeing his friend now dead, started to get up from behind. Zalenda picked up the club he forgot to take with him. He was a tall giant of a man and came confidently forward, expecting an easy victory. He saw that she was tall for a woman, beautiful and statuesque. He would only hurt her a little then he would use her and share her with his friends. He was actually smiling when her first blow from the club hit him on the knees. He fell in front of her. The second one smashed his skull.

"Now will you believe you must behave when the lady tells you, or would you rather play your stupid games and end up dead like your friends?" Rahana threatened the other four. They shook their heads, indicating they did not. "OK, now watch and learn."

"Ha-ha!" Benic snorted. "The queen bitch herself. Have you come to play with me? You will find me very accommodating. I promise you will like it before you die." Just then Pender and Pipa approached from the side. "What a wonderful surprise, the prince himself and another plaything for me. This night is getting better and better. Come and join me, gentlemen." He waved to his four bodyguards to come forward. "I promise you can have the princess here and the little black piece there—it will be fun." But they did not move. The little black piece had the club, and she knew how to use it.

Pipa moved over to see if Somer was still alive, but it was obvious that the stroke had killed him. She was on her way back to Pender when Benic moved with amazing speed for such a big man and caught Pipa by the throat. Now he baited Zalenda. "You will move back or she dies now."

Pender said, "Do not hurt her. Take me instead."

"No, no. I see she is your weak link. No, I am going to keep her. I have plans for her. Tell your little black piece to drop the club or"—he tightened his hands around Pipa's throat and lifted her off her feet—"I will kill her now." He got the words out of his mouth, but that was all. Pipa had been watching Zalenda's eyes and read what she was to do. Benic was about to put her down again when Pipa elbowed him in the face and at the same time stamped down hard on his foot. He let her go with an oath and tried hard to see past his broken nose.

Zalenda was on him like a wild thing kicking him hard to inflict the most pain but not to kill him. She was so fast with her kicks that it was impossible to register which one did the most damage. He slumped down whimpering like child, "Please do not kill me. I can tell you things. I can help you. I can pay you. You can have these miserable guards of mine."

Pender came and stood over him, looking down at him in disgust. "Is this the great Benic who knew better than his father and mocked him when he lay dying? Is this the same person who boasted what he was going to do to these fine ladies here? Look at him crying like a baby, a coward, pleading to us not to hurt him, a spoiled baby man. Pipa, would you like to question your would-be rapist?"

"I would welcome that opportunity, and I believe it might be profitable to stand on his groin right here." Benic screamed in pain. Pipa let off the pressure just a bit. "Now tell us what we want to know."

Pender asked, "Why did you come here, and what was it you were after?"

"We came here expecting to receive women slaves from your tribe and to meet my brother, Rolf, and one of the elders. They were going to help us take over a number of tribes in this area and revenge ourselves for the damage you have done to our business."

"Who are the two men you came to meet?"

"They were paid informants, friends of your uncle Abbi." Pipa stepped away from him just as he aimed a kick at her, but Zalenda had been watching his eyes. Her kick caught him under the chin; his neck breaking was the last sound he heard.

Rahana made Somer's bodyguards carry out the corpses of their dead masters with their dead friends out on to the moor to feed the vultures.

Pender and Zalenda turned their attention to the two informants who it seemed had ties to Abbi and his friends. They were shaking with fear as Zalenda approached them. Pender asked what the purpose of their meeting with Somer was. They said that someone had been allowed by Castor to visit the elder when he was supposed to be in a prisoner in a room on the island. The elder had been laughing and drinking with his friends, and he told this contact that this message was to be sent to Somer as quickly as possible. The message was that the first plan had not worked, but he the elder had taken care of everything, and he would soon have his women and the others for slaves.

"We were to be paid to deliver the message but were held up a whole day because the new chief would not let anyone from the tribe leave the settlement until they had been vetted. We do not belong to the tribe, so we were allowed to carry out the instructions we were given. We had no idea that we would be involved in anything like this."

"What else can you tell us about this mysterious person who met with the elder?" Zalenda asked, this time standing in front of them as if she was ready to strike.

They pleaded with her not to hurt them. They had told them all they knew. "We know nothing about this man, only that he was a friend of Abbi's."

"Is there anything else you should be telling us?" Pender asked.

"We did hear a discussion that we probably were not supposed to hear. Apparently, they found out that four young women were going to spy at Slave Island, and a message was to be sent to the Nuits to go and kill them."

Pender thanked them for their information and told them they could go back to their families on the condition they told Abbi's friend they had completed his instruction, but they must not tell anyone that Somer and his son were dead. "If you do, this lady here will visit you and your family, and what you have seen here today will be nothing in comparison to what she will do to them." They went with great haste, not waiting to pick up their meager belongings, and got on their horses and rode away into the morning.

The four returned with Rahana, who no longer carried the club. She seemed to enjoy giving the men orders and watching them carry them out, and they did not question her authority. Their next assignment she gave them was to go with her to bring the horses from the hide. Pipa questioned the wisdom of allowing her to go on her own with them because it would be easy for them to steal the horses and take Rahana as their prisoner.

Her fears were short lived, however, because they soon returned with the horses and the supplies, Rahana riding and the men leading the rest of the horses. It was quite evident that they were trying to outdo each other to please her, and she was enjoying their attention. There was a competition among them to see who was going to have the privilege of assisting her off her horse, and she played the part perfectly, the lady being served by her admires.

"What are we going to do with her lackeys?" Zalenda asked Pender.

"I think she has answered that question. It looks like our dark mysterious lady of small stature and the beautiful crown of black hair has won for herself a cohort of loyal followers." Pender helped Pipa and then Zalenda on to their horses, and he mounted up. It was important for them to get to Mari's hiding place at Slave Island before the Nuits did. As they rode up onto the moor, he turned to look behind. Rahana was well protected; she had two admirers riding on either side.

The morning of hard riding passed without incident. Just before they reached Slave Island, Rahana led her men in a charge to the hide. By the time Pender arrived with Zalenda and Pipa, she had the place turned inside out looking for the girls. She pointed to the ground. "Four horsemen, just as the informants said, the trail is leading north into the Nuits' territory. Josh, change our horses. Put that sheepskin on mine. My bum is sore riding, it will be a lot sorer tonight. If these bastards lay a hand on my girls, I will kill them with my bare hands. Remember we will need supplies for three days. Now let's go. We have no time to waste." As she was saying this, she commanded Caleb to lift her up on her horse, and she left without looking back.

Zalenda looked at Pender in wonderment. "That is one tough little lady. What has gotten into her?"

"We are her family, not just friends. She treats us younger ones as her daughters. She tells us that every time we are in the hot springs with her. I guess they were not empty words," Pipa said, the tears running down her face. "I doubt very much whether Rona's or Morag's mothers, knowing them, would have done the same. She is very special."

Pender said, "Where are the dogs? They were supposed to be here for the team's protection. Let us go and see if they went off duty with Mari and Zari."

"Should we not check on Becca's team first," Pipa asked, "in case the Nuits have sent assassins after them?"

"They will be on their way back today, so the chance of us finding them inbound is small. At this point, I think it is more important to see if we can contact Mari and Zari to find out if the Nuits have them. We may have lost the whole team—that would be disastrous. Rest and feed the horses. Meanwhile, check out our situation here to see if we are being watched. From now on, it is critical that Abbi's friends do not know we are coming after them. We will eat when we get to the Great Forest." As he was speaking, Pender was meticulously examining the ground to see if it yielded any clues as to how the Nuits had been able to get to the girls while they were watching. "The girls were lying here looking out under these branches. See, there is wool from their sheepskin jackets. Their vision range is wide to the front. Their attackers must have come from behind."

Zalenda said, "Here is something." She got down onto her knees among the scraps of the girls' breakfast and picked up a wooden drinking flask and put it to her nose. "That explains everything. The girls were drugged. Whoever prepared their supplies in the settlement was in on this, and now they don't know that we know." Pender went immediately and checked their flasks, smelled them, and handed them to Zalenda. she checked them and found nothing suspicious.

Pipa said, "That is because Elecia and I did our stuff. Rona wanted to take pies from her mother, so their supplies could have been tampered with there."

When they were satisfied that they were not being watched, they mounted and were soon on their way west toward the winding river. Pender led the way, Pipa in the middle and Zalenda in the rear so she could check regularly that they were not followed. The sun was getting low in the sky as they approached the Great Oak Tree. Zalenda took care of the call up the tree. as she was quite well known to the residents. Soon their horses and supplies were taken care of by two young men who eyed Pipa admiringly. She was unaware of this because ascending up into the forest fort was new experience for her. Pender was now impatient to find out how his friends had fared and what had happened to the dogs. His guides knew nothing of these things, as they had not been on duty when the ladies returned. They hurried to the room that they normally occupied and found Mari and Zari and the dogs collapsed in a drug-induced sleep.

Zalenda went to get water and wet towels to try and revive her friends. It was some time before they were sufficiently in control of all their faculties even to stand up. They were absolutely astounded when they realized what had happened and how near they were to have been prisoners of the Nuits. They decided to let the dogs sleep off the effects of the drugs till the morning. Zari, when she was able, wanted to know what they were going to do to rescue Rona and Morag. While Zalenda and Pipa went to find food, Pender related to them their adventures of the past three days and how they had learned of a plot for their team to be killed by assassins. When they had discovered Rona and Morag missing, Rahana was extremely angered, and this had led to her riding off in a terrible rage with her cohort of followers, determined to overtake and kill the Nuits. She had done this on her own initiative without any consultation, inspired by her deep love for the girls. "It did not seem appropriate at the time to stop and argue. Some of us were going to have gone, and she volunteered herself with the men."

"It does not seem possible—Rahana riding off with four men! How did she turn them from enemies into faithful followers?" Mari exclaimed.

Pender replied, "Honest, Mari, you had to be there to see it with your own eyes. She was simply marvelous. These men are willing to die for her—we were astonished."

The ladies returned with the food, and as they ate, they decided that all of them would return to the settlement in the morning. As a result of the recent events, no one outside their group could be trusted with anything, information, food supplies, or any kind of equipment. The evidence of a further traitor or traitors in the settlement must be dealt with right away, of course, with Cisi's permission. "We cannot divide the team again because we cannot afford to lose anyone. As soon as it is possible, we will follow Rahana's lead and deal with this new threat from the Nuits."

Zalenda said she wanted to pursue a new avenue with all of the women in the group—that was to make sure all of them were trained in combat. "We cannot leave anything to chance. I cannot always do these things on my own. Should I get cut down, I would like to think we could carry on. One other thing, we must invest time in acquiring red dye for our hair. One advantage the Nuits have is they know when we are coming because of our different hair color. I aim to take that advantage away and using it to our benefit. We will consult with Elecia as to the best shades and who should go undercover."

The three ladies were excited at the prospect of being the new Zalenda and could not wait to start practicing their kicks, but Zalenda assured them it would be all in good time. "It is more important that we get to sleep now. We will be moving out early in the morning." Extra cots had been brought into the room so that they would all get a good night's sleep. Pipa, in particular, looked forward to that, as she did not enjoy sleeping outside, and doing so up high in the trees, that was something special.

The dogs finally awakened and were keen to get out into their own environment, but they had to wait till everyone was fed and for Mari's trained watch girls to tell them that the forest area was clear to travel. It was the best day of the spring so far. The air was warm, and the horses seem to realize they were going home. Tarag went away ahead to make sure the road was clear, and Toto trailed some distance behind. They would never be taken by surprise again.

The settlement was just beginning to wake up when the group made its way around it to stable the horses and feed the other animals. They pulled themselves over to the island, so no one knew they were there. Elecia was serving breakfast to Cymon, Nena, Becca, and Ester, and immediately went and set five more places and brought in more delicious food. It was obvious that she enjoyed being mother, and she relished the opportunity to display her cooking skills. Ester came and kissed her brother and looked quizzically at him, holding up two fingers. Pender whispered later, "We will all talk. Let's eat and rest for now."

Everyone relished their wonderful breakfast and were complimenting Elecia on it and was about to leave to clean up when Pender told her to wait; she was needed in the meeting. Pender asked Nena to report on their mission to watch the actions of Raymond, the transporter, to see if there was any action on the river. She told the group that they had watched for three days, and during that time, they had observed no movement at all. She indicated that Cymon would report about some information he had been able to find.

Cymon had watched some men fishing in the river, and when they were bringing their catch in, he went to talk to them. During their conversation, he discovered that Tamor, the chief of the Nuits, was about to rebuild the Slave Island compound and also build a fort around it. The building materials for this project were being purchased at the Big River mouth, and it was expected that they would start shipping the materials in long barges in the weeks to come. Tamor would be moving his own men down to do the construction, and he had offered the fishermen work in the stockade as guards. They did not want to turn down such a powerful man, so they said they would think about it, but really intended to be long gone before the work started.

Pender thanked Cymon for that very valuable information their mission had provided, and this would be something they were going to have to consider in the near future. Pender then gave all the details of their dealings with Somer and Benic and how they had learned of the mole in their midst who had been giving information to the Nuits. He then informed them of how Rona and Morag had been drugged and taken by four Nuits, and how Rahana had gone to their rescue. It was suspected at this time that the drug had been put into their drinking flask by someone in Rona's household. He would ask Cisi to be allowed to investigate this situation and deal with the mole at the same time.

He also announced Zalenda's combat training program for every member of the team and that there might be a need for all of them to consider dying their head red in preparations for missions against the Nuits. If this became necessary, he was asking Elecia to be the adviser on this project and to provide background information. Becca wanted to know if the four men with Rahana could be trusted, so he asked Pipa and Zalenda to tell them how Rahana had changed these men into her loyal followers.

After days on horseback with only sheepskins for protection, the ladies wanted nothing else than the hot springs before bed. The meeting was adjourned for this purpose.

Cymon and Pender waited till the ladies were finished in the hot springs before they went for their time of relaxation. They had been considering where the links in the Nuits chain might be at its weakest. The discussion on where the Nuits were likely to be more vulnerable continued in the hot springs, so there was little time for real relaxation. Cymon believed that they should not wait but to plan for a strike to rescue the girls should Rahana fail to get them both. When Tamor brought his men down to rebuild the compound, the Nuits could be open to attack. Although their lands were vast and had a large population, they had no real natural protection.

Pender said that was a valid point, but it was very unlikely that they would be able to recruit enough people to launch an invasion against the Nuit lands. We will have to come up with a more ingenuous plan for a small team to do an undercover mission, with good intelligence, that will move in quickly and return without attracting attention. The major difficulty with that kind of operation is we must do it soon.

Cymon was thoughtful for some time, and Pender began to think that he was sleeping standing up. Then he suddenly broke the silence. "What we need is three teams of three that would have red hair, medium build, and look and talk like the Nuits. Elecia could be our tutor. She could be involved in all our preparations. The first strike team would have our best trained combat people, the second well trained in cover action and ready to move in should the first team fail. The third team would move in first to find out where the girls were being held and give information to the other two teams. What do you think of that plan? Does it have any merit for further discussion?"

"Cymon, I believe that is exactly the kind of thinking we need to do. Let's go and sleep on it, and we will talk again tomorrow. Good night. Sleep well."

Chapter 16

Rahana's Revenge

When Rahana and her four riders left Mari's hide, she was consumed with anger and a thirst for revenge against the Nuit raiders who had taken the girls, but more so against the people who had ordered it. She rode recklessly following the trail left by the raiders' horses, urging her mount forward with great energy. The men who followed her let her do this knowing full well this pent-up rage would soon evaporate, and it did when she saw the clues. The raiders were leaving to guide some yet unidentified members of their group to where they had their lair.

The first clue was Rona's jerkin, then her pants, then her underwear, and then it was the same with Morag's, and Rahana knew the girls were naked. She wept with anger and fear—what was she going to do? What would Pender do? What would Zalenda do? She ordered Caleb and Josh forward to scout the trail ahead—that's what Zalenda would have done. They had ridden a little further ahead but soon came back to tell her that they could see smoke rising from a small hillock some distance toward the north, so the Nuits must be heading home.

Bart had been gathering up the girls' clothes. He suggested that he should ride on and pretend to be the person they were expecting. Then Caleb, Josh, and Rahana should come at full speed. Aron would stay and cover their back and intercept anyone coming behind. "How will we know when to come?" Rahana asked.

Bart put his hand inside his coat and brought out his pet pigeon. "When you see her go up, come in a hurry." He turned to go.

Rahana said. "Stop! You cannot go, you are not redheaded."

Bart pulled down the sides of his cap. "Now they can't see, and I have no beard," and he was gone.

They waited and waited, and Rahana was getting impatient. Then they saw the pigeon ascend into the night sky then the three galloped like the wind. Aron was about to sit down when he heard the sound of riders coming from behind. He peered through the bushes and saw two riders coming fast up the pathway. He realized he could not let them past. He had kept the rope that had been used to tie them up when Zalenda had killed Benic. He fetched it from the supply horse and tied it between two trees. The first rider was almost on him when he finished and just got out of the way. The horse stumbled against the rope, spilling its rider on the ground and sending the horse careening off to the side, just as the second horse hit it. The rider had no chance; he was trapped in a melee of horse legs and hooves. He received a kick on the head, which killed him. The horses were injured but were able to run away into the bush.

Aron went forward to the badly injured rider from the first horse and was about to help him up, when the rider took him by surprise, rolling over and pulling a long flint knife from his belt, and slashed down on Aron's leg. The knife cut through the bindings Aron used to tie his pant legs tight while he was riding, but did little real damage. "Friend, I was about to help you, but for that, you get this," so saying, he picked up a club the second rider had lost in his fall, and hit his attacker in the face, which kept him quiet for the rest of his time on earth.

Rahana burst into the clearing with Josh and Caleb on her tail and rode straight at the redheaded giant who was holding a naked Morag by the back of the neck. She rode her horse into him, lifting Morag at the same time. He was so startled that he let go of his naked hostage. The element of surprise only lasted seconds, but that was too long; he was bowled over, the horse taking him down. Caleb and Josh were on top of him before he could move. The man was winded, but even a giant cannot do much when someone is standing with his full weight on his throat. Two much-smaller broader men were holding Bart, but not for long. When they saw the giant on his back, they hastily let him go; they did not want to suffer for this beast who treated them the way he treated slaves.

Rahana clung to Morag, not wanting to let her go. "My precious girl, what has he done to you?" Morag was frozen cold. She had been stripped naked by the giant and tied over a horse. Rahana rubbed her vigorously all over to try and get some warmth into her, while Bart brought her clothes. They soon had her clothed and sitting by the fire. Rahana approached the two redheaded men who wanted to escape in the worst way. "Where is the other girl you took?" They tremulously pointed to the giant and said he already sold her to one of his friends. "Do you know this man's name? The truth now, remember I am black and I am small, but I have a big temper as you will see in a moment."

"No, we don't know. All we know it was someone from her own tribe."

Rahana told them to move over to where the giant lay. "Now pull his legs open and stand on a leg each." They were afraid, but after a struggle, they complied with her instructions. She went and stood on the giant's crotch. He tried to scream, but his throat was obstructed by Caleb's weight and Josh standing on his arms. "Let's see if he will tell us the truth, so just enough weight off to let him speak please. You did something very wrong when you took my friends. Now tell the truth please. You are going to die right here—I can make it easy or hard, you choose."

"You little black bitch, I will not tell you anything," he said, trying to snatch a breath or two as he was talking.

"I was hoping you would say that because now I can do this." She jumped up and down on his crotch. He screamed and threw up everything he had eaten in days. When he had subsided into sobbing and pleading for mercy, she asked him again, "Do you know where my friend is?"

"The man who bought her was delivering her to the chief of the Nuits as a present. That is where she will be now."

Rahana put her bitch look on again. "Thank you for that information. Now it is time to pay for your despicable behavior. You have the privilege of being the first slave trader I have ever killed."

"Morag, please come now, you have an important job to do. I want you to think of all the suffering this man has caused you and how much more it would have been if we had not come along. Then I want you to think of all that Rona has suffered and will suffer. Then I want you to get angry and kick this pitiless piece of rubbish as hard as you can right there," and she let up on the giant's crotch. "Now kick." Morag did exactly that, and Rahana went and stood on his throat till he was dead.

Rahana turned to the two redheaded Nuits, who were absolutely stunned by what they had just witnessed. "Now I want you to take a message back to your chief. Tell him the small black lady will hunt him down should he hurt one hair of my girl's head, and I will kill ten of his family should he consider taking her life. Tell him how his giant of a friend died at my hands with one kick from a girl he ordered killed. Convince him of this, and I will allow you to live. Now go and do it!"

Rahana sat with Morag, feeding her from her food supplies and comforting her. Morag cried with embarrassment, knowing that everyone had seen her naked. Rahana assured her that these men did not take any joy from having witnessed her humiliation but were more moved because of that to protect her and get her home. After some time passed, Morag got up and said, "I am ready now. I will go with you and work to free Rona. There is something I must tell you, it might be worth thinking about. I have suspected Rona's younger brother is involved with some unscrupulous characters in our tribe but refrained from saying so because I did not want to offend her."

They cleared up the area and put out the fire. Caleb went ahead, and Bart followed behind to make sure no one trailed them home. It was well past midnight when they crossed to the island, but Rahana went immediately to report that Morag was safe home and that Rona was still missing.

Rahana went to the hot springs with Morag and spent the time relaxing in the heated water. She was sore and tired and needed to sleep, but she would not leave Morag to her frightened dreams. Once they were dried and comfortable, she took Morag to her room and then showed the men to the spare rooms. Only when she was sure everyone was set for the night did she go back to sleep with Morag in her warm custody.

In the morning breakfast was a crowded affair. Elecia had to go and get more food so that everyone could sit and eat together. It was a completely new experience for the four men that had come home with Rahana. Caleb was telling anyone who would listen how fearless Rahana had been in dealing with the giant. Mari asked her, "How did you know what to do, Rahana?"

"I didn't. I just said to myself what would Pender and Zalenda do, and the answer was take control of the situation. I watched her do it with Somer and Benic. She did not hesitate but went right in. I just copied her, and it turned out right. I think I require more lessons before I do something like that again, and, of course, my guys were great."

Morag came in just then, and everyone welcomed her. She thanked the team for coming and rescuing her, especially Rahana, but reminded them Rona was still a prisoner of the Nuits. She now understood how they had been drugged and where it originated. She had other suspicions that she would discuss later.

Pender said, "Just for the period of this breakfast, I want everyone to enjoy what we have to eat and the good company we have here, and I especially would like to introduce to you four young men who have recently joined with us through Rahana—Caleb, Josh, Bart, and Aron." The men were so glad to be recognized and were so happy to be working with a group like this.

Zalenda reminded everyone that unarmed combat training would begin today, and only Pender, Ester, and Morag would be exempt, as they had business at the settlement.

Elecia also reminded them after the combat training was finished, she would be giving out important background information on the Nuits' customs and culture, which would be important to all should they have to go undercover in that tribe. She would also talk about dying their hair red, which would be needed to fit in with the Nuit Tribe environment.

Pender, Ester, and Morag left after conferring with Rahana about the possible identity of the mole in their midst. They decided that Pipa should go with them.

On the way over to the settlement, Morag spoke of her suspicions and mistrust she had for Rona's younger brother, who she recalled was the only person around when their supplies were being prepared. It would have been simple for him to tamper with their drinks. It was a well-known fact that he disagreed with the selection of Cisi as chief and was totally against women being given any responsibility. He often took his spite on his sister for being part of the watch team and belittled her in company because of it.

Pipa said when she was on watch she often saw him hanging around with Abbi's cronies from the elders' group. Ester felt that perhaps her sister, in an effort to cause as little upset as possible, had erred in reinstating that group after Castor had removed them for good cause.

Ester went to the place that Cisi was using as her temporary home and requested a formal interview for her, Pender, and two other young women according to their new working agreement. As it was weeks since they had met, she agreed that they could meet informally over a flask of this new spiced cider she had just purchased. Cisi greeted her brother and the girls with hugs and kisses, and they chatted about how things were going for her dealing with tribal issues.

After they had exhausted that topic, she asked them why they had really come. Pender told her Somer and Benic were dead, but did not say how he knew or where it had happened. She could now dispose of Rolf's body, as it was still in cold storage on the island. If it was her wish, he could do it for her. She felt the less that people knew about it, the better it would be, so they were in agreement that his body should be disposed of as quickly as possible, burned without ceremony on the island.

Ester told her about her recent mission and what she had discovered about Tamor's future plans to rebuild a new compound and fort at Slave Island. This information should be circulated through all the family tribes.

Cisi asked what this super fort would mean for the family tribes around here and in particular this one. Pender answered very soberly, "All-out war. We are going to try and hinder him as much as possible, but they have too many men to call on while we are very limited. I plan to visit as many of the tribes as I can to see if they will consider helping us in this matter. When I have formulated a plan for a united effort, I will inform you.

"Now for some time more imminent, and this is where Morag comes in. Four days ago, two of our watchers were taken by Nuits raiders who were instructed to kill them. Rahana was able to follow them and rescue Morag, but Rona is still missing, we fear for her life."

Pender let Morag tell Cisi all the terrifying details of her ordeal right to where Rahana made her kick her giant abuser in the crotch prior to his death. "The reason I am here is to tell you I strongly suspect the person who put the drug in our drinking flask was Rona's brother, Remi. Prior to the preparations of our supplies for our trip, he was in and out of the room where we were working. I went out to check on our horses. When I came back, he was just leaving. He had a very guilty look on his face, but I could not find anything amiss. I know he was very derisive of Rona and her work as a watcher and believes women should not be involved in anything in the tribe, except looking after the interests of their own men. He also said you would not last very long as chief and that you had proved how stupid you are by reinstating the group of elders that had existed for no other reason than to aggrandize themselves and wield the power in the tribe."

Pipa told Cisi that while she was on watch duty in the tribe, she had often seen Remi hanging around with two of Abbi's friends and some of the present elders. This all began to make sense when one of the men had been sent by the elder, even before he died, to tell Somer that his original plan had failed, but everything was going to work out just fine, since he had taken care of everything. This man admitted that he knew that there was at least one mole still working on behalf of the slavers in our tribal council.

Pender waited to let this sink into Cisi's mind then he said, "I would like to advise you as your brother to remove these threats to your reign as chief right away. I would suggest that you attack the weakest link, Remi, Rona's brother. I think he should be advised to give up the person who got him to place the drugs in the flask. The threat of exposure and what he has done to his sister must be revealed to his family. They are honorable people, and he must know if he does not cooperate, he dies."

Cisi said, "This is what we must do—tonight I want Remi removed and taken to the island for interrogation. Once we have found out who the mole is, I will convene a special council of the elders. Whoever is responsible will be punished immediately. The more serious the crime, the more serious the punishment. I will need men available to arrest the guilty parties."

"I can provide you with trustworthy men," Pender promised.

Chapter 17

Remi's Treachery Revealed

Pipa, Morag, and Ester waited until it was dark and then visited Rona's family. The family was just finishing their evening meal when they arrived. Pipa excused their interruption but said they had sad news they had to pass on to this family.

She let Morag tell the story, how when they were on watch, they had drunk from their flask of honey cider, not knowing that someone had put a drug in it so that they would be easy prey for four Nuit raiders that were sent to kill them. The raiders decided that because they were virgins, rather than kill them, they would sell them, and Rona would be taken to the Nuit chief as a present. They were stripped naked on the way so that their clothes would be left as trail markers for the buyers. But Rahana, when she heard what happened, rode full out with her four friends, and she was able rescue her and kill the Nuits. She allowed two of them to live so that he could go and tell the Nuit chief that if he harmed Rona in any way, she would kill ten of his women in revenge.

Rona's father exploded with rage. "Who in our tribe would do such a thing? I will hunt them down with their friends and make sure they are punished beyond the law."

Her mother cried in anguish, "My daughter, my lovely daughter, given as a plaything for despicable men—who did this!"

Ester looked around the table to Remi, who was looking very guilty, and with Pipa and Morag pointed to him and said he did it. Remi's parents were shocked at the accusation and were looking at him in disbelief. "Did you do this!" Remi did not answer.

Morag said, "Unfortunately the evidence against him is difficult to deny. He was the only one who had access to the flask. He hung around your kitchen till I went out for a moment, and as I went out, he went in. When I went back in, he was doing something with our pack. I did not think too much of it at the time, but I do recall he looked as he does now—guilty!"

Remi sputtered out his words, "The little bitch got what she deserved. She with her important airs about her, she was a watcher for that other bitch woman, doing things that men were meant to do—watching my friends in the elders! The real people in charge, not your bitch sister," he said, looking at Ester. "They asked me to do this thing. It's how real men act, so what if we sell a few bitches to the Nuits? We profit."

Remi's father got up from the table and slapped him in the face. "You ungrateful little wretch, your sister loved you and served you hand and foot. How could you conspire to do such a thing? Take him away out of my sight before I kill him."

Quietly and under the cover of the night, Remi was removed from the settlement. He was escorted to the ferry by his father and mother, his hands tied behind his back, his mouth covered so he could not shout for his friends. As he boarded the ferry and Pender started to pull, he looked back at his parents, but they turned their faces away, ashamed of their boy who had betrayed their daughter.

The full complement of the team was in the hall waiting on his arrival. Rahana wanted so badly to extract the information from him on who his associates were in the elders. But Pender believed after Remi's outburst against women, it would be better for him to begin the questioning.

Pender began as soon as everyone was settled. "Remi, we know that this idea to deliver your precious sister naked to the chief of the Nuits was not yours, but by putting the potion into her drinking flask, you are convicted of it all. We have decided that the penalty for such an act is to be torn slowly apart by these dogs. Rahana, bring the dogs in."

Remi's eyes were like saucers, wide and unseeing; his breath came in great gasps of fear and terror. "Wait, wait," he wailed, "please wait.

If I tell you who gave me the potion and who took the message to the Nuits and who are the members of the elders who are plotting against your sister, will you take away the dogs please, please!"

Pender pretended to confer with Zalenda and Rahana. "We think that is a very good beginning, Remi, but you can see our problem. Tomorrow when we denounce these people before the council, they will simply deny it, and you might change your mind if the dogs are not there."

"I promise that I will speak before the council and identify those responsible for all their underhand dealings that are not in the best interests of this tribe, and I will point out the person who gave me the potion."

Pender addressed the team, "You have heard this young man. Should we trust him to do as he says?"

Cymon spoke on Remi's behalf. "If he does as he says he will, it would mean we can now work without the fear of the Nuits knowing ahead of time what our intentions might be."

"What will happen to him after this council? Won't the relatives of those he identifies try to kill him?"

Becca said, "I suggest he stays with us and trains to be on this team, that way we can keep our collective eyes on him. Put him in the team that is to rescue his sister, that would be true redemption.

Morag joined in. "Perhaps it would heal the breach with his parents."

The discussion went for some time. Bart thought he should be punished as an example. "I saw firsthand what his pettiness meant for his sister and Morag. I don't think I can forget it."

Zalenda's participation brought things to a head. "The first thing is we need him to identify those yet faceless people among the elders who dreamed up this plot. They can only be convicted and punished. If he confesses that he put the potion in the flask, according to their instructions, we have the word of the two paid messengers sent to Somer and Benic. They heard these same as yet unidentified people tell others to notify the Nuit raiders that the girls were to be killed. I remind you that it also included Mari and Zari. Had they not gone on a break, they would have been taken and sold."

Pender said, "I agreed with most of the things that you have said, so let me sum things up like this—we need him, and we must use him tomorrow at the council. Then depending on how well he does, he could be trained to be on our team. If he lets us down, then the dogs will play with him. Cymon, you will take charge of taking him to the council in the morning, but do not bring him in till Pipa comes to get you. Caleb, Josh, Bart, and Aron, you will be in the council with us, and when Cisi, my older sister and chief of our tribe, indicates that these men are proved guilty, you will arrest them immediately and bring them here for further interrogation then we will hand them over to Cisi to be punished."

Cisi had called the council meeting for midmorning, and there appeared to be great interest among the people as well as the elders. When Pender and his group filed in, the tension among the elders was almost boiling over. It was obvious they were spoiling for a fight with Cisi and had chosen today to press the issue to have her removed as chief. Cisi opened by saying she had scheduled the meeting to consider some important information that had come to her attention, regarding traitorous allegations on the part of some people who were members of the council as elders.

One of the elders stood up and called for an immediate dismissal of the chief's agenda, and instead he would introduce a motion to have the chief removed from office in favor of a male to be chosen by the elders here and present. It was their contention that a woman could not hold this office because everyone knew women did not have the ability to understand the importance of the issues facing an important tribe like theirs. To do this, only members of the settlement community should stay, and all the rest should leave, as this was not their business.

If he had expected his motion to be popular with the people, he was mistaken. The people, male and female, stood up and shouted him down, stamping their feet and shaking their fists at the speaker. He tried to continue, but no one would listen.

Cisi waited till silence prevailed and quietly said to the speaker, "Sir, I believe your motion has already been defeated. Now to our original agenda, will you please bring the young man in?" Everyone in the audience suddenly were very interested, especially the elders. Pipa brought Remi in; he was already shaking in his shoes. He had heard the crowd's raucous reaction to the elders—what would they be like with him? Would they take justice into their own hands and string him up?

As he was milling this over in his mind, Cisi asked him her first question, "Is your name Remi, Rona's brother?"

"Yes, I am her younger brother."

"Why is Rona not here today?"

"She is not here because I helped betray her to the Nuits."

"You betrayed your sister?"

"Yes. I was asked by members of the elders to put a potion in her drinking flask."

"Did you know what was in the potion?"

"No, no one told me what was in it or what it would do."

"Are the people here today who asked you to do this?"

"Yes, they are. They are right there with the elders," he said, pointing to three people.

"Where is Rona now?"

"She was to be killed by the Nuits, but the men who were supposed to do it decided they wanted to sell her and her friend. The person who bought Rona wanted instead to give her as a present to the Nuit chief. That is where she is today."

"Did you know this was the plot these elders had made?"

"No, I did not."

Cisi said, "Thank you for your evidence. Will the people who are here to arrest the suspects please remove them now?" Caleb and his friends came in and led away the three people identified by Remi, who then were led out by Pipa.

Chapter 18

The Mole Discovered and Punished

"The next order of business is very important because it is concerned with the upper echelons of our elders and their illegal activities in conspiring with well-known slave traders, in this case Somer and Benic. I can tell you that both of these very unsavory characters are now dead and no longer are a threat to us, but the people here today who provided them with help and information are certainly still dangerous to our tribe. Have the two men whom our elders paid to take information to the slavers been found?" Rahana, who had been searching for the men, brought them in to the meeting.

When the two men were brought in, it was very obvious that they were uncomfortable. The very essence of their business as paid informants was to remain inconspicuous at all times. Now their cover was blown, and they were very much on public display.

Cisi began by thanking them for coming and giving up their time. "My first question to you today is, do you recognize the men here who paid you to take a message to the slave traders from the head elder, who at that time was imprisoned for his part in the plot to kill our chief, Castor the Great?"

One of the men answered, "We did not know that man, but the people who paid us to take the message are certainly here." He pointed to the elder whom the people had shouted down.

"I want to be perfectly clear—this man you have identified gave you goods in payment for your service in carrying that message, is that correct?"

"Yes, that is what happened. He gave us half when we left and half when we came back."

Cisi asked the second man if he agreed with his friend about how the business was conducted.

"Yes, that is how things were done."

"Have you ever carried messages for them before?"

"Yes, we often did business carrying messages for this man to Slave Island."

"One final question—did he ever tell you what his authority for giving you these assignments?"

"Oh yes, he often boasted about the fact that he was the real chief, and he would soon remove the bitch chief."

Cisi thanked the men for their testimony and said they could leave.

Cisi then said to the meeting, "I want to warn the people of this council that the three people who have given testimony today are under my protection. Anyone who might consider harming them on behalf of the men convicted today will be dealt with by public hanging—this is not an idle threat! Will the men responsible for arresting the criminals please remove them at this time?

"The next thing on the agenda, in light of what has happened, is to dissolve this group of elders. Although some of them have not been tarred by this scandal, they all certainly knew what was going on. So I pronounce them dissolved on the grounds of treacherous dealings with known criminals."

Cisi now turned to the penalty that must be passed by the whole council on those that had been charged with conspiracy against the tribe and those who conspired to have Morag and Rona murdered by others. Since she had prorogued the last group of elders, this whole council would be responsible for passing the sentence on these men. She asked that all those who were not a member of the settlement tribe to retire so justice could be done. All of Pender's team left except Morag and Pipa, and returned to the island to consider what their next move to rescue Rona would be.

Later that evening Morag and Pipa returned with the news that the sentence had been passed by the council, and the conspirators had already been hanged in the settlement square; the judgment had been unanimous.

As was now the custom, the ladies went to the hot springs after they had eaten, then the men, so it was almost midnight before Pender and Zalenda had the springs to themselves.

Chapter 19

The Team to Warn the Tribes of Tamor's Plan

It was well into the following afternoon before Zalenda's combat training classes were completed. When everyone was available, they met to discuss who would go undercover in the Nuit Tribe to locate and rescue Rona. It was decided that a small team of four would go, two women and two men. They would pose as two couples looking for a lost relative, and their main purpose was to locate Rona. If they believed they could rescue her without risking their own lives, they had permission to try. Another group of four was to gather information about how susceptible the Nuit Tribe would be to a small highly trained force designed to take out the chief Tamor. They would pose as traveling sheepskin sellers. Pender and Zalenda would travel around the other tribes to see if they would provide help if things should denigrate into full-out war with the Nuits.

Pender then tried to determine who would be in the teams, but before he could ask, he was bombarded with volunteers. Nena and Elecia wanted to pose as the wives of Cymon and Bart to go undercover inside the Nuit Tribe. The team posing as the sheepskin traders would be led by Rahana because she already had experience in this area, Becca and Pipa as watchers, with the men Caleb, Josh, and Aron. Morag was to visit the mystic lady to see if she could provide them with red dye suitable to dye the heads of Nena, Cymon, and Bart. This decision having been made, everyone went back to their training.

That night after everyone had settled down, Pender and Zalenda were visited by Mari and Zari. They wondered if Pender had noticed that they had not volunteered for any of the missions. Previous to the meeting, they had decided to ask permission to go back to Slave Island and establish a new hide, from which they could observe the reconstruction of the Nuits' new fort. This might prove valuable if it became necessary to make another raid.

Pender thought this was an excellent idea, but he cautioned no one at the forest should know what their true purpose was, and they must have cover at all times. Perhaps the girls whom they had been training could provide that help. The other issue was that they must always prepare their own food and supplies. "We have learned an important lesson, and we must not fail in that aspect of our preparations again. Zalenda and I will come on a regular basis to get any information you might gather because we cannot put our young women into dangerous situations traveling the roads. Be ready in the morning, and we will travel with you. We may as well start our survey of the tribes there."

Early next morning as they were having breakfast, Ester arrived from the settlement to tell them that two Nuit men wanted to see Rahana. They were being held as prisoners, but according to Ester, that did not seem to upset them. Rahana had gone for an early morning visit to the springs, so they had to wait till she appeared for breakfast. Meantime, Ester brought news of the new council. The people had chosen four men and four women, one young man and one young woman, and she was that young women. They had been busy establishing new rules for doing business inside the settlement and with outside traders. As the island had its own laws for these types of things, she did not think there would be many changes there. Rahana finished her breakfast, and the six of them left for the ferry.

Rahana asked Pender to interview the two Nuits with her so there would be no suspicious dealings suspected. When the men were shown in, Rahana recognized them immediately as the two men she had sent with the message to the Nuit chief. They looked as if they had been badly beaten, and in fact, that was the story they told. When they could not produce Morag, the chief's men were ordered to kick them and beat them until they could not stand up. Another of their number cut off their beards and shaved their heads; now they could never return to their people. Like Rahana, they wanted revenge, and they would like to help her.

Rahana listened to them carefully and said, "I like your story, but you know it's just a bit too convenient. We have trouble locating one of our people, and you and your friend here think I am dumb enough to accept your offer of help when I know you were instrumental in her being taken in the first place! It is true I did upset the cruel plot and killed the rest of that bunch of cruel bastards. Take your clothes off!"

The men looked at each other in amazement. The spokesman said, "Why would we do that?" "It's fairly easy to take a few slaps on the face to help your cover story, but kicks on the ribs, well, that is a different matter. Sorry, guys, go back to your masters and tell them that I am not as stupid as they think. Take them back to prison and keep them on bread and water—it may help them to tell the truth." She stood up to leave. The men started to take off their clothes until they stood before them naked. Zalenda inspected each of them in turn. She examined them back and front and said to Rahana, "Rah, my dear sister, these are all consistent with a person being badly kicked. See here, you can see the imprint of a hard object having struck this man, probably a hard leather boot. Notice here, this rib is broken and requires to be tightly bound. This man must be in severe pain." She turned to the other man and continued her inspection. He was bruised and marked low down on his spine. She turned him around and lifted his penis with a rod. "Yes, see here, this is the result of this man being kicked in the balls. Look, they are turning black. The rest of his crotch is badly bruised. If we don't get this man into the springs and get him pumped full of water, he will die."

"Thanks, Zal. Gentlemen, put on your clothes. I am sorry I had to submit you to that humiliation, but I had to be sure. You are coming with me so that these injuries can be properly treated. You need to be cared for and fed. Welcome to our team. Oh! and so you are prepared, I will be rubbing salve all over your naked bodies. I will do my best not to enjoy it too much," she said in her normal joking manner.

Pender made a call to see his sister Cisi, who was just about to start an interview. They kissed, and she whispered in his ear, "This is more than I bargained for."

He whispered back, "You can do it, sis, but I am glad it's not me."

The four of them picked up their horses and were about to mount when Becca appeared. "Special delivery, fed and watered," and Tarag and Toto agreed they were keen to be off.

They rode round the lake and then out over the great moor toward the Big River. As they climbed a hill that overlooked the river, they were never conscious that in centuries to come, a great tower keep would be built on the ground they now walked on. Mari and Zari laid down a sheepskin cover, and they sat beholding the glorious sight of the winding river and the mountains beyond. When they turned around, the only thing that was moving on the Big River were small fishing coracles. These were small round boats made of wickerwork, made watertight and propelled with a paddle. Pender wondered where these men got the courage to go out on this river with its changing tides. He could not forget that had it not been for Becca, he would be dead right now. He shivered within himself, and Zalenda drew him to her, having read his mind. The dogs were impatient to get going, so they packed up everything and moved on. Zalenda had not wanted to stop at that spot because they were visible from a long way, almost to Slave Island. For the rest of the ride, she was watching the forest and the sky for any telltale signs of being followed or watched until they arrived at the Great Forest.

As they neared the spot they normally took to the Big Oak tree, Zalenda stopped quickly. She heard noises ahead. She put her hands to her lips, and they all held their breath. She moved on with the dogs, telling them to go and kill. Tarag went straight for a man's throat, who was kneeling down peering through the rough trees. He did not see death coming. Toto's method was her normal straightforward grab for the crotch and wait to see what would happen. The other two men were holding a rope, but the surprise attack by the dogs and what had been done to their comrades made them vulnerable to Zalenda's attack. She kicked one in the head and the other in the back; they both went down. Before they could recover, she had them tied up with their own rope.

The dogs let go their prey and waited for instructions, just as Pender and the girls rode up to the ambush area.

Pender said, "Well, isn't this interesting? We only gave your informant the information yesterday, and you were in place today waiting on us. Now, gentlemen, you are going to tell us exactly where your source of this information is and who it might be."

The men whom Zalenda had tied up claimed to know nothing. "You killed the wrong man. He knew everything."

"Zal, give the dog the order." Toto went back to the man lying on the ground and grabbed his crotch again. "Now harder." The man screamed.

"Is he telling the truth?" she asked him.

"No, that one there,"—pointing to the one who had just lied—"he is the boss."

"My name is Mac of the redheads. I am not really the boss. It's just the fact that I come from the same part of the Nuits as the chief does. We have five separate parts of the Nuit clan, all having red hair, but we have only a loose fealty to the present chief. My family is more conservative. We don't believe men and women should be seen naked in front of our families, but it is very common among other parts to have communal nude bathing. I tell you that so that you will not judge us all as being the same. Many of us are adamantly against the business of slave trading, but this chief has great power and forces his will on us by threatening our families if we do not conform to his will. We would all rather be home working on our farms. If I refuse to do his dirty work, my wife will become his plaything, dancing naked for the entertainment of his guests. This would be a terrible shame to me, so I conformed.

"The one your dog has is Donald. His brother, Cam, is the one who identified me as the boss—thanks Cam. They are both farmers like me but from a different part of the clan. They despise the present chief, but like me, they are here because if they refuse, their families will be sold as slaves. The one who was killed by the dog was a despicable rascal. He would sell his mother and his only child. There is one in each team who informs on us all. I am glad he is dead."

"Why are you here, Mac? What is it you are supposed to accomplish?" Pender asked. As he spoke, Mari and Zari began to lay out food for everyone. The men looked on in amazement as they realized they were going to be fed. As they sat down to eat, Pender said, "I am Pender. This is my lady Zalenda—most people call her Zal—and this is Mari who is serving you, and this lady just coming back from feeding our horses is Zari. Now please answer my questions."

"This food is good," Mac said. "Could we eat first then I will tell you everything you want to know?"

While they were eating, Zalenda was moving around checking their position, forever the meticulous guardian of the flock. When she was satisfied, she returned to her food, but never off guard, her eyes watchful, going from one face to the other of their prisoners.

Mac finished his food and began his story. "We were ordered here by the chief's inner cabinet of Lackeys to patrol around all of the tribes, to gather information on any movement between the tribes. I think they must have nightmares thinking what would happen if the other tribes united against them to stop the slave trade."

Zalenda spoke for the first time. "Please think hard and be truthful. Did anyone from the settlement contact you and give you any information about the possibility of us coming this way?"

"Lady Zal, I can tell without any hesitation that no one contacted us from the settlement or any other tribe. We were taken by complete surprise when the dogs came in. By the way, where did you learn to kick like that? We were here by chance. There are another five teams out watching the other tribes, and some will probably pick up travelers to take back for slaves."

Pender asked another pertinent question. "Mac, how much of the five-part clan would you say firmly support their chief in his endeavor to rebuild the fort at Slave Island and control the slave trade?"

"There are already rifts developing. The slave trade is only one of many issues. Last year he tried to take over all the business. Farmers could not sell their own produce. It had to be sold to an agent of the chief, and he controlled the price and what they could grow. When it was proved that the agent was crooked, the farmers refuse to cooperate, and the thing fell through, but they have not forgotten. The chief is absurdly fond of himself to the point of insanity. He believes that he and he alone is the sun, and everyone else pales in significance. Nothing can be done. Even the smallest mission must be controlled by him through his cronies, and every mission or tribal council is subject to his control. The people only relax when he leaves to go on his grand tours, and the only way to get anything done is to continually praise him. Four out of the five parts of the clan are firmly against anything to do with the slave trade, but to come out openly and say so would mean you and your family would be on Slave Island the next day."

Mari asked, "Mac, have you seen or heard anything of one of our young women who was taken from here a few days ago? Her name was Rona."

"Mari, by an amazing coincidence, the man the dog just killed was the one who brought her to the chief. I understand from that jerk there, she is to be kept as a bargaining tool. That is all I really know."

"Mac, what would you do to you and your fellow Nuits here if you were me? I have no wish to harm you, nor your families, yet I know if it were this dead scoundrel who was in charge, we would all be taken as slaves, and there are many like him you would have us believe still in your tribe."

"Pender, I have no wish to die for the scum we are supposed to represent. I would gladly die to protect my family, and that is the only reason I am here. I will never divulge any information that I have learned about you or your team's work to bring down the slavers, nor will I report your location now or in the future. I and these two men here will, when the time comes, open our homes and means to support you in bringing down our present regime."

"So, Mac, you are suggesting that I should let you go now? Well, that is all right, for that was my intention anyway. Stay here in position but do nothing to report on or take action against the people of the forest. Zal and I and the dogs will check on you tomorrow. See that you keep your promises, I may collect on them in the near future."

Mari and Zari had everything in order for the horses and the dogs. They shook hands with the Nuits and left.

When they were safely established in their room in the forest roof, Pender said to Mari, "Do you still want to watch the builders at Slave

Island? You now know it will be by far the most dangerous mission you will ever undertake."

"This experience we have had today makes me more determined than ever. We will watch our new friends as well. I know what is at stake here, and if we are going to stop the construction, our information must be accurate and detailed."

Zari said, "I still feel responsible for the loss of Rona, which I cannot purge from my soul. I will draw from that, and this opportunity I embrace, I can still make a difference. This is what we discussed back at the island. We knew then what was needed, and nothing we have learned since has changed."

Zalenda pondered the events of the day. "We started off to prove that Remi would betray us. We were sure he would, but we were wrong, and because of that, we know a great deal more about the Nuits and the personality of this chief Tamor. We must verify this information. How do you think I would look as a redhead, my love?"

Three voices said, "Spectacular!"

Pender addressed the four, "What is it we do best in trying to stop the slave trade?"

Zal said, "We excel in well-planned short missions with the minimum of people. The sinking of the barge and the freeing of the prisoners and destruction of compound are good examples."

Zari said, "Yes, that is true, but look at the success with the dogs we have had just responding to situations as they happen. Today was unexpected, but brilliant, because of Zal's abilities. Isn't that why she is training our people?"

"You both are correct. I think I may have been looking in the wrong areas. I was looking for help from the other tribes to counter the size of the Nuits. The five-part clan numerically is their biggest advantage, but it is also their biggest disadvantage. Mac kept saying to us over and over today, and I was not listening—they are farmers, and they have no skills in construction or training in war"

"My love, what is it you are trying to say?"

"Well, the plan is still in its infancy in my mind, but what if we continue this circuit just to keep them spread out thinking we are trying to forge alliances with the other tribes? But in fact all we do is make them aware that they are being watched. One exception to it would be when we visit the queen of the Warrior Women to see if we could borrow, say, ten of their trained women. With them, and counting our trained group, we would have two highly trained strike forces that could strike simultaneously at two different targets."

Zari said, "That sounds really exciting, but would it help against a fortified position?"

"That is the other part of this infant plan. What if we let them build the fort on Slave Island, let them spend all the money, do all the work, then we take it from them? Remember, Mac said they were farmers, not construction experts. You two will carefully watch them and note everything they do. You will detect the weakness in their construction. Remember while we were scaling the walls of the old compound, Rah was going through the sewer with the dogs. That is what we have to do, and when we have done it, we give it to the Forest People as a permanent home."

"My darling man, I think you have just come up with something that we are capable of doing. We must adjust our intelligence gathering not for an all-out assault but for two very narrow, important strikes that will cause the maximum amount of damage to the Nuit chief and turn his own people against him. That is not minimum results but maximum!"

"Let us rethink our plans, but not tonight. I think I smell food coming, then it's bed for me."

"And us," the ladies responded.

In the morning, they spoke at great length about the new dimension that was now added to the watch at Slave Island. The girls must make sure they were never taken by surprise again, so they must organize the girls whom they had already trained to watch them while they were watching the construction. At the first hint of trouble, they must withdraw immediately; their safety was paramount. Pender and Zal would continue the circuit of the other tribes so that the Nuits would believe they were preparing a joint endeavor against them. On the way out, they would visit the place where Mac and his fellows were supposed to be, but they would be careful in their approach.

The security of the forest fort was just behind them when Zal sent Tarag ahead. She knew that he instilled fear in the Nuits, and she wanted to use that to test them. As they were advancing toward the place where they had left the three Nuits, she stopped several times to check to see if they were being watched; there did not appear to be anything to raise her suspicions, nevertheless she decided to go in from the side. When she entered, the three men were deathly quiet staring at Tarag, and Tarag sat staring at them. "Oh, thank goodness you are here," Mac said. "I thought that the dog was here to kill us." Pender noticed the body of the villain had been moved. "We threw him out into the scrub. Our story will be he was killed by a wolf. We have to be on watch here until tomorrow then we can go home. We will report that you spent time among the Tree Forest People and then moved on. They can take what they want out of that."

"In what area of the Nuits land do you farm?" Zal asked.

"My land and that of my family have been cultivated in the northeast of the Nuit territory near the foothills for generations past. There are plenty hiding places there."

"That sounds inviting," Zal said. "We might see you there in the future."

For the first time in three years, Zalenda was on her way home. She rode with a sense of expectancy that going home always brings. She wondered how she would be accepted by the new queen. Being forewarned of the five other Nuit teams reporting on intertribe movement, they were being exceptionally careful not to run into one by accident. For this purpose, the dogs were kept behind them, while Zal scanned the horizon ahead as it shimmered in the midmorning heat. They were nearly halfway there when they cut down to the river to water the horses. They allowed the horses to wade into the shallow water, while they stayed mounted. The dogs ran and played. After the animals were satiated, she carefully rode the horse up the banking. She was about to turn back to warn Pender about the loose shale when she heard a scream somewhere ahead and to the right.

Pender joined her on the bank and at her signal silenced the dogs. It happened again, a woman crying and men laughing. They really did not want to interrupt their journey, but they could not ignore a cry for help. They spurred the horses into action and covered the distance very quickly and burst into a clearing, where they saw two tall beautiful blonde women being assaulted by four Nuit men and one younger blond man.

One of the women had been stripped of her clothes, and a Nuit was holding her down, while another mounted her; she was screaming with anger and frustration. The two men holding the other women turned in surprise, but did not let her go. The blond youth smirked at Pender, saying too late to save a queen. He made as if he were about to strike Pender with a club when Toto grabbed his arm and hand he was holding the club with and pulled him to the ground. The dog showed him no mercy, first, tearing at his arm and then his throat. He still had the smirk on his face, but his blond hair was red with blood.

The man raping the woman did not want to stop. Tarag pulled him from the back and savaged him, tearing his genitals from his body. The woman whom he had been raping finished him off with a kick to the head.

Zal had already freed the other woman. The two Nuits were bent over serving their last meal to the flies. Zal went and brought water and began washing off the blood that had sprayed everywhere on the woman's body from the wounds and mutilation of her rapist. The man who had been holding her was in shock, unable to speak or make a sound. His eyes glazed over in unbelief.

The other woman joined Zal in her ministrations to clean up and dress the queen of the Warrior Women for so she turned out to be. They had been out for a ride and were led to this spot by the young man, whom Zal now recognized as the son of the last queen. It had been for him the last queen had exchanged Zalenda and sent her into slavery.

Pender did not really want to talk to the other three Nuit men, but he was obliged to because the three women were deep in conversion discussing how they had trusted their betrayer. He was fed up with the perfidy of men, and he now knew their story before they told it, or so he thought. He lined them up with their backs to the women and the two dogs in front of them.

"Gentlemen, you are about to tell me you really are farmers and the only reason you allowed your dead comrade to rape this woman is because if you did not do this, your families would be sold as slaves, is that right?"

"No, that is not right. We are part of the chief of the Nuit's family, the inner circle, and we have the right to take any women we want if they are part of the coalition that is against us. If you should think to harm us, you will be hunted down, and that beautiful woman will no longer be yours—she will be shared with many of my colleagues."

Pender said to the dogs, "Kill them," and the dogs did.

They did not waste valuable time cleaning up. They left that to the vultures and to the other scavengers. Pender wanted to get the queen and her lady back to the safety of their tribe before they could be intercepted by another Nuit team.

Zal led, with Tarag out front, then the queen and her lady, and Pender was behind with Toto. Pender saw a group of men riding to their right at a very fast pace. He made Zalenda aware of the situation, and she told the queen she must ride faster. The queen said she was too sore to ride any faster and they must leave her and save themselves.

Pender sent the dogs out to bring the horses down and delay the attackers. He waited at a place where the two trails would join. The dogs went back along the hedge-covered trail unseen by those in pursuit. The dogs ran straight at the horses, which suddenly veered to the right through broom and hawthorn bushes, unseating their riders.

It was a disaster. The men went down with broken arms and legs, and the chase was abandoned. Pender called the dogs back in, and they went back together in safety.

Pender arrived to a hero's welcome. The queen had already told the story over and over again to her friends and to the whole tribe, who were gathered to celebrate her survival from the ordeal. Zalenda was feted as one of their own and given the place of honor beside the queen.

Chapter 20

The Breakup With Zalenda, the Queen in Waiting

Pender sat beside Davi and Jona and many of the young women with whom he had worked the last time he was here. They were very positive about their queen and wanted to know all the details of that adventure and how she had held up during her moments of terror. One of the young women wanted to know if he was in the act of raping her went they caught him. Another wanted to know if the queen was absolutely naked. "She is very beautiful. We see everybody in the tribe nude when we swim together, but never the queen—that must have been special."

That night Zal did not come to his bed. He waited for her but soon fell into a very deep sleep; the events of the day had taken their toll.

Next morning an invitation came from the queen to have breakfast with her. He was about to refuse on the grounds his clothing was stained by yesterday's action, but new clothes were soon provided for him. He was shown into the queen's presence and sat beside her at a table for four, but the other guests had not arrived yet.

"Pender—may I call you Pender?" she asked. He nodded his assent. "I understand you were on your way to warn us of the new danger that is posed by the new policy of the Nuit leadership. I wished I had not been disarmed by the last queen's son. That treacherous little rascal was out to depose me in favor of his aunt—we found that out last night. As you saw, I was given to the Nuits as a plaything, and who knows what would have happened if you and Zal had not been watchful? Then you saved me a second time when they were in hot pursuit, so I have much to thank you for, and anything I can do you only have to ask."

"There is one thing you might be able to help with. I will need perhaps ten or twelve of your exceptionally well-trained Warrior Women for about four or five weeks. I have a plan to stop the Nuit chief."

"I also have a plan in mind that involves Zalenda. We talked about it last night. I would like her to stay here and retrain my women. They have become lazy and difficult to handle. When she feels they are fit to protect us, then you may have your team. You should also know that I offered her the position of queen in waiting lest anything should happen to me, and she has accepted."

Pender was speechless. Now he understood why Zalenda had not come to him last night—she had got a better offer.

"I intend to return to my other team. We have important work to prepare." His words came out staccato, disconnected, and abrupt, like someone speaking in a new language for the first time. "May I speak with her before I leave?"

"Yes, of course, after all you are good friends. Wait here. When she is finished with her morning cleansing, then she will see you."

As the hours passed, Pender became more confused and angry. Had he completely misinterpreted their relationship? The binding of their hands with Rahana's hair and their bathing together were supposed to mean a lifetime commitment, or was it? She had never spelled it out. She called him her love, but was that only for a time until she found someone better? They were a team, but they could not be when she was the queen. Better to leave now when he had doubts than wait and be completely humiliated. He picked up his equipment and headed to the stables.

He was allowing his horse to amble on without any direction. If the Nuits had been around, he would have been there for the taking. Now his anger was in spate; he could taste the bile in his mouth. "I should have waited and given her a piece of my mind." He spat angrily on the ground. He looked up, and she was there. The white horse she was riding showed signs of being whipped and driven severely.

"Where do you think you are going? Were you not asked to wait for me? After all, you did make the request."

"So that is what this was about—your queenship? You decided not to come to our bed last night. You talked with your queen, and now you are the trainer of an elite team, and the queen in waiting. I must cool my heels while you cleanse yourself. How long was I supposed to wait—till you decided you could spare me a moment? Why waste your royal time on the likes of me? I left to save myself any further embarrassment and humiliation. I thought you loved me and we were together forever, but I guess I am a fool."

"Yes, you are a fool for leaving. You grudge me my moment in the sun? Should I have come and kissed your brow and made you feel better? Well, it's not going to happen. I ride after you, and all I get is pity myself, Pender. Now you can ride on. When you have grown up, we might talk again, but certainly not now." She turned in a cloud of dust and rode away.

By the time Pender made the crossing at the ferry, he had convinced himself that this was the best outcome possible. He was heartbroken, but time would heal that. He would concentrate all his time and effort into their original mission without Zalenda and her warriors.

His friends were curious to see him home alone. "Has something happened to Zal that she is not here with you?" they asked. Pender decided to tell them the truth. He told them the whole story of the rape of the warrior queen by the Nuits and the part played by the ex–queen's treacherous son. He told them he had ordered the dogs to kill the three Nuit goons and how they had helped the new queen to escape. He mentioned how he had foiled another attempt by a different group of Nuits by having the dogs run at the galloping horses and causing the horses to veer into the bush, unseating their Nuit riders. The queen reached the women warriors' tribal lands safely.

He explained to them what had happened during the interview with the queen—that the queen had asked Zalenda to stay and train her women warriors, and she offered Zalenda the position of the queen in waiting. She had agreed, but Zal had made no contact with him to give him this information. The queen said that Zalenda would come to speak with him after her cleansing. He waited for hours, but she did not come, so he left to spare himself any further pain. He told them as he was riding home, he became very angry. Then Zalenda rode up, they had a quarrel, and they parted. "I do not believe I will see her again. It is painful, but in these circumstances, we must carry on without help from that tribe."

"I will take two days to rest from this ordeal then I would like Rahana and Becca to come with me to warn the Cave People and the Water People of the Nuits' new operations and strategies."

Pender then left to go to his room amid a buzz of whispered conversations, which he did his best to ignore.

Pender took his two days quietly reflecting on the situation, spending most of his time with Cisi on the settlement. He confided in Cisi all the details and happenings leading to his breakup with Zalenda. Like Pender, Cisi thought there was something strange about Zalenda's decision making in that she had not tried to share with him the queen's desires and offers. She felt that her ride after him and what she said was done only to exonerate her actions in her own mind. He was right in deciding to keep himself apart for now—perhaps over time she may reconsider her choices; he must move on.

They talked into the night of what he could now accomplish with one team, instead of the two. He had counted on getting some help from the other family tribes, particularly the Warrior Women. Now that this was unlikely; his choice of missions was critical. He stayed the night with Cisi and crossed to the island in the morning. He was impatient to get back to business, and Rahana and Becca got up late.

After they had eaten, the team got down to business. "For the present, we will restrict our missions to rescuing Rona. Our first priority is to get an accurate location of where she is held. The undercover team will leave as soon as they are confident that they will be able to blend in to the Nuit Tribe. Elecia, how are things going on the preparations for this missions?"

"We have received what we think is suitable dye from Carla, the mystic woman. We will be trying it out on some of the men today. I think that everyone involved has a good understanding of the Nuit culture, and as I am heading the team, I can help guide them on site. As soon as I feel the dye will work, we will be on our way."

Chapter 21

Gena and Lacey Join the Team

"The second team that we had intended to send for information gathering we will cancel for the meantime, because Becca and Rahana will be leaving with me today to warn the Cave People and the Water People of the new strategy being used by the Nuits."

Pender attempted to calm himself as he waited for Becca and Rahana to change into appropriate clothing that would allow them to ride for the next three days. They also needed more supplies than they had allowed for in their original mission. Nena was inundated with requests and was having great difficulty adapting to Elecia's new role as supplies chief and at the same time looking after Zalenda's job in charge of training. It was well after midday before they reached the stables in the settlement. As Pender was waiting for the ladies to collect the horses, he was approached by two young women. They said they had heard that he was forming teams to fight the slavers. They were fully trained from infancy in combat as young women in their tribe, the Warrior Women. Pender asked if Zalenda had sent them. Their reply startled him. "No, the old queen has died. She had been ill for a long time." They had heard a rumor that she had been involved in an unfortunate accident, and it had aggravated some internal trouble from which she never recovered. Zalenda was now the new queen. As the new queen, she had released the present cohort of trained warriors so she could personally finish training a new set that would swear fealty to her."

When Rahana and Becca came back, they were introduced to Gena and Lacey and were informed that they would be joining them on this mission. They rode as a group while the introductions were made until they came to the hill above the settlement, where it was necessary to ride in line.

Pender wanted to test the competency of the new recruits and had Gena lead and Lacy cover the rear. The geography of the land changed here to a rift valley where the long winding river flowed from east to west. It was a steep descent that made it necessary to dismount and lead the horses down. Gena was looking ahead toward the hills where she saw a large party of riders riding parallel to the north side of the river, apparently looking for somewhere to cross. She turned around and guided the group into the tree line for cover.

Pender asked Rahana if she thought they could outrun the approaching riders to her rock and access to the caves. She felt that they had already been seen by the riders, and that put them at a disadvantage. It was a big force, and they could easily split up and they would be intercepted no matter how fast they rode.

Gena suggested that she and Lacey should lead their horses downhill, mount them, and lead the party of riders on a merry old chase so that Pender, Rahana, and Becca could complete their mission. She explained that their horses were specially bred for speed, and it was highly unlikely that these riders could keep up with them. Later they would return and pick up their trail and meet them at the caves of the Cave People. Lacey was excited at the thought of real action. "Please let us do it." She looked imploringly at Pender and Rahana. So it was agreed that they would wait in position till the girls had led the riders away.

Gena and Lacey led their horses down the slope, apparently oblivious to the coming storm of dust and dirt created by the advancing horsemen. They appeared to be quite unconcerned to the danger they were in.

Pender believed they must be taken and already regretted his decision to allow them to play their game when suddenly, they kicked their horses forward just enough to keep their would-be captors interested in the chase. When they felt they had cleared the way for Pender's party, the girls gave their horses their head and soon were just a cloud of dust on the horizon. The rest of the journey was uneventful, and they soon arrived at Rahana's rock.

She led the three horses away to a hidden rock den, and then they ascended the steep bare volcanic rock up to the middle cave. As they carefully climbed upward, Pender asked Rahana what she thought of the new recruits and the possibility of getting more like them from the Warrior Women Tribe.

She was about to reply when Becca broke in, "I wish I could ride like them. If they can perform like that in other areas, we need more of them." Rahana said she was impressed by their readiness to get involved and how quickly Gena evaluated the situations and came up with the solution that worked.

Pender said, "I was thinking the same thing. A pity we probably will not see them again."

"Oh, we will. I told them which cave to come to and where to leave their horses. They will be here," Rahana said. "I really did not want to lose help like that! It will most likely mean that we will require to change our methods. We have followed a fairly constant pattern, you know, Zalenda then the dogs. Do not think for a moment I am being critical of Zalenda's talents, but with new people, we will have to adjust."

Pender nodded his assent. "And we will be dealing with bigger groups."

Rahana was greeted by her people with great enthusiasm. She now was their hero, and they were ready to celebrate her return. A feast was planned for that evening, so Rahana and Becca were whisked away to be prepared for it by the young women of the tribe.

Pender met with the elders and warned them of the tactical changes the Nuits were now using to capture slaves for their new venture at Slave Island. Instead of buying slaves from the tribes, the raiders waited on travelers or unsuspecting farmers and shepherds, capturing them and making them slaves. He told them that he had a plan to stop the Nuits that did not involve a full-scale war. But if things should get out of hand, he hoped he could count on their support to show up to make it look like he had a big army. After a long discussion, the elders came back and said they would support him in any way, but to remember their people were shepherds not trained fighters. Pender was satisfied with that commitment.

Gena and Lacey turned up just as Rahana had said. They were taken straight away to be cleaned up for the celebrations and emerged later with their long blonde hair plaited and gathered on their heads like a crowns. Pender had heart pains because they reminded him of Zalenda. The young men of the cave people were taken by their beauty and served them all evening. Rahana was the main source of adoration and took the place of honor, sitting at the head table among the elders. No woman of the tribe had ever been given this place, and she did it gracefully. Becca and Pender sat a table reserved for the guests and enjoyed the food, music, and dancing late into the night. After the guards were set, everyone slept in the middle cave where they had danced.

The morning came to the middle cave, but only the cave dwellers were aware of it. Pender would have slept on, as would the girls, were it not for Rahana wakening them to have breakfast. A great coal fire was blazing in a natural rock fireplace that was vented into chimney formed for escaping volcanic gases eons ago. Women and men were busy cooking at the fire, and the food was immediately served from the stone table to rows of eager mouths that consumed it with great enjoyment.

Rahana took Pender and the girls deeper into the cave where they could hear running water. They crossed over two other tunnels into a large spacious cave where the rock gleamed with a natural light. Unlike the other caves, this one sparkled, and the floor was flat and level. The rock seemed to have a heat source. The water that streamed over the rock was pure and warm. Rahana ordered everyone to take off their clothes and wash off the last two days in the saddle. The girls complied right away; in their tribe this was normal, so they were not in the least embarrassed.

Not so Pender's, however. Becca and Rahana soon solved that problem by going to him and stripping his clothes off. As usual he was hesitant, but Rah and Bec grabbed his hand and took him to the warm showering spray, where they shared its cleansing refreshing comfort. Bec and Rah took turns at scrubbing each other with a flat, round, white stone that seem to have cleaning powers. Then they started on Pender, who seemed to be struck with paralysis, as he was before when Zari introduced him to these tribal services. To complete their ablutions, Rah rubbed a salve made from lamb's blood on their bodies, which was most refreshing. New clothes were brought from their packs, and it was only when they were fully clothed. Rah pronounced them ready for breakfast.

Breakfast for Pender was different than anything he had experienced before—long strips of lamb meat roasted crisp served on a flat oat meal biscuit. Gena and Lacey loved it and gladly went back for refills. Pender suggested they should ask for some to augment their own food supplies because they had not expected the girls to be with them. Rah made that request, and they soon had more food than they could possibly eat.

Two sheep herders that Rahana knew came to speak to Pender about the route they were going to take. They were concerned because they knew that the Nuits were closing the main roads that the herders normally took. They suggested that to get to the Crannog, they should carefully use the bottom of the hill's pathway because it was tree lined. Pender thanked them for their concern and information and made ready for the journey. Rah and Bec had some fun at the expense of Gena and Lacey, when the same two young men turned up to help them mount their horses.

When they left Rahana's rock, instead of going downhill to the rift valley, they turned east along a little used path that was covered on the hill side by thick broom bushes and on the other side by tall pine trees. Gena remarked it was as if they were still in the caves. She smiled ruefully and wondered out loud whether there would be some nice young men at the end of their journey to assist them off their horses. Becca could not let that one go. "Of course, there will be, and they will even rub your bums for you."

Rah said, "Do not worry, Gen, I have heard that one before. The young men there do not even know what salve is, so relax."

It was past midday when they dismounted to give the horses a rest. As they sat down on some rocks to eat, Lacey went off into the wood to take care of business. When she returned, she was leading a little girl by the hand. The child was crying quietly. Lacey gave the child to Rahana and asked Pender to go with her. They walked a little bit off the path to where three bodies were lying, a husband and wife and an older person.

The husband's body was lying protectively over his wife, while the third person, a woman, had a sharpened branch sticking out of her stomach. It looked like they had been dead for several hours. Pender and Lacey wondered who might have killed them, and why? It was when they were lifting the woman's body into the gorse bushes that they noticed the woman had been raped. Lacey asked, "Who would do such a thing!"

Pender replied, "Men, rogues, despicable men! I hope I meet up with them. I wish my dogs were here."

Rahana wrapped the little girl to her with some outer garments from her pack. Pender and Becca helped her up onto her horse, and they rode straight for the Crannog, the home of the Water People. When they were still some distance away, they could see they were under siege. A group of riders were chasing people from the Crannog who were trying to make it to the bridge of their wooden island home.

Becca slipped from her horse, stripped off her clothes, and told Pender she would swim to the wooden island and tell her people that help was on the way. Before Pender could answer, Gena and Lacey kicked their horses and went off to attack the raiders. Pender and Rahana followed at a slower pace. The raiders were on top of the fleeing men and women who had been working in the fields.

Gena and Lacey took them completely by surprise. They rode alongside the riders and then jumped from their own horse onto the back of the raiders. In one quick move, they took them by their heads and broke their necks, and the men did not know what had happened; death was instantaneous. The girls went in search of other victims, but the raiders, instead of forming up ranks, broke and ran away, cruelly lashing their horses in abject panic. By the time Pender and Rahana rode up, the girls were off the horses, helping the people who had been beaten by the Nuits. When Pender and Rahana with the little girl got near, he could see a naked Becca lowering the bridge so that the people could gain the safety of their homes. Soon help came from the Crannog to aid Gena and Lacey with the injured. Rahana took clothes to her naked friend, who was so overcome with the cold that she almost collapsed.

Pender held on to her while Rahana vigorously rubbed her. Rahana was somewhat restricted by having the little girl tied to her, so Pender was left to finish the job. A number of younger men came out and led the horses away to hidden safe stalls, where they were fed and watered, and all the packs were brought to the lake fort.

The elders came and welcomed Pender and his team. They could not believe how the young women had ridden so fearlessly into the melee and turned back a superior force and rescued so many of their people. They were pleased to note the part played by Becca and went out of their way to congratulate her on her long swim of the lake in such cold conditions.

Rahana wanted to know if anyone in their number were missing who might be the parents of the little girl. If no one could claim her, she would take her back with her. The elders said they would make that known and have an answer for the next day.

The next morning after a good breakfast of the Water People's roasted fish specialty and really tasty oat cakes, Pender sat down with the elders to discuss their problems with the Nuit raiders, specifically the fact that the Water People had to cross to the land for farming and herding their cattle, goats, and sheep. In fact, if it had not been for the trained watchers Pender had advised them about the last time, they would have lost a lot of their people. This time Pender suggested he might be able to get them some trained help. He brought in Gena and Lacey to meet the elders.

They talked with them about the type of training they could provide, but on the condition that they could stay there and make it their home. First, they would have to go back to their own tribe and make suitable arrangements, but they would come back within the week. Rahana and Becca were not thrilled about losing the girls because they had grown to like them in the last week. Gena and Lacey promised that they would recommend to their friends, who like them had been made redundant by Zalenda, that they would find a welcome for their skills with Pender.

The elders reported that they had not been able to trace the parents of the little girl, although they said there were many families willing to adopt her. In that case, Rahana said she would keep the girl herself. Becca was given the opportunity to stay but declined the invitation, saying she had committed herself to Pender's team to help defeat the

Nuits. The elders said they would support Pender in any way they could in his campaign against the hated Nuits.

Pender decided that they would use the fastest way home over the great moor. The paths were narrow and no use for a large group of riders like the Nuits were now using. As they rode, Rahana and Becca tried to convince the girls to stay and send the new girls to the Water People. Gena explained that during their training and life as Warrior Women, they had never been allowed to socialize with men. In the field yesterday while they were providing help to the wounded, they had met two young men who were trying to get them to stay. This opportunity to train them might lead to something more interesting. Becca teased them mercilessly all the way home. The riders left their horses at the settlement and crossed to the island, where they went immediately to the hot springs; even the little girl was introduced to its wonders. She had not uttered a word since they had picked her up.

They were not the only ones who had returned; Elecia and Cymon had returned from their undercover mission in Nuit territory and Mari had sent a message from Slave Island. Pender waited till the ladies had retired before he resorted to the hot springs; he needed time to think. He decided that he must face Zalenda. If his two-strike strategy was to work, he needed top people to work with, and right now he had ten partly trained, faithful, dedicated people. For the best result possible, regardless of his own pain, he had to go with Gena and Lacey tomorrow on his own to ask for Zalenda's help. After giving it much thought, he made up his mind he would do it.

In the morning after they had eaten, Elecia and Cymon reported they had located Rona, and she appeared to be in good health, though she was well guarded. She was left alone at night with very little real security. The actual rescue then would be quite simple; getting her out of the tribe would be another matter. Cymon felt there was something big happening because the Nuit hierarchy was on the move, and they were conscripting farmers out of the fields to be their foot soldiers. A large cavalry unit had gathered and was waiting daily on orders to move.

The message from Mari was that a barge laden with wood had arrived at Slave Island under heavy guard, but they seemed to be waiting for something because it remained anchored in the river.

Pender asked where the four men and Remi were. Nena said they left three days ago and never returned. Since they left with no supplies, she believed they would be coming back.

Pender announced he would be leaving later to go and see Zalenda to ask her permission to employ the young Warrior Women she had no need for at present. Rahana and Becca said they were going with him, but Pender tried to object on the grounds that Rahana needed to stay to look after the little girl. She told him his older sister was already considering adopting her, and that was the best possible outcome for the little one.

The word from Morag and Pipa was that the whole area was clear of the raiders. They seemed to have moved over to the great moor above the river. Pender and his four women, as Cymon called them, were off as soon as Nena had the supplies ready. They traveled all day, only stopping to water and feed the horses. They ate well and drank from their honeyed cider flasks.

At night they found a small low-lying camp where it was safe to make a fire now that the Nuits were gone. The cold was bone chilling at night, so they slept side by side with as many sheepskins covering them as they could bear.

Chapter 22

The Bitterness of the Bile of the Soul

When the morning came, the cold held till the sun was fully up in the sky. Rahana joked, "Who's going for a skinny dip in the river?" Not even Becca took her up on her offer. Breakfast was served around the fire. Toasted bread was high on the menu and boiled bark tea to warm the insides, which was quite a feat considering the cold. The horses were loath to get going, so they had to walk them for a while. The white frost on the grass made the pathway slippery, so they had to tread carefully. At this rate of travel, it was going to take them all day to get there. Very slowly conditions improved, so they were able to mount the horses and move a little faster. The girls' faces were rosy red, and their hands that held the leather reins were frozen. They had not expected this cold, so they had no gloves. By midday the cold had not abated, so progress slowed again. Pender called a halt so that the horses could rest, and they all needed to relieve themselves, which they were loath to do in this cold. Pender soon had a fire going, and they huddled over it, seeking its warmth. Again the hot bark tea warmed them, and after they had toasted more bread, they felt better. The sun steadily warmed the afternoon air, and their progress was much better, but it was well into the evening before they reached their destination.

Gena led them into the stabling area for the horses and then took them to the special facilities for the Warrior Women, where they were able to wash up and eat. She asked one of the officials to take a message to the queen, which she haughtily refused. Then Lacy said, "You go right now and you tell her Pender is here."

They all waited on tender hooks wondering what the outcome was going to be, when Zalenda walked in. She went right to Rahana and hugged her, saying, "My little sister, I am so happy to see you," kissing her on the lips. She did the same with Becca and then asked everyone to leave except Pender.

The smile left her face as soon as everyone had left; it was replaced by a steely stare. "Why are you here?"

Pender spoke with just as little emotion; he had rehearsed this all night. "I have come with a request for your help."

"Why would you believe that I would consider helping you?"

"Because the help I require is not for me personally. I believe that you once had a desire to stop the slavers and that you may still like to take part in a plan to do it."

"You are mistaken. I have no interest in having any dealings with you on any matter."

"You are inviting me to say the same thing, but I will not, nor could I ever say that. To do this we need not meet again if that is your desire. I understand you have no use for the young women who were trained as warriors under the last queen. Allow me access to these young women, and I promise you that you need never see me again."

"I will give you my decision on this matter tomorrow."

Pender left with a heavy heart, being so near her and yet being unable to touch her or even ask how she was doing.

She left the room with tears running down her face being so near to him, but she was the queen—she must hold her position. Trained in every aspect of war had not equipped her for solving the problems of he own heart, and she was at war with herself.

He was soon joined by the girls, who wanted to know if they had permission to go back to the Water People and a chance at a normal life, but he couldn't tell them anything.

Rahana and Becca wanted to know how the interview went. When he said icy cold, they couldn't believe it. They were all tired with the long day in the saddle and the terrible cold they had experienced. Pender slept in the same room as the girls. Becca teased him, "Does Zalenda know you sleep with four beautiful young women every night? No wonder she was icy cold."

Pender answered back, "Sorry, Becs, that was last night, different night different women."

Zalenda sent for Rahana and Becca in the morning. They were invited to have breakfast with her. They were delighted to see that she was treated just like a queen, and she played the part to perfection. The women around her were all tall, blonde, and beautiful. They were exquisitely dressed, and they treated her with the greatest respect. Rahana and Becca could hardly believe that this was their Zal.

She dismissed her attendants so they could talk. She asked how Cisi was doing. They told her about all the missions and how they had found Rona and the plan to rescue her and what the Nuits were doing to rebuild Slave Island. Then they told her how great Gena and Lacey had been and why they wanted to go back to the Water People.

She told them she was going to let the girls go and that they would have twenty of her best trained people to fight the Nuits. They asked her why she would not see Pender to tell him. She looked miserable. "I cannot! I just cannot!" and her voice trailed away.

Becca shook her. "Zal, you are miserable, and he is heartbroken. He called your name in his sleep all last night. You two are perfect together. There is just no one else for you, can't you see that?"

"I know, I know, but I cannot." Then she broke down and cried. Bec and Rah held her while she sobbed and bitterly cried. After some time they helped her compose herself, lovingly washing her face and kissing her fingers. "Promise me you will come again. I will always love you both. Now please leave me."

They went back to Pender to tell him he had twenty of the best trained women to fight the Nuits and the girls could go to the Water People. They never mentioned Zalenda's breakdown nor that she still loved him. The three of them left in the morning; the other girls would come later.

On the way back, Pender was deep in thought; he could not make sense of Zalenda's attitude. Why would she give him more than he asked for yet adamantly refused to see him? He had quizzed Rahana and Becca, but their lips were sealed.

This whole thing started when they rescued the old queen; therein was the problem, if he could only fathom it. Rahana and Becca wondered why they were not stopping; they had to stop. They were sore, and the horses needed rest. Becca rode up to him, and he looked as if he was asleep. She leaned over and pulled his horse to a stop. He did not flinch when she shouted at him to wake up, so she led the horse to the nearest place where they could hide. They dismounted and tethered the horses and watered and fed them; still he did not wake up. Meanwhile, Rahana was trying to start a fire but did not have Pender's skill with the flint. It took her a while, but she finally had lit a few flames.

They were glad it was not as cold as their journey was to see Zal, but they still needed a good fire. The fire grew and burned stronger, so they were able to toast their bread again and drink the hot tea. They found a fairly comfortable spot to sleep for the night. They laid Pender on the sheepskins, and they cuddled him from both sides. But he was still unconscious while they enjoyed the contact. Becca wondered how Zal would react if she knew what they were doing to her lovely one.

Pender seemed to have recovered by the morning. He was up early and had rekindled the fire, watered and fed the horses, and was toasting more bread by the time the girls awoke from their troubled dreams.

Rahana had dreamed all night about Zalenda's grief torn face and her forlorn miserable wretched words: "I can't, I can't."

Becca's mental faculties seemed to have been undulled by sleep. She had looked into her friend's eyes and saw the bitterness of love once realized, now denied, and she had cuddled them both in an effort to rescue them from their desolation.

To say that they were both surprised by Pender's seemingly quick recovery would have put it mildly. But they suffered in speechless silence and gladly accepted the toasted oat bread and ham he offered them. Rahana pointed to the rising smoke and questioned the wisdom of kindling a fire here where it could be seen for miles.

Pender smiled. "You did a good job of doing it last night, and we are still alive. No, Rah, we are safe from the raiders. I suspect the Nuit chief has called them all in as of yesterday to protect the builders at Slave Island. That is why we are going to rescue Rona tomorrow. Are you ready to dye your hair? We are the only ones left to do it, and we will—that I promise you."

When they arrived back at the settlement, they saw Cymon leaving in a hurry. What was particularly worrying to Pender was that he did not even acknowledge them. Elecia was waiting at the crossing, tears streaming down her face. Apparently, she and Cymon had quarreled and he had left in anger. She told them that after the last mission, they had decided that they would become husband and wife and raise their own family. It was when she had told the girls this news and everyone was congratulating her that Cymon suddenly took cold feet. He had accused her of manipulating him into a corner, and they had argued bitterly. Now she felt that he had left for good.

For the third time in as many days, Rahana and Becca found themselves trying to comfort their love-smitten friends. Becca said to Rahana, "I hope I never fall in love—it's too stressful."

"Too late, Bec, you already are," and she looked at Pender.

"In that case, so are you." To that Rahana had no witty reply. That night they both slept in Pender's room there by invitation, but not in his bed. He said he had grown accustomed to their presence, and he slept better, less haunted by Zalenda's absence.

Chapter 23

The Mission to Rescue Rona

Breakfast next morning was a joint project between Nena and Elecia, Elecia cooking and Nena serving. Morag and Pipa joined them, now freed from their responsibilities as the settlement watchers. They had dyed their hair red in anticipation of being included in the mission to rescue Rona. Becca wanted to know if they would help her and Rahana do theirs. She quipped, she just cannot wait to see a redheaded, beautiful black lady.

The after-breakfast meeting was all business. It was decided that the rescue attempt would take place within the next two days. They would use the same route as Elecia and Cymon had used earlier. The team that would get into place during the day would be Elecia, Pipa, Becca, and Pender. Elecia would assume the lead role, since she knew the area well. Becca and Pender would have their hair dyed that evening to the Nuit shade of red. The rescue would be done at night. Ester and Morag would watch their backs and take out any pursuit that may happen. Becca and the dogs would be their emergency strategy if the guards proved difficult to deal with.

Nena would need supplies for eight people and at least eleven horses for three days. Rahana would look after the requirements for the dogs. Ester pointed out they would also require hides for tent coverings and sheepskins for the ground because of the cold and rain. Suitable winter clothing and an extra sheepskin coat would be required for Rona. The number of horses was then increased to thirteen because of these extra loads.

The next day was filled with preparations, and when the girls were not involved with this, they were practicing the maneuvers taught them by Zalenda.

Pender's and Becca's hair were much admired, especially his well-trimmed red beard, which made him even more handsome. They looked like a strange couple—he now as tall as his brother, Kain; she small and slim with brilliant red hair. Rahana said she was jealous; she believed red hair would have suited her very well.

The next day the rain made the journey miserable, and at night they were very thankful for the hide tents that Ester had insisted they bring. As was now usual, Pender, Becca, Rahana, and the dogs shared one tent; Elecia, Ester, Pipa, and Morag in the other. By the time Pender had finished covering the area where the horses were tethered, and tying the hides securely in place, he was soaked literally to the skin. It was useless to try and get a fire going, so they had to eat their food cold.

When Pender was finally able to go to his tent, the girls had to strip him. His leather jacket and breaches were stiff with the rain and cold. He was now used to their ministrations and was beginning to enjoy them as they rubbed him down with clothes. Becca, as was her bent, was always trying to get the last rub; of course, Rahana could not allow her that luxury, so the drying process was prolonged. Finally, they got themselves wrapped up in sheepskins and slept the whole night, as warm as Queen Zalenda would be in her courtly bed.

The rain had abated by morning, and a watery sun hung in the sky. It was hard to take down the tents and the horses hide because the leather hides were stiff and waterlogged and difficult to fold. The horses were loath to leave their comfortable place of refuge for the cold blowing winds. The dogs were wet and bedraggled, and it was difficult to get them up from their nice warm sheepskin beds.

Everyone had to scrape the mud off their boots because that would be a dead giveaway to any observant Nuit. It seemed that everything was going against them—the elements, the horses, the dogs, the rain, the wind, and the cold, but they were determined to press on to accomplish their goal.

Elecia guided them through the Nuit territory with great precision so that both teams were in place to strike by the middle of the afternoon. When Elecia was satisfied that the Nuit raiders were gone, she went forward to check to see that Rona was still in prison in the same place. She casually approached the guards and offered them a skin of special beer for their evening meal; she cautioned them that they should only drink it with food because she didn't want them to be found drinking on duty. They thanked her for her kindness and promised they would do as she suggested if she would visit them when they went off duty. She said that could be arranged. Then she asked if she would need more for the rest of their friends. No, he said, they would not be sharing with the other two miserable cranks.

Elecia made her way back to where Pender, Pipa, and Becca were waiting. They were the center of attention of a group of Nuit women, who were eyeing Pender and wanted to know to which family he belonged. Elecia soon took over the conversation, explaining that they were her family from up north. They were invited to go for hospitality to a home nearby, where they were very well treated. The ladies wanted to know why Pender was not away with the rest of the men guarding the chief. He told them that he had just come back from a mission within the Warrior Women Tribe and had expected to see the chief here.

The women wanted to know about that tribe and if it was true that the women were all beautiful and tall and that no man was allowed to take them. They were fascinated at the stories he told, how the men worked the fields, worked in the home, and looked after the children, while the women trained for war. One very red-haired lady wanted to know if he would like to come to her home and she would look after him.

Becca told her he was very well looked after, and since he had been away on along mission, she would make sure that he was even better looked after tonight. The ladies all appreciated her sense of humor, and when it was time to go, they were invited back the next time they were in the area.

Elecia led the team in the pitch-black night back to the prison where Rona was kept. They approached quietly and carefully. Happily the guards were sleeping peacefully; so far the plan was working perfectly.

The last time Cymon and Elecia were here, the moon had been clearly visible in the sky, so it was easy to calculate the time when the guards might change. Now in this black night, all they could do was wait in the cold. Pipa took a sheepskin jacket out of her pack to be ready to put on Rona. They waited a long time, and Pender was about to signal to give up and let the day team take over when a guard suddenly appeared. He was about to shake his two comrades awake when Becca rolled her body into him at his knees, as Zalenda had taught them. He tumbled down, and Pipa hit him with a kick, which hurt him but didn't stop him. Elecia finished him off with a club left down by the sleeping guards. She and Becca then gagged and bound them, but in their drugged state, they would not be a danger this night.

Pender quickly changed into the guard's jacket, and he and Pipa went into the prison. They found the inside man putting on his clothes to go home; his arms were half inside his jacket, so he could not protect himself. Pipa kicked him in the groin. He groaned in pain but could do nothing to relieve it. He fell down on his back. Pender knelt on his chest with his hands around the man's throat. "Where is the girl?" he asked softly. The man shook his head in defiance. Pender increased the pressure on his throat till he almost choked. "Where is the girl?" he asked again, this time with a more threatening voice. The guard signaled with his eyes to a door behind him. "Where are the keys?" Pender inquired. The man looked down at his belt. Becca appeared with rope and a gag for the guard, and soon he was bound and gagged, like the rest. Pender got the wood slot keys and opened the door. Rona was inside, beaten and possibly raped. Pipa went out and picked up the club and smashed the heads of the three guards. Pender and Becca carried the bodies of the guards into the room that Rona had been beaten in and piled their bodies where she had lain.

Elecia attended to the barely conscious Rona, and soon she was dressed for the road. Pender carried her on his back all the way to where Ester and Morag waited. They took over the job of carrying their friend. Elecia and Pipa went ahead to tell Rahana that they had Rona, and they went with her to get the horses. Pender and Becca took over the carrying of Rona, and he was beginning to wish he had not sent Elecia, for she alone knew the road. Tarag and Toto showed up, their breath sending off steam in the cold air. Following the dogs made it easier, but the four of them were rapidly becoming exhausted carrying Rona. When Rahana appeared out of the dark with the horses, they mounted up and rode all night, stopping only to rest the horses. It was essential that they get Rona home as quickly as possible. Her injuries were serious, but her state of mind was even more dangerous. They did not stop the next day. Tarag and Toto provided their normal coverage during the journey because the teams were long past being careful, and they drove the horses and themselves mercilessly till they got to the stables at the settlement.

To their great surprise, Nena was waiting for them at the stables and had been there all night. She told them Remi and the four men had returned very drunk the night before. In their drunken state, they boasted how they had taken care of the little bitch and no one would know; soon they would be very rich. Remi had arranged everything—the Nuits would come and take all his damn tribe and family to Slave Island. Nena was uncertain whether this was idle boasting or the truth, so she thought it wise to come and wait for the team to come back and warn them of this potential danger. Pender's immediate reaction was to halt all thoughts of returning to the island until they had verified the truth of this information, so they took Rona to Cisi's house.

Chapter 24

Remi's Treachery Punished

Rahana was ready to go to the island and finish the men off before they recovered from their drunken state, but Pender wanted to hear what Rona would say. Ester, Morag, and Becca went with Cisi to clean Rona up and try to get her to respond to them. They bathed and pampered her and put salve in her wounds. They massaged her body, and, yes, there was evidence that she had been raped, and according to the bruising, more than once.

When she came around, she would not stop talking, right from the moment she recovered consciousness after the sleeping draft right up to her beating and rape by her brother, Remi, and his men. No Nuit had touched her on pain of their lives—that was the instructions she heard the head guard give to his men. In fact, they treated her quite well, but now she could not wait to get her hands on her brother. Becca asked her if she was ready to confront him now because he was on the island and did not know they were back or that she was free. She replied, "The quicker I get this over with, the better I will feel and get back to some semblance of normality."

"Would you want your parents there to support you?" Cisi asked.

"No, I will deal with them later on my own. Let's find Pender and Zalenda. I want to deal with this now." Morag quietly told her Zalenda would not be here; she would explain that later and bring her up to date with the way things had changed.

Cisi took Pender aside and warned him how fragile Rona was, but he needed to listen to her story. When the truth of what Nena had heard was confirmed in every detail, the only thing they could do was to confront the culprits and punish them.

Cisi decided it was her responsibility to inform the parents because there was no way Remi was going to escape this time. This could not be blamed on his youth.

Pender led Rona into his home and into the main hall where the five scrofulous scoundrels were sitting. Even in their drunken state, they knew their lives were over. Quickly Rahana and the team rendered their ability to even move, so quickly were they trussed up and gagged.

Pender pronounced judgment on the four, calling them profligates of honor, spending something they did not own. They had been accepted by this group, encouraged by this group, and protected by this group—that trust they had all betrayed.

Pender asked Rona to remove Bart's gag. "The young woman whose life you sought to degrade is here in person. What do you have to say for yourself?" Bart slurred his words and blamed everything on Remi. "Would anyone here accept this excuse for what this man did to this young woman?" Pender asked. The answer was a resounding no. Rahana lifted her club and hit Bart on the head; he fell backward dead. The process was repeated for the other three, and the bodies were carried out of the hall.

The gag was removed from Remi's mouth. He sobbed and cried like a baby. Rona came round from behind him and looked into his eyes. "Was it worth it, little brother? Was it worth it to act the big man? To sell your people, your mother and father, to the Nuits so you could strut like a peacock in the hen's yard, and then you had to destroy the bitch—that is me—is it not?"

"Yes," he shouted. "Acting like the savior of the tribe, walking around spying on me and my friends, you got what you deserved, you bitch!"

"You are condemned by your own mouth, little brother." Then she took the club and smashed him in the face repeatedly, as he had beaten her. The last thing he saw in this life was his sister's gentle face. "I did not want anyone to have to do that for me," she said. "Ester, Morag, Pipa, please take me to my parents so I can tell them what I have done."

They decided they would not eat in the hall that night, so Elecia and Nena went to prepare in the minor hall. Pender sat with Becca and Rahana, who was visibly upset with the demise of her men friends. "Was it the drink, or did they feel devalued when I did not include them in my team? Did I do this, Pender? They had every opportunity to kill me on the road or rape me in the woods, but they did not. I thought they were good men, but they were faithless, treacherous, and bought with the promise of riches. How could I have been so wrong?"

Pender and Becca drew her to them and held her while she cried. "No, my love, it was not you. You have done nothing wrong. It was the perfidious nature of these men." Pender sighed softly.

No one slept well that night. The indwelling and recurring picture in everyone's mind was not of Rahana's systematically killing of four men who once were her friends, but of Rona killing her brother. No one ever expects to have to do to that, but she did it. One of them was going to have done the deed, but she did it and then went to face her parents—what unmitigated courage.

Pender wakened in the night. He was lying beside Rahana, with Becca on the other side; they were both holding Rahana as if by doing that they could keep her from her dreams. Pender knew then he had to bring all the girls home, Mari and Zari from the watch at the Slave Island reconstruction, the girls from the settlement, and the crossing had to be made one way from the island side for them to be safe. Cymon had gone rogue, or had he? That question had to be answered. No mission could be attempted until he was found or eliminated.

He must have dozed off to sleep again, for he was wakened by a very tender kiss on his cheek; it was Nena telling him breakfast was ready. He looked and found he was alone in his bed. Had he dreamed the whole thing? No, it could not be; the pillow beside him was wet.

There were five places set for breakfast, and his coming to the table made it complete. No one wanted to talk or even establish eye contact. Finally, he broke the silence. "Elecia, do you have any idea where Cymon is?" Pender asked. "Because I believe it is absolutely necessary for us to find him or eliminate him."

"That is rather strange, Pender," she replied. "I was just thinking he is a loose end who knows how we work. Perhaps he did not leave because of me. Maybe there was another reason I think we must find out."

"Then that is the first thing on our agenda. The second is we have to get all of our people here for their safety. No one can be left unprotected. The third thing is we must control the crossing, and it must only be controlled from this side. Becca and I will leave this morning to bring Mari and Zari back. At the same time we will be on the lookout for Cymon. Nena, you will get all the girls from the settlement here—stress it will be permanent. Rahana must stay here and rest. Elecia, you are her nurse, so make sure she stays. We need her at her best."

Becca exclaimed, "Oh yes! I can just see you and me arrive at the tree fort with this color of hair. We could say something like this: 'We are two Nuits looking for a tree to climb,' and you know which tree it would be, in the land of your dreams. I think we should all have a hair washing day first—I wash yours, you wash mine. Oh, and that goes for the beard as well."

"I did not know you had a beard, Becs."

"I have, but I did not find it necessary to dye that one." They all laughed, and the tension of the long night was broken. It took a number of washings before the dye came out of their hair, and Becca's returned to its natural beautiful reddish-blonde color. It was decided that it would be better to wait till the next day before leaving for the forest fort and the Tree People.

During the afternoon, all of the girls arrived from the settlement to make the island their permanent base for the duration of the Nuit war, as it was now called. Rona was quite subdued, but she asked Pender not to leave her out of a mission because of what happened to her; her experience only made her more determined to fight slavery of any kind anywhere. Pender asked her how her parents had taken the news. She said, "My mum cried because of what I had suffered, but more for what I had to do. My dad hugged me and said he would have done it in any case if he had known, and that when he had a daughter like me, he did not need a son like Remi."

Pender discussed the new living arrangements with Elecia and Nena. Elecia said this was her family, and she loved belonging to it. Nena felt that getting the food supplies over from the settlement would be problematic but not impossible because of the ferry on way restrictions.

Early next morning, Pender and Becca were in the process of pulling their way over on the ferry when Becca looked over to the landing and saw Mari and Zari waiting to be picked up. Pender said, "That was good timing. We were just coming to get you. Why are you here?"

Mari answered, "There are some important developments we think we should discuss, so we came right away."

"That was good thinking," Pender agreed. "Let's go back. We have had some things that have happened here that need explaining." Becca hugged the girls, and Pender, who was pulling on the ropes, said, "Give them another one for me. It's so good to see you both here safely."

When they got into the hall, breakfast was just being served, and Elecia went for more food to serve the late arrivals. Mari sat down beside Rona. Not having expected to see her, she almost fell off her seat. She was so exhilarated, she danced around clapping her hands, shouting, "Zari! Zari, see here, Zari, it's Rona! Oh my darling Rona." Poor Rona was almost suffocated by two ardent female bodies that could not get enough of her. Mari and Zari led Rona to the fire. They were still cold from their journey and had just taken off their outer clothes. When they were joined by Morag, the team was together again.

Chapter 25

Cymon and Zalenda Switch Sides

The meeting started right away because Cisi had to get back to the settlement. Pender asked her to give the news she had about where Cymon had been located. She said, "Friends, it is with great sadness that I have to tell you that Cymon has gone over to the enemy. He apparently met a group of Nuits, and for information about this team, he betrayed your trust and now is at Slave Island working on the construction of the new fort there. The information is accurate, for their conversation was overheard by one of our people in the free market where they were buying supplies for their journey."

Elecia went out weeping but soon returned, for she had to give an account of the part she and Cymon had played in going undercover in the Nuit territory. Cisi had to leave, but she waited till Elecia joined her in the main hall. She apologized for breaking the news publicly, but she felt it had to be done. Elecia thanked her for her kindness, but her sadness was greatest when he left; nothing could make it worse. "He was obviously not the man I thought he was."

Pender came in at the end of the conversation to say he was puzzled by Cymon's ability to change sides so easily. *Can things get any worse?* he wondered to himself. The next meeting would reveal something even more sinister.

The team reassembled to hear about the rescue of Rona from Elecia, Becca, Rahana, and Pipa. Each had a different aspect to report on from the planning, undercover work, and the actual rescue from the prison. Pipa told them how Rona had suffered at the hands of her own brother and his treacherous friends. Pender told them of the danger these traitors had put the whole team in and why it was necessary for Rahana and Pipa to put these men to death. This was the reason that he had recalled everyone here today because of this treacherous behavior.

Mari then confirmed that Cymon was indeed working for the Nuits, and that was one of the reasons she had come to warn the team of his treasonable conduct. She then spoke of the construction of the new fort and how quickly it was being built and that all of the living quarters were already in use. The main hall was in the process of being roofed and would soon be completed. However, they were running out of lumber for the palisade and the bridge. They would need another barge load before the winter came. Pender asked what they were doing with the wood from the old fort. "From their observations, she said they were just building over the top of it.

"I have very serious news now to report. Zalenda and the Warrior Women have joined with the Nuits. We have seen her there several times, so it is a certainty." The promise of twenty of her best trained women was a lie, and this is the ultimate betrayal.

Rahana and Becca were struck dumb, as were the rest of the girls. They said, "Surely this cannot be. She was teaching us, and we loved her." Then they were speechless.

Pender said, "I knew there was something wrong, but I had not anticipated this. I never expected to get any help from her. I felt these were empty words, but I never thought she would become a slaver." He announced to the group, that it will take some time to digest this information and that they would meet again tomorrow. "In the meantime, I suggest, ladies, you retire to the hot springs and relax both mentally and physically."

Once Pender was alone, he felt his whole world had crashed and burned. No matter how he viewed the situation, it was difficult to find anything that might be construed as positive. The enemy knew their tactics and that they were only ten in number. Could ten people stop the mighty Nuit chief? What was it that Mari had said? They were waiting on a barge of wood. What if the barge did not arrive? What if they could not build the palisade? A plan began to formulate in his mind, daring, dangerous, but doable. This plan would require the watchers to be watched, but not completely. The watchers would have to be fooled, and he thought he knew how it could be done.

Next morning he met with Rahana and Becca to discuss some of the ideas that had been percolating overnight in his mind. The question that had to be solved was, how could they stop the barge with the load of wood from arriving at Slave Island? They decided it could not be done using the same methods as the last time. It was too cold to swim to the barge, and it would be much better guarded than the last time. What if they could approach it from the other side? There were two possibilities. They could ride west a long way and cross the Big River through the morass and back down the other side, opposite Slave Island.

Pender recalled a second method from a past report from Cymon. If they could locate the fishermen Cymon had talked to, they might be able to borrow their small boats and board the barge from the other side away from the watchers. The only way they could destroy the barge and its cargo of construction material was by fire.

Pender asked Rahana if the black rock that burned, the same rock the cave women used for cooking, could be transported, like she had done when destroying the Nuit army. Becca suggested if the guards were eliminated, the rock could be placed around the barge and the cargo then ignited, and the whole thing would go up in a glorious inferno of fire. Rahana said the rock can easily be broken down and carried in bags, but there would have to be two teams involved—one to take out the guards and one to place the rock and ignite it.

The second team would have to go to the Cave People for training, and that training would have to be done at night, in the cold, the same conditions that would be on the barge. They could then return here and continue practicing until they had reached a high level of competency. Becca said the first team would require excellent skills to take the guards out. She suggested she should go to her people and get Gena and Lacey to assist them. She could leave in the morning, Pender said, because everything would have to be done at night in the cold. Everyone would be required to be fitted with warm black clothing. Cisi would be needed to buy the material in the market, but they would have to be made here. "Did any of the ladies here have that kind of skills?" Pender said he would head up the team to go and locate the fishermen and find exactly where the barge was and where it was likely to be anchored. He proposed taking Pipa and Rona with him.

They decided they would wait till all the training was done before selecting the people for the mission. A special team might be required to hit the secondary target, which would be to set fire to all the old wood left over from the fire that burned down the compound. Nena and Elecia would have to be alerted to the great amount of supplies that would be needed for these things to happen.

The team meeting that morning was much more positive than the day before. The general talk during breakfast was of another opportunity to strike back at Tamor, the Nuit chief. Pender announced that they were considering trying to stop the barge from delivering its cargo. "This would be a very cold, difficult, dangerous affair, demanding absolute commitment from everyone on the team. Before it could be attempted, those involved would be required to undergo specialized training in the handling of fire and in eliminating guards at night in very cold conditions. They would need to row small boats onto the site, board the barge, and then one team would eliminate the guards while the second team set fires on the barge and in the cargo. These two teams would have to be dressed in black so that they would not be visible from a distance. If anyone had experience in that kind of work, please make it known. Three groups will leave tonight on information gathering. Pipa and Zari will go with me to find the fishermen and find out exactly where the barge is. Becca and Rona would seek help at the Water People's Crannog, and Rahana, Ester, and Morag would journey to the Cave People to learn about the burning rock."

As the meeting was breaking up, Nena and Elecia came to Pender with a novel idea that no one had thought of—instead of making new black garments, why not just dye their winter sheepskins black? They are warm, already at size, and dye perfectly, problem solved. Pender thanked them and said, "Ladies, good thinking. This is how we will stop the slavers."

The three groups left later that night with the firm intention to be back in the dark three nights later. Rahana took with her Tarag, and Becca took Toto. Pipa and Zari where well bundled up against the cold, and as they rode, their new sheepskin head coverings also covered their mouth. These were presents from Cisi, and they were now very much appreciated.

Pender was not as fortunate; his gloves and an old scarf were all he had to fight the biting wind and the extreme cold. They made progress, nevertheless. By daylight they were almost at the Big River. During the darkness, they had walked the horses most of the time because it was not a good path at places grown over with weeds and bushes. Now in the light of morning, they had to be more careful, stopping every so often to check the way ahead and the trail behind. They stopped on the hill overlooking the Big River and moved off the pathway into some cover where they rested and ate from their packs of food.

Pipa waited on watch while Pender and Zari rested. She crawled forward through the long grasses till she had a clear view of the river. A way downriver to her left, she saw the barge moving very slowly and sitting very low in the water, the rowers laboring against the cold and the strong flow of the river water on its way to the sea. She was about to go back for Pender when she saw a lone rider coming along the brow of the hill a long distance away. She carefully retraced her way back to her resting friends to warn them of the approaching rider. Zari fed the horses and led them down the hill into a large pine forest. When she returned, the three of them carefully crawled to Pipa's observation point. The rider was much nearer now. Pender's heart almost stopped when he recognized the white horse—White Flame! He knew the rider even from that distance; it was Zalenda. He whispered to the girls to remain perfectly still because Zalenda would notice the slightest movement of the grass and they would be discovered, and he did not want a showdown with her here.

Zalenda just had to get away from Tamor and his lunatic behavior. She could not understand how the Nuits could stand him as their chief, and so she had sought this excuse to go and find the barge, and the chance of a good long ride. She sat looking down the river, sitting very still as if she were some frozen silent sentinel. As she looked over their heads, Pender could see the same hopeless lost look on her face he had seen before that first day in the compound of the slavers. After what seemed like an eternity to the cold stiff watchers, she turned and rode back the way she had come.

Zari stretched out her cramped legs and almost screamed in pain but managed to stifle it behind her mouth covering. Pipa looked at Pender, wondering what was going on in his mind. "What do you think that was about?" she asked.

"I think she was wondering how long it would take us to put it out of commission, and she did not appear to be too happy. We had better rest here till she is well out of sight." He did not require to say that a second time when he looked, the two were cuddled down fast asleep. Pender allowed his mind to dwell on the hopeless look on Zalenda's face, and somehow he was filled with a fresh hope.

The girls wakened from their sleep ready to take on the rest of the day. They were back leading the horses down a steep incline down toward the river before the cold had chance to set in. The situation with the barge had not changed; it was still low in the water, and it looked as if it had not moved. Pender wondered at this, since the Nuits were clearly in a hurry to get the construction finished before the ice and snow stopped the work for the winter.

Chapter 26

The Destruction of the Barge

He could see to his left downriver what looked like wood thatched hovels. This must be the fishing village, so they would head in that direction. Zari climbed up into a tree to check their forward path and their trail behind. She reported seeing a large group of men walking away from the barge and heading downriver. Pender decided that they should go carefully, so they mounted up because it would be quicker should they have to retreat. Now they were near enough to see four small boats and two larger ones tied up on the riverbank. Pender was much encouraged when he saw this; his plan might indeed be doable.

As they neared the village, two men came toward them. By their garb they were obviously fishermen. They hailed Pender, who stayed mounted while they conversed. They told him if they were looking for the rowers, they had left because they had not been paid and would not be back. Pender thought, *This is getting better and better.* Pender assured him that they had nothing to do with the slavers. As a matter of fact, they were very much against them. They had come to see if they could borrow one of their boats to board and burn the barge and its contents.

The men's eyes lit up at that prospect. "Come, come with us to our humble abode and let us talk about how we can help you."

Pipa and Zari were just too glad to oblige. The major attraction was a nice cheery fire they could see blazing inside. Pender produced two skins of beer that he had the foresight to bring with him, and they sat down to the very pleasant smell of fish soup two ladies were making on the fire. The men explained this was only their summer place and that they would soon be moving inland to their permanent homes for the winter. The slavers' activities on the river had cut into their fishing time, so they were trying to get as much from the river while they could.

Pender told them why they were there and what they hoped to achieve—if they could borrow one of their boats for a night strike. He could pay them in oats, sheepskins, and beer. The men said they could not allow them to borrow the boats because the currents here were treacherous, but they would be pleased to take them out to the barge, and they would be glad to take them tonight. They knew the rowers from the barge had beat up the guards before they left, so the barge would be easy takings.

Pipa and Zari said that would be a great idea, but they did not have with them the fire starters they would need to start the blaze. The men went and brought in two wooden barrel-type containers, saying, "This is the best fire starter you can find." It was oily fish parts in a slurry of fish oil that they used for starting all their fires. Wood shavings are immersed in the slurry to soak them in the oil then they are held in place and then ignited.

Pender told them he would give them all the supplies they had with them and the spare horse for their help in doing this tonight, but they would require to leave right afterward, for the slavers would take them if they stayed. If they needed more supplies for winter, they would need to come back with them to pick them up. The men said when they came back from the barge, they would bury their boats in a pit and take down their temporary home. This horse would be a huge help in packing and moving. They had never had one before, and it would more than compensate them for their help.

Zari told them that they had some rough oats for the horse that she would give them, "but this one liked to forage for himself."

Pipa asked how they would ignite the fish slurry once they got it on board. The two women took the girls outside and showed them how to put the fish oil in place, take the dried wood shavings, and light it with a flaming torch. They also gave them ropes to get over the barge sides and large flaming torches that they would use to light the fire, and they would also be able to see where to put the fire starters in the dark.

Night came quickly, and they needed two boats because the women came as well with torches, ready to light from the lit ones they were carrying. It was a tough row out against the current, and Pender was becoming more and more appreciative of the help they were receiving from the fishermen and their wives. When they got to the barge, Pipa and Zari climbed up onto the barge and threw the ropes down that they had taken with them to pull up the supplies. One of the wives handed up the torches so that Pipa and Zari could go looking for the guards. They found them lying in the stern severely beaten and dead. "The Nuits should have paid the rowers," Pipa said. "Now let's start a fire." They started at the stern and laid out the fish oil slurry and the wood shavings, working quickly in setting it down on either side. The wind seemed to be favorable because it died down just as they put the wood shavings on the slurry and set it alight with the torches. In a very short time, the whole barge and its contents were a flaming wall of fire.

Pender was the last to leave. As soon as he was in the boat, they pulled away using the current to their advantage. The whole night was lit up by the roaring inferno, and the wind picked up speed just in time to send great shivers of smoking light up the river. When they ran aground, Pender helped the men up to the pits with the boats where they already had the smaller boats entombed. The larger boats were placed at right angles and covered with sheets and then the sand pushed on top and covered with mud. The girls were mounted and said good-bye to their new friends, while Pender delivered the supplies he had promised and then mounted his horse. They rode west, while the fisher folks went east to their homes.

The first signs of dawn began to light the sky when they reached the top of the hill. They stopped and looked back at the blazing structure that once carried the ominous threat of slavery, which was now collapsing piles of ash. "You know they will blame the rowers for this," Zari said.

"Do we care?" Pipa said, pumping her fist in the air. "We did it! We stopped them."

"Without our plan, it would still be there."

"Let's go home," Pender said.

Chapter 27

The View from the Top

Rahana arrived with Ester and Morag at the home of the Cave People. She had to leave Tarag at the rock because he would have caused panic among the shepherds and the sheep. The girls were fascinated with the caves, and of course, they enjoyed the attention of the admiring young men.

Rahana still was viewed by all and especially the elders as their hero, so when she requested a meeting with them, it was granted right away. But first of all, the young ladies had to be fed, so they enjoyed the hospitality and dishes of the Cave People, which for Esther and Morag were novel and new. Rahana remembered her friend Tarag at the rock and took him down a generous portion of the leftovers.

Ester and Morag were inundated with offers to take them up the hill to view the valley and the mountains to the north. Ester thought it best to tell Rahana that the young men had offered to escort them for an evening climb. Rahana told her to wait until she had spoken to their escorts first because in this tribe, there was going up the hill and going up the hill. She soon found these willing fellows and told them in no uncertain way that these young ladies were very precious to her, and if they touched or said anything unseemly to them, that she had a dog down at the rock that would tear their genitals off. They agreed to be on their best behavior.

Rahana spent the rest of the afternoon speaking to the women about the burning rock they called coal. It turned out there was no real secret to the process. First, you had to make a fire of leaves and small twigs then ignite it with a flint and pile on more wood. When it was really hot, put on small pieces of coal. As these were burning, larger pieces of coal were added. Here in the caves with good ventilation, they could cook all day by just adding more coal. They also burned their refuse outside summer and winter using this method, and it also kept the wild animals away. Rahana practiced the process for some time and was able to spark a good blaze, and although she realized that this was a valuable tool, it would take too much time for their purpose.

The girls had a wonderful time up the hill and could not believe how helpful the young men had been. They were interested to find how big this world really was and how beautiful the mountains and the lakes were. They were excited that they had seen the Great River and the barge like a little stick floating in the water. That night they sat around a fire after a very good evening meal listening to the storyteller. Some of the young men came and said good-bye to them as they were going up the hill to watch over the sheep and to watch for raiders. The girls were tired with the journey the night before. The climb up the hill, the good company, and the good food made an early night a good idea. They went to their cots and soon were off to sleep.

Rahana's meeting with the elders produced good results. She exacted an agreement that if Pender required a show of force and support when he went up against the Nuit chief, that they would come to his aid. After the meeting, she went down to the rock to feed Tarag with several sheepskins, and she slept there at her rock. The rock that had changed her life.

Rahana had finished her morning shower under the ice-cold water of the hill stream that mysteriously found its way into a back cave, where it poured out of the rock. As she joined the group for breakfast, she listened to the excited chatter of the young men as they told of seeing a huge blaze during the night over on the Great River, where a big barge had been sighted early yesterday. Rahana knew immediately what had happened—somehow Pender, Pipa, and Zari had done it! They must get back as soon as possible. She went and told the young man to bring their horses, as they were leaving for the island immediately. Then she told the girls to pack up their equipment in a hurry because they could be required for another mission as soon as they got back. The women brought her four bags of small coal and helped her carry it down to the rock. The girls said good-bye to their new friends and hurriedly mounted and left for home.

Chapter 28

Becca Is Wounded on Her Mission Home

Becca was having a hard job convincing Gena and Lacey to come and help Pender and the team to go on a strike against the Nuit chief. They said they were finished with that kind of life and just wanted to settle down with their men and have a normal life with a family. They did say, however, that if the tribe was mobilized against the Nuits, they would certainly be there.

That night Rona revealed to Becca that she had seen a man at supper whom she recognized as having been in contact with the Nuits while she was a prisoner. She felt they could be in danger because she was sure he had recognized her. Becca went and brought Toto from the kennel where she had left her and brought her inside. If they were going to have a visitor during the night, the element of surprise would be theirs. For good measure, Becca went and borrowed a club and made a bed for Toto at the door.

During the night, the door opened slowly. Toto responded with a low warning growl and launched herself at the intruder. The person screamed; it was a woman armed with a long bladed flint knife. Toto caught her by the arm and would not let go.

The man behind her aimed a kick at the dog, but in the dark, he did more harm than good. He kicked the woman on the leg, sending her down on her back. Toto quickly changed her grip to the woman's throat. The man turned to run. For a few seconds, he was silhouetted against a very faint light. Becca saw it and struck with the club; it was a glancing blow. Her club hit the door lintel and then the man's shoulder. He turned and struck at a shadow with his knife, cutting Becca in the side. Becca fell to the floor in great pain, the man poised to kill her, when Rona kicked him hard in the groin as she had been taught. He was on his way down when her second kick caught him on the throat. He gasped, but the third kick hit him in the chin, forcing his head back and breaking his neck. Rona ordered Toto to kill the woman, and she did.

The alarm was sounded somewhere, and people came running with lights. They removed the bodies of the man and woman who were identified as merchants there to sell their wares to the people. Becca was taken to have her wound treated. The healer lady cut off her leather jerkin and was able to stop the bleeding and put bandages on the wound. She was given leaf tea with a special bark in a potion to kill the pain and make her sleep. Rona stayed with her all night and, against the healing lady's wishes, kept Toto at the door.

In the morning, the elders held a meeting to investigate the incident, and Becca, still in considerable pain, was asked to attend. She took Rona with her so she could answer the questions. The elders wanted to know first of all why they were there. Becca explained that two of the young women who were until recently with their team trying to stop the slave trade had decided to come and live here. They had fallen in love with two young men at that time and wanted to settle down and live a normal life. She had come to ask them to return with her for one more mission, but they had declined. This was the only reason they had come, so it was their intent to return home today.

The elders asked Rona why she had killed two people. She said it was a case of kill or be killed. She had recognized the man as a person who had been exchanging information with the Nuits when she was in prison there. One elder asked why she was in prison. Rona told them she and her friend were drugged and abducted by the Nuits, who were ordered to kill them, but instead they were stripped of the clothes and taken naked to be sold to the highest bidder. Pender and his team rescued her friend while they were pursuing the Nuits. Unfortunately, they were too late to bring her back. She was humiliated and beaten and every day threatened with rape. Another raid on the Nuits by Pender's team freed her, and now she had completely recovered from the ordeal.

She had just finished speaking when there was a great commotion outside. A woman broke into the meeting room. Men were trying to drag her back outside, but she was determined to be heard. "You tell them, you tell them," she kept shouting and kept pointing to the speaker. "They were ordered to kill the young women."

The head elder said, "This is unspeakable, a woman shouting in this assembly, remove her from this place. Sir, you need to teach your wife her place."

"No! No! No!" was the chant that resounded around the hall as one after the other elders stood to voice their disagreement. "We have been saved in the past by Pender and his friends. We will not betray them now on the account of this dishonest person. If she has information that these two people were here in our community to kill our friends, we want to hear about it."

The elder knew that he was not going to prevail, so he turned to the speaker, but the assembly did not want to hear from him. They wanted to hear from his wife because they did not trust him to give the whole story. "We want the woman! We want the woman!"

"Gentlemen, this is very unusual."

"Rubbish!" they cried. "We want the truth." Very grudgingly he signaled to the woman with his hand and sat down in disgust.

"Sirs, my husband took payment from these two Nuit informants to deliver these young people here into their hands to kill them. The plan was he would identify them and show the would-be killers where they would be sleeping overnight. They were to be killed, and my husband was to help dispose of the bodies. After this attempt failed, he went across the bridge early in the morning to the mainland and informed two men who were waiting there that the killing had not taken place, but another attempt should be made when they left this morning to go back to their home."

A number of men ran at the speaker and threw him down and beat him, calling him, "Despicable, obnoxious, contemptible worthless trash." His wife also joined in beating him with a brush, telling him he would never beat her again. The elder spoke again. "Although I do not agree with your methods this man is indeed dispiteous, I want him interrogated so that he will tell whom the men he gave this information to and where they will be lying in wait and who is behind this nefarious action. Then he will be imprisoned for the rest of his life or until a new committee passes judgment. My dear lady, I apologize for my earlier remarks. Please forgive me. You were absolutely right to bring this matter to this committee. For the safety of our friends traveling today, I am sending the two ladies you have requested and the two men they have chosen to be with. I trust this matter is suitably dealt with."

Gena and Lacey were not happy that they were being sent as protectors for Rona and Becca, feeling that they already had shown they could protect themselves, but at least they would have their men all to themselves for four days. But they were very disappointed when their men friends refused to go with them. Apparently, they did not want to put themselves in danger. Lacey asked them, if it were the case that she and Gena were in danger, would they come to help? They said no, they would be on their own. Gena was angry that these two men who were trying to get them to settle down with them would take no responsibility for their welfare should it be required.

The four women left together. Becca, still in pain from the knife wound, found it very difficult to ride. Gena led the way with Becca and Rona in the middle, with Toto bringing up the rear. They rode at a steady pace, requiring to stop frequently to allow Becca to rest. They made their usual stopping place for the night, and while Gena looked after the horses, Rona attended to Becca. Before they kindled a fire, Lacey climbed a tree to scout the surrounding area. It was well that she did; she saw a fire behind them about an hour's ride, and one in front of them about a half hour's ride. It was obvious that they were being followed and someone had tipped them off with the information at what time they had left and which path they had taken.

"No wonder these treacherous little bastards did not want to come," Gena said. "They were the only ones who knew. They actually asked which route we would take, and I, like a trusting fool, told them. We were being played, sister. If Becca had been able to ride at our normal pace, we would have been in their trap."

"Let's use this to our advantage," Becca said. "Let's get the horses and lead them well east of the path in the dark. We will follow that star right there," she said, pointing to it. "When we are clear, Lacey can stay and start a fire then follow us quickly and quietly. Toto will cover your back."

They ate quickly then Lacey went into action gathering leaves and twigs for her fire. When everyone was set, they moved out to their unknown path. Gena led the way, feeling the ground in front of her before taking a step. It was very slow progress. An hour had passed, and they could see the fire of their forward foes well behind them and to their right. The middle fire that Lacey had kindled was now burning brightly. In the shadows, she had arranged piles of leaves to look like sleeping people then she crept quietly away. Toto remained as if she was on guard. Everything looked inviting to the would-be murderers, and they fell into the trap.

The forward group arrived a few minutes before the group from the rear. The fire had gone out, and in the dark under the trees, they mistook each other for their prey. It was some time before they realized that these were not women they were fighting, but it was too late—one man was dead and three badly injured; the dead man had no genitals.

When Toto arrived covered with blood, they knew it was safe to return to the path, and with Toto leading the way, they made good progress. It was morning when they reached the settlement. Lacey and Gena looked after the horses, while Rona took Becca to her mother's house for treatment. Later she would bring the mystic woman to attend to the stab wound. The four women crossed to the island and went straight to the hot springs and then to bed. The long walk and ride had exhausted their young bodies. Tarag and Toto lay outside their bedroom door.

Morning breakfast was a very exciting affair. Rumors abounded—the barge had been destroyed. Morag and Ester had been on a mission with Rahana to the Cave People. Before they returned, they had been up a high hill where they saw great mountains to the north and the Great River to the south. It was thrilling to see so much of the country from high up, but even more so when they heard of a great blazing on the river. The young men who were their escorts had noticed what they took to be a large barge earlier in the day somehow it had gone on fire. They looked to Zari and Pipa for confirmation, but they would neither confirm nor deny this.

The meeting that morning was eagerly anticipated by the whole team. Pender was his usual low-key self and refused to get drawn into the excitement that was so palpable in the room. He first asked Rahana about her experiments with getting the burning rock to ignite. She said that it was fairly easy to do but would take too long for the planned project. She had brought four bags of the rock with her for further experiments. She was most careful not to mention the great blaze that the girls had heard about.

Next, Becca reported on her visit to the Water People. She told of her discussions with the elders, and he could see both girls named were here this morning. She went on to tell how she had been wounded by night intruders who had attempted to kill them. She was forewarned by Rona, who had recognized the man as one she had seen while in the hands of the Nuits, and she was sure he recognized her. They were prepared for a night attack with Toto on guard at the door. Because of this preparation, they were able to thwart the attack and kill one of the attackers. In the action, she had sustained a knife wound in the side. In an inquiry into the incident, it was revealed that the visiting merchants had been paid by the Nuits to kill them. A further attempt had been made on their way home by a group bent on their murder from information the killers had received from two young men they had trusted.

In a brilliant piece of work by Lacey, their attackers were duped into fighting each other in the dark. In the fight, three of the men were wounded, and one was killed by Toto. "The team took really good care of me, and we escaped two attempts on our lives. The Nuits are getting afraid of what we can do and will do anything to stop us, even using our friend to betray us."

Pender asked Zari and Pipa to report on their mission. Pipa opened by saying, "It is true—the Nuits' barge with its cargo has been destroyed." Everyone stood up and cheered. She paused before she continued. "The official report must be that it was caused by disgruntled rowers who burned it down because they had not been paid. In fact, they had a huge part in it. They had not been paid, and they were told they were now slaves of the Nuit chief, so they beat up and killed the guards and left the barge undefended. With the help of some fishermen friends who transported us to the barge, we were able to set fire to the barge and its cargo using a type of fish oil. The fishermen and their wives left at the same time as we did. We helped them cover our collective trails behind us by burying their boats and stripping down their summer huts. They left east, and we came west. Everyone must know it was the rowers that did it. Is it feasible that one man and two girls with help from local fishermen could do that? Impossible!—not really!"

Everyone stood on their feet and chanted, "We stopped the slavers! We stopped the slavers!" It seemed that the chanting would go on forever; it was so exhilarating.

Pender waited till the chanters had exhausted their moments of sheer joy. "Yes, indeed we stopped the slavers." The chanting broke out again. This time he waited and waited till it subsided. He brought Pipa and Zari up to the front and said, "Ladies, here is your team that did it!' Zari danced around with her hand in the air. Pipa looked embarrassed.

Everyone shouted, "Dance, Pipa, dance!" and Pipa joined in, while everyone clapped in time to Zari's timing. Just then Cisi came in and went to the front and joined the dancers. That was the sign for everyone to get up and dance; even Pender managed a clumsy step or two for which he was heartily cheered.

The fun ended when Pender put up his hands. "Yes, it is true we stopped the slavers, and it indeed was a notable victory, but the Nuit chief will not rest now. If it becomes known that we were responsible for this great setback to his plans, he will come for us—we are all in danger."

Cisi stood up and addressed the meeting; as chief that was her prerogative. She said, "It is that danger I have come to talk about. The Nuit chief would like to call a halt to all hostilities and declare a truce with all the family tribes in our area. He would like to talk to all the chiefs and elders about the cessation of the slave trade in our area. To this end, he has sent a representative to talk to this team because it is well known I cannot speak on your behalf in these matters. The representative is now waiting to cross to the island from the settlement. Will you hear this person?"

Elecia signaled to Pender that lunch was ready to be served, so he called the meeting temporarily halted, and the decision to hear this person was delayed till then.

Cisi was given the place of honor and deliberately did not sit beside Pender so she could not be accused of influencing him on the coming vote. The discussions around the table were upbeat and positive. The general feeling was that the destruction of the barge had brought about this change of heart, but others asked what about the attempts on Rona's and Becca's lives.

Cisi left the room so that the team could discuss the matter. Pender stood up and asked if anyone had any objections to hearing this person. Mari wanted to know if the cessation of slave trading was to be restricted to only their family tribes. Pender said that was a good question and one he would address to Cisi; she should ask this of the representative. "First, we must agree to hear this person and then decide on our strategy." The vote went eleven to one. Gena and Lacey were allowed to vote. Elecia voted against on the principle that she would not trust this Nuit chief to do anything or uphold any agreement.

Cisi came in and was informed that the team would hear this person. She asked Ester to go and bring the person in. When Ester returned, she led in Zalenda.

Chapter 29

Zalenda's Return and Reconciliation

There was a deadly quiet. All eyes turned to Pender, who was visibly shocked. Zalenda looked down at the floor. The hostility in the room was reaching boiling point. Becca and Rahana felt that this could finally destroy Pender and were ready to lead an assault on Zalenda.

Then Pender spoke. "As the representative of the Nuit chief, you are welcome to our humble abode to address this team. I am asking my team to address this person with the utmost civility that is due to her position."

Cisi stood to say, "I speak as the chief of this family tribe. You are welcome to address this group." Then she led Zalenda to the center of the platform and said, "You have our attention."

Zalenda looked around the room at all her friends and gazed for a few moments at Pender, who steadfastly made eye contact with her. "I suppose that you all are shocked and disappointed to see me here today as the representative of the hated slave trader, Tamor, the Nuit chief. It is all the more difficult to understand when you remember that it was the father of your present chief who delivered me from the slave compound. You also know that I have worked with you bringing down other vile people like Somer and Benic. Then you all understand that the man I have loved and will always love is the one who leads you in all your endeavors. Then you ask, 'If all of these things are true, why are you here?'

"The first thing is this unscrupulous villain holds over me information against my mother that I find it impossible to expunge. If this were to be exposed, it would cause havoc in my people's tribe, the Warrior Women, whose queen I am. At the same time, it makes it impossible for me to be Pender's wife. This is the burden I must bear. The more important reason, if there can be one, is that by appearing to want an agreement with all the family tribes in this area to cease taking slaves from among them, he hopes to isolate this team from any protection it would have and enjoys from your friends in other tribes. If he gets this agreement, it will give him every reason to bring the full force of his might against this team. This I believe has already been demonstrated here in the last few days by the would-be assassins he has sent after Becca and Rona at the Water People's Crannog.

"I know that it was this team who stopped the barge. I stood on the hill overlooking the Big River, and I saw the rowers leave it. I saw the dust of their trail as they walked away, and they did not have the good sense to set it on fire. I sat on my horse feeling miserable, thinking where is Pender when you need him, what an opportunity! He was there all right, hiding in the grass with his girls somewhere. Someday he might tell me how it was done. All I know is by the time I got back, the night had turned into day, and the Nuit chief was having one of his fits of rage. He will never hear the truth from me—that I promise you! He thought that this was a great embarrassment for me to come here—that is how his evil mind works. He threatened to expose me to Cisi if I refused. I played the part because more than anything else, I wanted to come to warn you. But I cannot lie. The real reason I wanted to come was to see you all and bathe at least one more time in the hot springs. Will you allow me to do that? There is one more request—will you allow me time to handle it in my own way, the threat of exposure that this brute man has over me?"

"Cisi, can I spend some time with your courageous handsome brother? There are some things I must say to him that I was stupid enough not to have said to him before, and I cannot live without saying them now."

The meeting was finished, but the buzz of voices went on as Cisi led Zalenda and Pender out into another room. Cisi spoke first with

Zalenda quietly away from Pender. "Zal, I have a lot of questions about what you have said. I must know what your plans are, so later tonight, I want to have a long talk with you before you leave." Cisi left to a deafening silence.

Zalenda was the first to speak. "You are too far away from me. Please come nearer." Pender stood his ground and said nothing. "Pender, my heart is broken. Sadness like a cloud has enveloped me since I sent you away. I know you tried to understand because that is who you are. The lady we rescued that day, the lady we saw raped, was my mother. It was not the first time. Twenty years ago in your time, eighteen in mine, she was raped by three men, the details of which I now know—who the men were and what the revealed truth would mean to me and my tribe, the pain and havoc it would cause to others who are innocent of all wrongdoing. Tamor, the Nuit chief, somehow knows all this and daily in his insane rages threatens to expose me to my tribe. I care little for myself, but unfortunately my mother died the queen and made me queen in her place, so the dishonor would be on the whole tribe. When I sent you away without explaining my motives, I thought if I could make you hate me, I could hide in the dark, and I would never be your wife. Now I want everything to be in the light between us. I want you more than being a queen. I only care about being your wife. Can you forgive me? Can you take me as your wife forever? I love only you."

The stillness in the room was slowly breaking her down. She thought she had lost him—had she succeeded in making him hate her? Had he fallen in love with someone else? Her heart seemed to have stopped, and she could not breathe.

Pender said at last, "Zalenda, my love, I saw you on the hill looking down at river when you were looking at the barge. You seemed so sad that it gave me hope, and I began to live again inside. Zalenda, I know everything. The day you left me, I was sure it all started with the queen. Rahana and Becca thought I had lost my mind, but I had to solve the thing that was tying my heart and my mind in knots.

"Then I remembered a story that Brini told me about how my father and Somer and another friend got into big trouble for getting drunk and raping a well-respected young woman from another tribe. I believe that young woman was your mother, the woman who became queen, the woman we saw being raped by the Nuits raider whom we killed. When you went and joined the Nuit chief, I thought you had betrayed me. Then I realized that Tamor might have been the third man, and that was the hold he had on you. He told you he could be your father, or was it Somer, or perhaps Castor, the man whose son you loved? Let me call my sisters please and allow me to show you something that I believe to be important."

Zalenda's heart was choking her, at least it felt that way so she could only nod her head, acquiescing to his request.

When Cisi and Ester came in, Pender asked them to stand beside him. "Zalenda, I want you to notice something. All of the women in our tribe are smaller in stature, but Cisi and Ester are medium for our tribe, which is below the normal. Their hair is black, not brown. Their eyes are black, as were my father's and my mother's. In fact, there is not one tall, blonde, blue-eyed person in our whole tribe. Brini hinted that the reason my father was not severely punished for his indiscretions was that he was too drunk to have performed any physical activity, even rape. Of the three named—or was it four?—Tamor, Raymond, Somer, and Castor, only one had an offspring who had blond hair and blue eyes, and that was Rolf. I noticed this when I moved his body.

"I do not believe I am your brother. nor do I care. The moment I saw a young woman in the compound on Slave Island was the moment I fell in love, and I still love her, and I hope one day she will be my wife. I say this in the presence of my tribal chief and sisters—they are my witnesses. What is it you want me to do?"

Zalenda stood immobilized, the night of her sadness, crying, hopelessly alone all falling away. What she had heard and saw was away beyond her wildest dreams when this day started. How had she been so blind to the obvious, how she had tortured her soul and his? Why did he not speak of this before? Then she realized she would not have listened. *I have been a fool.*

"What I want right now is to kiss you and hold you and let me love you again." Cisi and Ester tiptoed out. She came to him with open arms, and he took her in his. Their eyes locked in wonder and amazement, the hurt and bewildering sorrow forgotten. Nothing would part their hearts again.

Pender could not believe that his dreams had come true. He was now thankful that Abbi and Brini had told him stories of his father's experiences as a young man and his inability to drink beer and ale to the extreme without becoming totally unconscious and unable to function. Their stories, of course, had been more like lectures for him personally so that he would not enter into that type of lifestyle. But they need not have bothered. His time working in the brewing house had made him intolerant of the stuff and anyone who drank it. It was the memories of their stories that had helped him work out Zalenda's parentage problem and brought her back to him.

They had two hours of unspeakable bliss before Cisi came and interrupted them. She came to tell them that there were people waiting to see them on matter of extreme importance. But before she would let them in, she wanted to know if she could tell the team of their reconciliation. "Better still—Cisi, could you bring them in? I want to tell them myself of our wonderful news," Zalenda said, a smile lighting up her beautiful face.

When the team came in, there was no need to say anything; they could read the joy on their friend's faces. Becca shouted, "This is the best news ever, you two are one again! Is this not what we longed for, girls, but dare not hope? It's wonderful!" and she ran to Pender and Zalenda, hugging and kissing them all over. This was repeated nine more times as each of the young women expressed their joy and love and danced with sheer exhilaration.

But that joy could not last, and in fact it became very quiet when Cisi showed in the visitors. To everyone one's surprise, Cisi brought Davi and Thomi from the Warrior Women's tribe to the front of the gathering. Cisi introduced them and said they had some important information to share with the team.

Davi was inexperienced at speaking in public, especially in front of women. He made several vain efforts to start but was quite incoherent. Rahana came from the back and held his hand. "Now, Davi, tell me, why are you here?"

"I came to get Zalenda."

"Why is it you need Zalenda?"

"We need Zalenda to come back with us to our tribe right now," he stammered.

"Why has that become necessary, Davi?"

"Tamor, the chief of the Nuit Tribe, claims he is her father, and as such he can take over the chief's position. We do not want that to happen, and we are all prepared to fight against him. We need our queen Zalenda to lead us."

Everyone looked shocked. There was a long exhaling of breath; euphoria had turned into apprehension and joy into trepidation, and they looked expectantly to Pender and Zalenda for answers.

Pender came to the front. "This is a lie. Last month the story that Tamor wanted to tell the world was that Zalenda and I were brother and sister. This is what he held over her to keep us apart. This goes back to a story I heard how three young men brutally attacked and raped a woman from the Warrior Women Tribe when they were drunk. One was my father, the others were supposed to be Somer and Tamor. According to Abbi, Castor was one who could never hold his drink and was judged by our tribe on his word to have been totally incapable of rape. This was a well-known fact of Castor's youth. He was punished for his drinking by the elders but not for rape. The only one of the three who had an offspring who had blond hair was Somer's son, Rolf. Now judge for yourselves. Cisi and Ester, come forward please." He went and stood beside them. "You have seen my father and my brother, Kain. Now, Zalenda, come and stand beside us please. Is there any similarity between the four of us or what you remember of my father or Kain?" They all shook their heads. "Thank you all, neither do I!"

"Tamor is trying through his lies to influence the Warrior tribe to reject Zalenda as their lawful queen because he needs their support to get to this team—that is what this about. Somer died from a stroke caused by drunkenness, apoplexy, and unreasonable rage. It is possible that of the three, he was the only one who could have raped the young woman, who was Zalenda's mother. Do I care who her father was? No. I love her unreservedly, as I am confident that she does me. Please excuse us for a few moments, she and I have strategies to discuss."

Zalenda and Pender left and went into another room.

When they were alone, Zalenda said to Pender, "You were magnificent in there. Thank you, my love. But do you appreciate that I will have to leave you for a little while to go back to my tribe to fend off Tamor's latest rants? It will not be pleasant being without you because I love you. I would never voluntarily be parted from you again. Tell me you understand," she said with a quiver in her voice.

"We are back as one again. Yes, you must go back and deal with this situation. Things are obviously changing in your tribe when they sent Davi and Thomi. I wish I could spare Rahana. She has a great influence with these men. But I am afraid I will have to gather the girls and leave when you leave. Tamor sent you here for a reason to lead his murdering squad right here to get to our team. Perhaps we can arrange a surprise meeting."

Pender went into the meeting room and called everyone to order. Davi and Thomi appeared to be in a deep conversation with Rahana and Becca, so it took a little time for order to be restored. He announced that Zalenda would be returning to the Warrior tribe with Davi and Thomi tonight, as he was sure that Tamor had sent one of his groups of assassins here to murder them and this team. *Now we know this, perhaps we can arrange to provide a little surprise for them.*

Chapter 30

The Dogs Bring Victory out of Disaster

"Becca, do you believe you and I could swim across just north of the crossing and scout out where the assassins are and come up behind them with the dogs?"

Becca replied, "Under normal circumstances anywhere else. This would be impossible in winter conditions. We would die with the cold in the attempt, but the crossing, as you know, is always heated from the springs. However, the Nuits do not know this and would never expect such a thing. Yes, I can see lots of possibilities. We can do this."

Davi and Thomi said they were both excellent swimmers and they wanted to be in on the action. Pender was glad of this kind of help because they had no knowledge of how many Nuits there would be.

Zalenda with all of the young women she had trained would wait for Pender's signal and start pulling themselves across. When they were almost there and the Nuits showed themselves, Pender's team would strike from behind. Zalenda asked if she could have Toto, and this was readily granted.

Elecia said she would look after the supplies Zalenda and the men would need for their return journey.

Pender indicated that the mission would start immediately, so everyone was dismissed. Rahana asked what will happen if no one turns up. Becca quipped, "Oh, then I will have a nice swim with two available men."

Rah said, "Do you not mean three men?"

"Listen, sister," Bec said, "that one is definitely not available." They all had a good laugh, and the team was one again.

The mission started off with a complete disaster. When Pender and his team got into the water, an icy rain began to fall, and it came on harder as they swam. The wind was blowing directly into their faces. Pender was having trouble, and Becca stopped to help him. Davi and Thomi swam on only to find that a group of Nuits were already in position to intercept them.

They were on the point of turning back when Tarag, who had reached the main land unseen, attacked the Nuits from behind. He tore the arm of his first victim, who screamed in pain and went down with blood streaming from his injury. The would-be attackers stopped in their tracks and turned around in horror as Tarag took his next victim in the leg. Davi and Thomi pulled out their short clubs as they came up out of the water and began beating the Nuits from behind. The Nuits tried to reassemble around their beleaguered comrades, but just then Becca and Pender came out of the water screaming with the cold. The Nuits mistook them for some terrible water monsters coming to take them. They broke and ran, leaving their wounded friends to their fate.

Tarag watched the prisoners, while Davi and Thomi went to assist Becca. They dragged her and Pender out of the storming rain into the cover of a hide the Nuits had erected. Pender helped remove her clothes, and the two men dried her off with clothing left by the fleeing Nuits. Slowly her body recovered from its ordeal. Pender quickly dried himself, and frozen as he was, he went to warn Zalenda.

He was too late. The girls pulling on the ropes heard Becca's scream and mistook it for Pender's signal, so they came on shore right into the path of the second group of killers, whose orders were to kill Zalenda. Tamor was bent on taking over the Warrior Women Tribe, and he needed Zalenda dead. Before the girls could recover, four of them had grabbed Zalenda, while a fifth drew his knife to kill her. "Kill her, and we will take the rest to play with," their leader shouted.

The man lifted the knife to make his thrust when his arm was torn to pieces by Toto, who timed her jump perfectly—no one was going to hurt her mistress. In seconds, the whole situation changed. Pipa, Rona, Ester, and Morag were kicking at the knees of Zalenda's captors, who let her go to defend themselves. That was a mistake; her anger was now kindled. She broke two men's necks within seconds, and the girls kicked the other two into submission, while Toto finished off the knife wielder. The leader turned to run, but Davi and Thomi were in his way. He drew a club from his belt along with a knife. He was so busy doing this that he did not see Tarag till it was too late. Tarag took him down by the groin, Toto's favorite place. The man tried to beat him with his club, but the pain was excruciating, Davi hit him twice on the head with his club and was about to hit him a third time when Pender intervened, saying, "Keep him alive for now. We need him for information."

They stood around, the ice rain forming on their clothes. "Let's go home," Pender said, "but bring the prisoner." Pender could hardly speak for it was cold, and Becca was looking terrible. Zalenda and the girls brought the almost unconscious men, and Davi and Thomi brought the leader.

Zari ran ahead to warn Elecia that they would need lots of sheepskin covers for the frozen teams and lots of hot cider and honey water. The kitchen was the only heated area at this time of day, so Zari had the rest of the girls bring in cots for those suffering from the frozen conditions. Becca was the worst case; exhaustion from the swim and the extreme cold ice rain rendered her almost unconscious. She was barely breathing when Zari stripped off her clothes and started rubbing her vigorously with hot clothes.

Chapter 31

The Great Storm

Pender staggered into the kitchen and collapsed on a cot. Someone had already taken off his outer garments. He was blue with the cold and breathing erratically. He kept mumbling, "It was me. I am at fault. I never took into consideration the weather conditions. Becca saved my life again, and I have taken hers." He wept and wept inconsolably.

Davi and Thomi carried in the lifeless body of Tarag. He had absorbed cruel blows from the Nuit clubs in his efforts to chase them off and later had drowned trying to swim back home. The members of the team who were still able to move wept at his demise. Nena signed to them not tell Pender because it could finish him.

Gena and Lacey came in with Zalenda, who went immediately to Pender's cot where she tried to take his hand and reassure him that although things had gone badly, everyone had survived and the Nuits had failed.

Toto was smelling around the body of her lifetime mate, crying and scratching the floor. Zalenda came and took her beside Pender and lay down cuddling Toto to her. Gena and Lacey went to help Davi and Thomi remove their clothes and dry their frozen bodies. Then they had to go to their packs and find dry clothes before they could settle down for the night.

For two days, the storm raged without letting up, the wind and rain obliterating everything from site; even the settlement could not be seen from the island. The temperature went down again so that the ice-cold rain turned to snow. For ten days, the snow piled up on the frozen ice of the lake, making any movement in and around the island impossible. Strange ice sculptures appeared at the western tip of the island carved out by the eerie whistling wind. The opposite end was a wall of white five to six feet high with only a small clearing where a strange cyclone of wind whipped the snow upward off the ice covered lake.

Inside, the kitchen was still the main living area because it was the easiest to heat. The floor heated by some deep subterranean volcanic action from the distant past had always made the space comfortable in the winter. But it also had excellent natural flues, which carried the smoke away from the heated cooking surfaces. The sixteen cots needed for the extended team to sleep on were all jammed in at night; fourteen were moved out during the day to give Nena and Elecia room to prepare the food.

During the past twelve days, Pender's health had improved slowly, but he could not get rid of a heavy chest cold and was confined to his cot most of the time. Zalenda seldom left his side, and when she did, Toto followed her. They had discussed every aspect of the fateful mission that was the cause of Pender's great grief. He now knew that Tarag was dead, and he could see Becca's was desperately ill. Her temperature was dangerously high, and despite everything they had tried, it was to no avail. The girls had told him that Zalenda would be dead if Toto had not deflected the knife wielded by her would-be assassin. He was absorbed by guilt and could not concentrate on the problems at hand. In the light of this, it was left to Zalenda, Nena, and Mari to start to plan for the next few days.

Nena's concern was that they would soon run out of food and other supplies. It was therefore necessary to make an emergency trip across the snow to the settlement. But how could this be done in these weather conditions?

Rona and Pipa had been out looking at the snow and ice and reported that they could walk over the snow because an icy surface on top of the snow was weight bearing. They had found the section where the cyclonic action of the wind had cut a somewhat easier pathway off the island.

Rahana suggested that she should lead an expedition over the lake to get supplies and find the mystic woman to try and get a potion for Becca. Ester, Morag, Pipa, and Rona could stay there for the duration of this emergency, as this would make it easier on the island's food supply with four less mouths to feed. While they were there, they could concentrate on finding out what had happened to the remaining Nuit attackers to see if they were still a threat.

She would take Davi, Thomi, Gena, and Lacey with her to carry back the food supplies. Gena and Lacey would go to the stables and find out if the men there could fit snowshoes on their horses for the journey back with Zalenda and the two men back to the Warrior Women Tribe. While she was waiting for the supplies, she would contact the mystic to see if she could come and administer her potions to Becca. Rahana said she believed it was critical that these things should be done now.

Zalenda and Nena said this was a good plan, but this time those involved must be properly dressed for the cold weather conditions. They set about immediately to prepare for this to happen the next morning, if the weather conditions were suitable. Rahana went and informed the people who would be going with her to get themselves ready. Rona and Pipa would lead the way, since they had looked at the situation and were best informed on which way to travel.

While Rahana tried to sleep, Mari and Zari hovered over Becca, nursing her through the long night. Often they were sure she was about to die, but as the night gave way to morning, her labored breathing could still be detected. Elecia and Nena were up early preparing the breakfast for the group and had already been outside. They reported that the wind and the blowing snow had stopped and the sun was shining, so it looked as if Rahana's relief expedition could cross the lake.

After everyone had eaten, Pender joined them for the first time in the meeting room since he became ill. Zalenda supported him as he walked. His whole attitude had changed with his improving health, and now he was keen to participate in this meeting. He wanted to stress to the team that at the first sign of trouble, they were to immediately abandon the crossing and come back. The other thing he wanted to remind them was to keep space between each other on the ice, as the water on that side was usually warmer than the other areas on the lake. He asked Davi to make sure they carried a rope in case of emergency.

Rahana had already given her team their assignments, so when the meeting was finished, they donned their winter sheepskins and ventured out onto the ice. Rona and Pipa led the way, moving carefully out along a fairly clear passage they had scouted the day before. Everyone followed at regular intervals, but the sandwich of thick ice, snow, and then even thicker ice was solid under their feet.

As they approached the settlement where the warmer water from the island passage met the lake, the ice was bare. Rahana saw two men's bodies frozen in the ice. She got as near as possible to see if they were people from the settlement. The bodies were frozen face up, and she recognized them as two of the would-be assassins sent to kill them. They were not Nuits, which meant that Tamor was hiring killer squads from outside the tribes. She decided that this information should not be shared with this group till she had spoken with Zalenda and Pender.

The settlement had survived the storms but not without damage. The eastern palisade had collapsed and now lay under piles of snow and ice. Men were already working on removing snow from building roofs, while others had been assigned to help repair their neighbors' homes.

A large contingent of men and women was busy clearing the snow and ice from the roads and passageways between the buildings so things could get back to normal as soon as possible. Cisi was working with the people shoveling the snow when Rahana's group arrived. Rona, Pipa, Morag, and Ester went immediately to assist in the snow clearing, and Gena and Lacey went to check on the horses. Davi and Thomi asked Cisi if they could help, and she assigned them to the building repair team.

With her team now all involved, Rahana had now time to go in search of the mystic. Cisi gave her directions to where she might be found but warned her that because of the cold weather, she might be out attending to the sick.

Rahana was determined to find her and get help for Becca. She wanted to take the mystic back with her but understood this might not be possible When she found her, she was treating a number of children. This woman was not what she had expected. She had expected some old wizened hag of a woman dressed in black with a sinister air about her. This woman was younger than she expected, tall with beautiful black tresses that reached down to her waist. When she looked up, Rahana realized this woman had the whitest skin she had ever seen; her features were perfect, dominated with the greenest of eyes.

"You are a friend of Pender's here to ask me to accompany you to the island. You are from the Cave People. What is your name?"

Rahana took time to get over her surprise before she replied. "You are correct in both questions, and my name is Rahana."

"Well, Rahana, before this day is over, you and I have much to do. I must go now to the island with you and speak to the wind. Pender and his company are in grave danger. I will treat your friend because you must all leave the island as soon as possible. I must go with you to guide you into the safety of my people where your enemies will never find you and you will all be safe. Now go to Cisi and get your supplies for Zalenda. I will talk with her and tell her what she must do, but we must all cross to the island while the sun is still strong. I have important information for Pender that is vital to his team's survival."

Rahana found Cisi, who was struggling with all the added pressure of being the chief in the middle of these difficult times; she discussed with Cisi what the mystic lady had revealed to her and what needed to be done. Cisi saw some positive things for her in it. It meant that Cisi could return to the island when the team left for the duration of the rebuild here in the settlement. Although it would mean she would have to travel back and forward every day, some of the homeless families could live in her home.

Cisi gave Rahana permission to take whatever food supplies they would need from the food storage area. Rahana went and collected Davi and Thomi from their work and explained their predicament. She made a list of the food that they would required packed for Zalenda's five people for three days and then what would be needed for eleven people for six days. They would need food for cooking on the island for at least the next four or five days. This had to be done quickly, as they would have to cross to the island before the sun started to go down today. Rona had to find the girls because they needed to go and pack warm winter traveling clothes and be ready to leave to go back to the island just after lunch. Her next stop was at the stables, where she informed Gena that they would require sixteen riding horses and four pack horses. Gena said they only had twenty horses, all told. Rahana said that would do; the mystic woman would bring her own pony.

At lunch Rahana gathered everyone together and told the group what she had learned from the mystic lady and why it was necessary for all of them to leave. Everyone was full of questions. Rahana said she did not have the answers yet; they would learn more at a meeting tomorrow. She inquired if everything was in order for them to leave within the hour. Lacey said most of the horses had not been trained yet to walk with snowshoes. Rahana replied that they will be walking very slowly. The training will have to be done tomorrow or later in the journey.

The sun was still high in the sky at the crossing edge when the mystic lady joined them on her pony. Davi led the parade of horses with Thomi at the back, and the pack horses were led by Lacey. The mystic lady rode her pony, and the rest of the party walked some distance apart till they reached the safety of the island shore.

Pender and Zalenda wanted to know why they had all come back. The mystic lady replied she would give them a full report later; it was critical that she see her patient right away. Zari and Mari took her to where Becca was lying still looking very ill. The mystic asked her nurses to take her clothes off so she could examine her properly. Mari and Zari looked on with great interest as this was being done. The lady straightened up. She smiled at them, saying, "I can allay your greatest fears—we are in time. Now one of you go and tell Rahana, since she grieves so much for her friend. Mari, may I call you that?"

Mari smiled from ear to ear. "Yes, please do."

"Then please call me Carla. Now, Mari, let us go and prepare a special poultice so we can apply it to her chest and back. We must apply it while it is still hot."

Zari was back with Rahana to help lift Becca onto her back first, while Mari applied a slurry of foul-smelling stuff to her back and then her chest. When this was done, Carla tied a soft cloth that none of the girls had seen before around Becca. This was done with great tenderness, which the watching girls appreciated very much. She then produced from a flask of strong-smelling liquid, which she proceeded to pour into Becca's mouth. Becca choked a little at first but managed to drink it all. "Now, ladies, we must leave her to sleep. We will check on her progress every hour. I know you have already been doing this, but I do not expect any further problems."

Carla met with Pender and Zalenda before meeting with the full team. She told them her name was Carla and that she had grave news for them. "My news is about the man called Tamor. He will try to depose Zalenda as queen of the Warrior Women in an attempt to take over the tribe. I suspect that you already know this and that he has hired murder squads to kill you. What you probably do not know is that he has suffered a great setback. The storms that have raged these past weeks have almost completely destroyed his Slave Island fort to the point where there is very little of it left. He blames you for all his misfortunes, including a broken leg that was caused by falling building parts. I have been called to reset his leg, but the pathways to his fort remain impassable. He is to be carried along the Big River beach, and I have to meet them at the moor road. I have to be carried there by one of his teams that will arrive the day after tomorrow. I suspect, Zalenda, that among this team will be a new group of assassins who have been ordered to search the settlement and the island thoroughly and kill anyone they find whom they believe is part of your organization. This is why you must leave tomorrow with your friends. The pathway south of the winding river is your best option. The night winds will cover your tracks and make it difficult for them to find you. I know you are a competent leader and queen. Do what you must to strengthen and defend your people."

"Pender, in the morning, you must leave with all of your team—even Becca must go. I will give your young women instruction in her treatment and the administering of the medicines. I am sending you to my people a long way from here where you will be safe. Tonight I must speak to the wind, because in the morning, I must instruct you how to get there. You must not come back till the tribes call you, and they will, I can assure you of that. Now I want to visit your wonderful hot springs. I leave you to prepare. Sleep well."

At the team meeting later, Rahana told them of finding the bodies of the two men frozen in the ice, and she stressed they did not have red hair. This would support what Carla had said about Tamor having gone outside his tribe to hire a new band of killers. It would appear then that the two separate groups that come against them at the crossing were perhaps hired by different people. The one that faced Pender and Becca were definitely Nuits, yet the others who were after Zalenda were not—what did this mean? Were the two men she saw in the ice killed by the rival Nuits? If not, how did they turn up dead?

Pipa said the men whom she and her friends had kicked to free Zalenda did not speak a different language, just with a different cadence and inflection in their voices. It would be good to know who their enemies were.

Zari just joined the meeting having come from nursing Becca. She was interested in what Pipa said. She thought that the language might not mean very much because among the Tree People, it was quite common to hear different dialects. Most of the people there came from many different tribes and areas. None of them, however, had any skills or training with weapons or in combat.

Rona wanted to know if they had been able to gather any information from the prisoners; if not, what were they going to do with them when they left? They all looked expectantly at Pender, but it was Zalenda that replied.

"This is a very interesting and intelligent conversation we are having. I congratulate all for how you have matured as warriors and leaders. You have grasped the essentials of the preparation a leader must do before undertaking any kind of mission. Pender and I have had a conversation with Carla, and she has been able to give us valuable intelligence that affects us all. Carla was able to tell us that Tamor has received a very serious blow to his plans. The storms of the last weeks have completely destroyed his fort. This means a certain amount of his plans are delayed. Unfortunately, they do not include his determination to kill me so he can take over the Warrior Women Tribe, claiming he is my father. Nor do they mean he will let up in his efforts to kill Pender whom he sees as his main rival in taking over all the tribes in this area. The result of this intelligence is we all must leave our home here.

"This decision causes me great grief. I have just been restored to the man I love, and now I must leave him again. For me this is unthinkable, but it is absolutely necessary for the well-being of my people and the tribes in general. Gena, Lacey, Davi, and Thomi will leave with me in the morning. We must be ready and packed to leave at first light. Carla has given us the trail we must use, as the others will be well watched. I will ride my white stallion because he is used to Toto lying across his shoulders. Make sure we have enough supplies for three days and have extra sheepskins for sleeping out at night."

Pender said, "I also am saddened because Zalenda must leave me, but she is correct—the evil forces that are come against us in this winter make it impossible for us to defend ourselves here. The ice on the lake makes our normal safe home assailable on three sides, and we cannot defend it with our small numbers. Tonight Carla will climb the Doan Stone and speak to the wind. I do not pretend to understand what this means, but she believes it is essential to our survival. I trust her because she is coming with us to guide us to the home of her ancestors and family friends. I do not know at this time where this is, but we must leave tomorrow, as Carla has to be back in time to journey to the Big River, where she has to set Tamor's broken leg.

"In answer to Rona's question, Zalenda said that her assailant has succumbed to his wounds and died. We were unable to get any information from him. The other two prisoners were very helpful. At first, we thought they were talking drivel. They told us that Tamor had promoted a new captain from outside the Nuit Tribe with special powers to recruit and arm a special squad from outside his tribe to track down and kill me and all of you. This has caused conflict inside his upper echelon, which later might prove to be valuable to us. We have decided to allow the prisoners to return to their families, as they have no intention of rejoining the death squad. Tonight we will meet at the Doan Stone to hear Carla speak to the wind, but pack all the things you might need for this journey and, of course, extra sheepskins, as we may have to sleep outside for a few nights."

Everyone gathered at the Doan Stone when the winter sun weakly gave into the darkness. Even Becca and the prisoners were there, Becca dwarfed by the large sheepskin she wore and the prisoners silenced in wonderment.

Carla dismounted from her pony and with amazing alacrity and sight found the footholds cut by the hammer when Rolf damaged the stone. She climbed to the top and stood very still; the night and the wind stilled with her. They all witnessed the incredible look on her face as if she had become a different person. It appeared as if year upon year seemed to pile on her, changing her before their eyes from Carla's beautiful face into a visage that was marred and scarred by time.

Her eyes gave the impression that she was no longer with them but that she was searching some far-off universe with these searching searing eyes. What she was looking for she must have found, because her throat began to emit the strangest sound like an ass baying at the moon, but there was no ass and no moon. Her voice gradually increased in sound and volume as it climbed the scale till it echoed out over the lake across the waters, the valleys, and the hills, this screeching, whistling sound that made them cover their ears.

They were trapped in the stillness of time, and not a sound was heard but the high-pitched sound that now warbled into some ancient language. As she spoke in this unknown tongue, winds began to whip around the island at gale force speeds in a great crescendo of sound. They could see the snow and the ice being blown like a blizzard, but they were wrapped in a cocoon of peace and silence. She stopped her talking to the winds and raised her arms. The winds slowly fell. She dropped them back to her sides, and the quiet night was restored.

Carla lithely climbed down the stone and stood at the base where she told the gathered company that she had spoken to the wind, and the news was they would all travel to their destinations safely. The winds had agreed to cover their tracks in the snow so no one could follow them, but only if they left tomorrow.

She told Pender's group that she would accompany them past the Water Gate, but they would have to traverse the Valley of the Flies on their own. This valley was where the old people left their dead. They did not bury them or burn them like other tribes did. As a result, great cloud of flies feasted on the decaying carcasses. If they disturbed the flies, the result could be fatal. When they passed a standing stone at the entrance to the valley, they would see another one at the end. Everyone in the group must fix their eyes on that stone and ignore their surroundings and walk carefully through the valley; in this way, they will not disturb the flies. "I have spoken to my people on the wind, and they will welcome you and keep you all safe till I recall you to continue your missions. After I have checked on Becca, I will leave, for I have other patients to care for. I will meet you all in the morning."

Pender met with his team to briefly discuss what they should do with the prisoners in the morning. He said that he had indicated to the men that his inclination was to allow them to return to their families and asked if everyone agreed with this solution.

Pipa suggested that the men leave with them in the morning, but that they be held at the settlement for two days before being released. This would mean that they would have no information to give to anyone who might be interested. Everyone liked this idea, so it was agreed they should be alerted to this now so that they would be prepared.

Rahana wanted to know how Becca was to be moved because she did not think she could go for a long ride on horseback in this weather. Pender said he was taking the biggest and strongest horse, and Becca would be wrapped and tied to him at all times. Zari joked. "Could I please have the same treatment?" They all laughed and went to prepare for their long journey.

Carla and Zalenda were conducting an examination of Becca when Rahana came to prepare for her friend. "I have great news, Bec. You are to be wrapped to Pender for the whole trip—not even Zalenda has had that treatment!"

"What do I do when I want to pee?" she quipped back.

"That is our problem. Right now you are not doing enough of that," Carla said. "Rahana, see that she drinks from this flask three times a day till she returns to normal. Now I must go. See you in the morning," and she left in a hurry.

Zalenda said, "I am glad I have you two alone. I have never thanked you for the care you both took of Pender when I left him. I know I broke his heart, but thanks to you two he made it through. Thank you for saving him for me. As a Warrior Woman, I was never allowed to care for anyone, and when I am alone, I doubt myself. I doubt how Pender can love me. I am not skilled at relationships, and when I am forced to leave him, I cannot find an anchor in my soul, and I make stupid decisions that leave me alone and adrift in my misery. I should never leave him, and this would not happen, but life has transpired so far to frequently keep us apart, and now I must leave him again, and I am afraid."

The sincerity in her voice prevented them from making any quick quips. "This is the reason I wanted to talk with you. If in the next weeks—could be years—something happens to me, I want you to take him as your husband."

"Zalenda, please do not talk of this. Yes, we both love him, we have come to know that, but no one will ever be able to take your place in his heart," Becca said, sobbing each word into her sentence. Rahana came and cuddled them both to her; her small stature meant she hugged their chests and held them tight, tears streaming from her eyes.

"You promise?" Zalenda said.

"We promise" was the muffled reply.

They held on for a long time till Zalenda said, "I must go to him now—it may be our last night together. Yes, I know I am fortunate and unfortunate at the same time. Remember what I have asked of you."

Pender was already lying down in the cot because they were all still sleeping in the kitchen area. She carefully maneuvered herself in beside him, taking care not to disturb the covers lest she let the cold in to him. He turned to kiss her, and they held that position even in their sleep.

Elecia and Nena were up early to cook the last breakfast there perhaps for some time, so there was no opportunity to stay in bed longer. The girls went to the hot springs for their morning wash, taking care to have all their winter clothes with them, while the men fed the horses and got them ready for a long day.

At breakfast Pender told them what they must expect this day, and he thanked them all for the care, courage, and devotion they had all shown to their cause and mission. He said because of the early hour, they would have a little longer to clean up, and they would meet at the stone in two hours.

The temperature had not changed since the storms, and as they gathered at the stone, the horses' breath and that of the humans milling around seemed to create their own rising fog. It was determined that Pender's group of ten and Zalenda's four would stay together until they reached the south side of the winding river. Rahana would ride ahead with the two prisoners and put them in Cisi's care, where they would be put to work for at least two days. Carla and Rahana would meet them outside the settlement on the west side, where they would be hidden from view of any prying eyes.

Rahana rode off with the two men, carefully retracing the path that they had used the day before across the ice and snow. The pack horses were made ready, and the two teams hugged and kissed at the stone, promising each other they would meet here sometime in the future on this spot and remember this day. Everyone mounted, and there was some delay in leaving because Becca had to be lifted into position ahead of Pender. The horse moved under her while they put a large sheepskin around them. Nena and Elecia had sown it together so it could lace up the front. When it was in position, Nena then laced it up, pulling her back against Pender, where she could ride in spite of her great weakness.

They moved out onto the ice and followed the recent tracks made by Rahana, Pender and Zalenda leading the way. Toto lay across the great white stallion's shoulders, seeming oblivious to everything around her except her ever watchful eyes on her mistress. They rode in a column of two with Davi and Thomi at the rear. Within the hour, they were in position beside the settlement waiting on Carla and Rahana.

Rahana and Cisi came out first. Cisi came to say good-bye to her brother and sister, and Rahana to ride beside Becca. She carried with her the flask Carla had given her to administer to Becca along the way. Ester dismounted and went to Cisi. They hugged and kissed and then made their way to Pender. Ester put her hands together so Cisi could step into them to get up and kiss her brother. Cisi then made her way to Zalenda, who dismounted when she saw her coming; they embraced and kissed. Cisi said to her, "Go and do what you must do. I know this is difficult for you, but please come again and be my brother's wife. He will only exist without you."

"My dear sister, that is now my only ambition."

Carla came on her pony, and they remounted and were gone, Cisi watching them go with tears in her eyes. "Brother and sister, will I ever see you again?" She knew only time could answer that question.

Davi and Gena led the way, following a path that night animals had carved in the snow to get to the open water at the island crossing.

Gena discovered she liked being with Davi; he was so thoughtful and attentive, always there to lift her on the her horse. At breakfast he always got her food first and cleaned up after them. He had carried her pack this morning and laced up her coat when her hands were too cold to do it on her own. She knew it was normal for men to serve the women in their tribe, but this was different. It was the way he looked at her when he was doing it, signaling to her that he wanted to do it not out of duty but of admiration and love. There she had thought of it, and she wanted it to be true.

He was smaller than her in height, broad shouldered, and had very masculine qualities that seem very appropriate in him, even in the way he conducted himself in company. He was strong but not overbearing, slow of speech, especially to her, and she could see he had few social skills. She found he had a very handsome face with hazel eyes that dominated his every expression. Yes, she liked this man, more than any man, with the exception of Pender, and he had a long line of admirers. She was going to love this whole journey and hoping it would take the three days so she could make him love her when she had him all to herself.

At the back of the line, Lacey rode with Thomi. She would have preferred to have been somewhere else with someone more talkative. Thomi was unbelievably shy, unable to converse with strangers especially women. He could not believe that for three days he was trapped with this very beautiful young woman, the type he dreamed about but could never speak to in anything but single syllabic words. It was obvious to him that she disliked him more and more as the journey progressed. She displayed this by always riding a little further ahead so that she would not be required to speak to him.

It was that, however, that probably saved her life. As they passed under a large tree, he saw something big and black pounce on her from above, taking her off her horse onto the ground. She screamed in terror as the big cat tried to subdue her. Thomi was off his horse like a flash and tearing the animal off her with his bare hands. The animal turned ferociously on its attacker, prepared to defend its prey. Thomi had his club out and began beating it on the head. By luck, one of his strokes caught the animal on the paw with which it was holding Lacey. It let her go roaring in pain and limped away in to the woods.

Thomi did not take time to be shy. He picked up Lacey and with great tenderness removed her glove to reveal a great gashing wound on her wrist and hand. When he saw it, he ran forward, and as he went shouting for Carla, he ran all the way explaining to everyone what had happened to this precious girl. The whole company stopped, concerned by what they saw and guided Thomi to where Carla was dismounting from her pony. When Pender realized what had happened, he ordered them to circle up and stop for a lunch break.

Thomi held Lacey while Carla examined her wounds. Lacey was in shock and shook uncontrollably. Carla told Thomi to hold her even tighter, as she would have to clean the wound and sew it together. Ester went and got Carla's emergency kit from her pony and brought it on the run. Gena came to help her friend, with Davi in pursuit. They discovered that Thomi had everything under control. As Carla cleaned the wound, Lacey held Thomi. Carla was about to stitch the wound, but before doing so, she wanted to give Lacey a potion to curb the pain. Lacey indicated that she would only take it from Thomi. He was very careful in administering the draft while Lacey drank it with her eyes closed. Thomi thought to himself, *Even now she cannot look at me.* Lacey, like all Warrior Women, had been trained to resist pain, but having an open wound sewn in this cold was excruciating. She blacked out, going limp in Thomi's arms. He took her whole weight and did not falter. This allowed Carla to stitch the wound tighter and put more stitches along the torn flesh; this she felt would help the healing. She finished and sterilized the wound and then held a cloth with a smelling concoction to Lacey's nose, which she inhaled and slowly brought her back to consciousness.

The group had managed in the extreme cold to get a fire going, and they were busy heating drinks for everyone and toasting oat bread. Gena went to get a drink for her, but Lacey would only allow Thomi to nurse her; this he took great pleasure in doing. As the draft wore off, Lacey became more and more talkative, telling the story of her mishap over and over again. Each time she told it, the more poetic she became of her brave companion who had saved her life and carried her miles to get help. Now as she talked, her eyes never left his face.

Ester, noticing this, said to Rona, "I think our Lacey is smitten."

Rona replied, "Perhaps that is a good thing. Look at the other two—it looks like Zalenda is going to have a pleasant journey home with all the loving and cooing that will be going on."

Becca was temporarily loosened from Pender's care and had begun to feel stronger, though not able to ride on her own. She watched Pender while he sat with Zalenda, with their arms intertwined, whispering in each other's ears; these were moments no one could encroach on, and she was not inclined to do it. Her mind wandered to what might be ahead and to the promise she had made to Zalenda. She knew neither she nor Rahana, nor both of them together could ever replace Zalenda in his heart; they loved him, but could he ever love them? In her reverie of thoughts, she had not noticed Zalenda and Pender approaching, nor had she noticed that everyone was packed up and ready to go. She was glad they all put her inaction down to the draft she had been given, so she did not have to explain herself.

Pender and Zalenda were trying to figure out whether she needed to be bound to Pender or if it was possible for her just to ride behind him and hold on to him. Zalenda put her inaction down to physical weakness and suggested to Pender that it would be better and safer for Becca to be strapped to him for the next two days till she was fully recovered. Davi and Pender lifted her up in position, and Zalenda tied her in place.

Zalenda then went and checked on Lacey, who was already mounted and belted securely to Thomi and very happy to be there. She whispered something that no one else heard, and he leaned forward and kissed her neck. They both appeared to very happy with this arrangement. Zalenda watched with envy, wishing the next few moments would never come, but she went to face the inevitable—her parting with Pender. She mounted the stallion. Toto was already in place and moved to where Pender was at the head of the procession. She rose up from her horse and leaned over and grasped him with both hands and kissed him full on the mouth. He did not have time to respond. She sat back down and guided her group of three mounted horses, one extra horse, and the two pack horses away from the main group heading west. She did not look back.

Chapter 32

The Journey to the Palace and Establishing the New Order

Gena was happy to be on the way home. She rode beside Davi and was still exhilarated by the time they had spent at the break and especially the loving way he had lifted her up on to her horse as if she were the most precious thing in the world. She was confident of his love, and now she was sure of her own feelings. She loved him and did not care whether it was right or wrong for them in the eyes of her tribe. She would go anywhere with him so they could be together.

Davi, who rode right alongside her, kept his eyes on the road but also scanned the terrain ahead for any signs of possible trouble. He too was elated with how Gena expressed her love for him. This was a new experience; he had never been in love before. This young woman was so high above his station, yet she loved him. Unthinkable, unbelievable, yet true, there might be problems ahead, but they were strong and so was their love. He turned and looked into her eyes, and he saw the source of their strength—their love.

Lacey's arm and hand were hurting, yet she did not complain; she was secure in this man's arms. How foolish she had been in looking to these two traitorous rogues for something that was here all the time. She was thankful to have escaped that kind of relationship. Her own ingrained tribal customs had almost robbed her of this precious experience of loving and being loved. They had both admitted to each other at the break that he loved her and she loved him. He had believed that to be impossible. She had convinced him it was not just because he saved her life—and that was big—but more than anything, it was the love he had shown afterward. No one had ever wanted to do that for her. She loved everything about him, even his reticence and difficulty with words, which he more than compensated for with his actions. She loved him. *And I do not care who knows or what they may think,* she said to herself. *We will be happy in our love no matter what happens.*

Thomi held her close to him as he rode. She was so wonderful to hold like this, and this was the first time in his life anything good had happened to him. Just hours ago he thought she despised him and would not even look at him. Now she gazed into eyes, and her eyes spoke of love. If the big cat had not attacked her, he never would have had the courage to touch her hand, never mind kiss her on the lips and hold her. He had watched her on the road all the way to the island, and all the time she was there, unable to even stutter in her presence. Now everything had changed. This was beyond any dream he had ever dreamed. When he worked in the fields, women passed him by, ignoring him completely, yet here he was holding his dreams in his arms.

Zalenda kept her eyes focused ahead of her as mile after mile the big stallion covered the snow. On either side of the river, the snow was piled higher than anywhere else; yet here on the south side of the river, they had a fairly easy passage. She wondered again how Carla, the mystic lady, had known this was how it would be. At the break today while they had waited on Lacey being treated, she had gone to check their trail, and sure enough, just as Carla had predicted, their trail had been covered.

She was conscious that her tears had dried on her face. The cause of these tears was manifold. She wept because she was riding away from the man she loved right from that moment she looked up and saw him outside the palisade on Slave Island. How had she ever sent him away? How could she have believed that he would not understand the lies that Tamor circulated? How could she have ever doubted him? He had loved her through it all, and now she was riding away from him. Being a queen was not worth this. She would reorganize the tribe, and then when it was working well, she would go right back to him; this was her resolve. She would be the best wife ever. Would she ever be able to give him children? No women warriors that she knew were ever wives or had become pregnant. Would this become a big problem in their relationship? Would he take Rahana or Becca as second wives so they could have a family? All these questions haunted her as she rode. She kept saying over and over, "Pender, I love you, I love you." She was unaware that she was shouting this at the top of her voice.

Thomi and Davi rode up quickly to find out what was the problem, but they found that in her deep need, there was nothing they could do to comfort her or provide any consolation.

Davi decided that as the horses were tired, they would stop for the night. Thomi unpacked the tents and the ground covers and set them up, while Davi attended to the horses. Gena went and gathered materials to start a fire and after many attempts got it started. Lacey took Zalenda into the newly erected tent and with her good hand wiped away her tears. Thomi came in and said it was too difficult to get the second tent up because of the sloping ground. Zalenda suddenly came to her senses and said that was all right; they would all sleep together in one tent. She went out and helped Gena make the hot cider and toast the bread. During the day, the temperature had gone up, so they were able to sit around the fire in their sheepskins. Zalenda put down a sheepskin for Toto and ordered her to be on guard. She then organized the night watch, as they did not want the wild animals to harm their horses.

Before they went to sleep, she went over with them the plans for her return to the tribe. First of all, the five of them would go immediately to the palace, and she would order the substitute queen and her cohorts out. They had tried to form an alliance with Tamor, hoping he would leave them alone to rule the tribe, but she knew he had other plans. He knew that she was the legitimate queen, and the way his mind worked was like this: if he had her killed, he could claim she was his daughter and set himself up as the legitimate ruler.

Two days from now, she would call the tribe together in the great square at the statue of the Great Queen. The four of them would stand together, and she would announce the new order of governance. This new order would recognize the equality of men and women. The practice of raising women warriors would cease, although training for defense of the tribe would continue, but men as well as women would be trained. This was to reflect the changes of their time. Armies no longer relied on highly skilled people who used their bodies as a weapon. The new armies who would come against them are people trained in the use of weapons, long poles with harden points called spears, and shorter weapons called swords—weapons that can hurl stones great distances that rain down on ill-prepared tribal armies who rely only on their physical prowess. "We will prepare ourselves for such attacks."

"The laws governing our society will change. Men and women will make their own choices as to whom they will have as a husband or wife—children will be protected. The production of food will be put back in the hands of families, as will the work of trade and trading. All people in the tribe will be seen to be equal, and there will be no special class to create their own privileges. The government will be done by an equal number of men and women who will represent the family tribe, appointed initially by her but later would be chosen by the people. In the interim period, she would make all the decisions as is normal for the protection of the tribe. She would then call on Davi and Thomi to take hammers and smash the Statue of the Great Queen. She would then take Gena and Lacey and lead them to Davi and Thomi and proclaim them husband and wife. They would be the first recipients of the new order.

The two couples were beside themselves with happiness. They could openly show their love, but would it all work? "That," Zalenda said, "is our task. Are you with me?"

"All the way" was the answer.

"Now let us go to the tent and sleep. We have much to do tomorrow."

In the morning, Zalenda was up early working on the fire. She was having difficulty getting her little pile of leaves to ignite in the cold morning wind. Toto looked on with great attention. She had a vested interest in this fire, both for the heat it would generate and the food that would come her way. Finally, after many attempts, the spark caught, and she was soon able to add the twigs and branches, and the fire blazed. Breakfast was just under way when the others emerged from the tent. The men had worked the night watch to allow their partners to sleep. Lacey was having problems dressing, as her arm and hand were still painful. Thomi was pleased to assist as her dressing maid.

Zalenda had no skills as a cook, so she was very pleased when Gena took over that responsibility. Davi went to a small tributary of the river and broke the ice to get freshwater for breakfast so they could all have a wash. To do this, he had to increase the size of the fire because they only had smaller-sized stone containers. They needed enough hot water for the ladies to bathe with and the men to wash in. Zalenda felt that they had to establish a good impression when they went into the palace, and being unkempt might give her adversary an advantage before the court.

Thomi fed and made the horses ready for the day's journey, and then he went and helped Lacey bathe. When they were finished, Davi took down the tent and packed everything ready for the road. Toto did not want to assume her normal traveling position in front of Zalenda, and when they moved out, she went to cover their trail. Zalenda was not sure whether she was reverting back to her old habits or perhaps she was wary of this part of the pathway because of the increased tree and bush cover. Davi also felt this was significant and suggested it would be better if he and Gena took up the rear position, seeing Lacey still needed Thomi's support to ride.

Late in the afternoon as they were approaching the territory of the women warriors, Toto barked out a warning and took off over a small rise in the road. Gena stayed behind while Davi went to investigate. He came back to report that their way ahead was blocked by four riders who definitely were not Nuits or men from their tribe.

They all agreed that these men had only one purpose—and that was to kill Zalenda and stop them from getting to the palace. Zalenda believed they were not hired by Tamor; he still had to have his leg reset and would be behaving like a big baby, and everyone would have to concentrate on keeping him happy. Her instinct told her these men came from the palace, hired by the temporary queen to kill her so she could make her position permanent. As such, they would not be as well trained as Tamor's hired killers would have been, so they were going to use this to their advantage.

"Lacey will stay here in cover with the pack horses. We will ride along the trail as if we are expecting nothing, and we will hail them like travelers do. Then at my signal, Davi and Gena will ride to the left of them, and Thomi and I will ride to the right of them. We will come at them with as much speed as we can. On this snow, their horses will not have hide shoes like ours, and they will be standing still. We will ride into them. Toto will be somewhere around, and if they are unhorsed, she will deal with them. Remember, we want them alive."

They deliberately slowed their pace as they rode over the rise to give their quarry time to recognize them, and they nonchalantly stopped and talked and pointed toward the palace. Zalenda was watching the would-be assassins' eyes as they sauntered toward them. Thomi shouted a greeting and moved his horse slightly off the path, distracting the men. Zalenda gave the signal, and the four kicked their horses at speed right into the waiting wall of arms and legs trying to get out of the way. The four men landed on the ground, with Zalenda, Thomi, and Davi on top of them. Gena stood back as the winded men were punished and subdued. She then roped them together for the walk back to the palace, already disgraced in their task.

Thomi went and brought Lacey and the pack horses forward for the hour ride to the palace. It was then that Toto decided to show up; it looked like she had been hunting. "Where were you when you were needed?" Zalenda said. Toto looked at her and wagged her tail, ready to assume her ride in front of Zalenda.

On the way through the fields where until recently Davi and Thomi had worked, their friends were out getting bales of hay for their animals. As they went, Thomi told his friends to get everyone and gather at the palace—big things are about to happen. The men could not believe their eyes or ears. Why was Thomi riding behind the queen, with a well-known Warrior Woman on his lap, and he was holding her! Why was Davi escorting these four scoundrels all trussed up! and why was that Warrior Woman acting like he was her man!

They went and got their friends and secretly sent messages to the young women who had helped the last time Pender and Rahana came to warn the tribe, and they all congregated outside the palace.

Gena and Lacy's friends in the Warrior Women brigade came to support Zalenda, their true queen, and together the whole throng walked and rode down into the palace grounds. The palace guards could do nothing to stop them, especially when Zalenda ordered them to follow her. She did not even dismount as she rode into the queen's council chamber, which was in session. The young pretender rose in anger and shouted, "What is the meaning of this inexcusable interruption of this court's business?" Her voice trailed off when she saw Zalenda and her four hires trussed up as her prisoners. She turned for help from her councillors, but they studied the floor.

Zalenda's voice was icy cold when she ordered the guards, "Take hold of this young woman. I have much to say in her presence and these scurrilous rogues I made to act as council in my absence."

The guards moved into position but did not lay hands on anyone. "What have I to do, dismiss the palace guards as well? I told you, take hold of her. Do it now or I have men here who will do it for you and you can join these in prison," she said, waving her hand at the council.

"We have orders from Tamor himself."

"Tamor, Tamor! Who is this Tamor? Is she a queen who answers to all of the requirements of this tribe?"

The spokesman for the guards spoke again. "No, my lady, he told us you were dead and that because of the shameful behavior of your mother, the last queen, he was your father and rightful chief of this tribe."

Zalenda asked the council, "Do you people have so little common sense that you did not understand what his real motives are? Are you so easily blinded by his promises of power he might give you but won't? Look at what he has done to create his slave trading empire. I have been in Slave Island. Have any of you? Who else were there? People like you who believed his promises. If I had not come back, you would all be there within the next few weeks."

She turned to Thomi and commanded, "Bring forward the prisoners. It was not Tamor that ordered these men to kill me—it was you. It was this council and this little impostor here who paid informants to find out when I would be on the way here and then paid these men to kill me and my friends. Should I have mercy on you? See how much I have on them."

She took Thomi's club from him and walked forward and smashed the head of each prisoner; with four strokes, they were all dead.

The councillors shrieked in fear as she turned to the spokesmen of the guard and said, "Arrest this council and put them in prison, and if you refuse, you will join them. These people here"—she turned and pointed to the throng from the fields and the young women warriors—"will surely like the opportunity right now to obey me." The guard moved immediately to do her bidding.

"Now I have a very important announcement to make. When my friends and I have had time to wash off the dirt of three days of travel, we will meet at noon in the palace square in front of the statue of the Great Queen. I will announce then some very exciting changes in how we will govern ourselves in the future."

Zalenda led her four friends through the palace to her rooms. As they went, they wondered at the opulence of the place. Soon they were being served by the servants who were part of the queen's retinue. The three ladies were pampered in every way, but Lacey secretly wished it was Thomi that was doing it. After they had experienced this spoiling, new clothes were brought for them to approve, and once they were dressed, they ate at the queen's table.

At noon Zalenda led the four friends out before the people of the tribe, Davi and Gena on one side of her, and Thomi and Lacey on the other. The four friends were in mortal fear of the presence of the whole tribe; every eye seemed to be fixed on them. The people were wondering what was happening. Nothing had happened like this before their queen not backed by council but four people like themselves; their interest was piqued by it all.

Zalenda soon put their minds into another whirl of thought entirely as she asked them to come nearer and dismissed her guards. "I have come today with my four friends, people like yourselves with whom I have shared these plans for the future governance of our tribe—they were excited, I hope you will be to."

"In my travels among the tribes around us, I have come to realize that the greatest danger to our people come from within when appointed chiefs and queens organize the government of their people not for the greatest good but for their own personal comfort and benefit. I firmly believe that this is one of the reasons that slavery flourishes among all tribes.

"Today I am announcing a new order of governance for this tribe. We will no longer be called the Warrior Women Tribe. We will be known as the People of the Plains. In the past, young women were taken from their families because of their appearance and the likelihood that they would grow up through a rigid regime of strenuous training to enable them to kill their enemies with their bodies. This, for our tribe, has been successful in the past. I was trained in these methods, and I have killed many people, mostly men.

"Recently I was attacked by an assassin who was armed with a new weapon. I escaped because my dog distracted him long enough for my companions to capture him. We can no longer depend on our old methods. Tribes and enemies coming against us will be armed with long polelike sticks with hardened tips that will kill at a single thrust. They will protect themselves by wearing layers of hardened leather at close quarters and fight with short, pointed wooden weapons called swords. To soften resistance to a gathered army, they will use stones and sling them into the air to rain down on their enemies, causing havoc and killing many even before they attack. We must change if we are to survive as a tribe, as a people.

"Today I am announcing a new type of society, one where men and women will be equal in all things. Men and women will be trained in these new methods of war and will fight side by side. Men and women will be free to choose their own partners for life, and they will not require any approval from the council. Children will be protected in this new order, and no child will be taken from their parents to act as servants or soldiers to this tribe. Slavery will not be allowed in any form within this tribe. Workers will be paid fairly, and men and women will work in the fields. Farmers and artisans will be responsible for the sale of their own products, but intertribe trade will still be controlled by the council.

"To make these changes possible, I am announcing a new form of governance. We will no longer be ruled only by a queen and a council appointed only by her. I am officially putting an end to that right now." She nodded to Davi and Thomi, who picked up their hammers and smashed the statue of the Great Queen and her artificial standard until it lay in ruins on the ground.

The people gasped in astonishment and looked fearfully at where the palace guards were formed up, expecting them to rush the five people on the podium, but they did not move.

Zalenda spoke again. "Men and women of this family tribe, let me introduce to you your new council. When I call your name, will you please come forward and join me here?" She called out the names of ten men and ten women; some were farmers, some were ex-Warrior Women, some worked in the fields, others in the market place, two were from the former council, and one from the guards. She formed them up on either side of her and told them to take each other's hands. The famous four, as people were now calling them, stood behind her. Zalenda then indicated with her hand that this was their new council. She asked them each in turn to tell the people their name and their occupation.

When this was completed, she went to one side and said, "People of this tribe, I present to you your new council." The people cheered and cheered until Zalenda held up her hand. "Thank you for your support. I want to let you know that I have picked this council to represent you for the next two years, but in the future, you will pick your own council. During that time, I will stay as your queen, assisted by my four friends. When I believe you have a capable government, I will resign as queen and leave you to go and be the wife of the young man you know as Pender, the man whom I love with all my heart." The people were silent in awe of everything they had seen and heard.

Chapter 33

Pender and the Lost World

Meanwhile, Pender was struggling leading his horse uphill through a steep, very secluded narrow valley, which he had not even seen from just a short distance away. To make the journey more difficult, a hill stream wound like some wriggling serpent slashed into the hills, its gushing water slowly but surely eroding its rock-filled passageway. He looked back at his team, now strung out as they maneuvered from one side to the other. They were tired and needed to rest, but Carla and her pony kept moving on. His feet were slipping on the wet, icy snow. The hide shoe covers he wore were of little use in these conditions, but they did keep his feet warm, and that was something in this cold, wet environment.

As he turned the next corner, a large mountain rock lay in the way, and the path went around it, so he had to slip and slide down to the stream again. This time he heard the unmistakable sound of a large volume of water falling from a great height. The rock had blocked it from view; it was beyond his imagination—a very wide, very high gate of water falling from a great height at an ever-increasing speed into a large deep pool of water. There was no way around it. He stood for some time, mesmerized by the falling water, before he realized that to the right of him was a large open space where Carla and her pony were waiting. She already had a fire under way and oats cooking on a flat rock. His horse saw the open space and without being urged moved over, ready for him to tether it to a rock.

Although he was tired and sore, Pender went back to help his team. Becca was up the hill looking down at Rahana with a look of abject despair on her face. "This horse will not move. I have tried everything. I am tired, and I am sore. Where is Pender when you need him?"

"I am right here, Your Majesty, willing and able to carry you down this slope so we both can have a bath together in this frozen water," Pender said, poking his head around the rock. "I can tell you that just around the corner, there is a fire and oats cooking."

Rahana led her horse away to the fire but not before she heard Becca say to Pender, "All right, you take the horse down, and I'll slide down on my bum."

"But you will get a cold, wet bum," Ester said, who was next in line.

"Yes, but that gives me an excellent reason for standing with my bum to the fire."

The rest of the team had laughed at Becca but saw the sense in what she said; each person who went down was making it more treacherous. They passed along hides from the pack horses and laid them on the slope. The horses were enticed down with oats, and everyone, even Elecia, benefited from Becca's cold bum.

When they were all rested and seated on rocks covered with hides enjoying the fire and the good food Carla had provided, she stood up and said, "Today I must leave you to go back and attend to Tamor. His men will be at the settlement waiting to take me to him so I can set his leg properly. I will probably be required to rebreak it to do this. You can be sure I will make it most painful experience for him so he will not be able to get up to his evil antics anytime soon."

She turned and pointed to the waterfall. "This is the Water Gate. We must go through it. This is the gateway into the Lost World. You will wear these," she said, picking up a strange-looking cape and put it over her head and pulled a hood on to cover her beautiful hair. "You must leave your horses here. My friends will look after them till you require them again. Take with you only the things that are essential. People will feed you along the way and keep you safe, but you must do what they say—they know what is best.

"Remember what I told you about going through the Valley of the Flies, the valley of corpses. The rules are stringent—all of you must obey. Should one of you be enticed to look around, you will all suffer. When you move into the valley at the first standing stone, you must set your eyes then on the standing stone at the end of the valley and never take your eyes off it. Pender will lead. You follow him and walk confidently. Do not look down. Just walk till you are past the stone and safe in the cave at the end.

"In the cave, at the end, you will be met by my people, often called the Old People or the M People, so named because everyone's name begins with the letter *M* and their tribal last name is Mac. They are very different from you and me and have suffered much in their existence in the past from other tribes. They are honest and good and will be good to you. They will keep you safe until I come again. You can repay them by accepting their hospitality with genuine grace and thankfulness. Only a few people know of this lost tribe, and fewer still would be able to find them. You can rest here free from fear of the assassins that hunt you.

"Now I must open the Water Gate. Do not be afraid of the falling water. I will turn it off. Your capes will protect you from the spray. Take your shoes off—the water is warm."

Carla led them into the waters. By the time she had traversed the pool, the last person in the team was entering the water. Pender could see that they were walking along a ridge of rock, and the water was shallow and warm, but on either side was a deep abyss of frozen turbulent water. The Water Gate was a waterfall divided into two parts, one large wide section with thousands of gallons of roaring water falling down at a great rate, and a lesser fall, narrower one, which Carla now walked behind. She did something, and a sliding circular door opened, and the water was temporarily stopped. The team filed through the door just sprinkled with a few drops of water.

When the last member of the team was in the cave, she touched the rock at the side. The door rolled shut and the water fell, and the gate was closed. She told the team to gather around her. Because of the falling water it was difficult for her to be heard. Carla told them she must leave them now and go back. They must carry on no more than sixty paces into the cave from where they were. She warned them of a bottomless gulf ahead at about a hundred paces. "When you get to the sixty paces, Pender will guide you to the right into a long corridor that is lit by luminous rock, where it will be nice and warm." Then she kissed Pender and hugged each of the girls and was gone.

Pender counted out the sixty paces very carefully, and just as Carla had said, when he turned to the right, he could see the corridor with its strange light. He waited while all of the girls passed him then followed them into the corridor. It indeed was strange; the rocks glowed with a brilliant incandescent light, and yet the air did not feel like the cave that had been cold and inhospitable. The air here was warm and ardent, so warm in fact that the girls were stripping off their outer clothes. They walked further along in this magical world till they came to larger cavern where warm fountains gushed up out of the floors. Around the sides of this area were warm rocks to lounge on, and they made full use of them. This was the first time in four days they could rest in safety and comfort.

Although Becca was not yet fully recovered from the terrible cold and breathing problems she had suffered, she was the first to strip off her clothes and stand in the middle of the fountains. Her friends soon followed, quick to enjoy the comfort and heat. It was also nice to be able to bathe and wash off the accumulated days of traveling dirt, so they ended up washing each other's hair. Only Nena had thought to bring salve for the hair and skin, so she was in much demand.

To give the ladies privacy, Pender decided to find out where the corridor led, and as he walked, he wondered if he would ever see Zalenda again. He knew of her plans to change how the tribe would be governed and how its defense would be organized. They had also talked about her plans to make men and women equal and free them to make their own decisions and take full responsibility for their families. But what worried him the most was the two years she had set aside from her own life to do it. At the end of that, would she still love him? Would he still love her? As he mused on these things, he hadn't noticed that he had walked out into natural daylight into a new type of life.

The first thing that caught his eye was that he was in a very tight valley with volcanic mountains on either side that were completely denuded of any kind of plant life. From these mountains, streams ran down on either side and were gathered into fairly fast-flowing narrow rivers. In between, on a kind of raised plateau, there were about sixty round random-rubble small-stoned buildings with semispherical topped roofs covered with turf. They were not very high, indicating that the people who lived in them were not very tall. He observed at the far end of the valley beautiful verdant green hills sloping gently down into the valley. Even from this distance, he could see flocks of fairly large sheep congregating near a fold wall. Eagles circled above, and Pender thought that the shepherds must have trouble with these birds during lambing season.

While he gazed around him, he was approached by some really small men and women who were very interestingly dressed. They all wore black leather calf-length boots, with wide-legged pants tucked into the top of their boots. Their leather jerkins were tight to their bodies which gave the women a very voluptuous look. A very broad leather belt held everything together. Men and women wore their hair in three long pigtails down their backs tied together at the bottom and tucked inside their belts. They gathered around him, looking up at him with expectant faces. Their leader asked him, "Where are the ten women we were told would be here?"

"The ladies were tired and dirty from their long journey, so they decided to enjoy the pleasures of the warm fountain waters."

"Oh, sir, that is not good news. These fountains will leave their skin yellowed, and they will require sleep for two days. Did the mystic not tell you?" He turned to his friends and said, "Quickly, quickly now, folks, take ten cots and put them in the big hall. We will need them immediately. Now, sir, go and rescue the ladies before they all fall asleep."

Pender hurried back along the corridor to where the ladies were putting the finishing touches to their hair. "Quickly, ladies, we have to leave these fountains because they have an iridescent effect on the skin. Then you will all fall asleep for at least two days. The people are now readying cots for your long sleep. Hurry please!"

He led them out into the light where their hosts were waiting to take them to their beds. Becca, of course, was excited when she saw the curious glow from her skin. She said, "I always wanted to be a sunshine girl."

Rahana laughed. "Then I must be a moonlight girl—that is much more romantic." Within a few minutes, they were all in bed fast asleep. When Pender checked on them later in the night, they were still glowing.

Pender was tired with all the happenings of the last few days. The stress was beginning to tell on him. He wondered if Zalenda felt the same. These were his last thoughts as he surrendered to the peace of the valley and sleep.

Pender awoke to the bleating of sheep in a state of utter confusion. He could not fathom why there would be sheep on the island. He made the supreme effort necessary to move, expecting to feel the cold of the winter blast. Instead, it was warm, and he was in a strange room with eleven cots on which there slept ten glowing bodies. Slowly his mind cleared, and he remembered everything! He put on his clothes and stumbled out into brilliant sunlight to see the source of the bleating. It was the sheep he had seen the day before being herded out of one of the stone buildings to go to the hills for the day's grazing.

But it was the sheep herders who caught Pender's attention. Young women who were very petite, with attractive complexions and happy smiling faces, darted around the sheep, keeping them in order. They were laughing and giggling no doubt at his expense. Never before had they seen a man of his height, virile appearance, and handsome features, and when he smiled at them, they pretended to swoon. The happy laughter rang out amid the bleating of the sheep. It came to a swift end, however, at the approach of the headman Pender had met the day before. The young women suddenly focused all their attention on the sheep and began to move them out, but not without taking one or two last peeks over their shoulders at the handsome stranger.

The headman joined Pender as they watched the sheep head toward the hills. "You are wondering why we bring the sheep in every night when we have adequate folds on the hillsides." He looked at Pender questioningly. Pender nodded. "The wild animals, wolves, bears, cougars, and eagles. The biggest problem, though, is not animals, but the raiders."

"Raiders?" Pender exclaimed. "You have raiders in this most idyllic of situations, how? Where do they come from? How do they get here?"

"They are a people who have lived here before the rains made the hill fall into this valley. They are the nomadic Auits. They move from place to place. They never put down permanent roots, and they live by hunting and stealing from other people. This group has been here since the sun ruled the summer skies and had stolen sheep from us twice already. Their men and women raid together. They are a very beautiful fit specimen of a people. They never walk or ride but run fast everywhere they go, whether it is uphill or downhill. This makes it difficult to catch them. The women pick out the sheep, and the men pick them up and run away with them. They are very strong."

"Do you know where these people are living right now?" Pender asked. "I would like to go and visit with them and perhaps work out a trade agreement with them. What would they have that you would trade a few sheep for?"

"I could show you where they are, but I will not go there. I am in fear of them. As you can see, we are very short in stature, and they would not show any respect for me or my people. That is why they just take what they want. They are hunters and have beautiful bearskins. They wear really nice bearskin hats that don't let the rain in. We could trade for these, my people would like that."

"When my team wakes up, we will pay them a visit. We will gain their respect. You know, my name is Pender, but you have not told me your name."

"It is the custom of my people that we must know a person three moons before we exchange names. The day after the young women wake up, I will introduce you to my people. You will find it interesting that we all are named after the four brothers who sired our people, and every name begins with the same sound of *M*. Now you must come and eat. The small people will have many questions to ask you."

Pender followed the man into one of the stone buildings and was immediately the focus of about fifty pairs of eyes. He tried to sit down at one of the stools but found his knees were in the way. One of the men went and brought a stool with very short legs. When he was seen to be comfortable, two ladies came and brought food and a drink to him on a wooden-type platter. His breakfast consisted of long strips of crispy burned meat, and the drink in the flask looked like a very black beer. He was pleasantly surprised the meat was delicious and the beer very satisfying and strong, which made him decide not to drink too much of it.

When he was quite satisfied and finished eating, the interrogation began. He was bombarded with questions mostly from the women who wanted to know whether he had a wife or was spoken for. He told them about Zalenda and how he had met her and where she was at present. Another woman wanted to know if he needed to be comforted at night. They all laughed but listened intently to his reply. Then the questioners wanted to know about his team—Why were they here? What did they do? Who was special to him?

He told him about the slavers and their plans to kill both him and Zalenda and what they had done to Rona and Morag. Then he spoke about what his team had accomplished in the past keeping the family tribes informed and how they had burned down the Slave Island fort and set the prisoners free. It was because of these activities that the slavers had hired bands of killers to pursue them, kill him, and take the young women to be sold to the highest bidder. They were warned by the mystic lady, Carla, to leave their home as soon as the storm was over, and it was because of her powers that they were safely here.

Then the questions became personal—What was it like to be taller than anyone else? What was it like to have to kill your own brother? Why was his sister chief of their tribe and not him? He and his team had killed a lot of people; was it worth it just to save some unfortunate people who could not fight their own battles? He took the time to answer all their questions fully.

At the end, one of the bolder ladies requested that he pick her up and kiss her. Pender picked her up and kissed her on the lips, and she responded with great enthusiasm. He put her down to the cheering of all the assembled group. She became the center of attraction among the ladies.

As he left the breakfast gathering, the men and woman came up to him, measuring themselves against him. They looked up into his face and told him they now understood why the mystic lady had asked them to help them on their way and how much they were looking forward to meeting the team.

The leader of the M People, as he had now labeled them in his mind, suggested if he wanted to go up the hill to find out where the raiders were, now would be the best time to go. The young shepherd ladies would be pleased to guide him to their encampment, but it might be better to view them from a distance.

Pender was keen to take this opportunity, as he would have little to do until the girls woke up. He went to his pack and changed into his leathers because the sheepskins were way overdressed for the weather in this valley.

He took the same path toward the hills as the sheep herders had done with their flocks and soon began to appreciate why the M People were so susceptible to the frequent raids of the sheep stealers. The fields where the sheep grazed were on a very low slope at the point where the hill and the valley intersected. It meant that the flocks and the shepherds would be easily visible from above, and they had built the sheepfold against an abutment for the sake of cover from the weather. All the raiders had to do was to come down the steeper part of the slope in the gray of the morning or evening, grab the sheep, and because of their superior strength and running abilities would be gone before the shepherds could react.

The shepherds saw him coming, and the sheep were forgotten for the time, as they seldom got visitors. The men were curious about this very tall person dressed in leathers. The shepherd girls knew exactly who he was and were interested in the leathers for a very different reason.

One of the girls told the men who the stranger was but did not know why he would be here. Pender soon explained what he wanted to do and that he had permission from the headman to take two of the female shepherds as guides. The girls all volunteered to guide him, so the men very sourly told him to take his pick. He picked two of the very cheeky ones from earlier in the morning.

They were no sooner out of safe hearing distance than the girls asked what his name was and what they should call him. "My name is Pender, and that is what you should call me."

"Our names are Mina and Marta. I am the beautiful one, she is the cheeky one. It is very confusing for strangers because all our names start with the same sound,—she sounded—"mmm," and then smiled with her sparkling smile. Marta pursed her lips and blew a rasp at her friend. They both giggled. Pender could see that he was in for a very interesting afternoon.

It was good to be out in the warm air. The past days had been very unpleasant, but the hill was steep, and he soon began to feel the strain. As the girls led the way up, they made sure that as they leaned into the climb, their very attractive rear ends were adequately displayed. Pender could see he had another Rahana and Becca in the making. He did, however, enjoy their nonstop chatter.

They climbed steadily for some time until the girls called for a rest. They had food packs and were ready to share them with Pender. As they were eating, he asked the two Ms if either of them had seen the sheep stealers. He was about to go on when the sound of a pheasant, disturbed further up the hill, pushed him into action. He quickly pulled the girls into the cover of some ferns and broom bushes. The girls were about to protest when Pender signed to them to be quiet and pointed uphill. Mina took off crawling at an incredible rate through the broom but taking care at the same time not to disclose their position. After a few minutes, she returned with the news that a raid was about to happen; three men and three women were coming down the hill. Pender said, "Good, let's go to meet them." The girls looked at each other and confirmed that they were ready for this new adventure. "I will lead the way, and you two follow right behind me."

It was the sheep stealing women that raised the alarm first. They saw this very tall man rising out of the hill in front of them and turned to run, but their path was blocked by the men hurrying down the hill. They spilled right into the men, knocking them off their feet. This raid was not going according to plan. Pender was on them quickly. He picked up a man by the throat in his left hand and a woman in his right. He told the two girls to come forward and stand on the groins of the men on the ground. The other two women wept in fear, choosing to stay on the ground beside their men.

This was the first time they had been apprehended in the act of stealing sheep, and they were in awe of this big man dressed in leathers and had no idea how to react. Pender roughly threw the woman down on the ground but took the man by the throat. "Now, sir, you are going to tell me why it is you are stealing other people's sheep when you could just as easily trade some of your bearskins for the sheep instead."

The man refused to answer, but the woman lying beside him did. "Our hunters are away following the traveling herds of big deer, and we have no food left, and the children are dying, and it was easier to steal the sheep than watch them die."

"Is this true?" Pender demanded, speaking to the woman he had just thrown on the ground.

"It is, sir. I have lost both my children."

The two Ms came to Pender and said, "We cannot allow babies and children to die because they have no food."

"What do you suggest we should do?" Pender asked, knowing full well what he would do, but he wanted it to be their decision.

Mina replied, "The first thing we are going to do is to give the rest of our food pack to these poor people here to keep their strength up. Then I think we should take this lady here down to our people and let her explain to them why they have been forced to steal our sheep."

Marta chimed in with her beautiful lilting voice. "Yes, and we should try and get them some emergency supplies right away. I will stay here with the other two women, but I suggest you, Mina, take two of the men to carry back the food they will need for today. Then when Pender's team wakes tomorrow, we can arrange a trip up the mountain to these people's tents and care for them properly."

She looked imploringly at Pender. "Can we do this for the children?"

Pender nodded and said, "I think that is a very good solution." As they were talking, Mina was handing out the food from their packs, and the men and women were eating ravenously.

"Oh, please, please, yes, I will gladly trade anything if you can save the children," the woman whom Pender had thrown down said, with tears running down her face.

Pender said, "Then it is decided. We will leave when these folks have finished eating so we can get food to the children before it gets dark."

Marta and one of the men and two women followed them down the hill as far as the sheepfold, while Pender's party went to meet the head of the Ms.

Pender stood back and let Mina speak on behalf of the sheep stealers. The headman listened intently to her plea and looked inquiringly at Pender. "Do you think if we help them, we can forge an agreement to trade instead of them stealing from our flocks?"

"Yes, I do believe this is possible, but right now we are more interested in saving the children, and we would like to take the emergency supplies right now before it gets dark."

"Come now, let us go, and I will speak to the people so that they will be informed of our intentions."

Mina spoke very persuasively to her people, telling them that as they spoke, children were dying; she could not live with that, could they? "What I want from you is permission to go to our emergency stores and take as much food as we can carry to help these starving children and their parents. If Marta and I find a child that requires extra care, we would like to bring it here for even better care. Can you in all good conscience deny us what we are asking?"

The speaker said he was in full agreement with Mina and believed they should immediately answer this grave situation. No more children or people should be allowed to die when they had more than enough food to share.

Mina got the answer she wanted, and without waiting to be dismissed, she and her small band of carriers were on their way, supported by a host of volunteers laden with food, milk, and beer.

Pender carried medicines that the M women brought him to help the suffering and clothes for binding wounds. It was well into the middle of the afternoon when they reached the tent encampment. Marta chose the best of tents to clean it thoroughly and set it up with cots Then the weakest of the children were brought in, and the volunteers washed and bathed each child. She wept when she saw their small, thin emaciated bodies and the worn suffering on their faces. They were too weak to cry, but when the milk teats were put to their lips, they drank eagerly. One little girl could not respond. Mina went and advised Pender about this, and he decided that this little one should go down the hill for emergency treatment; perhaps one of the new mothers could attempt to breast-feed her.

Mina came and reported that all the children had been bathed and fed, and the complete group of adults, fourteen in number, was presently at the table. She had been able to find out that eleven children and twelve adults had died through starvation. She had seen the bodies of some of the adults but could not look at the bodies of the children. Two older ladies probably would not make it through the night; the three women who had been in the raiding party were caring for them. Mina said she had decided to stay with Marta and some of the volunteers to continue nursing the children and the adults who were ill.

Pender gathered the rest of the volunteers, and they took the baby girl with them and went down the hill. It was getting dark as they passed the sheepfold. Pender went with the little girl directly to the headman and explained her condition. Within minutes, his daughter came and took the little one away and reported later that all was well, the little one was feeding, but they would watch her through the night.

The volunteers were so happy at what they had been able to accomplish and were so proud of Mina and Marta and their friends. They told everyone of the great things the food that they had sent had done and the lives they had saved. Pender did not require to say a word.

Before going to bathe before dinner, he went to check on his team and was surprised to see Mari and Zari up and dressed. Besides the glow that seemed to surround them, they seem remarkably well rested. They asked when the next meal was because they were absolutely famished. He asked them about the rest of the girls and was told they were still asleep. Zari said that was because she and Mari had spent less time in the fountains than the others. She joked that Becca would probably not waken till next week because she was first in and last out.

At dinner that night, Mari and Zari were very much the center of attention. They had done each other's hair in the Zalenda style with their beautiful long plaits circle on their heads, making them look taller than they were. Zari, in particular, seemed to bedazzle the young men with her sparkling charm, while Mari as always was her usual sedate self, breathing tranquility into the sometimes raucous conversation. When she spoke, the people stopped to listen as she quietly explained how ordinary people were stolen from their tribes by ruthless men who wanted to profit by selling them as slaves. But it was left to Zari to tell them how Pender had seen a beautiful young woman in a slave pen and how that had changed his life and theirs as they became part of his team dedicated to fighting slavery.

The older women at the table tried to push Pender into explaining why he had chosen only young women for his team. A voice from the doorway said, "He didn't, we chose him," Elecia said. "I never speak because I like to stay in the background, however, I must tell you this—twice this young man saved me from being beaten and sent to be a slave, but I am here of my own volition to serve and to help defeat evil men. The men who joined our team betrayed us. The young women have been faithful in every way to our mission."

The women who had asked the question rose from the table and took Elecia by the hand and brought her into their group. They hugged and kissed her and told her how welcome she was among them. Others rushed to bring her food and drink. She, who only wanted to serve, was being served; she was aware of the irony of the situation.

As the four of them returned to their quarters, Pender was the only one who needed sleep. He was tired with the hill climbing and the stress of dealing with the starving people. As they reflected on the strange things that had happened to them since they met Carla, Pender fell fast asleep. It was the first time he had gone to sleep without thinking about Zalenda. The girls talked late into the night.

Pender woke to the clamor of beds being dragged around, folded, stacked, things clanking together as the water pots were moved, all this with the noisy chatter of female voices. Sleep tried hard to drag him back into its pleasant comfortable confines, but his brain would have none of it; he had to open his eyes to see what Becca was up to. She had already plaited her hair into three plaits down her back, her sheepskin trousers were tucked into her boots, and her jerkin was held in the middle by a wide towel, and as she walked, she aped the gait of the M People. Pender could not fathom how she ever noticed these things given how tired she was when they arrived. Now he had to be cross with her; he could not have her offend their hosts who had been so hospitable to them.

He said to her, "Meca, please change back to Becca, we need her back. We have much to do today without offending our hosts."

"Meca?" she exclaimed, "I never thought about that," as she continued her exaggerated playacting toward the door. Rahana and Rona grabbed her and proceeded to change her clothes right there without consideration of her privacy. Becca puffed up her cheeks, pretending to be angry, and they all collapsed in laughter. Unfortunately, for Pender, the only bed left for them to collapse on was his, so they all piled on top of him. Becca, in her unclothed state, said, "I must be the cherry on top," so she climbed to the top of the pile.

It was some time before order was restored and the laughter abated. Pender asked them to hurry and get their belongings packed and their temporary quarters brushed out and cleaned so they were ready to leave for the next part of the journey.

When they went for breakfast, the headman introduced himself as Merca and was about to guide them to a separate table when the girls asked if it would be all right if they sat with the people. Merca was astonished at the request but was delighted to comply. Some of the girls went and sat at the empty table and were soon joined with eager people from the community. The rest of the team joined the much larger group and were soon engaged in conversation, Pender was intent on spending time with Merca to find out as much as possible about the way ahead.

The team formed up ready to leave, which took longer than Pender anticipated, because now they had all made friends that they wanted to say good-bye to. As they were involved in this, a small group of ladies came forward and said, "We heard you must go through the Valley of the Flies, so we made these for you. Each one of you should wear these masks, and as you walk, you must hold on to this rope. We have tied a ribbon every ten paces so you will not stumble. The mask for Pender is the only one with eye holes. You must trust him completely and follow his lead." Rahana thanked the ladies for their thoughtfulness and assured them that they had learned from past experience to trust Pender implicitly with their lives and he had never let them down.

The M People volunteers left with the team to carry more food up the hill to relieve those who had waited overnight caring for the sick. When they came to the tents, Mina and Marta came out to greet them, and the girls bonded right away. Mina said they would have loved to join them on their next adventure, but for now, they were committed to caring for the children. Should they come back this way, they would be interested in helping them in their mission against the slavers. Rahana thanked them for everything they had done and assured them they would be welcomed on the team.

Pender had been talking to the men whom he had helped the day before. From them he discovered that they and the men and women who were away hunting were all that was left of what once was a very large tribe called the Auits. A plague several years ago had wiped out more than half of the tribe, and what was very serious about it, most of the women of child-bearing age had died. Stronger tribes took over their ancestral home and lands, and they were forced to become nomadic. This latest tragedy would have finished them had he and the two young women not spoken on their behalf to Merca and brought them food, and for this, they would always be grateful.

He told Pender that it would be better for them to wait here for lunch because on their way to the Valley of the Flies, there was no water available. It would be better for them to fill up their water supply before they left then stop at the far end of the valley for the night at the place where the rocks turned red. In the morning, they should start the walk through the valley. As well as wearing their masks, they should put bread in their ears, and they should make sure that everything was tied tightly to their bodies. Even the flapping of a piece of clothing could start the flies swarming, and they did not want to live through that. "Make sure the rope is kept taut, and everyone must walk at the same pace. Practice it before you enter the valley."

Pender gathered his team together after lunch, and they practiced walking with the rope. When he was satisfied with their performance, he introduced the masks. It was decided that it would be better for them to arrange the walkers according to height. This meant that Becca and Rahana would be last in the line; however, Elecia volunteered to take the last position, and she would adjust her step accordingly. By nightfall they were at the place where the rocks turned red. Pender was glad he had been informed to fill up with water before they left because this part of the valley was like a desert. They put up their tents for the night, and Pender wished he had Tarag to be on night watch. He missed the dog; he had been such a faithful friend, and he blamed himself for his death. Zalenda had helped him bury Tarag. That had been a sad time, and he was glad she was there to share his sorrow; he could not have shared it with anyone else. Now he missed them both. He was so tired, and it would have been so nice to have them with him right now to go to sleep with Zalenda beside him, Toto at the top, and Tarag at their feet. Now that would never happen again.

Elecia wakened him in the morning with a flask of hot bark tea in a strange mixture of black beer, which quickly brought him back to consciousness. She told him they needed him up and dressed because breakfast was being served. Pender emerged from his tent to the mock applause of the team, while Elecia served him breakfast. They regaled him with imaginative tales of their great prowess as a team. As usual, they always finished with Becca telling some monstrous story of her delivering the boss because of her ability to charm all his enemies. Rahana playacted the end, bowing low in front of Bec and kissing her feet. The team loved these two playing the fools and laughed till they were sore. Pender hoped they would be as cheerful after their journey through the Valley of the Flies.

They finished breakfast, and Elecia cleaned up and packed the food while the rest of the team struck camp and made ready for the last practice walking with the masks on. The practice went very well, and it was arranged that Elecia would signal when she was safely in the cave past the second standing stone by pulling on the rope. They were to stand there for a few seconds until they adjusted to their new surroundings.

It was time now to go. Pender told them this was not going to be easy. They must be calm and trust each other and concentrate on taking one step at a time in time so that no one would have cause to stumble.

Chapter 34

The Valley of the Flies

Pender lined them up. They all took the rope, holding it with their left hand, and put their masks on and remembered to put the bread in their ears. Then they were off into the Valley of the Flies. Pender guided them toward the first standing stone and then looked and set his eyes on the second one across the valley.

As well trained as the team was, nothing could have prepared them for what followed; even with their ears plugged, the noise was incredible. Great swarms of flies, millions and millions of them, large and small, filled the air with buzzing and whirling of wings. Each species fought for air supremacy in an attempt to take over command of the airspace. The larger flies had already established their land claims on the small scraps of decaying flesh left on the rocks. When they felt their territory was in danger of being invaded, they rose to meet the challenge, their angry buzzing creating more and more noise. The bare volcanic mountain walls echoed the resulting sound and magnified it by a thousand times a thousand.

The smell of decaying putrid flesh assailed the senses of the walkers. They were even more grateful to the M women for providing them with the masks, for they helped filter out some of the stench. What they could not see with their eyes, they saw through their imaginations, which conjured up pictures of the destruction and decomposition of death. It was their nostrils that inhaled the rot of putrefying human corpses left in the open, which was the most offensive to their senses.

But as sickened as they were with the smell, all they could do was to keep walking forward, taking the same carefully measured steps, holding the line and taking care not to stumble.

Pender could see forward and reckoned they had walked about halfway to the second stone when disaster almost overtook them. The first thing they were conscious of was a change in the air around them as thousands of beating wings caused new currents of air to whirl above them. Flocks of large birds came to feed on the flies, crows, ravens, rooks, starlings, and countless other species, adding their raucous cries and high-pitched screeching, creating a crescendo of sound that was ear shattering.

Nena felt nauseated and wanted to vomit. Her stomach heaved, and she knew she was in danger of fainting. Everything in her wanted this to end. She felt like ripping the mask of her face and running for her life. The unending noise and the horrible stench were closing in on her conscious mind. To run or not to run?—that was the question that played over and over with each step she took. Then she thought of her friends and the terrifying torture they would experience if they were attacked by the swarming flies. She calmed herself and tried to breathe deeper into the rhythm of the walk and held on to the rope as if it were a lifeline from this sea of sound and scent of corruption.

Pender kept his eye on the goal and controlled the urge to increase the pace when a large bird flew into his face. He flinched but did not stumble. The bird turned on the wing, curious about his reaction, and lined up to fly into his masked face again. From the corner of his eye, Pender could see the bird maneuver but knew he dare not attempt to defend himself. He steeled himself for the attack; it never came. As the bird was about to launch itself at him, at that exact moment, someone decided to throw a human corpse off the mountain wall. Birds, bees, and flies became a tornado of mouths and beaks determined to join in the feeding frenzy. Pender's attacker saw and heard the commotion and decided to seek his prey elsewhere and quickly overflew Pender to get its share. At the front of the line, Pender could see the standing stone with its mysterious markings and was filled with renewed energy. Not so at the back of the line, where Becca was tiring rapidly. She was not yet fully recovered from her bronchial problems, and her breathing was labored and her steps unsteady. Rahana could tell by the tension on the rope that her friend was in trouble. She increased each of her steps by a few inches while keeping the same tension on the rope. After about thirty paces, she was right behind Becca. She picked her up with her free arm and carried her the rest of the way. Elecia knew there was something wrong, and she did the same as Rahana had done until she was at the position behind Rahana. She whispered to Rahana that she would help with Becca if it was required.

Pender passed the standing stone into the coolness of a cave. He had to keep walking till everyone was inside. When Elecia felt the cold of the cave, she immediately signaled by pulling on the rope. It had been arranged they were to stop and wait for a short time until their eyes adjusted to the darkness inside before leaving the rope. Elecia did not obey this instruction but instead went to help Rahana with Becca. She pulled out her sheepskin from her pack and put it over Becca where she lay. She had kept a little bit of water for such emergencies. She offered it to Becca, who drank it thankfully.

Nena's nausea was reduced by the cool air that circulated through the cave and getting rid of the mask. Zari and Ester attended to her, walking her around till she regained her strength, and dressed her in winter clothes. Becca also was recovering from her ordeal. The cool air helped her breathing, and the strength was returning to her legs. Rona, Morag, and Pipa were busy putting up a tent for the temporary treatment of their friends so they could rest. This was no easy task because everything had to be held together with ties and boulders they found in the cave. There was no wood or other materials to make a fire, and candles were their only way of producing light, but they soon had it quite comfortable because their packs proved invaluable as seats.

The conversation was all about the walk through the Valley of the Flies and the horrors of the sound and the smell. Pender told them how proud he was of them; their courage, tenacity, and training had brought them through a very difficult trial. He said they should take the time to rest and recover, as they had some more walking to do through the tunnels of this cave.

They walked for most of the afternoon going from one labyrinth of caves and tunnels into another. Pender began to wonder if his information was correct, but he persisted. It soon paid off: one cave tunnel they entered was lit by luminous rock that formed the ceiling. The walls were an ancient art gallery with lined pictures of people from long ago, beautifully etched into the rock. The girls slowed down to admire each scene until they came to one that depicted the Valley of the Flies. They saw portrayed on the wall what they had just experienced. Now they could see the corpses with sightless eyes staring at them from down through the annals of time. One single fly represented the millions of the swarming pests, and one single crow the flocks of its gluttonous carrion feasters. Although they felt nauseated as they relived the sounds and smell of the valley, they were strangely held by the power of its representation.

Pender broke the spell of the picture by calling them to see a new wonder. In the passageway, a latter-day artist was at work. His depiction was of a village of circular structures with cone-shaped roofs and small human forms in the front and face upon face behind. His work was painstakingly difficult, as each line was first scored into the rock then carefully picked out to form a V-shaped channel. Circles and arcs were particularly hard to scribe, but his calm, persistent demeanor was a testimony to the dedication he had for his work.

The team stood in awe of the man, but he was quite oblivious to their presence and continued to work absorbed by his subject. When he stepped back to check his work, he almost fainted with shock when he realized he was the subject of so many eyes. Pender helped him to recover from the fright, holding his hand and telling him who they were and why they were there.

Pender introduced the girls, and they were all intrigued by his placid nature. He told them his name was Eram, and he was chosen by the Mystic People to leave their history on the wall of the caves. He was expecting them, and they should follow him to a place where they could get out into the light and enjoy the sunshine.

They followed him through a maze of intersecting tunnels and caves to emerge into a beautiful green level field surrounded on all sides by hills and mountains. Birds rose from this pleasant meadow to fill the air with their songs, which was diametrically opposite to the last valley they had been in. The air was fresh, light, and perfumed, and the girls ran around enjoying the freedom of the space. Eram led them to his daytime home, a wall-less tent where a fire was burning and a pot was simmering. He showed them where a cool spring of water lapped constantly, and the girls lay down on the grass and drank then rolled over and laughed and giggled as Becca attempted to drink from the fountain, but every time she positioned her mouth, the water sprang up somewhere else and soaked her.

They enjoyed the stew Eram had made and shared the oat bread they had been given by the M People with him. Elecia was busy serving the girls, and Eram asked if she was the group's slave. She told him that as it was his delight to etch on the walls, it was her delight to serve her family. He was baffled by that answer. So she went on to explain how she had been beaten by people from her own tribe and on her way to the slave market, when she was rescued twice and made part of this family. She loved every one of these girls as if they were her daughters and Pender as her son. "It is now my source of joy and happiness to serve and care for them, and every day I am thankful for this opportunity to show them how much I love them."

Eram said, "You are a most remarkable woman, Elecia."

"No, Eram," she replied, "just a very happy one."

As they sat resting in this nirvana of quietude, it was easy to imagine that the happenings of the last weeks were nothing but bad dreams.

Eram wanted to have a private conversation with Pender, so he invited him to walk out to the edge of the field, where he showed him a large valley that was covered with ice and snow. "This field here is protected by the mountains and heated from underground streams and rivers year round—that is why I love working here every day of my life. Down there, things are different. For many years, we, the Mystic People, have enjoyed an idyllic lifestyle, protected on all sides by high mountains. This has allowed us to develop our own laws for living and the sense of respect we show to one another and for the very few strangers we meet. It is for these characteristics, I believe, that strangers call us mystic. While it is true that we have developed many potions and treatments for disease, infections, and wounds, and converse in ways others find strange, we are at best ordinary people. That is why we are perturbed when evil men seek us out to serve them.

"Recently, a man came among us from the sea, looking for information about a man named Pender and a group of young women. Carla had informed us you were coming and that we should welcome you and keep you safe. She guided you through the Water Gate, the caves and tunnels, the Valley of the Flies, and through my labyrinth to this beautiful place. The man of the sea came through there." He pointed to the only exit from the valley, an opening in the mountains where a river ran out to the sea. "It would have taken him at least five days to get here. Someone had given him information that this is where you would be found. He searched all our villages asking questions that our people chose not to answer, and as he could see he was not welcome, he left, but waits for you a day's walk from our gates."

Pender said, "I would like to see this person and perhaps bring him here for interrogation to find out who gave him this information. Would that be possible?"

"While I am a nonviolent person and would choose not to be here when you catch him and bring him here, I will support you in this endeavor. You will need a small team, so the rest of the girls can stay here with me. I will bring more supplies up from the nearest village to the bottom of the hill tunnel, and the girls can help me bring them up. I have seen your tents—they will be ideal up here. The girls can start erecting them now."

Pender got the team together and told them what he had learned from Eram. He said he and Rahana would require two volunteers to take this person down and bring him here. The girls suggested Pipa and Rona, as they were the best in Zalenda's classes at combat training, These two were excited to have been chosen and said they were ready for action. Becca knew she was not mission ready, so she decided she would supervise where the tents should be placed, and Elecia and Nena would coordinate supplies with Eram.

It was very early in the morning when Eram led the team out of their camp back into the caves, and as before, they went from cave to cave, but this time on a downward slope. The light was poor, and it made the descent difficult and dangerous; even Eram, master of the caves, had considerable difficulty.

Then they came to the longest staircase they had ever seen. The risers were shallow, and the treads very wide, so it was not as tiring as it might have been, but it was a long way down. Finally, they came out into a bottom cave that was very dark and then into a tunnel where light came in from the side. Eram ordered them to stop and rest and put on their winter coats and pants; it was going to be cold outside. They walked for some time in the bitter biting wind, looking around as they went at the strange-shaped buildings they had seen before pictured on the cave walls. The place seemed uninhabited. Where were the people who lived here? That question was soon to be answered.

He led them to what appeared to be a gathering place for the people. A number of fireplaces heated the circular building, and the smoke went straight up to chimneys, which kept the atmosphere inside free from its contamination. They were taken to an anteroom, where they removed their outside clothes, but before they sat down for breakfast, they were welcomed to the table by a family of smiling-faced people.

The people had expected to see all of the team for breakfast and looked wonderingly at Eram, who said the rest of the team would stay in the caves for the next two days. He introduced the team and made sure they were comfortable before going to the food storage to order food for the next days for the rest of the team.

Everyone at the table wanted to talk to the girls, especially Rahana, as she was short like them with the most beautiful hair, and her darker skin enthralled them. Pipa and Rona attracted the young men who admired them from a distance for their confident personalities displayed in the way they talked and conducted themselves. The fact that they were both beautiful with long flowing tresses—they had combed out their plaits—and fair complexions that accentuated their blue eyes captivated their male hosts.

The ladies unashamedly stared at Pender. They had never seen anyone as tall and handsome yet so comfortable in his own being. He made a point of going around the tables and talking to all of them. They whispered to each other that Carla was right; this young man was special.

Pender and the girls went to their sleeping quarters that had been prepared for the whole team. They lay on their beds fully clothed with their outer wear ready for the night. The plan was when it was dark, they would leave and follow the path out through the village gates onto the sea road. They hoped to locate their target in the dark and the cold of night by his need to have a fire. Eram had informed them that they were likely to find him in an old ruined shepherd's cottage that was built into the ridge rock, located near the junction of two paths. Since these were the only paths in the area, they should have no difficulty finding it; however, they should be aware that as the cottage was built into the rock, there was only one entrance through the front, and that is where the fire was likely to be.

They waited until they were sure everyone was asleep before they moved out into a freezing cold wind. This was going to be a long torturous walk. Rahana had conceived a second use for the masks the M People had given them. She had sown sheepskin onto them so that they made excellent face coverings against the piercing biting winds. Pender led the way, adjusting his normal stride so that Rahana could hold on to his belt. Rona and Pipa walked behind, keeping frequent checks on the back and the sides, looking for possible signs of light from a fire.

They stopped often for group hugs to try and keep warm; although this was not as successful as they would have liked, it made them feel they were all in this together. They passed the crossings of the paths, and sure enough as Eram had thought, they could see the rock ridge, and to their left, what was left of a smoldering fire, which gave off just enough light to be seen from this distance.

Pender's plan was quite simple: they would try to catch the spy asleep, tie him up before he wakened, rekindle the fire until they were warm enough for the return journey, and then go directly to the caves with the prisoner. In the off chance that the spy was awake or someone was on watch, Rona would walk off to the left about twenty paces from the door, Rahana would do the same from the right, and Pender with Pipa would approach from the front twenty paces. At that point, Pender would make one clap with his frozen hands, and they would move in.

At the sound of the clap, a man wrestled himself to his feet. He had been on watch from the doorway, so Pender's instincts were correct—there might be two spies sent after him. The man spoke in a belligerent voice. "Who are you, and what do you want?"

Pender replied quietly and coldly. "I am Pender, the man you have been sent to kill—that is why I have come to kill you."

The man charged at Pender, determined to catch him before he could turn and run. Pender allowed him to come to him. The frozen air quickly had the man gasping in an attempt to breathe. He stopped short of Pender, hung his head downward breathing hard, then charged again. Pipa was behind Pender where the man could not see her. Zalenda would have been proud of the perfect kick she aimed at the man's left knee just at the right time. He went down gasping and groaning, but he was intent on taking Pender as his prize. Even on the ground he was brandishing a large club, swinging it around, trying to ignore the pain in his shattered leg.

Pender stood over him, hoping to take him alive as the swinging club came perilously close. Pipa timed her next kick to connect after one of the man's futile swings; his head went back. He was now completely defenseless, but he took one more swing. The next kick hit him in the throat. A snapping noise was indicative of a broken neck; he lay back and died in the snow.

A shout from Rahana attracted their attention, "Look who we have here." Pender looked up. He was shocked to see a very well trussed-up figure between Rona and Rahana; it was Cymon!

Pender went and picked up all the firewood he could find to rekindle the fire. Soon it was blazing, and the girls began thawing out a little. They had to rest because they knew the effort that it would take going back. This time, however, the wind would be at their back.

Cymon sat sulking and feeling sorry for himself. He had no delusions about what would happen to him. After all, he had betrayed their trust. Pender left him as long as possible, ignoring him completely, but knew he had to find out sooner or later whether there were more spies sent by Tamor.

When the fire was at its brightest, Rahana went and stood behind Cymon, brandishing in her hands the big club. He saw her from the corner of his eye and tensed up. Pender had arranged with Rahana the next move. He went and stood in front of Cymon, looking directly into his eyes then at Rahana, and nodded. Cymon expected to be hit on the head and drew his shoulders up and head down in anticipation of the blow, but it did not come. Instead he talked over his shoulders to Rona and Pipa, saying, "Bring the ropes. We may have to burn his hands in the fire if he will not tell me what I want to know."

Cymon spoke for the first time, blurting out in fear, "Please do not do that. I will tell you everything."

"OK Cymon, that is good. The first thing is really easy. We need five drinking flasks. I want to make some bark tea to heat our insides so that we will be comfortable for the return journey."

"You will find them inside on a shelf. I cleaned them myself, but there are only three." The moment he said it, he knew he had been tricked.

"That is very good, Cymon. See how easy this is? You really don't require to be burned. Now tell me, where is the other spy Tamor sent, or were the three of you supposed to assassinate me and the young women? The truth please, the fire after all is very hot right now." Pender moved a little to his right so that Cymon could see the fire.

"You will find his body in the snow, over there at the ridge." Cymon nodded in the direction. "These two had a fight. Last night they got drunk, and he"—indicating the dead man lying over by the door—"spilled out Tamor's whole plan. I was sent ahead last week on information received from one of the elders from your sister Cisi's council. You apparently had his friend poisoned. The information was that your whole group left accompanied by the mystic woman. She is currently a prisoner of Tamor. He has a broken leg that will not heal. I am told it is a festering mess. She will not treat it nor give them the potions to clear up the infection until she is guaranteed a safe passage home to her people. These two were the next in command to Tamor. They couldn't care less about you or your team. All they wanted was to wait until Tamor's leg kills him so they could take over the business. The fight started last night after they tied me up. The winner would get Zalenda, and the loser would have Carla, the mystic woman. They were so drunk, they could hardly stand up. There will be others in Tamor's troop who will replace them, but right now they will be in disarray as they fight for position. I was sent because I was the only one who could identify you and your team."

Rahana went over to the ridge and found the body where Cymon had indicated it would be. She examined the body and found a lot of blood and bruising around the head, which might be consistent with being hit by a club.

"It appears as if our onetime friend is telling the truth. I think we can cut the ropes from his hands and feet. He won't be wanting to go back to report to Tamor anytime soon."

Pender used his knife to cut Cymon free and invited him nearer the fire, where Rona handed him a flask of hot tea made fresh from a pot still on the fire.

Cymon said they should feed the horses before they started back to the home of the Mystic People. "We have horses for the return trip?" Rona asked with great excitement in her voice. "That is great news, but where are they? I didn't see any in the building."

"We brought three riding horses and two pack horses with us. They are on the other side of the ridge in a hide. I don't believe the two goons have fed them today. The oats are in the hide."

Rona and Rahana got up to investigate Cymon's claim. This would be good, for their tired bodies if this were true. Pender warned them to be careful. He was not about to allow Cymon to divide the team or trust him in anything he might say. Pipa moved over and stood behind him, ready to strike if necessary, and Pender picked up the club. While he was doing this, he made sure that Cymon was aware of their precautions.

Rahana came back to report that there were indeed horses there, and Rona was at present feeding them. They were well equipped with leather and sheepskin saddles and excellent horse covers for this bad weather; the pack horses had covers but no saddles.

Pipa went to assist Rona to get the horses prepared and ready for the ride back. They soon had picked the ones they were going to ride. They returned to the fire, delighted at the prospect of riding rather than walking in the snow.

Pender said they should drink up the last of the good tea and then get on their way. The fire was allowed to burn out while they cleaned up the site and moved the bodies onto the ridge, where the wild animals would feast on them. The girls led the horses out while Cymon slung the remaining supplies onto the pack horses. Pender checked to see they had not left any clues of their having been there, when he heard a mewing from the corner of the hide. When he went to investigate, he found a newborn wolf cub ready to suck on his fingers. He just could not leave it to die of starvation, so he put it inside his jerkin, where it curled up in the warmth and went to sleep.

Pipa and Rona were already mounted, but Rahana liked Pender to lift her up into the saddle. She quipped this would be the first time she would be pleased to have a sore bum when she got home. Cymon and Pender had to ride the pack horses, but that was judged to be better than walking.

The sun was beginning to rise when they reached their destination. They were surprised to see their hosts up ready to care for the horses and the wolf cub, while they stumbled to their beds and fell fast asleep.

Chapter 35

Zalenda's Search for Pender

Zalenda wakened with a start. She had been dreaming; it was a dream she had not had in some time. In her dream, Pender was with her in her bed, and she had reached out to touch him, and he wasn't there. She cried out in bitter disappointment; she was sobbing and wet with tears when Gena came in from the next room. Gena looked at her inquiringly and said, "Pender?" Zalenda nodded.

Gena went and held her while she wept uncontrollably, saying over and over, "Oh, Pender, where are you? Where are you? I need you, I need you." Gena stayed with her while Zalenda told how foolish she had been in telling Rahana and Becca that she knew they loved Pender and they should be his wives and have babies with him.

"You said what?"

Zalenda nodded. "When we parted, I went and kissed him, I was resigned in my mind that I would never see him again. After all, what virile, handsome, young, desirable man could be expected to chain himself to me for at least two years and remain true and celibate, especially when he can take his pick from anyone of ten beautiful women?"

"The only man I know who would not do a thing like that is a man called Pender, and he does it because he loves you, and if you had any sense at all, you would leave us here to carry on and take some leave and go and find him. In the last year, we have changed the whole fabric of the tribe. We are better governed than we have ever been. Our defense has become better trained and armed, and the people are happy. The council can manage without you for a little while—that is what you have trained us for. Get on your horse and go and find Pender so you can be happy in your love, like I am."

"Do you think I should call a meeting of the inner council and announce that I am taking a break to go and visit the man whose wife I want to be? Would they think I was being selfish?"

"How could they possibly think that! You have given up the position of being queen of the Warrior Women, the supreme ruler of the tribe, so that we could become the self-governed People of the Plains. In the process, you have made every man and woman equal and made us a self-sustaining people that no enemies would want to tangle with. To accomplish this, you have put your own life on hold, sacrificing your love in our service. You are the least selfish person they will ever know. If they don't know this already you can be sure I will tell them at the meeting tomorrow."

The next morning, the inner council met, and Zalenda made her announcement then went to prepare for her search to find Pender.

The famous four were there to see her leave after breakfast the next day, Davi, Tomi, Gena, and Lacey along with the people of the full council and many of her personal friends. She mounted her white stallion and rode off in the nice air of spring time, Toto in her now familiar place in front of her mistress.

Zalenda rode back along the north side of the river, retracing her journey of two years before, keeping clear of any wooded areas so she could see and be seen. It felt good again to be free from all the burdens of living only for other people and solving their problems Now for the immediate future, she was on her own with only one problem to solve, and that is, where is Pender? She made frequent stops to check her surroundings and to feed White Flame, her stallion. Toto took off whenever she was released to chase rabbits; she had been cooped up in court too long, and she relished the freedom to run.

By evening she was in the same hollow she had used before, just north of the river. She circled it twice before deciding to camp there for the night. She thought it strange that she had traveled all day without seeing anyone, so she was cautious in everything she did. She let the fire go down and made a figure out of her spare clothes near it then moved further into the hollow into a more defendable position. She tethered White Flame near her and put Toto on guard, only then did she settle down for the night.

In the morning when she awoke, she found everything as she had laid it out the night before. Nothing had been moved, and there was no sign of any human movement.

She had a quick breakfast and dressed for the day in her leathers, the same type she wore when she first met Pender. She put on the leather hat that Castor had given her and mounted her beloved stallion and rode toward the junction of the rivers. She was determined to ride all day until she reached the settlement, where she expected to find out from Cisi where Pender might be found. A spring rainstorm late in the afternoon foiled her plans, and she had to stop and shelter from the sleet and rain. By the time the storm abated, she knew she would have to spend another night in the open. This time she chose a spot near where she had said good-bye to Pender. She took the same precautions as she did the night before and went to sleep and dreamed again of Pender at the slave compound when he had stolen her heart forever.

She awoke when the dark of the night was slowly giving way to the light of day. The silence of the night was broken by the morning songs of the birds. She heard it all but could not understand why her unconscious mind fought with her conscious to drag her back into her dreams. Then Toto came and licked her face, and the world of her beautiful sleep of dreams was gone forever. She checked her site thoroughly before kindling the fire and making herself hot cider and honey. She baked her oats on a slate like Elecia had taught her and settled down to the comfort of her hot food.

Toto came back from her hunt quicker than she normally did. Zalenda recovered quickly from her reverie of thoughts; the birds had stopped singing. She moved quickly to put the waning fire out and dressed in a hurry. White Flame snickered as he waited for her to mount, and Toto's hair rose along her back; all signs she read correctly. She carefully moved on foot to where she could get a view of the river junction. A column of men was in the process of coming up out of the next valley where they must have spent the night. They were heading north away from her. It took all her considerable self-control to remain in cover where she was and not to ride away south. The sound that such movement would have made could have tipped them off, and if they were Tamor's men, they would recognize White Flame. She waited till they were lost on the horizon before she slipped away into the morning sunlight.

Zalenda knew to time her arrival at the settlement in the midafternoon, long after the people had eaten their midday meal. She wanted to get there as unobtrusively as possible, so she rode around to where the island animals were kept. When she stabled White Flame, she noticed there were only four horses in the stable. That was a bad omen; it meant Pender was still away from home.

She went in search of Cisi and was told Cisi used the Island as her home and was there at present with some men who said they were from Tamor. Zalenda decided she would go there right away to see if she could help Cisi. The young men who pulled her across told her they had been there all morning waiting to see Cisi.

Zalenda entered from the back and quickly and quietly went and stood in the upper hallway overlooking the great hall where she could see and hear everything.

Cisi was speaking. "How dare you come here and dictate to me and my council what we should do or what we should think. We have heard that Tamor is dying from the infection brought about because you withhold treatment from him. We know the terms of her treatment that Tamor has agreed to, but you scum who want to replace him will not allow it to happen. So do not come here pretending to represent him because you do not. You are here to represent your own interests."

"I can assure you, missy, that you will comply with all of our requests. You do not have your brother or his little band of virgins to protect you and your tribe now. We have sent a whole army after him. This time we will find him and kill him and take his precious band of young women for our own." The four men produced big wooden clubs and waved them in Cisi's face, saying, "Now who will be first?"

"Perhaps you should start with me," Zalenda said in an icy voice, walking slowly across the hall floor. The four were startled, as were everyone else in the room.

"You," one of the men said and charged her with his club, lashing the air around him but hitting nothing. Zalenda stepped to the side, and the man's charge led him past her. She kicked him in the side of the knee with such power that he went down in a pile. She picked up the club and smashed his head, and he was dead.

The three turned in horror. Zalenda said again, "Start with me, gentlemen. I heard you threaten my sister and these dear people here. Now there are three of you and one of me. Do you feel lucky?"

The men dropped their clubs in dismay. They backed away looking for an escape route, but there was none. Zalenda said, "Now tell my sister here who really sent you and what did you hope to achieve." She picked up a second club and did some conjuring tricks with them, keeping her eyes all the time on the three men.

The men broke down completely. They were not trained soldiers, just people who worked in the slave business selling slaves. They were sent by people who were fighting to take over the business and who did not want Tamor to live but did not have the guts to kill him, so they would not allow the mystic woman to treat him, but because she is so talented and beautiful, they want to keep her and sell her.

The men in the council led away the three to prison. Cisi rushed to Zalenda, crushing her, saying, "You were magnificent. How, why, when did you get here?"

"I came to find Pender. I cannot live any longer without him. I have just been existing. My people in the last two years have become very independent and well able to look after their own interests, so I have left them to be with the person I love. I will not be easily separated from him again. Do you know where I can find him?"

Cisi said, "Zalenda, my dearest sister, first of all, I cannot thank you enough for coming just in time to save me and my council from that awful man. You killed the killer when we were at his mercy. One of my councilors very foolishly allowed him into our meeting, but for you, who knows what might have happened? But listen to me, going on when you need to be looked after right away. We will go to the hot springs first to bathe away the stress of your days in the saddle. Then we will have a meal brought to my bedroom. You must sleep with me tonight so we can talk. You heard what that man was talking about? I will tell you what I know."

Cisi had her own maids to help her. It was obvious that they were more friends than servants because after they had bathed her, she did the same for them. Zalenda's maid was very young and shy, and it took her some time to pluck up the courage just to touch Zalenda's beautiful naked body, never mind sponging it all over. She was so short, Zalenda had to go down on her knees; she did not mind a bit because she could luxuriate in the heat of the springs. This was what she had longed for during her long ride.

Cisi came and rubbed her with a nice creamy lotion and plaited her long blonde hair and set it in her usual style; she, as a queen, had always been well treated but never with such love. They retired to eat in Cisi's room and then lay on Cisi's big bed, where she was plied with questions about her last years in what was now called the People of the Plains.

Then Zalenda told her about the last time she had seen Pender. At that time, she had been sure she would not see him again and how unreasonable it was of her to expect him to wait two years for her. "To make matters worse, I told Rahana and Becca that I knew they loved him and that they should be his wives and have babies with him. It has always troubled me that I have kept it secret from him that I might never be able to have children because of the potions we were made to take to stop our monthly fluxes when we trained to be women warriors."

Cisi was dumbfounded. "Zalenda! You who are so smart, with so many talents a woman of action, fearless in combat, a young woman who has transformed and archaic regime and made it workable for the people, yet you are so terrible at relationships.

"I was certain the last time you and Pender were apart that he would find someone else to love, but through it all he loved only you. I don't think you have any comprehension of what it cost him to ride away from you, to protect his team from the assassins Tamor sent to kill you both, in fact to kill the whole team. That was a choice you both had to make, and you did it for the greater good, not because you did not love each other. The shy young awkward man who declared his eternal love for you is still inside the grown man. At the time when he made that conscious choice for you, the circumstances made that love seem impossible. Then you met his father, and you told him you loved his son whom you had never met. Just consider what you have done together—it is a marvel that people still talk about. He loves you, you love him. That is not the end of the story, There are many more chapters to be written." She pulled Zalenda to her and cradled her in her arms, like Brid had done to her when the world disappointed her as a child. Now she was the tower of strength to her friend who was traumatized by the torture of her own mind.

Early in the day, Cisi had to go over to the settlement to verify the statements of visitors who had claimed they had information that Carla was in danger. When she had dismissed the council yesterday, she had sent two of her most trusted people to find out where Carla was being kept. She had to wait some time before the news came in that Carla was currently being held on Slave Island but was likely to be transferred to a stronghold of the new slavers' faction. She knew she had to do something immediately to get Carla out and have her treat Tamor to frustrate this new group, but she did not have the resources. It was with a heavy heart that she returned to the island.

Zalenda had slept long and had just finished breakfast when Cisi arrived to break the news of Carla's predicament. She listened to Cisi's assessment of the situation, and to her amazement, the lost child of last night was gone. That person was now replaced by an insightful woman of action who quickly concocted a plan to rescue Carla. Zalenda was determined to go on her own in disguise. First of all, she would visit the Tree People and take time to study the situation before moving to infiltrate their system. While the infighting among the slavers was to their advantage, in the short term, it would be better for everyone if Tamor retained control even with his erratic behavior. She would rescue Carla and in the process destroy the reputation of her captors and allow her to treat Tamor. Once that was completed, she would take Carla to Abbi's hide up on the hill, where she and Pender had caught and killed Kain. They would need supplies kept there so that she could go and find Pender.

Cisi listened and marveled at Zalenda's perception and plan. The only objection she had was that she felt it was all too much for one person. Zalenda countered, saying if she failed, Carla would be no worse off than she was now, and no blame could be traced back to Cisi.

The first thing she needed was another horse because White Flame would identify her to her enemies. Then she needed a whole set of men's clothes and if possible a false beard and a hood that would completely cover her hair. She would also need something to darken her complexion and two male companions to ride with her to the Treetop People's fort. They would stay overnight and return the next day.

Cisi said she and her cousin would dress as men and go with her because she did not trust her elders with any matters involving the slave traders. They should ride out as women and change on the way. Their cover story would be they were going to visit her mother's relations for a couple of days. They would leave tomorrow evening when the pullers at the crossing went off duty; they would need that time to prepare. She would go back to the settlement now and set things in motion and to alert her cousin of the coming mission.

Zalenda had to accept Cisi's proposal, for it made good sense, and she would be more comfortable taking Cisi to the tree fort rather than divulging the secrets of its access to men Cisi could not trust. She spent all afternoon training her body and mind for what lay ahead, kicking and punching the air till she felt her body was tuned to perfection. She practiced swinging clubs at hanging targets from every conceivable position while dodging weights hanging from the ceiling. She went over every possible contingency in her mind-setting goals. This mission must not fail. If she was to find Pender, she must have the best information of the fort's defenses to find away in to free Carla. If she freed Carla, she had to get Tamor treated and back in charge then bring Carla back home. If she could get Carla home, she would find out where Pender could be found. But it must all be done without causing any suspicion that Cisi was involved or that the Tree People were still watching the daily happenings at Slave Island.

Cisi came back from the settlement the next morning with Tina, her cousin, a very pretty lively girl the same age as Ester. They had great fun modeling themselves in men's clothes, especially playing around with the false beards and the stuffed waistcoats. Zalenda's pants had to be taken in at the waist and lengthened in the legs. She decided that the beard was too uncomfortable to wear, so she settled for a darker skin color. Cisi had her own seamstresses make the alterations rather than give the people in the settlement cause to gossip. Zalenda was having fun with the girls. It was a good release to playact. She suddenly became Becca, as Pender, the way Becca would have done. They laughed and laughed till Tina said, "I wished Pender was here."

Cisi said, "He is right there." They laughed again. Zalenda was smiling on the outside but crying in the inside.

They waited till the crossing was left unmanned then crossed over to the settlement with all of their supplies. Toto followed them rather indifferently; she was just becoming used to being at home. They went directly to the stables, and Zalenda said good-bye to White Flame and rode out east to go down the winding river valley. They changed into their male clothes in a nice little hide that Zalenda knew about from her many travels on this route. They decided they would stay there for the night.

They soon had a fire going, and while Cisi attended to their evening meal, Tina and Zalenda put up the tent and laid out their beds. Before they settled down to eat, Zalenda took Tina with her to check out their surroundings in case they were being observed. When she was satisfied, they went back to enjoy their meal and sat beside the fire till they were ready to sleep. Zalenda ordered Toto to watch while they slept. Tina had never done this before, and she was excited to be sleeping outside for the night.

The next day they traveled without incident to the Great Forest and made their entrance at the Big Oak. Zalenda had to take off her head covering so they could confirm her identification. The girls were amazed at their travel up to the rooftop and their subsequent walk across the roof of the forest. Zalenda went right away and talked to the young woman now in charge of the watch, who took her to the new watch position. A new walkway had been constructed right out to the very edge of the forest, ending up in one of the largest oaks Zalenda had ever seen. The young woman informed her that they very often could hear as well as see what was going on below; as a result, they had been able to frustrate some of the evil plans Tamor had tried to carry out against them.

Zalenda asked if she knew the mystic lady, Carla, and if so, did she know where she was being held? She pointed out a small hut that at one time had been inside the compound. She said a black-haired lady had been placed there as soon as she arrived on her pony. Her guards appeared to be deathly afraid of her and treated her with great respect. The young woman had other duties to attend to and asked Zalenda when she wanted to be relieved. Zalenda said she would watch for the rest of the day.

The Great Fort that Tamor had built was in a shambles. The big storm, almost two years ago now, had reduced it to piles of broken wood, and no attempt had been made to clear it or rebuild on the site. It was a strange feeling to look down on the place where she had once stood as prisoner on a spot now covered with kitchen garbage. The whole site was a mess, the guards unkempt and slovenly, the huts in need of repair. The columns of men she had seen going north to hunt for Pender had not originated here. There was not enough room to house them or feed them. By watching the servants carry out food from the kitchen, She soon identified the buildings where Tamor held court and where Carla was imprisoned. In between, there were three buildings where Tamor's captors where living. She had to get Carla out and over to Tamor. Then she had to take the buildings between them out of the equation. She thought about getting down there barring the doors and setting them on fire, but that could backfire. The large piles of broken wood from the destroyed fort would go up and endanger the Great Forest and all the people living there.

It was then she remembered Abbi's secret elixir—she believed it originated here in the forest—some type of bark poison. There might be possibilities that it could work here; she would pursue this further tonight.

A young woman came to relieve Zalenda because it was the custom of the watch to be there until all the lights were extinguished in the fort's buildings. Zalenda followed her back to the room she had shared with Mari and Zari and found Cisi and Tina already in bed, but not yet asleep. They were in wonder at what they had seen of a people who, by necessity, invented this new way of living and were in awe of it. Cisi announced that she and Tina intended to stay until Zalenda freed Carla so that they could escort her home to the settlement. Zalenda told them that perhaps it would take another two days before that would happen. The prospect of staying here and being involved in the rescue seemed to excite them both. Cisi said she found it exhilarating to be free from her chief's duties and being able to help.

When her two friends fell asleep, Zalenda went in search of some of her friends from the elders' council to ask them about the bark poison Abbi used to such great effect. It took a great deal of persuasion for them even to talk about it, but they said they would introduce her to the people who knew about such things in the morning, on the condition that she did not make it public what she intended to do with it.

It was difficult for Zalenda to sleep, for she kept rehearsing the plan that had been formulated in her mind—to use the bark tea on the guards. She would attempt the next night to somehow introduce it into either their drinking water or their beer. To prepare for that, she would require to solve two problems; the first was, where did they keep their supplies, and how would she find access to it? The girls on the watch team would have the information on the guards' schedules and habits, but she would have to watch all day tomorrow to locate the best entrance and the most likely place where the skins of beer would be kept. Round and round in her mind, the possible problems circulated in her head. She wished Pender were here; his quick mind would soon find a solution. "Where are you, Pender, when I need you? Why did I let you go?" With that question still unanswered, she fell asleep.

Chapter 36

The Plan to Free Carla

Zalenda was surprised to find the next morning that it was three women who were introduced to her as being the experts in the production of the bark tea poison. When she explained to them what she hoped to do with it, they quickly dashed her hopes of killing the guards with one application. First of all, there was no use putting it in the water, for it would be much too easy to detect. Second, they were not allowed to keep on the premises large-enough doses to kill fourteen men. She would have to allow them to drink at least four skins between them of good beer and then administer the poison to the next six. This would not be enough to kill healthy men, but it certainly would be enough to induce a sleepy sickness that would render them incapable of speech and action. They suggested she take ten skins from their supply of a very potent beer made from malt barley, oats, and honey. They could make up the mixture now in six of them, and it would be almost impossible to taste the difference. This was the best they could do for her, and Zalenda accepted it with much thanks. It would now mean, however, that she would need help to move them into place. She went to find Cisi and Tina to discuss how this could be done. Tina immediately volunteered first of all to move them along to the watch station and then help put them in place.

Tina and Zalenda found their way to the watching point that overlooked Tamor's ruined fort. The young women on watch reported that she could account this morning for a total of twelve men; two were on constant guard all day on Tamor, two on watch over Carla. They would change with their colleagues for night shifts, which meant four were on duty during the day in what was left of the compound. Tonight when they placed the skins of beer in place, they should have eight sleeping men in the three huts. They were hoping for a little moonlight so they would be able to see where to hang the skins.

Zalenda concentrated all her attention on which building the cooks were working in so she might find their supply shed. They were about to break for lunch when two men arrived with four pack horses carrying bags of vegetables and sacks of meal. Tina was excited when she noticed on the last pack horse skins of beer slung down the animal's back. This horse was led to a smaller hut almost below their viewing post. Zalenda could hardly believe their good fortune; this might be easier than she had thought. The three watchers noted that before he started unloading the beer, he went into the hut and spent some time inside. Zalenda climbed down the tree, taking great care to remain in good cover to a branch where she could see his movements inside. She could see the rack where he was moving the beer already on it to the front so that there would be room for the new supply at the back. Tonight she was going to move ten of those at the front and replace them with her own doctored ones.

Later on in the day, Tina went and collected the beer and carried it to the watch station. She had carefully marked the four ordinary beers with a leather lace that they could feel in the dark. They warned the new girl on watch that no one should be allowed to drink any of it.

The night was almost perfect for their operation, warm and airy with about a quarter moon showing just enough light for them to see their way down the tree. The young woman in charge of the watch came to help them with the rope, first, to lower Zalenda onto the ground then Tina. They both took the good beer with them. When they were safely on the ground, she lowered the rest of the skins. The rope was kept in place in case they had to make a quick exit. Zalenda went and easily opened the door to the hut. She went in and started to move the beer around so she could put theirs in the right place. Tina brought the six treated skins to the door of the hut so Zalenda could put them in the correct order for their purpose, and then she went to stand guard.

The moon was hidden by a cloud, so Zalenda was taking longer to sort the beer that they had allowed. Tina was fretting about this and was about to leave her post when two very drunk guards emerged from Tamor's quarters. They saw her at once and started a very unsteady amble toward her. Tina realized she had to distract them or, as drunk they were, they would raise the alarm. She smiled at them. They could see her now because the clouds had moved. She slowly removed her top, showing her beautiful breasts. They stopped short in amazement as she stepped out of her pants and underwear, beckoning them to come to her with her hand. She slowly moved backward away from them. They moved in unison with her. Twice she led them around the pile of broken lumber. The third time she picked up her clothes and ran for the rope. Zalenda had just finished her chore when a naked Tina burst past her. Then she saw the reason why—the two drunks were in pursuit trying to chase her down. In their haste, they ran into one other and fell in their drunken state and could not get up. It seemed to Zalenda that as they could not get up, they had decided to sleep right there. She waited for some time before she continued to the rope and her way back to the forest fort.

Zalenda climbed onto the watch platform just as Tina was being helped into her pants. She was shivering all over, not from the cold but because no man had ever seen her naked before. She could not believe what she had done, so she explained to Zalenda that it was the only way she could think of at the time to distract the men from giving the alarm. Zalenda helped her to put her top back on and thanked her for saving the mission. The other young woman called Tina heroic and said she wished she had that kind of courage. They went to bed feeling that they had made a good start in their mission to free Carla.

The final preparations were made the next afternoon when the watch girls located Carla's pony. Zalenda knew that Carla would not leave without her faithful little friend, so arrangements were made for the watch girls to pick up the pony at Mari's old hide. Zalenda would go alone and make sure that all of the guards were taken out or disabled before Tina came down the rope. They would wear their male disguises. Zalenda did not want a repeat of Tina's exploits to be required tonight. Their horses were to be ready to leave as soon as the signal was given that the operation was successful so they could leave at first light. During the day, the watch would be on the lookout in case the army returned from searching for Pender because that would require the cancellation of this attempt to free Carla.

Zalenda slipped down the rope that night into what was left of the compound. It was very dark, so she moved very slowly over to the hut where Tamor was being kept. She circled the hut and quietly proceeded to the only window. The hut was lit inside by three candles. She could see Tamor asleep on a large cot in one part of the hut and two men apparently asleep in the other corner. She took off her shoes at the door and then entered the hut and stood for a few moments. She listened to the rhythmic breathing of the men and noticed there were no skins of beer or drinking goblets in the hut. This meant she would have to kill them.

She approached the first man who was sleeping on his stomach. She placed her knee in the middle of his back and took his head in her hands and jerked it quickly to the side and upward. The cracking noise indicated to her that she had broken his neck and that he was dead.

The sound of movement from the other bed and the floor creaking alerted her that the other guard was awake and aware of her presence. The shadow on the wall told her he would soon be behind her and that he was armed. She moved backward at speed and drove her elbow into his midriff. The man stumbled backward and fell over his bed, but not without striking her on her arm with his knife. She had learned long ago in her training to disregard her pain and close in for the kill. The man was attempting to get up when she kicked him hard in the knee, knocking him back down on to the floor. He knew he had to get up and stab her again with his knife, which had fallen on the floor behind him. He was struggling to reach for it when she kicked him twice, once in the throat and another in the head. He died where he had fallen.

She was bleeding from the wound in her arm, and she knew she had to get to Carla as quickly as possible, but first she had to check on the condition of Tamor. It was obvious to her that the same knife that had wounded her had killed him, so now the slavers were under different control.

She was losing blood quickly. When she got to the small hut where Carla had been held, the guards were asleep near the door. She gagged them and tied them together so that they would not be able to get up. Carla woke with a start but was soon in control of all her faculties. Zalenda explained to her why she was there and what had happened while she had tried to rescue Tamor.

Carla moved quickly to stem the flow of the blood from her arm and sowed the V-shaped wound together then applied some kind of leaf from her kit and coated it with a foul-smelling ointment. She ordered Zalenda to sit down and drink from a flask because she was feeling lightheaded. Carla was busy gathering her belongings together and soon announced she was ready to go. She assisted Zalenda to the rope and helped her tie it on so it would not interfere with her wounded arm. Tina descended first so she could arrange Carla's possessions for pulling up with a second rope. The quicker they were all up in the tree fort, the less likely they would be of being detected.

Zalenda was pulled up first, followed by Carla and then Tina with the rest of their equipment. They went directly to the room where Zalenda explained it was necessary for them to stick to their original plan and leave immediately. The three of them would go in disguise and use the coast road, for it would be faster. They would pick up Carla's pony on the way at Mari's hide.

Carla said it would be better if they left the pony because all of the slavers would recognize it as hers, and she did not want to endanger her friends by insisting on taking it with her. Cisi said she would have one of her trusted people pick it up later to avert suspicion and bring it to the settlement. One of the watch team would go with them to the hide and bring it back to the forest. After a quick meal, they left the Forest People, and the four of them rode out into the night, with Toto on duty guarding from behind.

They had an uneventful ride out over the coast road, and daylight was pushing the waning night out of the sky when they began the long climb up over the moor. It was then Cisi noticed that Zalenda was gradually slipping down on her horse. She rode alongside and called a halt right away. Even with the artificial coloring on her face, she looked pained and unhealthy and very weak. With great care, they got her off the horse, but she could not stand on her own. Carla removed the wound dressing and saw that she was still losing blood. It was now essential that they get her to the settlement as quickly as possible. She took a powder from her kit and sprinkled it on the wound then she placed fresh leaves on it and tightly bandaged it with fresh clothes. She then made a mud pack and put it over the wound to keep pressure on it and finished by cutting the sleeve of her own jacket and sliding it in place. As Tina was the lightest, she rode behind Zalenda to support her in the saddle.

As they came to the brow of the hill between the river road and the Great Moor, Zalenda asked Tina to ride ahead with her so she could check to see if the road was clear or if they were being observed from the river. She looked first toward the Big River and saw that all the river birds were feeding on the mud banks and swimming contentedly in the water; this was a good sign. To the east, as far as she could see, nothing stirred, although there was evidence that the fishermen had already set their nets; everything was at peace. Inland over the moor where it touched the horizon, she could see a fairly dense cloud of smoke rising in the clear morning air; this was indicative to her that the cause was either a moor fire or a rather large group of people traveling in their direction, most likely the latter.

Tina rode back to the rest of the party, and Zalenda reported her findings and her suspicions that the group out on the moor might be the army that the slavers had hired to find Pender. She suggested that they should ride another mile on this road, past the entrance to the moor road, where she knew of a safe covered hollow on the riverbank that the team had used before. She knew that after the night's happenings, the girls were tired and weary with the ride and needed to rest. A good breakfast was something they all needed.

She dismounted carefully and sat down on a log. She reflected on the last time she was here looking longingly at a big barge full of construction lumber that was intended for Tamor's Great Fort, wishing that someone would come and burn it. Pender had been right here watching her, and when she rode away, he found a method to do just that and frustrate Tamor again. The question that now filled her mind was one that had festered there since she had observed the plume of smoke; had Tamor's hired army been successful in finding Pender? She had to find out.

Tina and Cisi had been busy finding wood and starting a fire, while Carla prepared the food for cooking. Once the food was ready, they all sat down together without speaking a word till they had cleared their plates. It was then they realized they had not eaten since the mission started.

Zalenda confided her fears to her friends that the army ahead might have found and captured Pender. Carla was quite sure that this was impossible because she alone had the power to open the Water Gate, and unless this army was trained in mountain climbing, they could not enter the valley where Pender and his team were in hiding. If they tried to come in from the sea route, her people would frustrate them in the cave labyrinths.

"I will take you to Pender and to the rest of your team, but first, you must rest and get stronger. Here, drink this potent potion. We have many hours to ride yet, and I cannot risk your body becoming weak by the stress and strain of what you have endured to rescue me. You are my first and only concern." Carla spoke sharply to her.

The girls looked on with wonder. Was this the normally calm careful Carla that everyone knew expressing anger at Zalenda? It had its effect for Zalenda, who meekly accepted the brew and drank it all.

They were disturbed by the return of Toto, who had gone hunting but now returned in an agitated state, first, running up to Zalenda then back toward the road. "She is trying to tell us something. Tina, come with me. The rest of you, put out the fire and get ready to leave in a hurry," Zalenda said, suddenly coming back to her normal self. They all moved to do her bidding, and Tina followed her to see what Toto was trying to tell them.

It soon became evident what Toto's matter of concern was all about. Four riders were approaching their position, riding hard toward them following the river road. Zalenda recognized them from the way they were dressed that they were part of the troupe she had seen weeks ago riding north looking for Pender. They did not appear to have noticed the smoke from their fire because they were concentrating all their attention on the river. They rode past their position in a cloud of dust, making it impossible for the two watchers to see anything until the dirt and dust had settled.

Zalenda signed to Tina not to talk but to go and check the road; she pointed with her finger using a circular motion, meaning check all around. Toto followed her without orders or instruction; she seemed to appreciate the gravity of the situation and went to protect her new friend.

Tina moved carefully to a viewing point and saw the four riders stop just on the brow of the hill they had so recently come up. The four men were soon joined by the eight men from Tamor's ruined fort they had drugged the evening before with the beer. Some of them could hardly sit on their horses and appeared still in a drunken stupor. She could not hear what they were saying, so she moved forward and climbed a tree. Toto quietly waited for her.

The leader was gesticulating with his arms angrily, shouting that there was no money. "We killed the big guy, but there was no money! It looks like our bosses must have killed each other in a fight to the death, but we could not find the money! The woman has gone vanished in the night because these stupid idiots got drunk out of their minds, so there is no prisoner we can hold for ransom. Did your army find their man?"

"No, we did not. We have been in the fields and mountains for weeks and found no sign of him."

"Just as well, since there is no money. It is a good thing that we got half up front and all the provisions, otherwise, we would have been out of pocket. How did the two spy specialists and the informer do?" he asked sarcastically.

"No word, no report. With any luck, they will be dead."

"I hate these knife-in-the-night guys. Now it does not matter anyway. I hope they did not get paid."

"Why was the big guy so keen to get him and kill him anyway?"

"It seemed every time the big guy had something good going, this man and some young girls got in the way and managed to free all the slaves."

"That is what all this has been about?"

"That and the two women."

"What an idiot!"

Tina had heard enough, so she waited till they turned to ride for home and carefully descended from her perch and with Toto made her way back to her friends. What she was able to tell them from her treetop experience calmed some of their fears, especially Zalenda—to know that Pender was no longer in danger from Tamor's hired army. They decided to stay the night to give Zalenda time to heal and recover before the hazards of riding over the moor.

Toto wakened them in the morning to tell them something was amiss. Tina was assigned to go and check what was troubling her friend Toto. She had only gone as far as her tree when she heard the sound of horses' hooves clattering on the still-hardened mud moor pathway. They were still some way off, so she had time to crawl through the broom and heather planting till she was near enough to see their eyes. As they were passing, she was shocked to see Rici, one of her male cousins, riding in the middle of the pack. Her first reaction was to call out his name, and then the realization of the situation set in—he had been paid by Tamor to identify Pender. She choked back the bile that had risen in her throat, her own cousin, one who sat in Cisi's council, betraying his own family for a share of Pender's death money.

She sat down and cried. Money! What was money? Only the slavers used it. None of the tribes would deal in it. They still preferred to trade with goods. What did he expect to gain, a few pieces of metal to rattle in his pocket? To sell his cousin for that was beyond her understanding. Although she was still in a state of shock, she had enough wits left to check around her before she stood up. The area was clear, but she could see the army moving at speed toward the Big River down the sea road. Tina knew she had to go and tell Cisi her news. She sat back down and asked Toto, "What do I do next?" Toto licked her face and barked and turned to go back to their camp. "That is very easy for you to say in dog language, but you are in a right mind now. I need you to back me up." She turned and followed the dog back the way they had come.

Cisi received the news quietly, but everyone could see how hard it was for her to take. "What is wrong with the men in my family that they would conceive of such corrupt practices and to engage in the evil intent of others to murder my brother? I am resolved to take this family apart and punish severely all those who might even have suspected Rici, my cousin, was involved in this treacherous deed."

After the horses were fed and watered, they made ready for the journey home. Zalenda said she was now strong enough to ride on her own. This would help speed up their journey and save the horses becoming overtired. Tina enjoyed the responsibility of being in the lead. She had been trained while on this trip by Zalenda in all the nuances of looking at the road ahead and perceiving any possible dangers. She liked so much what she had learned that she was excited about joining Zalenda and Carla on their way to find Pender because she wanted to be part of the team.

Carla and Cisi rode behind, discussing the perfidious behavior of the men in her family, how on so many occasions it was the men who were prepared for personal gain to betray and consult with the slave traders, in this case to murder Pender. Carla said she was often conflicted between her vow as a healer and the sure knowledge that the person she was healing would go on to do unspeakable deeds of evil. She said she had found it so wonderful to observe the fidelity of the young women in Pender's team in their cause to rid their tribes of slavery.

They reached the settlement at midnight and went directly to the stables and left their horses in the good care of the stable boys. At the crossing, it was left to Tina to pull them over to their island home for the night. Cisi's ladies went and prepared a late evening meal for them, while they hastened to the comfort of the hot springs. This time Tina forgot to be self-conscious.

It was later in the morning when Cisi and Tina went back to the settlement to complete the myth that they had been away visiting relatives. They were very pleased to leave behind the evidence of their altered personalities as men. It was good to dress as themselves. Cisi convened a meeting of her council and pretended she was scrutinizing each member of the council and taking note of the absentees. In each case, she asked why the members were not present. She consulted her mythical list and then asked where her cousin Rici might be. Her mother's brother gave a long winded excuse for his absence. Cisi allowed him to continue till he ran out of excuses. Then she asked him, "Why are you lying?"

He looked down on the floor and looked embarrassed then replied, "I really do not know where he is."

"How long has he been away from home? Think carefully. I am speaking as your chief, not your niece."

"I think he has been away about sixty days, but I do not know where. He said he had some business to attend to." His voice trailed off to a whisper.

"Perhaps I can enlighten you all to the business he was involved in. He was being paid by a particularly vile man to identify my brother Pender so they could murder him."

She watched carefully the reaction that her statement had on the council and noted the furtive looks some gave as they looked around. She wrote names on a note and signaled to Tina to come and get it. She ordered Tina to stay where she was. Everyone knew this was unusual and waited with bated breath. Cisi waited while everyone shuffled uncomfortably. Then she spoke again to her uncle. "Would it surprise you to know that he was seen yesterday riding with a hired army of men whose job it was to search for Pender and his team, which included my sister and some of your daughters? They were to be killed because they have been frustrating the slave traders. I have information that some of you knew of this matter and were prepared to allow it to happen for personal gain. Each one of you here swore fealty to me and this tribe. I promise I will punish the offenders without mercy. I think you are despicable." She paused for a few moments then turned on her family. "Uncle Seth, you and your family are under house arrest. You must have absolutely no contact with any traders, visitors, or family connections from other tribes. You will be watched night and day, and should you attempt to get other members of this tribe to act for you in contacting Rici, you and they will be imprisoned at my pleasure in the island prison. I have no patience left for this family's treachery."

Chapter 37

The Missions in the Lost World

Pender watched the departing army pack their tents and prepare to leave the valley away below their hidden mountain home, thankful for Carla's care in getting them to this place of safety. During the time spent here, he had observed the movements of their leaders, as they had divided up the army into smaller groups, which ranged far and wide in an attempt to locate his team. To make sure they were not caught unaware, he had organized watch groups day and night in case an attempt was made to scale the mountains. Food was prepared back in the caves, so no fire or rising smoke would be visible from below. These precautions seemed to have been worthwhile, for now the army appeared to be moving out; however, he had decided not to relax these safeguards for at least another two days. Then he would take a small team down the mountain to check and make sure the danger was past.

On this watch, he was joined with Rahana and Becca. They had sought him out because it was difficult for them to discuss sensitive matters when living in such close proximity with the rest of the team. They were very concerned about how the slavers had obtained the information that Pender and his team could be found in this area. Rahana's main cause of concern was, what if something had happened to Carla? Could it be that Tamor and his thugs had beaten the information out of her? Becca was suspicious of Cymon, who seemed to be too good to be true, always there to help, and she did not like the way he was ingratiating himself back into Elecia's favor.

Pender explained to them his plans for the next few days and told them they would be in charge in his absence. He wanted them to pay particular attention to see how Elecia dealt with Cymon's advances. They were to take Rona, Pipa, Ester, and Morag to Eram so he could take them down to the village to watch near the gates, just in case the leaders of the departing army had also been given information by Cymon. The only reason he kept him around was so he could watch him. "We must use discretion in what we allow him to be involved in with us. I would be really disappointed if Elecia turned to him again, but love can breed strange relationships, so watch them carefully."

Pender met with Eram the next day to discuss the scouting trip he was proposing to take with Mari and Zari down the mountain to see if Tamor's hired ruffians had indeed departed. Eram said he would guide them out of the labyrinth and onto the plains below, but they must be back before nightfall so he could bring them back up. It would also be a good idea to take his young wolf cub with him.

Mari and Zari were delighted at the prospect of exploring the rest of the caves and getting out into the glorious morning air of the plains they could only see from above. Zari had become best friends with Rollo, Pender's wolf cub now over two years old. He was playful and friendly, which certainly belied his fierce appearance, and of course, he was bribed by the whole team with the scraps from the table. It was Zari, however, that he clung to, following her around like a personal protective bodyguard. Anyone who even spoke sharply to her was subject to his glare of hostility. He considered it his exclusive right if she should drop anything, to pick it up and bring it to her so he might be kissed on his head. At night he lay outside her tent on guard, and no one dare enter without her permission. He bore Pender's training with an air of resignation but nevertheless was becoming an excellent line of first defense when they went out on a mission.

Today he was trailing his three friends as Eram led them out of the caves into the open air. He was somewhat bewildered by this new environment, and instead of rushing ahead like Tarag would have done, to chase the nearest rabbit, he followed behind Zari. Eram left them with the warning to be back before the sun went down because these plains at night were dangerous to travel through because of the wild animals.

Pender had located a lookout spot he had identified from above that would give them the best view of the surrounding area. As they made their way toward it, a pheasant strolled in front of them. Rollo could not resist his inquisitive nature and rushed the silly bird, which immediately recognized him as an enemy and took to the air somewhat belatedly, leaving his tail feathers in Rollo's mouth. Rollo, the mighty hunter, was born.

After they had climbed to the top of the hill, they had to sit down, as it had been some time since they had anything that demanded such physical effort. They had been careful to approach the incline from the mountainside so they would not be visible from the plain side. Zari called Rollo to her as they lay on the ground overlooking a broad unbroken expanse of rolling countryside. Nothing stirred except nature itself; all of the movements they witnessed were related to birds on the wing and trees decorated with every type of bird. The slight wind was scented with smells of a thousand wild flowers all dancing in the breeze; it was if paradise itself was here in this beautiful climate.

The magic of the moment was broken by a strange human cry. They looked at one another, trying to locate its source. Pender stood up as the sound came toward them again and again. "Over there," Pender said, pointing to a small ridge. "Let's go and investigate." The road down was a little easier but fraught with sharp rock sticking up through the moss and hill turf, so they had to tread carefully. Not so for Rollo; now let loose from his earlier fear, he was running with the wind, stopping frequently to sniff the air and the small bushes that were abundant on this hillside.

They soon tracked down the source of the wailing when they came to some bushes in a small hollow. They entered carefully to see a terrible sight. A young woman had just given birth to a child that was hanging from her knees. Mari went straight to her, while the others held back. She called Zari to come and help and to bring Pender's knife. She told Pender to find water quickly and bring it on the run if this child and mother were to be saved. Pender gave her the pack he was carrying because it contained a flask of cider and honey. He emptied out a skin of beer onto the ground, which Rollo proceeded to lap up. With the empty skin in his hand, he went in search of the mountain stream they had just passed. He was feeling sick at what he had just witnessed, not at the blood and mess, but how someone knew this young girl and left her here to die here with a baby.

He found the stream and filled the skin with water and ran back to where Zari was already starting a fire. They only had a small pot they had brought to make tea in. Now it had to do to heat water to wash the baby and the mother. Mari believed she had given birth somewhere else and dragged herself and the baby here to hide. Judging from the dirt on the baby, it had been some distance. Mari cut the umbilical cord and tied it with thread from her hat and handed the baby to Zari. Zari gently sponged the baby's face, and Rollo came to observe. There was enough warm water ready, and Pender tore up his spare shirt to make a shawl for the little baby girl. When she was thoroughly washed, she was wrapped in the shirt nice and tight and given to Pender to nurse. He dipped a corner of the shirt in the honey and cider and put it to the baby's lips; it seemed to pacify her for the time being till they got the young mother comfortable.

Mari and Zari worked at washing the girl and giving her some of their spare clothes they had brought with them in case they got soaked with rain. There was no sign of the placenta, so Mari believed it had fallen out on the way. The girl was quite incoherent, so she did not pursue the matter. Once she was comfortable, Pender handed her the baby, and she started to feed her. As she was feeding the baby, she fell asleep; the baby, however, kept working on her breast till she slept.

Pender said, "We will eat here now, but we must return right away so these new members of our team can be properly looked after."

Zari was elated. She came to Pender, saying, "Oh, how wonderful is this! We were able to save a little baby," dancing as she went singing, "I am going to be an aunt, I am an aunt." Mari cleaned up the site, and Pender went and buried the bloody clothes. While they were eating, Mari suggested that Zari should wrap the baby to her for traveling. Zari said she would prefer to carry the baby, for that is what aunts do. She said Mari had more experience in these things, and she would be better looking after their sister.

Pender said he would require to carry the girl because she was far too weak to walk and they had better start back now. "It would be better if she were tied to my back so I can see where I am going. Take my jacket and put it on her. Now with my belt, strap her around the legs and rope them around me, and with the rest of the long rope, tie her around my shoulders." He stood up with his sleeping burden and was able to walk quite comfortably. The baby was wrapped around Zari with what was left of Mari's shawl, and they were off back to their mountain retreat.

The journey back went without incident, but they did have to stop for rests along the way. Mari was carrying their supplies, and although she found it tiring, she was secretly relieved that Zari had offered to carry the baby. Considering what had happened to her own child, she was quite bereft of feelings for babies now.

Eram was surprised to see them early. "We went away with three, and we are coming back as five," Zari sang. Pender explained to Eram what had happened. Eram suggested that he should take Mari's load, and he would lead Zari up the stairs with her still-sleeping burden so that she would not fall on the stairs. Mari took Pender by the hand and led him up the countless number of stairs. He was tiring rapidly but would not hear that the young woman should come off his back and walk on her own, as she was still in a deep sleep. After climbing countless number of stairs, they arrived exhausted at their home in the mountains.

Rahana and Becca rushed to receive them. Rollo kept beside his mistress's feet while the baby was unwrapped from her. Then he went with Rahana and the baby; he obviously had adopted it as his little sister. Becca had already gone to get supplies for the new members of the team.

While the girls were fussing over the baby, Elecia and Becca came to assist Mari unwrap the young mother from Pender's back. He was quite exhausted, not so much with carrying her weight but by the climb through the labyrinth. Eram said he would go and find from his people all the necessities that would be needed for the baby and her mother and bring more milk and supplies in the morning.

Becca had wakened the young girl, who now looked much younger than they had thought. She said her name was Lena and had been part of a small group of wandering people who had no land. They had been attacked by a band of men who had taken her people as slaves. She had been raped every day for months until she became pregnant. Then they left her to die in the bush. She had existed by eating last year's berries that had not yet fallen from the bushes and plants that had been part of her band's food supply for years.

Pender asked her if she had recognized any of her attackers. She said she had never seen them before, and they only used her at night when she could not see their faces; they laughed when she screamed and beat her if she made too much noise. The first man who raped her was named Rici. "I ran away when they first attacked my people. He ran after me and pushed me down and raped me. I was a virgin, and he hurt me very much. The only thing I know for sure about him was that he had a brown eye and a blue eye."

Pender's anger was evident to everyone in the room. Mari came to comfort him, but he spurned her ministrations. She retreated and signed to everyone to leave him for a few minutes till he recovered from what had obviously been a nasty shock.

Elecia was the first to venture near. She came to tell him that Lena needed a lot more medical help than they could give her. She had been raped back and front many times, and even her throat showed signs of scarring. The birth had been terrible, and she was torn and bleeding. She had endured multiple beatings and at least three broken ribs. Only great determination had carried her to the point of birth, and she would most surely have died if they had not rescued her. "I want to be assigned as her nurse. I have suffered like her, and I know what she went through. I promise I will bring her through this, and I will be with her day and night. Please say yes because I want to get away from Cymon. He is trying to get me to join him in a wild scheme against you and the team."

Pender finally spoke. "Yes, you may nurse Lena, but I want you to encourage Cymon in his treachery, but tell me about it. I will meet you here so we can talk. Tell everyone that Lena could be infectious—only you must know why."

The four girls returned from their watch at the village gates. They came straight to Pender and reported that their two-day watch had produced nothing. It began to look like that Tamor's searchers had indeed given up and returned to their base. He told them what had happened on his scouting trip with Mari and Zari, and how they had found Lena and the little baby girl and had been able to rescue them and bring them here. They all wanted to go right away and see the baby, but before they left, he gave them a new assignment. "First of all, I want you to switch your tent to the one nearest to Elecia's. Esther and Morag, you will carefully watch during the day Cymon's going in and out, and I want you to report anything you deem to be suspicious. You are watching Cymon, not Elecia—she will be nursing Lena. Rona and Pipa, I want you to do the same but during the night. Pretend you are out on our normal watch schedule. Pay particular attention to what Cymon does. Be near in case he should attempt to escape into the caves."

Early next morning, Eram returned with a baby's basket for the little girl to sleep in and all the clothes and supplies they would ever need. Cymon made a point of asking Eram if there were any other supplies for the baby or the mother that they would require; he would go with him to carry them up. Elecia said she would need Cymon to move her tent further away from the main group because she felt that Lena might yet be infectious, and as her nurse, she would be the only one allowed into her tent.

Pender admired Elecia's quick wit to keep Cymon around, but it also made it more difficult for his special watch team to function without being noticed. When Cymon went to move Elecia's tent, Pender called the team together down at the wall that overlooked the mountain abyss so that Cymon could not hear what was being discussed. He told the team that he had been able to identify one of the men who had raped Lena; it was his cousin Rici. The only thing that Lena could remember about her unfortunate experience was that the first person who had raped her was named Rici, and he had a brown eye and a blue eye. When Ester heard it, she let out a scream, which she immediately stifled. "I am afraid that there can be no doubt that he is the man responsible. This means that Cisi could be in danger."

That night Pender talked with Rahana and Becca for a long time. Then they were joined by Zari, who wanted to go alone to warn Cisi of this new problem. Pender said he appreciated her thoughtfulness, but the dangers of the last months were not over, and he could not sacrifice her for this new violation of his family's allegiance and treachery. They talked deep into the night about possible solutions. One after the other, they fell fast asleep, the four of them in each other's arms. The day had taken a hard toll on them.

Pipa and Rona were on watch when they observed Cymon creeping around making for Elecia's tent. They followed him very carefully and quietly, taking a parallel path to the same tent. Cymon looked around before entering. The girls quickly followed him into the tent. When they got there, Elecia was lying down on her face. She had been hit from the behind and was bleeding. Cymon was on top of Lena, trying to waken her. His hands were around her throat, saying over and over again, "Did you tell them that you saw me?"

Pipa said, "No, she did not, but we see you." And with that, she kicked him in the back. Cymon rolled over to avoid Pipa's second kick and tried to reach over to get his club, which had fallen behind him on the floor. Rona snatched it away and smashed him on the ear, knocking him back against the tent support, which fell and brought the tent down on top of them. Cymon, roaring with rage, disentangled himself from the tent only to see Pipa and Rona waiting for him. He turned and ran away from them toward the wall, with Rona and Pipa in hot pursuit. He dived over the wall into the abyss, where they could hear the thudding of his body striking the rocks below; his suicide was completed.

The camp was awakened from its sleep. Morag and Esther went to help Mari get to Elecia and Lena and to repitch the fallen tent. The skins were wet with dew and heavy to lift, but the rest of the team arrived, and they soon had everything in order. Elecia's wound was not serious. She described how Cymon had approached her from behind and punched her in the head. Then he assaulted Lena, who was further traumatized by that experience.

Pender blamed himself for having allowed Cymon to live after he had repeatedly abused their trust with his treacherous behavior. He had done so in the hope of gaining information about the strategies of the slavers, but it had all gone terribly wrong. Mari said, without his foresight in putting the watch in place, the result might have been quite different; no one could have foreseen the extent of Cymon's erratic behavior. Ester and Morag decided they would sleep beside Lena for the rest of the time; they were there and they would also help Zari with the baby. No one sorrowed for Cymon; it was good that he took his own life, which was fitting for such a treacherous man.

It was three days later before Lena had fully recovered from her ordeal and was able to get up and move around with the help of Ester and Morag. She never really had any contact with other young women before, and now to have two friends who loved her and called her sister was beyond her imagination. Her life had gone from hopeless resignation, waiting to be devoured by some wild animal in the open, far from help, to being healed by Elecia and spoiled by these two beautiful women. She was in the process of feeding the baby when Ester asked her if she had chosen a name for their little sister. Lena was embarrassed at first to speak, but after much prompting from her three friends, she said, "Among my people, it is the custom to name the firstborn baby after your mother or father, but I never knew who they were, nor did I ever have anyone who really cared for me. To give my baby a name, I would normally have had great difficulty, but now I was wondering if you thought Zari would mind if I named her Zarena."

Elecia took the baby from her and said, "Little baby girl, let me be the first person to call you by your name, Zarena. Now we are going to have to get you ready to introduce you to all your big sisters. I am your aunt Elecia." When she turned to Ester and Morag, she saw the tears of happiness on their faces. Then she said briskly, hiding her own feelings, "Come on, you two, get your sister ready for the occasion." The team was ready to sit down for breakfast when they entered the dining tent to a busy buzz of conversation.

Ester called for quiet then she took her time to let everyone notice who was with her. Then she said, "Team, today I take great pleasure in introducing to you the newest members of our team. The last few days of turmoil and tragedy have turned into ones of great joy and happiness. Now let me introduce you to our new sister, Lena! Morag brought Lena forward and paraded her around the table, where she was hugged and kissed by everyone until she came to Pender.

He picked her up and kissed her, saying, "Sister, I am glad you are here."

She kissed him back boldly and said, "Brother, I am glad I am here with you. Thank you for rescuing me and carrying me here on your back and saving my life." Everyone cheered her. Then Morag took her and made room for her between Zari and Mari. Ester waited again till she had their attention.

"Friends, I feel like I am going to cry, but I must not do that because this little one has gone through the most impossible odds to live and to bring us this great joy. Here is our very newest little sister, Zarena." Elecia carried Zarena forward and presented her to Zari. "This is a great wonder, your first grandchild." Zari cried with sheer joy.

Chapter 38

Zalenda's Journey to Find Pender in the Lost World

Zalenda brought White Flame to a halt underneath the tree from which she had heard Abbi and Kain plan their destruction. From here she would collect Carla's pony from Abbi's old hide. The young man Cisi had sent with the pony was pleased to see her. It had been lonely on this hill, and he was keen to get back home. He said good-bye to her as she led the pony to where she had left White Flame. She was careful to make sure he did not see in what direction she was heading. Carla and Tina were waiting for her, and they were soon under way heading toward the Water Gate. They made a much-quicker journey than Pender's team two winters past and were mesmerized when Carla led them through the Water Gate and into the caves beyond. The wonder's continued past the translucent rocks, where they rested in one of the many luminous rock caves. Zalenda worried about where they had left White Flame and Carla's pony.

Carla explained that she had made arrangements for her people to care for them and that they would be stabled with Pender's and his team's mounts for the journey back home.

Merca, Mina, and Marta waited for them when they left the caves to take them right into the dining area where dinner was being served. The M People were astonished when they saw Zalenda. She was so beautiful, tall and slim, with a glorious crown of blonde white hair, graceful and elegant in her deportment, yet possessing a strong confident cool air of being in control. Tina was quite the opposite; she was small, of clear complexion and jet-black hair plaited in one single strand and woven into crownlike circles on her head in the Zalenda style. She looked at everyone through her hazel-brown eyes with a sense of excitement that exuded an exuberance of joy and happiness in everything she did; they loved her from the beginning.

While Carla introduced Zalenda to her people, telling them that she was Pender's wife, they nodded their heads knowingly; now they understood. She was bombarded with their questions as they tried to make sense of why she had not been with him and why she had left him with all these beautiful women; she must trust him a whole lot. She was happy that Carla was there to answer them in accordance with their own customs and deflect the most embarrassing questions like, where were her children?

Mina and Marta took Tina under their wings and shielded her from all the young men who desperately wanted to make her acquaintance. They plied her with questions about working with Zalenda, and she told them about rescuing Carla, even describing how she took off her clothes to distract the guards. That night the three of them slept together, comfortable new friends.

Zalenda spent the night with Carla and was introduced into her world of being the mystic lady. It turned out there was very little mystic about it. She came from a long line of women who were sworn by a vow to help all people, friend or foe, who were suffering from illness or wounds. She had been trained by her mother, as she had been trained by her mother, in all manner of treatments for diseases, pustulant wounds, broken bones, and all types of fevers. Zalenda was enthralled by her knowledge and the rooms of leaves, potions, mixtures, and contraptions for setting bones. She skillfully guided the conversation around to her own problem because of the potions she was given as a woman warrior—would she ever be able to conceive? Carla examined and scrutinized her thoroughly. After she was finished, she said that she did not see any reason why she could not conceive. "I will prescribe for you a potion that will make your monthly flux restore itself, but I warn you it will be heavy and uncomfortable for the first three or four cycles. Be prepared for excessive bleeding and painful periods. Now go with confidence knowing that you have an excellent potential to be a mother." She admitted to Carla that she had slept beside Pender but was always afraid because she did not want him to know that she might never be able to be a mother. In fact, when she left her two friends, Rahana and Becca, she had encouraged them to be Pender's wives and have babies with him.

Carla took Zalenda to her and hugged her while she wept then said, "Zalenda, you who are so clever and adept at changing the whole government of your people, yet you cannot see what is so prevalent in your own life. Pender's whole team loves him. I could easily fall in love with him, but he loves you. When you meet him tomorrow evening, you will know this. You have given up much to find him. Let him find you again. The two years will mean nothing, but under no circumstances leave him again"—then she smiled—"or I may take him from you. Now we have a lot to accomplish tomorrow. Let's sleep and dream of better things."

Mina and Marta were waiting all packed and ready to go with them in the morning. They had obtained permission from their people and Merca to go and join Pender's team and were so excited at that prospect. Carla led them out with their masks and rope, ready to walk the Valley of the Flies. She had explained to them that no matter how they felt, they must keep walking. They endured the flies and the stench of the rotting flesh and the noise of the birds, and the girls would probably have thrown up had Carla not given them a special drink that prevented such mishaps; for this they were very thankful.

Like Pender's team many months earlier, they staggered into the coolness of the caves and collapsed. Zalenda helped the girls recover, while Carla produced some food from her pack. She would not allow the girls to eat, however, till they had first drunk a very powerful syruplike liquid from her flask, which made their eyes water and soothed their throats and stomachs. The three girls decided they could not eat because the stench lingered with them, but they were keen to continue with their adventure. Zalenda and Carla both enjoyed a modest meal and then made ready to leave. As Carla was putting on her pack, she warned them to watch each step because of the rough rock passageways that they would traverse for the rest of the afternoon.

They were quite cold and very tired, and it was well into the late afternoon when they finally came out into the late evening sunlight and saw the tents of Pender's team. Rahana and Becca were the first to see them and ran and threw themselves at Zalenda. When the rest of the team came to see what the noise was all about, they joined in till Zalenda was buried underneath a small mountain of female arms and legs. Slowly order and good sense returned to the group. Zalenda introduced Tina, Mina, and Marta as new team members and stood back as the rest of the team lined up to make their acquaintance. As Zalenda turned, she saw Pender coming out of the tent carrying a baby, with a large wolflike creature at his side. She gasped and fell fainting downward, a wailing sound escaping her lips. She would have hit the ground had Rahana and Becca not held her up. She kept saying, "No, no. I have come too late. It is my fault again. Now I have lost him forever."

It was Zari who made the connection first. She bent over Zalenda and said, "No, Zal, it's not like that at all. Come, do not distress yourself. This is our sister Lena's baby, Zarena. We found Lena in the wilderness dying alone giving birth to this beautiful baby girl. We were able to rescue them and bring them here to recover. They are part of us now."

Zalenda looked stunned as Carla came to help her. Carla said in a whisper, "Dear girl, you have jumped to the wrong conclusion again. Now get up and go and claim your husband."

Pender came to see what had happened. He recognized Carla first but did not see Zalenda. He came and embraced her and then asked her, "Have you seen or heard from Zalenda?" Carla signaled with her eyes over her shoulders. He said, "She is here!"

"Yes, now go and get her yourself before she dies with grief and longing. When she saw the baby, she thought it was yours."

Pender bent down picked Zalenda up and wrapped his arms around her and carried her to his tent. The girls followed, but Rollo would not let them enter the tent. He positioned himself in such a way that no one could get near.

Rahana and Becca stood beside Carla as she told them of their journey and how Zalenda and Tina had rescued her from Slave Island

and took her to the forest fort. They had disguised themselves as men to avoid being recognized, and she had someone else collect and ride her pony. This was all necessary because Tamor was dead, and others were fighting to take over his position as head of the slave traders.

On the way to the settlement, they had taken the river route over the moor and had fortunately recognized in the distance a group of men coming in their direction. It was necessary for them to know who these men were, so Zalenda, who had been stabbed in the arm and was still losing blood, sent Tina to try to identify what this small army of men was intent on doing. Tina had been able to get to a point near the intersection of the river and moor roads and observe the troop as they passed. While she was up the tree, men whom she recognized as being from Slave Island intercepted the larger group. She heard their discussions that none of the search teams had been able to find Pender. She also recognized her cousin Rici as being one of the hired gang of thugs. This knowledge had disturbed her very much because it meant they had been getting information from Cisi's council.

When they got to the settlement, Cisi tried to deal with the traitors in their midst, while Zalenda rested on the island for the journey here. Carla said she had spent time trying to treat Zalenda to get her ready for the ordeals of this journey. "Although Zalenda had shown amazing physical powers of recovery, she was still very much fatigued mentally. Her collapse when she saw Pender with the baby was testimony to this, although I had told her over and over that he loved only her. In her training as a woman warrior, she had been allowed no trusting human contact, and this has made it difficult for her to accept that she could be loved for herself not for the things she could do. We must constantly reinforce the truth of this to her till she is confident in his love. She is an amazing young woman, and we must make her comfortable in this knowledge. What she did for me coming into an environment where I was to be on sale to the highest bidder, watched day and night by at least a dozen men, yet she devised a plan with only Tina as her help to rescue me, and she did it. She is truly remarkable. I ask you two who know her so well to help me preserve her from this depression of her soul."

Chapter 39

The Mission against the Baldheads

Inside the tent, Pender was trying to revive Zalenda but was having trouble getting through herself imposed barrier of grief. Elecia noticed her wound was bleeding, so she immediately sent for Carla. Carla entered with Rahana and Becca, who helped Pender lift Zalenda onto a cot. Elecia went for the supplies that Carla required from her backpack to deal with the bleeding, while Rahana repeated to Pender how Zalenda had been injured but did not mention her mental collapse at the sight of him with the baby. Carla soon had the bleeding under control, but before she attempted to bring her around, she made it clear to everyone that Pender must be the first person she should see, and that Rahana and Becca must stay with him till Zalenda was fully recovered. Then and only then would she bring her around to a conscious state they all agreed to this. Carla applied a strong-smelling salve to Zalenda's face and nose, and soon she was sputtering under the influence of the concoction. Her unseeing eyes opened slowly at first as consciousness struggled to accept her surroundings. Then she saw Pender; she concentrated on his face for a long time. She asked in querulous voice, "Am I still dreaming?"

Pender knelt down beside her and said, "No, my darling, you are not dreaming. See here are your two best friends, Rahana and Becca. I wouldn't allow these two rascals in your dreams. Your dreams are strictly reserved for me." Then he leaned over her, kissing her tenderly on the lips. She responded gradually to his touch. Carla intervened at that point and said her patient required to rest and sleep, but she assured Zalenda that they would wait all night with her. When she finally fell asleep, Pender went and brought extra cots for the girls and Elecia to sleep on, while Carla said she had to go and sleep because she was so tired but to wake her if they felt it was necessary.

Rahana told Carla that the team was about to go out on a difficult mission to rescue four young girls who had been kidnapped by the Bald People. The problem was that they would be required to kill a large number of that tribe because they could not afford to take prisoners and keep the team safe. Eram had asked Pender to see if an attempt could be made today because these people would move on very soon. The team was about to leave when Carla and Zalenda had arrived with the other young women—should they put it on hold? Carla said it was important that the Bald People should learn a lesson that they could not steal people to be their slaves with impunity. The mission must go on as long as Pender was back by night. She had given Zalenda a sleeping potion, so she would probably sleep all day. Rahana said Becca had never fully recovered from injuries sustained in the past and was not allowed to go out on missions. She would stay all day with Zalenda.

Pender put Pipa in charge of the mission, and he went along only as one of the team members. These young women had come a long way in the last years and were more than capable of designing and carrying out this unplanned mission. For the last three days, they had carefully observed the habits and organization of the Bald People's camp and felt they had three problems to solve. The first was that the rescue attempt would have to be made at night; that was why it was necessary for the mission to be done tonight, the night of the full moon. The second was that they could not allow any prisoners to be taken; they had to kill immediately their quarries so that they could not raise an alarm. The third was they had to find a way of distracting the guards. The problems would have to be solved during the mission tonight. They would require to take out the leaders and the important people first whose tents were near the top end of the valley and the less important people at the opening of the valley where they would likely be first to suffer in any attack by raiders. One factor that could be in their favor was the tribe's custom to blow a horn when the sun went down. The purpose of this signal was that the whole tribe had to go to their tent for the night, and only the night guards were allowed to keep their vigil at the entrance to the valley.

Today Rona, Morag, Ester, and Zari would be in action. Tina would be on site with the two new girls, Mina and Marta. They had to find a way of distracting the guards, but nothing could be organized till they were actually in position. Eram, the wall artist, led them out into the caves down a long tunnel, with each person carrying their own supplies strapped to their back. After an hour of hard walking, Pender called a halt because with the weight they had on their backs, he did not want them to be overtired before the mission started.

At the break, Pender took Mina and Marta aside and told them that the team would make a further evaluation of the situation when they got to the site. When they had made a careful study of what was required, they would rehearse the plan of action, and those members present on site best suited for the job would be chosen for the rescue. Should things go wrong, the remaining members would be engaged. Their job today was to assist in dealing with the guards and learning the tactics used, but if any of the team were hurt, they would go with him to bring them out. The young women they were rescuing would probably have been stripped of their clothes, so they could be required to take clothes from the pack he was carrying and go and dress them before bringing them out to safety. Mina and Marta were excited at the prospect of being involved in their first mission. Pender said he was trusting them with this responsibility because he had seen their good work saving the starving people of the Auits nomadic hunting tribe.

The team assembled again and was soon back walking down the long slope to the outside world of human greed and selfish subjection of others, which was what today's mission was all about. Eram led them to a position on a low hillside that overlooked the camp of the Bald-Headed People. Pipa asked Rahana and Mari to go and watch the camp from the other side of the hill where there was more cover down low near the Bald People's tents. It was their task to identify the tent where the young women were being held.

Pender, Pipa, and Rona followed them to a point where they could view the layout of the whole camp. Pender could see exactly what Pipa and Rona had reported; the valley was indeed formed V-shaped tight against the hill. The tents of the important people he could see by the size and quality of the tents were positioned at the top of the valley slope where they had unobstructed sight lines of the whole camp. Families least valued by the tribe were in the poor-quality tents at the mouth of the valley, so they would bear the brunt of any attack by rival bands or tribes.

The rest of the team began to assemble ropes and supplies that would be required in this rescue bid, but it was left to Elecia to get a cold lunch to everybody. Tina was selected to carry the meal to Rahana and Mari and was to stay with them to act as a messenger between the groups. Mina was to accompany Tina as far as Pender's group and perform the same function. The reserve group of Nena, Ester, Morag, Zari, and Marta would be on call should they be required.

In the late afternoon, Tina reported that Rahana felt the rescue bid must be made tonight. They had identified the tent nearest to their position as the one where the girls were being held. They knew this because there was a continual stream of men visiting the site, which brought screams of pain from the girls. The men left with grins on their faces while pulling on their pants, so they were very certain of their target.

Pender and Pipa agreed with that assessment; now they needed a plan. First, they had to find a way of luring the men out of the tent so that the recovery team could get access to the girls. Tina told them how she had taken off all her clothes to lead the drunken guards away from Zalenda when they were rescuing Carla. She was prepared to do that again if it meant these girls could be freed. Mina said she would join her in this distraction, although she had never done anything like that before; two of them might be more alluring than one.

They came up with a plan to wait till twilight, then in that attack, Tina and Mina would tempt the men up the hill where Morag and Ester would kill them. Mari and Rahana would pull the tent down on top of the men still in the tent with the girls and, as they emerged, kill them. Elecia, Zari, Marta, and Nena would join in to bring the girls to safety. In the meantime, Pipa, Rona, and Pender would go down from their position and destroy the tents of the leaders and kill as many of them as they could. The Bald-Headed People would be taught a lesson tonight they could not ignore.

The team assembled and went to their positions. They were fortunate that the moonlight was perfect for the operation here in the foothills. The only people who left their tents after the horn had blown were those men looking to misuse the girls who were their prisoners. It appeared that the leaders overlooked this breach of the night curfew to allow men to rape these young women.

The signal for the mission to begin would be given by Pipa. She would light a candle, cover it, and then show it twice more. Everyone at the signal went into action. Pipa, Pender, and Rona rappelled down the steep slope coming to the Bald-Headed People's tents. Very quickly they cut the guy-ropes and knocked down the poles. When heads popped up, they smashed them with their clubs. Within minutes the operation was over. They moved swiftly to the next group of tents and kept moving the carnage downhill.

Tina and Mina very carefully moved to a point near the tent and waited for the guards to show. They could hear the terrible screams of the young women inside; these toughened their resolve. Six men were approaching from across the camp. Now was the time; their courage could not falter. They quickly removed their clothes under a tree, which housed Mari and Rahana armed with clubs. Their job was to lure the men there. Mina shivered with fright and cold, but the screams of the girls kept her going, Tina put on her act, signaling to the men with her hands and fondling her breasts. Mina took her cue and was soon absorbed in displaying her nakedness to tempt the men away from the tent. The guards were keen to follow for this new sport and were disarmed of all care and judgment by these temptresses who promised such pleasures. Ester, Morag, and Zari attacked them from behind, while Rahana and Mari took down those who were more agile at climbing the slope; they were the first to arrive at death. Elecia joined them, and together they went to rescue the girls. Rahana and Mari pulled down the tent, and as the men emerged, they were quickly set on by Ester and Morag, whose quick kicks brought them down, where Rahana smashed in their heads without sympathy or sorrow.

Elecia and Nena stripped the girls of their blood-stained garments and washed them as quickly as possible. Marta and Zari put on the new clothes they had brought with them, and in minutes, the first girl was ready to leave between Ester and Morag, who had to carry her up the hill. Tina and Mina arrived to escort the second girl up the hill. When she could not walk, she was carried. Zari and Marta took the third girl, and Elecia and Nena took care of the last girl, who was in a very bad condition.

Pender and Eram stood on the hill calling out to the Bald-Headed People so they would know why this judgment had been exercised against them. The people reluctantly left their own tents and stood outside, while Pipa and Rona ranged up and down, making sure the people inside came out. When some of the men would not obey a woman, they were kicked into submission.

When all was quiet, Pender introduced himself and Eram and told them what they had done to their leaders for attacking another tribe just like theirs and had taken four young innocent women and allowed them to be brutally raped by their leaders, by their husbands, by their brothers and sons. "You women are not excused. You heard the screams but chose to ignore them. Everyone of the men who died here tonight was killed by twelve young women who could not ignore the rape and brutality practiced against these young girls.

"We are leaving you to bury the dead. Learn this lesson well because should you allow this to happen again, we will pursue you, and we are resolved to leave none of you alive. These young women who carried out their mission tonight have vowed with me to seek out and punish the evil people who attack smaller tribes and take the poor to sell as slaves for their own advancement. Your leaders have done this—they took four girls from this man's tribe. We have rescued them and will take care of them, but be warned—you are all guilty. The only way you can expunge that guilt is to repair and change your humanity. You have an opportunity to elect from among you people who are strong in that humanity. Do that before you leave this place."

A man shouted at him, "Who made you our judge? We will do as we see fit. Do not threaten us. If we are strong, no one can stand against us. This has always been the mantra of this tribe." Pipa approached him face on.

Pender said, "Change that mantra now." Pipa made another perfect kick to his head, and he was dead. The people slowly filed back into their tents. They would bury their dead in the morning.

The team walked back with Eram through the caves to their camp. It was a difficult journey. Besides being uphill all the way, they had the added burdens of carrying extra equipment. Eight of the team were responsible for carrying the four young women who were so badly injured they could not walk alone. When they arrived at the camp, only Becca and Carla were available to minister to the young women, so they were moved in beside Zalenda, who was almost fully recovered. The rest of the team went directly to their tents and slept till the next morning.

Pender also had a difficult journey back. Eram was upset that they had killed so many men of the Bald People's tribe in freeing the four young women. Pender tried to explain that to have simply taken them as temporary prisoners would have not only put his own team at risk but also encouraged the Bald People to help themselves to more of his people anytime they felt like it. "You saw and heard the attitude of the common man whom we killed to reinforce what would happen to them if they attack your tribe again. Can you imagine what their leaders would have done if we had not killed them?"

Eram then grumbled that since these young women had been so badly raped, they would no longer be marriageable to the men in his tribe.

For Pender it was difficult to remember that they were guests of this man's tribe, but he did tell him with great candor that he should have made these foibles of his and his people known to him, and he would not have risked the lives of his team. In this particular situation, he would allow sufficient time for the girls to heal and then go back to their parents to say good-bye. If they chose, he would be pleased to take them back as members of his team. This would also provide enough time to see if the Bald People's tribe had learned the lesson that they had been given. They had no right to steal innocent young women and treat them the way they had without reprisals being taken against them.

Eram was angered at Pender's response and replied, "I told you I did not approve of violence, and yet you deliberately ignored my sensitivity in these matters. There are people in my tribe who will condemn me for allowing this to happen."

"Will you bother to tell them how badly treated these young women were, or should we have considered the sensitivity of the young men in your tribe who will despise them now that we rescued them? Perhaps I should apologize to their parents for saving them, or better still I should let Carla list the indignities practiced on these young women and see how your dignitaries will react."

"You have no right to talk to me like this. You have damaged my reputation. People will talk of this for years to come. I will not be responsible for resupplying your team with food from now on."

"Now we can see the real reason for wanting to rescue the girls. It was all to enhance your reputation. Go back to doing your pictures on the walls of the caves. Carve this story there and let history be the judge of your motives and mine, or would that interfere with your sensitivity?"

Pender was upset at himself for getting into such an argument with Eram and resolved to let Carla know everything that had happened so she could then judge whether or not he should apologize to the Bald People for the way they had rescued the girls.

That night he and Zalenda slept together, and she held on to him tightly the whole night. In the morning, she was her old self, confident, bright, and as beautiful as ever, just the way Pender needed her to be this day.

In the late afternoon, Pender met with Carla, who had been working nonstop since she arrived, tending to Lena and the baby Zarena, Zalenda, and now the four girls, Lilly, Lara, Ena, and Nanci. Elecia, Nena, and Mari helped her nurse them; in fact, they had little sleep all night and were resting in their cots.

Tina had made friends with Lilly and Ena and was presently their go-for girl. Mina and Marta were doing the same for the other girls, wiping their tears when they cried and assuring them they were safe and secure from further harm.

Carla listened carefully to what Pender said the team had done to rescue the girls and then his subsequent argument with Eram. He said he bitterly regretted what he had said but cited the tension of the mission and the fatigue from carrying so much equipment back from the Bald People's camp as motivating factors. "Everything we did in rescuing the girls was done to make him look good in the eyes of his friends, not for the benefit of the girls and their families. The important thing as far as I am concerned is that we have four young women who will live and survive because of what this team has done. We will wait four days till the girls are able to go with me to my people. I will show them the results. I will list the awful injuries they sustained and the mental and physical damage to their bodies, some of which might be permanent. Then I will present the cost to them, nothing! Just a few food supplies. Not one of them put themselves in danger—that is not sensitivity, that is cowardly. It is good that we can offer the girls the choice of joining us as full members of this team or to go back to their parents where they would be little better than slaves."

Zalenda said, "I noticed that you said 'us'—does that mean you consider yourself a member of this team?"

"My darling girl, when you came through that door and set me free, I made up my mind I would be with you to the end. Now let us get something to eat. Thank goodness Elecia and Nena are back. I am starving."

Lena brought Zarena into the tent where Pender and Zalenda had moved into beside Rahana and Becca to make room for the injured girls. Rollo followed wherever baby Zarena went, and although the tent was crowded, he insisted he be given entrance, so he lay down at Len's feet as guardian of his adopted family. Pender took Zarena and gave her to Zalenda to hold, while he moved a cot into a better position. It was the first time she had ever held a baby and did not know how to cradle her in her arms. Becca soon coached her in the proper position and practices. She had become the prescribed parent when Zarena fretted and needed to be soothed and comforted.

Rahana watched in wonder at her best friend's antics with this little one. Was this the same comedian who made fun of every situation, coaching the woman warrior how to display emotion to a child? Pender caught her incredulous look, and as their eyes met, they both smiled. Zalenda was healed, not by a potion but by a baby; she was finally home.

The team met to discuss the mission and to evaluate the results. Pipa, as leader of the group, felt that in spite of the fact that the team had gone into action with no prearranged plan, and because of the emergency nature surrounding the welfare of the young women, they had contrived a plan that had worked. This was their very first mission in which they were forced to kill so many people; some people will argue too much. "I today would have felt a great burden of guilt had I not seen and heard the screams of these girls and realized no one in that whole tribe, young and old, rich and poor, men and women, felt that this was not inhuman. I salute the new members of our team who were so inventive in distracting six men who were intent on inflicting further humiliation on these young women and then making sure they did their share in bringing them home." She asked Tina, Mina, and Marta to stand up and be recognized for their courage and imagination on a particularly trying mission.

Pender made them all aware of what Eram had said and how he had replied, but he would let Carla, who will be going to address her people on this issue, give them her evaluation of their work.

Carla began by giving them an update on the health of the young women. She reported that the girls were making progress from their horrendous ordeal. They are so thankful to Elecia, Mari, and Nena and the others for their thoughtful kindness in treating their wounds. But cannot believe that so many young people in this team, people whom they do not even know, put themselves in danger for their sakes, something their own tribe and families had not thought to do.

"In four days' time, when they have recovered enough, I will take them and some of the members of this team to address the issues Eram has brought to our attention. We will be leaving for home shortly after that. I will be traveling with you as a member of this team. The young women you have rescued will be given the same opportunity, if they so choose."

The team cheered these announcements. They were very excited at the prospect of returning home, and they were full of joy that Carla was returning with them. Lena was visibly upset, but Zari soon put her greatest fears to rest when she told her from now on wherever they went, she would be going with them. Zalenda reminded them that although they must prepare for returning home, it did not mean that fitness and combat classes were canceled. She expected to see everyone down on the field who had no other duties at present; only Becca would be given light training. "Ladies, I am back."

Zalenda had all the team out for physical defensive training; even Elecia, Nena, and Carla left their charges to attend and were as vigorous as the active mission members. For Tina, Lena, Mini, and Marta, this was their first introduction to this type of activity. Zari, Pipa, Rona, and Morag became their personal trainers, and as usual, Becca became the class clown when she gave them dry land swimming lessons.

Pender brought the four young girls out to watch the training class. They were mesmerized at what these young women were learning but were still very much afraid to say anything. Pender let Lilly hold Zarena, but not before Rollo had sniffed around to give his permission. The other girls were too shy or nervous to partake of this simple pleasure. Lilly asked him if the baby was his, so he told them the story of how they had found Lena in the wilderness abandoned by men who had raped her and made her pregnant and left her to die. The team members helped her and brought her back with the baby, and now they were part of the family.

Lara asked tremulously, "What will happen to us?"

Pender answered, "In three days' time, we will take you back to your people and families. If they are prepared to take you back and you really want to stay, then you are free to do so. If, for any reason, your presence will embarrass them, you will be free to return with us and become part of our team and family."

Lilly said, "My father will be ashamed of me. He will not even allow me to be a slave in our home. As far as he is concerned, I know he would rather that I had died."

Ena spoke for the first since she had recovered. "No man in our tribe will even look at us. We have been raped, which makes us a pariah, outcasts in our own families, not even allowed to sit at the same dining table, rejected by all of our relatives and resigned to be sold as slaves."

Nanci said, "I don't know whether I can take anymore. My body is damaged, but it will recover—my mind, that is a different matter. While one of the men was beating me, I could not get it out of my head that our families knew that the Bald-Headed People were continuingly stealing our sheep and livestock, and they still deliberately put us uncaringly into danger then did nothing to rescue us. We were worth the same as the sheep and the goats, an unfortunate cost of doing business. This realization will stay with me for the rest of my life. How can I ever recover from seeing the looks of complete distain on the faces of my family and friends? And that is inevitable. I will go with you and stare them all down, but I will not stay. I want to be like these young women right there. I want their purpose in life as my own."

Pender listened to the girls with great interest, for these were exactly the pictures he had conjured up in his own mind, that this would be the attitudes of their families and the futures facing these dear young people. His argument with Eram had revealed that they would have few desirable options, and he was determined they should not suffer for the conscienceless dictates of the rulers of the Mystic People. His whole purpose in life had been formed the day he had visited Slave Island with Brini to seek Castor. It was the first time he had seen what the future meant for slaves and was touched forever. His commitment to free his only love, Zalenda, from slavery had become a burning ambition to free all slaves and destroy human trafficking and the traffickers wherever he found them. He found these men and women so dispiteous that he had no conscience in killing them in cold blood. His attitude against rape had been formed when he found the two men about to rape Becca. His disgust for this type of person had enabled him to order the dogs to kill her would-be rapist without a second thought.

The Mystic People had made a vow to help treat and heal people from all tribes who where sick, hurt, and wounded, and yet would treat their own daughters as inconsequential without a modicum of protection. He would protect them and keep them safe.

When the training session was over, Zalenda brought the whole team to where Pender sat with the four girls. She introduced herself as Pender's wife and companion in the business of halting slavery and the rape of women. These young women with her were their team formed and trained for that purpose. She would let Pipa, their leader, introduce each one, and then they could spend time getting to know one another.

Lena came and sat down beside the four girls from the Mystic People tribe, and as each member of the team was introduced, she gave them a short account of what each one had done to help her recover from her ordeal. She said she could not believe how her life had changed in ten short days. It had gone from being raped by large groups of men, made pregnant, and left to die in a desert, into a family of beautiful caring people who were taking her home with them. "Did you see me out there doing all the kicks with the rest of the team? I feel wonderful. Maybe when you feel better and Carla allows you, we can help each other to join in the fun."

Nanci said, "I will make myself ready for tomorrow. Will you come and take me with you? I am not very good with people, and I do want to be accepted by all of the team so I can go with you to your home.

Lena said, "I will be there as your special sister, and you can hold my baby Zarena. We will be best friends for the rest of our lives." She hugged and kissed Nanci, who was a bit embarrassed; no one had ever done that before, and she loved the feeling.

The other three girls looked on with wonder but were noncommittal. Then Carla came and took them back to the hospital tent to rest.

Nena and Elecia approached Pender because now they had a problem. Since Eram had refused to bring them supplies, their present food would require to be rationed, and even at that, they would only have enough for two days. Pender said he would consult with Carla to see if they perhaps could change their leaving date to the second day, which would mean they would have to visit the Mystic People tomorrow. It would really depend on how well the girls were to travel. The team should accelerate their packing and be ready should things not change. They must have their masks and hoods available for the Valley of the Flies, and new equipment would be required for the new people.

He and Carla met in the hospital tent, where the four girls were sleeping, thanks to one of Carla's sleeping potions. She agreed that they should meet with Eram and her people to discuss the perceived slight Eram felt. She would give the girls another potion, but they were recovering quicker than she thought, thanks to their young bodies. When she addressed the whole tribe and the girls' families, she wanted the whole team to be there so the Mystic People would see the good they represented.

While she was there, she would pick up special potions for the expanded team, the baby, and the dog for going through the Valley of the Flies. She would also get some special ones for Becca, Lena, and the four girls if they wished to travel with them. She would contact some of her friends to make sure there would be enough horses for the journey to the settlement. This would be done once they were through the Water Gate; payment could be arranged for later.

Pender called a team meeting to inform them of the new deadlines. They would leave for the meeting with the Mystic People the next day after Zalenda had excused them from their training. Everyone had to be there except Nena and Elecia. He explained that this was necessary because they were running out of food supplies, so it was likely that they would leave for home the day after tomorrow.

The evening meal that night was sparse, reflecting the reality of the food shortage, but they decided to have one last big fire so that everyone could relax and have fun. Zalenda had all the team do their hair in what was now their special style. The new girls in particular were given special attention. Tina, Lena, Mina, and Marta had never experienced such treatment before, as Esther, Nena, and Elecia spoiled them, plaiting and twisting up their beautiful head crowns. Zalenda and Rahana did the hair for the four mystic girls who at first were not too keen, but when they saw the results were absolutely thrilled, especially when Elecia brought them new dresses to wear. They had never been so pampered and looked so beautiful. Zari, of course, started dancing. While she danced, everyone clapped in time. Then one by one everyone joined in, even Carla, whose gorgeous black hair was swept up on the top of her head; no crown could have sparkled more. Lilly and Nanci were the last to join in when they saw Pender stagger around with the baby; even Zarena had her hair done. Then they were entertained by Becca's impression of Pender's dancing style till everyone was laughing and just had to sit down and enjoy the fire. Before they left to go to their tents, Carla said she would like the ladies to wear their hair up and dress as they were for their meeting the next afternoon, so all last-minute packing should be done in the morning.

The next afternoon they assembled at the wall, everyone looking beautiful and confident. The four girls who had dreaded this day were looking like princesses and had gained that new confidence that the team possessed.

Pender spoke briefly about what they might express. Then Carla led them out into the caves. They had put on their sheepskin coats because of the cold in the caves. At first they walked slowly, but Nanci told Carla, "We are quite able to walk faster," so she increased the pace. After an hour, they filed into the gathering hall of the Mystic People, and Carla led them to the front and onto the platform, where Eram and his dignitaries where already in place. Carla did not give him a chance to start his rant. She instructed the girls to take off their sheepskin coats and made sure their daughters were right in front of them. Their parents and family gasped when they saw how beautiful they looked. Pender stood beside Carla holding the baby, Rollo lying at his feet.

Carla waited until everyone had focused on her. Then she began. "People of the Mystic tribe, I am here as part of the team that answered the earnest plea from one of your leaders to rescue these four young women, your daughters, sisters, granddaughters, and family from the Bald People. I understand that you sent out these young girls to watch your flocks without any kind of protection. This was an open invitation for evil men to take your flocks and these young girls to do what they wanted with them, and they did. But did you fathers demand from these men behind me to form a band to go and get these children back? What did you do? Nothing! What did these dignitaries behind us do? Nothing! It was these young people you see here who rescued me when I was a prisoner of the slave traders. They saw my need and responded, and I am fortunate to be alive. When they were being hunted by a large army of paid assassins, I contacted Eram here to give them safe haven, as is the stated policy of this tribe. The vows you made mean something that cannot easily be laid aside. They came here, and as a result, we have a baby who is here today alive with her mother. Lena, please tell these good people your story."

Lena was hesitant at first but told them of her terrible childhood and how she had been raped repeatedly by evil men, made pregnant, and left to die with her newborn baby hanging from her. "I was saved by this man and two of these young women, and now my baby and I have a future with this team. They are my family." She went and took Zarena from Pender and walked back to her place.

"When your daughters were being brutally raped night after night, you did nothing. Then we learned from Eram what the situation was, and that it was necessary to move quickly, for the Bald People were making ready to move. These young people quickly came up with a plan and put it into operation. They were guided to the tent where the girls were being held by a continuous stream of men and the screams of the girls as they were beaten and horribly raped. These young people knew that if the Bald-Headed People were moving, the girls would be murdered, so they distracted the stream of men and killed them so that they would not be able to raise the alarm. Two young women pulled down the tent on top of the men raping your girls and killed the men as they emerged. They then took the girls to safety. We killed all of the leaders of the Bald-Headed People. As a lesson that they had to learn— they cannot raid your tribe with impunity.

"Let me now show you how your girls are today after they have been treated and loved by all our team." She called to Lilly, Lara, Ena, and Nanci to come forward. Carla had expected the girls to look down on the floor, but as Nanci had said, she and the others looked for their parents and stared them out. "These girls were so badly beaten, they had broken ribs, torn and beaten breasts, multiple bite marks, bruises all over their arms and legs, and the most horrendous evidence of countless rapes. But you all did nothing! These girls are not for sale today. If they choose now, you will never see them again." Then she said lovingly to the girls, "If you want to stay with these people, just stay where you are, and I will arrange it. If you want to go with our team as full members, walk back into the line, and we will take you home with us."

Nanci looked right at her father and then turned around and looked at Eram and his council and walked back into her place. Lilly stood for a moment with tears streaming down her face then paused, looked around the hall face by face, then turned and went back to her place. Lara looked at her family then said to the people, "Today I hate you all equally. You allowed us to be taken and did nothing," then walked back into line.

Ena waited until the buzz had subsided after Lara's condemning words then said, "You sent us out to watch your sheep and goats but did not provide any protection for us. When the Baldheads stole the sheep and the goats, you did nothing. When we were taken and raped, you did nothing! We were worthless to you than the sheep. I hope I never see any of you again." She spat on the floor then walked back into line.

Carla waited again until the affront some people felt at Ena's action died down then spoke with great anger. "We have been asked here today by Eram to apologize for killing so many of the Bald-Headed People. Apparently, we damaged his dignity and sensibilities. He is proud of his nonviolent reputation. First of all, he did not take part in the planning of the rescue bid nor did he give any instructions. We acted as we did, first of all, to rescue the girls and to protect our team. The odds were fifty to one, and we did it. Second, it was our intention to teach the Baldheads a lesson they would not soon forget. Did it work? Yes! Word has just come that the Bald-Headed People have just moved out—your farmers and flocks are safe. You can carry on your lives without fear." The place erupted in cheering and stamping of feet as people patted each other on the back and were shouting with relief.

The team left the platform, leaving only Carla and Pender. Eram came forward and silenced the crowd then spoke with real conviction. "Mystic People, we have been taught a great lesson today. We must change and see the world as it is, not as it was in earlier times. Had these young people listened to me, we would still be living in fear. I was wrong to criticize their methods. I should have realized they knew more about these things than I did, and today we have that proof. You have our eternal thanks for what you have accomplished. Now for your journey home, ask for anything, and we will gladly supply it."

Chapter 40

The Journey Home

Carla thanked him for the kind words and suggested that the four girls would require clothes, personal care lotions, sheepskin jackets and pants, night wear, and skin coats and hats for rainwear. Perhaps their parents should be asked to provide these items and any others they may think they will require. "I will need access to your stores of ointments, potions, and other medicinal products for our journey through the Valley of the Flies. To give the girls more time to recover physically, we will require enough food supplies for six days and ten ground covers, supplies for the baby, and a carrier for the baby and dog for going through the Valley of the Flies."

Eram said if she gave him the full list, he would get his people working on it immediately, and she was welcome at any time to help herself to their storeroom of potions.

Carla noticed that there was great interaction between the team and her people. They were so thankful to be free from their oppressors and hugged and kissed Rahana and Becca. The parents of the four girls were in deep discussions with them, but when it was time to leave, they just hugged their mothers and sisters and left without looking at their fathers.

The team made its way back to the camp carrying some of the food they would need and Carla's kit back filled with new potions. The baby started to cry because she needed to be fed, so there was a temporary halt until she was satisfied. Nanci approached Pender to ask if they could carry their fair share of the loads. Pender thanked her for asking but said the long climb up to the camp would be enough for them today, and they should give their bodies more time to recover.

The next four days were spent in preparation for moving out and practicing for the Valley of the Flies. Carla and Pender decided because of the increased number, it would be better to have a double column. Pender and Zalenda would lead, and Carla and Elecia would be at the end of the line. Pender had procured a sling carrier from Eram for Rollo, and Zalenda had one for the baby that wrapped around her. She was delighted at this prospect. With Carla's help, they were much better prepared this time for their ordeal. Everyone would receive a potion in their drink before entering the tunnels, and she had devised a special-smelling concoction that was attached to their masks to alleviate their suffering from the stench. Nena in particular was so thankful for this, and she thanked Carla for her thoughtfulness.

Carla pronounced the four girls fit for the journey as long as their ribs were bound and they only carried half a load. Mina, Marta, Tina, and Morag decided they would take half of their kit. As the tents were well weathered, Pender decided to take them down and leave them in place. Eram was pleased to have extra storage, so they arranged to leave two for this purpose.

The last night on the site, they had a party to use up the extra food. They were surprised when Eram brought the Mystic People with him to say good-bye. It was made even more special when the team was all given special lockets to wear around their necks made from a rare stone. Each one was distinctive and different. The presentation was made by Eram and his council, and when each member of the team was recognized, the Mystic People cheered heartily. The four girls were last to be called. Their fathers came out of the cave and made their special presentation special.

In the morning, Eram turned up to lead them through the labyrinth of caves and tunnels because it had been a while since Pender had made that journey, and Carla was busy with her charges. It was well into the afternoon before they were ready to exit the caves and into the Valley of the Flies.

After they had rested and said good-bye to Eram, they lined up and drank their last potion in their flasks but kept one in reserve for the journey from the place of the red rocks where there would be no water. They donned their masks and special head coverings and followed Pender and Zalenda into the valley, each one of them holding on to the rope and walking in unison. The smell and noise were exactly as they remembered it and were especially difficult for the new girls, whose apprehension and trepidation led to panic attacks, but with great courage, they walked on.

When Carla and Elecia gave the signal, the column came to a temporary halt, while they removed their masks and head covers. Rollo had been given a sedative, so Pender had to keep on carrying his burden, while Zalenda kept the baby, who was asleep cuddled to her and would do till the baby would awake. The leather rope was greased and rolled up and placed under a rock in case of emergency in the future. Then they were off walking again till they reached the homes of the M People where Merca was there to greet them.

The ladies all collapsed in their rooms, but additional cots had to be brought in for the extra travelers. Nanci shared with Tina, Lilly with Ester, Lena with Rona, Ena with Morag, and Lara with Pipa. Rahana, Becca, Mari, Zari, Nena, Elecia, and Carla shared the second room. Mina and Marta when to their families for the night, while Pender and Zalenda were given their own room. It was the first time they had enjoyed this privacy in a long time but were too exhausted to take advantage of it. Everyone slept unhindered till morning, even Rollo, whose sleeping potion kept him quiet the whole night. Zarena had been given to Merca's daughter, who was pleased to nurse her overnight.

In the morning, they all woke up to a beautiful day and were welcomed into the dining room where the M People wanted to hear their stories. Becca starred in many dramas, but it was the stories told by Mina and Marta about the rescue of the four girls that gave their people the most pleasure. Pender recognized people who had not been there before; they were what was left of the Auit Tribe that they had helped. The hunters had never returned, so Merca had invited them to join with his tribe, and now they were an integral part of the M People because of their hard work. It was good to see such positive solution to what had been a matter of life and death.

They were persuaded to stay one more night so they could leave in the morning. Everyone was in favor, so it was an easy decision.

That night was special in many ways. After the cold of the caves, the sheepskin jackets and pants could safely be put away with the hats and hoods. The spring nights had arrived early, and it was hot even when darkness fell. The celebrating, the dancing, and the singing went on and on. The girls all got up and danced, and as they did, they were joined by the whole M tribe. There had never been a night like it; everyone danced for sheer joy and happiness. Carla even got up on a table and danced. Everyone clapped and cheered her exquisite performance. Then it was the talking and exchanging of stories again into the midnight hour. One by one the girls straggled off to bed to sleep naked, for the heat was intense.

Pender and Zalenda waited till they were sure the whole team was in bed before they made for their room, where they took off all their clothes to lie naked beneath a single sheet. Despite the heat and their tired bodies, they embraced and kissed, then kissed again; this time there was no interruption. They went to bed virgins, but that night was special—they truly became one forever, never again to part. Nothing could come between them; this was the consummation of their love, a love that started when he saw her in the slave compound and he threw his drinking flask to her, and she saw him and loved him and signed her heart to him, and he had loved her from that moment.

The morning came too early for everyone. Rollo was up and looking for Zarena; she had to be fed and her mother was still sleeping. But soon the delicate scents of breakfast wafted over the buildings, bringing everyone to life with promise of food to be savored and enjoyed. It was very successful, for soon the team was fed, packed, and ready to leave and saying good-bye to their friends. Mina and Marta found the parting difficult but stressed they were committed to the team and were ready and happy to be part of it.

Pender and Zalenda led the team into the cave tunnels again where it was pleasantly cooler and started their walk to the Water Gate. They stayed well away from the yellow fountains; of course, Becca had to amuse everyone with her antics of suffering from its yellow glow. They continued their walk through the translucent rock caves, where Mina, Marta, and the four girls were in wonder of everything they saw. The whole group lingered in the glory of this strange temple of the earth's majesty.

When they approached the Water Gate, Pender followed Carla to see how she controlled the door through the waterfall. He was amazed to see a large round rock wheel that slid in a groove cut into the side of the cave rock. He wondered at the skill of these long-ago cave dwellers who had designed and cut this water wheel with such precision that all Carla had to do was to move a rocklike wedge from one side to the other to open and shut the gate, turning the flow of water on and off.

The team passed through the gate out into the now very hot afternoon air. They all stripped off the extra clothes they had worn in the caves, and Becca even ventured into the falls pool for a swim. Carla went to contact her friends to bring the horses back for the rest of the journey to the settlement and the island.

Carla soon returned with her pony, White Flame, and Toto, who rushed Zalenda and was nonplussed to find a strange dog in her company. The two dogs sniffed around each other and must have come to some agreement of friendship, for they were soon cavorting and rushing around amid all the now-disorganized camp. A fire was set up, and Elecia, Mari, and Nena started a meal assisted by Nanci and Ena. The rest reorganized their kit for going on the pack horses and trying to remember which horse they had ridden on their hurried flight from their home. All of the horses including the extra ones Carla had ordered for the new team members arrived in the middle of the meal, adding to the general confusion.

Slowly order was restored, and the men who had brought the horse assisted in loading the pack horses, and the site was cleared ready for everyone to move out. There was a slight delay when the new girls said they had never ridden a horse before and were afraid of these large animals. Carla gave them a potion to calm them down, and after some time, they were lifted up by the men onto their steeds. This seemingly insurmountable problem was solved when the men offered to walk the horses along the path until the girls were comfortable and knew how to talk and guide their mounts. The men stayed with them on the narrow pathway, but when they came to the wider road through the hills, they left and went back to their homes. The team reorganized so that they were riding on either side of the new recruits. Pender called a halt for the night early in the evening because everyone was sore and stiff from riding. It had been two years since some of them had ridden. The next two days and nights were excessively hot, and the horses had to be well watered, but the midges and flies were troublesome to the animal and humans.

When they stopped for the next night, Carla went out and collected herbs, which she brewed overnight to form a paste. The next morning the team anointed it on their faces and on the horses' heads. The ride to the settlement next day was much more comfortable, and they arrived in good time for the men to be able to settle the horses in the stables. The men also assisted the girls in carrying all the equipment to the ferry. By nightfall they were safely installed back in their own rooms, and the new team members were issued their own places. After Cisi and her people had welcomed everyone to their island home and sat down for a meal, they were all ready for bed, but not before they visited the hot springs. Pender and Zalenda waited till they were all in bed before they went and had the springs to themselves.

In the morning Pender and Zalenda met with Cisi to find out if Rici had been back at the settlement and to tell her he had been identified as one of the men who had been paid to find Pender and the team. He had also been recognized as one of the men who had raped Lena, and they wanted to bring him to justice.

Chapter 41

Rici and Raymond—the Prelude to War

Cisi was delighted to meet with them because it was time for her to move back to the settlement. In the last two years, she had completely rebuilt it from the damage done by that violent storm. Her new home had just been completed, and it was much more conducive to the daily running of tribal affairs from the settlement. She was finding it was easier to get things done since she had replaced the old group of elder cronies because the people had seen what she had been able to accomplish and were very happy and satisfied. Since the fall of Tamor and the slave traders, intertribal trade was very good, and they were becoming quite prosperous.

Unfortunately, she had no information on where Rici had gone, but it was generally believed that he was working with the new boss of the slavers, Raymond. Raymond had apparently wrestled control of the slave trade from the group who had tried to take it over on the demise of Tamor, but because he was the transporter, he would not allow them to use his barges. It was a simple matter after that to mop up the opposition, so now he was the big guy and all the former groups were under his iron hand. No trade of any kind could be done on the river without his tax, but that was not all bad because the tribes were becoming more self-reliant; even the new weapons were being made at home by the skills of the Forest People.

Zalenda allowed the girls two days of relaxation before starting combat training again. She introduced them to attacking and defending against opponents with clubs using her own specialized training system. The girls were dumbfounded when they watched her strike her target and gracefully dodge the swinging weights she had suspended from the ceiling. Under her tutelage, the girls learned the hard way to time each thrust and move with quick hand-and-eye coordination while escaping the punishing maze of disaster the weights provided. The new girls found this form of preparation very sore on their bodies, and it was necessary for Carla to attend all sessions to treat their bumps and bruises. Carla took her share of bumps as well, as no one was excused. Becca cried foul when Rahana, because of her small stature, had no difficulty in dodging the weights.

The next day Zalenda introduced the team to using and defending against other weapons of warlike spears and swords. Her aim was to have her people excel in all these areas like she had done for her old tribe. This meant they had to acquire these weapons from Cisi; in turn, she provided the same training for the settlement's defense. At first, the men were loath to accept her because she was a woman; but after the beatings she gave them in practice, they slowly came to the realization that they needed her expert knowledge.

Pender wanted to inquire into how Carla was able to commune with her people so far away and why it was necessary to talk to the wind. Carla admitted that the whole standing on the Doan Stone was indeed a ruse to get his team to trust her and have confidence in her by appearing to have special powers. She had taken a powerful potion that had temporarily affected her features and she had spoken in her old language. She had preknowledge of the weather conditions because she had a wide network of people who delivered her potions. Even Rona and Pipa had accepted deliveries at the settlement on her behalf. The men who had looked after their horses were part of that network, so they had received information from her when the team was to arrive. They in turn had alerted Merca and Eram to be prepared for their arrival, and the same had held true for their return.

Carla suggested that because she had people in every tribe across all of the areas, this network could be invaluable to get information out quickly to these people without risking team members and without creating suspicion. "I could arrange for special flasks to be delivered to every tribe that would hold a potion and a stone that would have special significance for all of the tribes. If we had an emergency and required immediate support from them, this could be done quickly, quietly, and safely."

Pender said, "Carla, this suggestion has great merit. We truly could devise an excellent intelligence gathering system, but could we trust your people with this kind of secret communication?"

"I think they have already proved that they are trustworthy. They accepted the responsibility to stable your horses and equipment and for great personal gain could have divulged where you were to the evil men who were hunting you, but they did not. Besides, they never open the packages. I have sent thousands of potions to all people and all tribes without having one complaint. Should they open one, how would they know what the stone symbolized? I would like to take Rona and Pipa and the two new girls, Mina and Marta, with me so I can go around the tribes and explain the system and what to do in case they need help or we should need help. There are no real issues that we have on our horizons, and the new members of the team need some riding practice. This is a very good opportunity for them to broaden their relationships with the other people of this area. Rona and Pipa can be their mentors and further develop their wilderness experience. Do you think we could take the dogs with us? They have been quite constricted since we came home."

Pender said he would organize a team meeting for that afternoon to discuss these requests because he was so excited about all of these possibilities. He felt the other important issue they had to deal with was to find out where his cousin Rici was at present; as long as he was on the loose, the team would be in danger. They had not been home long enough to gather any kind of reliable information on Raymond, the transporter, and his new role as the big guy! This had to be one of their major concerns because he now controlled all the aspects of the slave trade and the support of his hired army. The good news seem to be that the redheaded Nuit Tribe had distanced themselves from the slave business since the death of Tamor, and they had also purged his cohorts from any position of authority within the tribe. We should consider including them in your trip around the family tribes; they might prove to be valuable friends in the future.

At the team meeting that afternoon even before the discussion got under way, Tina and Ester wanted permission to go and look for Rici, and Lena wanted to go with them as long as Becca or Zari took care of Zarena. Pender said this request would come under the full discussion of the team, as they had many other decisions that had to be made.

Carla made a very persuasive presentation on establishing a network of potion dispatchers who presently delivered to all the tribes. She described in detail how this system that had been in place for years; it could be also used to give warning to the tribes or to get help for the team without attracting attention. The other attractive feature was that in times of danger, team members would not be involved.

Everyone thought this would be worth pursuing, and Rona and Pipa were delighted that they would be traveling with Carla in the initial setup of the program. Mina and Marta were equally excited because they would get more riding experience and time in the field.

It was decided that the full-grown wolf Rollo would go with them, as Pender had been teaching him to kill and could now respond to that order on straw dummies. Toto was getting too old to go on long missions, and Zalenda in particular was happy at that decision.

The news from Cisi was that the whole area was at peace, and there was no sign of trouble anywhere. Mari and Zari, because of this, asked if they could go and get an update from the watchers at Slave Island to see if any rebuilding of the palisade had been done. Zalenda and Pender would accompany them to gather information on Raymond's intentions as far as the slave trade was concerned and what the extent of his manpower and hired armies was likely to have at his disposal.

The team to go after Rici would be Ester, Tina, and Lena, with Rahana to be in charge. They had permission, if it was safe to do so, to take him out without bringing him back for punishment. Cisi was quite in favor of this decision, although it probably could be viewed by her council as infringing on their responsibility to determine his punishment. She requested that she should have Morag and Nena as riders in case she required to communicate with anyone in the field. Becca would continue to finish the training of Lilly, Lara, Ena, and

Nanci. Elecia would be mother to Zarena as well as her normal position as mother to the team.

All the teams were to report back within five days except Carla's, which would need at least two to three weeks. For the visit to the Nuit Tribe, it was essential that Carla's team come back to the island to pick up Elecia, whose expertise would be needed to set up the network there.

Chapter 42

The Search and Apprehension of Rici

A cooler summer morning greeted the team groups as they loaded their supplies onto their horses. Pender reflected on the first missions they had undertaken when they had to walk everywhere, and the walking was fraught with danger. At least on these missions, if their information was correct, the girls should be safer, and they would be completed in less time. Nevertheless, he gathered them together before they left and warned them to be exceedingly careful in everything they did and to test each situation as it developed. If they became aware of anything that might become dangerous, they were to stop what they were doing and ride for home immediately. Becca, whose health still was not good, was to guard their island home with the four new girls. They were so happy to be there, as Becca took them every day to complete their riding lessons, but today was special because they were going to ride with Pender and Zalenda out onto the moor. This was big! The teams hugged each other and rode off in different directions aware of their responsibilities and not knowing when they would see each other again.

The conditions for riding over the moor could not have been better. The paths were clear, the early morning air was still cool, and a light breeze rose up from the river. Nanci talked the whole time till even Becca shook her head in disbelief. Rahana whispered to Zalenda, "We did a good thing there, sister."

Zalenda replied, "If that is all we have accomplished, it has all been worthwhile. Who would have guessed when I picked up that flask in the slave compound? Who could have predicted when you put your hair plaits in Pender's hands that we would have rescued so many and changed their lives and ours? It is a wonder."

They came to the river road crossing and decided to use the same spot they had rested in the last time Tina had seen Rici. The new girls went to work setting up the campsite while Pender started a fire. Rahana took her team aside and went over their new assignments. She had decided that it would be better if they accompanied Pender and Zalenda down to see if their fishermen friends had any useful information that would guide them in their search for Rici.

Zalenda did her usual checking to see if all was clear before they sat down for their meal. She was a little perturbed that Toto, who had been covering their trail all day, had not shown up. Pender put it down to the fact that she had not been out hunting for some time, having been restricted to the island for the last month.

After they had eaten, Becca and her girls went to pick up their horses from the hide. On the way back, they heard Toto making an uncharacteristic noise. Becca sent Lilly up a tree to investigate. She came down quickly and told Becca a group of men were coming down through the woods. They had Toto on a rope and were heading toward them. Becca immediately retraced her steps and put the horses back in the hide and told Nanci, Lara, and Ena to go quietly to Pender and tell him what was about to happen. Lilly was sent back up the tree and told to stay there and only to come down if she called her. She then sat down and waited for the men to come.

The men were tired and staggered into the clearing where Becca sat. When they saw her sitting apparently on her own, two of them rushed at her which was a mistake. It was exactly the reaction Becca had counted on; she wanted to distract them till the team arrived. Then everything went wrong for her attackers. They were hungry and tired and not thinking. Toto's captor let up on the rope. She turned on him and grabbed him by the groin. The man screamed in agony, and Becca's would-be attackers got tangled up in the rope. One of the men disentangled himself from the rope and was about to smash Becca on the head with a club when Lilly dropped from the tree right on top of him, sending him back down on the ground. Lilly recovered quicker than the assailant and kicked him as she had been taught in the legs; unfortunately, it was a glancing blow that hit him in the groin. The man howled and went down again. Her second kick hit him in the chin. He didn't get up again.

Just then Pender and Zalenda came in from one side, and Rahana and her team from the other. Lena, who was told to follow Zalenda, shouted to Pender that these were the men who had raped her. The girls moved in on the men with a controlled fury. The men charged and hit nothing. Clubs were swung, and no contact was made, and as the men became more tired, their efforts became more desperate. Ester and Tina had recognized Rici as one of the assailants and separated him from his cronies and were relentless in their pursuit of him. Zalenda had already killed two men and was busy dispatching at the third, while Rahana's club subdued another as the four new girls kicked and beat off their attackers. The unplanned haphazard attack was over very quickly. Pender with Toto's help held the leader on the ground. He was bleeding and beaten and in no shape to order further resistance. Things went very quiet when Ester brought Rici into the middle of the now-depleted group of men. When he recognized Pender, he spat on the ground and said, "Why, it's the girly boy, my cousin, and his band of concubines. I have been paid a lot of money to kill you all and then to go and kill that bitch, your sister."

Ester replied, "It is a great pity that you will never be able to collect it because today you will die for being a treacherous little coward and for raping this young woman here who is going to watch you die slowly."

"Sorry, bitch cousin, you will have to take me back to the settlement to have our tribal council pass judgment on me. That is our custom, and guess what, I have already paid them all."

"Thank you for that information. I will be sure to tell my sister that she has to hang the rest of your treacherous family, but you should know we have already obtained permission to make sure you die here today for your scurrilous behavior and despicable conduct."

"Now, Pender said, "let us begin. Toto, take and hold." Toto took and held Rici by the groin. "Now normally I would command Toto to kill and he would tear off your genitals, but not today. Today you're under judgment for being a traitor to your tribe and to your family, and for at least on two, now three, separate times being paid to identify me and my team so others could kill us. But further to that is your dispiteous despoilment of this young lady here whom you and your friends raped repeatedly, and when she was pregnant, you left her and her baby to die in the wilderness. These are the charges that we bring against you."

"Rahana, as leader of the team charged with the responsibility of finding and bringing this man to justice, what is your judgment?" Rahana consulted with her team and pronounced him guilty.

Pender asked Ester and Tina to come forward and stand on Rici's arms and then asked Ena and Nanci to stand on his legs; then and only then did he order Toto to let go of Rici's crotch. Held down in this way, Rici realized his end was near. He had always believed he could outmaneuver his cousins within the family, but not this time. He began to cry like the true coward he was, saying over and over again, "Please don't do this. I can help you. I know things you need to know."

Zalenda brought Lena forward and coached her, "This is the man, little sister, who raped you repeatedly and encouraged these men here to do the same. I want you to kick him three times, once in the genitals from which he raped you, once in the throat from which he mocked you, and once in the head to make sure he can never do it again to another young girl. If he still lives after that, I will take great pleasure in sending him into death."

The two men who were left alive watched as Lena coolly aimed her first kick; it was delivered exactly as she had been trained. Rici screamed in pain, and as he had been oblivious on many occasions to her screams of pain, she was now to his. Her second kick connected to his once-sneering face, smashing his teeth and mouth to pulp, reducing his nose to a bloody mess. He could no longer make a sound. The clothes they had propped up his head oozed with his blood. Her third kick caught him on the throat, and there was no need for Zalenda's expert dispatch of this criminal; he was dead.

The two men immediately began to beg for mercy, saying over and over again it was all Rici's fault—he had made all the arrangements, it was right that he should have died but at no time could they have identified any of Pender's team; they were just there as a show of force.

Rahana asked Lena if she could tell her if either of these men had raped her. She pointed to one of them and said, "He raped me, and even when they came back later when I was almost ready to deliver the baby, they all raped me again, and he was the one who carried me out and threw me into the bushes so the wild animals could eat me. They all laughed and joked about it."

Rahana drew her club and smashed it down on the man's head repeatedly until Zalenda intervened to stop her friend's frenzy.

The last man suddenly became coherent and said to Pender, "Raymond is coming to get you next week with a very large army. Some are trained, some are not, but he is determined to take and kill all your team. He will attack all of the tribes in the area and take men and women from here to be slaves. I have heard that it could be two weeks, as he is making himself rich attacking other tribes south of the Big River and holding them for ransom."

Pender asked him what he should do with him. "Rahana here is very good with a club, as she has demonstrated. All of the young ladies have been scrupulously trained to kill as you have seen. My dog with one command can render your male parts useless. My wife can kill you with one kick—what would you prefer?"

"I would like you to let me go so I can go back to my family. I can honestly say that I have not raped any woman, although with these bad men, there was plenty of opportunity. I can say also that I have never mistreated anyone or did any harm to or killed anyone. I was originally hired because of my knowledge of all of the tribes and to be a guide for these men. My former occupation was a traveling trader in all kinds of hand tools and pottery. This is how I obtained my knowledge of all the tribes and people, and for this I must die?"

"What is your name, sir?" Pender asked.

"My family call me Bobi," he replied.

"Bobi, I notice you have red hair. Does that mean you are from the Nuit Tribe?" Pender asked again.

"Yes, my family are from the most northern part of the Nuit territories."

"Now, Bobi, think carefully before you answer this. Were you at any time a supporter of the late chief of the Nuit Tribe, Tamor the Redhead?" Pender put on a grim expression as he spoke.

Bobi seemed to be relieved as he replied, "No, my family and indeed our people from the north did not like him, nor did they agree with his policies."

"Well, Bobi, you are going back to our island home as a prisoner of Rahana and Becca and their team of young women. If you try to escape, they will kill you without mercy. When you get to our home, a lady there called Elecia, formerly of the Nuit Tribe, will carefully test your authenticity, and if she agrees you are who you say you are, you will live and be set free. If not, she will kill you. Is that clear?"

"Yes, Pender, I understand perfectly. Thank you for listening to me."

Rahana wasted no time in setting Bobi to work pulling out the bodies of the dead men and disposing of them in the woods, while the girls cleaned up the site and made ready for the trip home. It was arranged that Rahana and Becca's teams would return home with the prisoner, while Pender and Zalenda went on down to the river to see if they could glean more information from the fishing people. Rahana marveled to the group how things had evolved this time in their favor, but what about the next mission?

Pender and Zalenda mounted and watched the girls in the team ride away back over the moor before they turned and rode down the road to the shore of the Big River. Pender knew that at this time his fishing friends would be safely in their quarters enjoying their fish soup. He approached the door and called to warn them he was there. They soon came out and welcomed him but were in awe of Zalenda, whom he introduced as his wife.

Chapter 43

Raymond's Army and the Coming Storm

They were soon ensconced beside a blazing fire enjoying a special fish soup and brazed fish on a flat black bread that was quite delicious. The eyes of his friends never left Zalenda's beautiful face and statuesque figure. When she rose to remove her leather jerkin, the women rushed to help. They asked her if they could unlace the leather ties and were careful in removing it from her shoulders and equally carefully in folding it and placing it on a bed. Then the questions started: When and where had they fallen in love? Where was she the last time Pender was here? Why did she give up being a queen? And what was it like to kill a man? The men were embarrassed at their wives' continual questioning of their guest, but the stories she told enthralled them. No question was too personal—and they were—that Zalenda did not answer fully and often with great pleasure. The fishing families had not spent an evening like this before, and nothing was too good for their guests.

When the stories came to an end, it was time to sleep. Pender and Zalenda were given the best bed and new hand-knitted sheets and covers, while the families chose to sleep on the floor.

Breakfast in the morning consisted of the toasted black bread spread with good-tasting fish paste and hot cider tea, which their two guests enjoyed very much. Pender knew that his friends would soon be going to attend to their nets, so he began to question them about what was the news on the river about Raymond and his armies. They told him they had learned from fishermen down the river that Raymond and his armies had defeated a number of smaller tribes and held their chiefs for ransom. Raymond's problem was that it was too early in the year for harvest, and no one could pay until the harvest was in. At the same time, he was having to pay his mercenary troops for doing nothing, so it would be next spring before he would be able to move upriver. Pender asked if they had any knowledge of how many mercenaries were involved. The only way they could answer that question was that the rumors were it took two of the largest boats built to move them, around 120 men.

Pender and Zalenda shared their supplies they had with their friends and left when the men and women went out in their little boats to check their nets. The morning air was cool near the river as they made their way up to the moor. White Flame broke into a gallop, and Pender had some trouble keeping up with Zalenda, who stopped when she saw someone coming in a hurry toward her. It was Ester who had spent the night at the settlement. She came with news that Seth's relations and friends on the council were trying to organize a rebellion against Cisi. She had sent word to Rahana to bring the team from the island, and they were waiting on Pender and Zalenda to lead them.

By the middle of the afternoon Pender, Zalenda and Ester arrived at the settlement and did not take time to stable their horses. Rahana came and told them that Cisi had barricaded her home against the friends of Seth who were trying to gain entrance. They were all armed with clubs and other weapons. Since Zalenda had been training the men of the settlement to use weapons for defense, these men were now dangerous, and she did not want to risk her small team because all their weapons were at home on the island. She had sent word to Becca to come with her team and bring all their weapons, but she feared they would not arrive in time before the men attacking Cisi would break through the door. Toto came bounding forward, ready to greet his mistress with a loud welcome, which she immediately stopped and brought her to heel.

"Pender, you take Ester quietly and quickly around to the other side of the building. I will ride White Flame down on top of the men with Toto. When they break to flee, you cut them off in the alleyway, kill them if you have to. They are a treacherous bunch and have not learned from the past." Ester led Pender around and into position. When Zalenda heard the door being beaten down, she went into action, charging Cisi's bellicose belligerent attackers at full force. They saw her coming too late. They broke off their attack, threw down their weapons, and tried to run, only to be ridden down by Pender and Ester coming from the alleyway. Pandemonium reigned as the men tried to escape the entanglement they found themselves in one of the horse's legs and a raging dog.

Becca's reinforcements arrived now armed with their weapons and Rollo, who joined in the melee with great excitement. The rebellion was soon over, but not entirely.

As the team turned their traitorous targets into a simpering weeping bunch of cowards, a new danger came into view. Cisi was led out of her home by two of her own guards. They had her trussed up, one on either side with a knife at her throat, demanding that their comrades be set free or they would kill her. For a few moments, it looked like things had reached a stalemate, until Nanci and Ena could be seen by Pender on the roof of Cisi's home. The position the men who were holding Cisi were in as they came out of the house now meant that their backs were to the girls. Nanci and Ena were armed with their throwing spears. They were by far Zalenda's best pupils at that art and could hit the practice targets nine out of ten times.

One of the men spoke directly to Pender, saying, "If you do not release these men and the rightful chief of this tribe, your uncle Seth, we will kill your sister right now."

"On the contrary," Pender said, "as you have only a few moments to live, I suggest you drop your knife and then plead for forgiveness from your present and lawful chief. She might forgive you, I will not."

Both men laughed. "We have the bitch, and we will slit her throat. What will you do then, son of the great Castor, cry for Zalenda?"

"No, I will do this—you have been warned." He nodded his head, and two short spears arced in perfect unison, striking their targets and piercing them through and through. The men dropped dead, their knife falling harmlessly to the ground. Now the rebellion was truly finished. Seth cowered in defeat.

Ester and Rahana ran to Cisi and held her while she recovered from her ordeal. She said, "Don't let the people see me crying or they will see it as a sign of weakness. Take me back to my house quickly please." Ester and Rahana walked with her into the house.

Pender commandeered some of the men who had observed the spectacle to remove the bodies and take them into the council chamber and put them on display; they were not to remove the spears. He then called for an immediate council meeting with all the elders present, and he indicated that he and his team would attend in case there were any other attempts on his sister's life. After this meeting, he would convene one for the whole tribe, as he had some important information to share with them. The traitors would be held in the council cells with four of his armed team and the two dogs to guard them till sentence was passed on them. He then left to go and consult with Zalenda, Rahana, and Becca, and alert Cisi on the arrangements he had made.

He found the four women trying to make sense of what had happened. Becca believed their stumbling on Rici and his men was no accident, as they had thought at first, but a plan that was put together by Seth. Rahana pointed out that the only way they could have come up with the team's movements was from the stable boys, perhaps overhearing the teams talking with one another on their different missions. Zalenda felt that this was a distinct possibility. She said as well as teaching them to read signs to gather information, they must impress on them that it is equally important not to give anything away in casual conversation with these young men.

Cisi congratulated Becca on her training of the four young recruits, especially in how they had conducted themselves in assessing the situation and then climbing on the roof. "The throwing of the spears! That was excellent. They saved my life, and they have my gratitude."

Becca said, "The spear thing, that was all Zalenda, but keep piling on the praise, I can take it."

Rahana said to Pender, "You know, I believe that this young lady is getting too big for her britches."

Becca, as always, had to have the last word. She retorted, "Well, my diminutive friend, that is one thing we will never be able to say of you."

Rahana pouted and pretended to be hurt but quickly relented when the food was served.

Pender explained to Cisi why he had told the people who had gathered to watch her arrest by her uncle Seth's cronies that he was convening a special meeting that afternoon to deal with two things: Rici's treacherous behavior in taking the pay of the slave traders to have him and his team killed and his repeated rape of Lena; and the second thing that had become self-evident, Seth's family's continual attempts to replace Cisi, the genuine chief of this family tribe. He had done this without consulting her because he did not want any further rebellious behavior from their own family. He had just received information that within a year, Raymond would launch an all-out attack on all of the tribes in the area with a large army of hired mercenaries. He felt that they would have to meet this threat with a concerted effort from all of the tribes, perhaps in forming a confederation of tribes to face this pending action by Raymond.

Cisi said she was still a bit shaken by what had happened, but she agreed that these issues must be dealt with right away. She would open the meeting and hand it over to him to try each case, but she would pronounce the judgment.

The whole tribe gathered that afternoon, spurred by rumors and innuendo, and for what they might learn in the light of recent happenings. It was a noisy and recalcitrant crowd that had gathered, with many of Seth's male followers present to make trouble. When Cisi and Pender's team took the platform, they booed loudly till Zalenda led the two dogs in; the effect was immediate. Everyone there knew that with one order from their mistress what havoc they could cause to the booing men; they covered their genitals and went silent. Seth and his men were led in bound hand and foot, and the gags were removed from their mouths.

Cisi stood before the people of her tribes and carefully looked around the gathered crowd. The men who had been the most raucous were now squirming uncomfortably. She began, "People of this family tribe, you who have sworn fealty to me, must now decide what we must do with the traitors in our midst. I regret to inform you that members of my own family have repeatedly plotted great treachery toward me, my brother and my sister. This in spite of the very specific warnings I gave them to shun away from any involvement in this type of treachery they have practiced today and throughout the last months—for this they will be punished now. My brother Pender will now bring the evidence and the extent of their despicable behavior."

Pender stood up and looked at Seth and then began. "People of the settlement and island communities, my people, my friends, my family, I regret to inform you of fresh instances of the treachery and cruelty of my own family against us and a young woman who is here today to give veracity to these charges. I absolutely abhor the behavior of my family, starting with my brother, Kain, who murdered my mother and our stepmother, sold his father to the slave traders, and hung his friend and uncle, and then hung me and left my sisters to die in the cold. You know this, for it was your daughters that saved not only our lives but also the reputation of the whole tribe. Then it was my uncle and my father who entered into vile associations with the same slave traders while pretending to be against them. You were witnesses to the evil that was acted out by one of the elders at the lifting of the stone, and that historic tribal custom was destroyed forever that day when my father upheld that custom before he was revealed to also be a traitor. My sister became chief of this tribe according to a new lineage that was necessary because of the destruction of the Doan Stone.

"In spite of the fact that she has been accepted as such, her uncle Seth has sought at every turn to have her removed so that he could become your chief. There is no need to rehearse before you today the evidence of his final act of treachery today. The two bodies you see lying before you with the spears through them speak volumes of the man's dastardly underhand cruelty. My sister, your chief, was standing before him, held by these two men there who held a knife at her throat and were determined to kill her no doubt at Seth's orders. As you can see, two of our newest well-trained recruits found a way to cancel that order and set your chief free. Later you will be asked to pass judgment on these men and in particular on my uncle Seth for his treachery and abject cowardice. Would you believe when he saw his ambitions thwarted and his men taken prisoner by a group of young women, your would-be chief sobbed and cried for mercy? In the light of his behavior, can you honestly grant him that? I cannot."

"Don't think you have won. This is only the beginning. Rici is coming after you with men I have paid to kill you and your little girls, so I will have the last laugh. You will never escape me," and he laughed with a scornful belly laugh.

"I regret to inform you, Uncle, that what you described will never happen. You see, Rici was recognized by his cousin Tina riding with your paid assassins. Tina will you tell your uncle and your friends of this tribe what you observed when you were watching from a tree." Tina stood and told her story and exactly who Rici had been riding with besides the paid killers; it was the slave traders.

Pender stood again and introduced Lena and Becca. Becca told the story of how members of the team found Lena in the wilderness pregnant and the baby hanging from her. She spoke of the baby being delivered and how Pender had carried her home tied to his back. When the young woman was questioned, she told them that she had been raped repeatedly by a group of men, one of whom had a blue eye and a brown eye, and his name was Rici.

Seth screamed, "That does not mean it was Rici. Plenty of men have that problem."

"I am glad you mentioned that, Uncle, because that is exactly why Lena is here to positively identify Rici as the man who raped her. On our way here today, while we stopped for a break, Rici and your hired band of murderers staggered into our camp. They saw Becca sitting alone and rushed to catch her possibly to rape her, but they were overcome by a small band of highly trained women. Rici was identified by this young woman as the person who raped her over and over again without any kind of mercy for her. Not only that, he shared her with his friends who continued to rape her when they knew she was pregnant and threw her out in the desert for the wild animals to eat. Unfortunately for Rici, he was positively identified as the cruel merciless rapist that he was. We killed all of his men. Your paid killers are all dead, Uncle Seth, so you wasted your money. Lena here was invited to kick Rici three times, once in the crotch from which he raped her, once in the face from which he laughed at her, and once in the head from which he thought to end her life, but by which she ended his.

"So, Uncle, Rici is dead, and he will never insult or maim any other young woman. You have made a terrible mistake. We now know it was you who has been behind all of the treachery of this family that has existed from the beginning. You are a slave trader and the mole among us. For this you should die. Your peers will pass judgment, not me or my team, I am sure they will do it well."

"No one here will believe the word of that little bitch. You killed my son on her word. It is you who should die for that killing of an innocent boy."

"Wrong again, Uncle Seth. We kept alive one of your paid people who was an independent witness who took no part in the raping of this girl and who identified Rici and the rest of his bunch in their dispiteous behavior—that is why they are all dead."

Cisi stood up and announced that she would convene a meeting of the full tribe tomorrow to decide the punishment of her uncle Seth and her attackers.

"Now I am going to ask Pender to come and give us even more serious news that will affect every tribe in our area. It is something that we cannot ignore. It is something we must all support."

Before Pender could take the platform again, one of the well-known merchants stood up in the audience and asked for permission to speak. Cisi nodded her approval, although she did not want the meeting to develop into a name-calling distraction; she recognized him as a good person.

The man talked quietly at first, so the people called him to go to the front so they could hear him. When he reached the front and everyone was quiet, he said, "People and friends of this tribe, I am greatly concerned that there might seem to be present among us an attitude of dissatisfaction with our chief and the way we are being governed. I am here to say that this is a misconception. I cannot remember a time when we have been more involved in what this tribe stands for and when our business inside the tribe and outside with other tribes has grown, like it has these last years. I attribute this to the leadership of our wonderful chief and her excellent council. Please do not let the work of a few jealous, evil men take this away from us. Let us express our appreciation for our chief, the lovely Lady Cisi!"

The crowd applauded and cheered, shouting, "Our chief is Cisi! Our chief is Cisi! She is the best! She is the best!"

Pender stood up, and the crowd quieted. He said, "Sir, I agree with you—she is the best!" The people cheered again and again until Pender went to the center of the platform.

"People of our tribe, in the days and months ahead of us, she will have to be the best, and all of you will also be required to give her your support. There is another evil man who is on our horizon, his name is Raymond. In the last few days, our little team of young women have been out gathering information about this man and what he has done to other tribes and what he plans to do here. This year alone, he, with his hired armies, has ravaged the tribes to the south and east of us, taking the people for his slave trading and holding the chiefs for ransom. The only reason he is not here now among us is that he must wait till the harvest is in before the ransoms can be paid. This has given us an opportunity to be prepared for his arrival expected in the spring. One of the reasons they were so easily a prey to his ambitions is that he faced only limited opposition from these smaller tribes. They were not prepared. They were farmers and had no training or means to defend themselves. If we are to avoid a similar experience, we must prepare now. All of the tribes in our area must come together and form a confederation to face this new threat to our tribes and people.

"Our friend Carla has been out among the tribes forming a network so she can better serve their needs for potions. We foresaw the day when this network might be required to keep the other tribes informed of situations like this. It is my strong belief that day is now. We must prepare and pick the place where we will stand together with all the tribes and defend our lands and our people. My dear wife, Zalenda, as you know, has been teaching the use of the new weapons for defense to some of the people here. She is prepared to extend that to all the tribes. Some of you here will be asked to assist her in this venture. We will give an invitation to all the tribes to send their representatives here to talk over these matters. We must come together to form a common front. We cannot allow past grievances to prevail, and we cannot give up our land and people without a struggle. We must destroy this man's evil ambitions, his might, and his slave trading empire."

The hall was quiet. This was serious; nothing like this had happened before. They could not believe their way of life was being threatened, but it was, and they had to get ready.

Pender and his team were ready to take their horses to the stables and then leave for the island, but before they left, they arranged to meet Cisi in the morning to discuss the ramifications of Pender's speech and to pass judgment on Seth and his cronies.

The part of the team that had remained with Pender and Zalenda were in deep discussion as they pulled themselves over in the ferry to the island. The topic of the conversation was one that interested Pender immensely—why had the spears pierced through the bodies of Cici's captors. It could have been the force they were thrown with, or perhaps it was the downward arc, or was it the wood the spears were made from?

Nanci and Ena said they were concentrating so much on just hitting their targets, they were not conscious of any increase in power they might have made in the actual throw, but the downward arc may have been responsible.

Zalenda said the downward arc could have contributed to the force, but she felt it might have been the new delivery of weapons they had received from the Forest People, who were now using their woodworking skills to manufacture their special brand of throwing spears. Pender said we must inquire further about this; it could be important for the future.

Back on the island, there was great excitement because of the return of Carla, Pipa, Rona, Mina, and Marta, who had traveled to all the tribes and had enjoyed a very good reception. They wanted to stay for a few days before going on with Elecia to visit the Nuit Tribe. Elecia had already vetted Bobi and had cleared him as being of good character, so they were all keen to travel together. The result of their adventures around the tribes brought about the best relationships that had ever existed in intertribal affairs.

Chapter 44

The Tribes Prepare for the Coming War

Later on that year, the representatives from all the tribes came together to discuss the preparations they should make to thwart Raymond's planned attack. Pender was able to give them an update on what the news was from down the river and the information on when they might expect Raymond to turn his attention on their tribes.

Pender and Zalenda had made it their mission to visit their fishermen friends every two weeks throughout the last months to keep everyone alerted to the present dangers. During the discussions, it was the unanimous opinion of all those present that Pender should be in charge of all the arrangements for the defense of the tribes. He would also be in charge of how the tribes would assemble and how and where they would line up for the battle.

Pender and Zalenda on their trips downriver had already spent a great deal of time carefully selecting where they might meet Raymond with all his force. To be able to land his army from two barges, he would require a fairly large staging area. In discussions with his fishermen friends, they had suggested because of the tides, the most likely place for such a large landing would be just short of Tamor's old fort. This was also the opinion of the watchers from the Forest People, who agreed at this time of the year the river tides were less troublesome on their side of the island and were therefore more conducive for such a venture.

With this in mind, Pender and Zalenda chose an area opposite this point where the terrain was most difficult for an army to march uphill in any semblance of order. Pender remembered the lesson of the arcing spears and the force that they might fall with from a height onto an advancing army. They would require a great arsenal of these spears to be made by the Forest People and people skilled in handling them for the team.

They selected the place where they would make their stand on a knoll that crowned the slope and brought the team members to practice the range and the force of the falling spears. The distance the girls could throw the spears with deadly accuracy was critical to their plan so they would know when to unleash this deadly hail of death. It was decided that only Pender and his team would face Raymond's troops to lure them into range and to provide them with a false confidence. Gena and Lacey would hide their cavalry in the woods and bush on either side and be ready to charge into the fight. Once again the timing of such a charge was critical for the safety of the riders, and it was arranged that Zalenda would make these decisions.

Rahana would hide out of sight with her Cave People, and soon as Raymond's mercenaries had passed, they would follow them as unobtrusively as possible. When the cavalry charge was completed, Zalenda would signal for them to unleash their own brand of deadly hail. The rest of the tribes would remain in hiding near the battlefield and would only see action if absolutely necessary.

Chapter 45

The Day of the Burning Rock

The spring of the new year had come and gone, and it was high summer when the news came from the spies that Pender had put in place that Raymond's ships were on the move. Carla's network had moved into high gear, and now the tribes were arriving every day. Pender had conveyed to them where they would make their stand and how the tribes would be arranged. He had taken great care to explain to them why this site had been selected and how the battle would be conducted. He was adamant to them that the tribes must remain off the field unless called upon by Zalenda. No chief was to take matters into their own hands and charge into the fight because that would only cause chaos and could prove fatal to their plans.

Now the morning was here. The tribes were in position according to their strengths. They were carefully hidden behind the mound, the cavalry on either end of the line, and the spear throwers in the middle. Gena and Lacey had brought all of the trained warriors from the Plains People and were in charge of all the mounted cavalry. The vast numbers of the Nuits were divided into four groups, again hidden carefully from view. Although they had no training, Pender had a role for them to play. As Raymond's army appeared coming up the hill, they would be suddenly surrounded by this sea of redheaded warriors, a frightening sight indeed and enough to instill fear into the hearts of the most hardened mercenaries. The Forest People had provided the Cave People with special long-shafted wood shovel-like tools to throw the lighted coals. Everything was ready now, only the waiting for it all to begin.

The ships came to a halt near Slave Island. Zalenda came and took Pender's hands as they watched. The soldiers slowly disembarked and began to form up into two divisions. Pender whispered, "They are putting the partially trained in the front to absorb any frontal attack. I am sorry to disappoint them. Come now, it is time to show ourselves. Let's lure them to us." The team stood up, one man with twenty young women and two dogs, not a very challenging sight, easy prey for Raymond's appetite.

The two divisions moved up the slope bent on doing Raymond's instructions to kill Pender and his team. When they passed through the hedgerow, unseen to them, Rahana's Cave People closed in behind them. Then the four columns of Nuits formed on either side of the marching troops, and Lacey and Gena's mounted warriors moved down into their positions. The Water People, the Forest People, and the M People came into a supporting role alongside the team.

Raymond now saw he had been outmaneuvered and was at a drastic disadvantage even to get up the hill. He could not charge or assail his enemy's position, so their short swords were of no use to them, and they were getting ready to switch to their spears. Zalenda waited till the marchers were in range then signaled to Becca, and the first salvo of spear arced into the sky and rained down Pender's deadly hail of death on the unsuspecting soldiers. The Forest People kept supplying the young women with spears, so each one was throwing and average of fifteen. As one was thrown, another appeared in their hands, and the killing continued, causing chaos and havoc in the front ranks.

The soldiers tried hard to move forward as Raymond continued shouting, "Attack! Attack!" Zalenda called for a halt to the spears then signaled to Gena to make her first run with the horses. They rode furiously into the depleted front division, bowling over the unorganized mess of broken and dying men. The rest of the men threw down their weapons and tried to run back to the second division. Lacey's led the second charge and wiped out the survivors.

Raymond was beside himself with anger. What had seemed an easy foregone conclusion, easy pickings, more slaves, more women, and bigger ransoms, was gone before his eyes. Then the air around him was filled with falling burning rocks. His highly trained mercenaries were falling over with hair and bodies on fire, and still the burning rock fell. The men looked for somewhere to hide, but there was none. Raymond tried to reorganize the ranks, but the day belonged to the burning rock; Rahana rained down on them. It was then Pender brought in the Nuits, who kept chanting, "Kill Raymond! Kill Raymond!" The remaining members of his army heard the chant and broke ranks to charge and kill him without mercy.

Pender and his team with the aid of Gena and Lacey and their trained people disarmed the fallen and broken army. Raymond was dead, killed by his own minions. His grand schemes for greater glory and riches disappeared in the ashes of coal dust.

The prisoners were escorted to one of the ships, and after they had buried their dead, Carla attended to their wounds, and the ship became their prison.

The tribes all came together to celebrate their great victory and found it rather incredible that other than a few broken bones and bruises among the riders, not one life had been lost. Pender and Zalenda were given full honors for their meticulous planning and foresight in putting it into action.

After the battle site had been cleaned up in the morning by the Nuits and the M People, the tribal leaders came together to dispose of the riches and goods that were left on Raymond's ships. It was decided that the prisoners could go free without any payment as long as they rowed the ships downriver. Pender proposed that the goods and supplies that Raymond had taken from the smaller tribes downriver should be returned to them to keep them alive through this winter and through to the next harvest. They discussed this proposal and decided a representative from each tribe would be charged with the responsibility to see this was done fairly. The success and victory was to be further completed by keeping intact the new federation of family tribes, and Pender was asked to be its first leader.

That night back on their island home, as the girls were in the hot springs, they noticed Zalenda was showing a little bump in the front. She was overcome with twenty naked women who just wanted to love her. Carla told them it was true—Zalenda and Pender were going to have a baby. As they were congratulating her, Zalenda's thoughts went back to that slave pen when a young man had thrown her a flask of cider, and she looked at him and loved him, and he loved her and would continue to do so forever.

THE END

The screaming stopped, but its echo reverberated throughout the sinkhole of the cavern of time in which I had been plummeted into by the stone. My senses were alive within me of all the things I had seen and heard of this lost world. I wanted to stay here lost in time for a little longer to record the end of the story, but the stones would not allow it. Suddenly, the cyclonic whirlwind of ear-piercing sound had me spinning upward and forward into my time, and I emerged back to a standstill on that large white stone. The island was its picture postcard self with its gorgeous green oak trees. I heard the laughter again of the harvesters in the fields, the singing of the birds, yes, and even the bawling of the cow. I wondered as I looked at the beautiful hills about where I had been—was it just a dream?

I retraced my steps carefully through the slough of decaying vegetation walking these stones of time, and I wondered, Would I ever see Pender, Zalenda, and the team again? I could never forget them because I have it all written down.

It was ten years since I had that strange experience, and my teaching assignment was coming to an end, and I had no intentions of renewing my contract. I decided that I would go in search of that lost world again, perhaps in a different time. Who would I meet? What would their issues be? How would they live? The prospects were exciting, but how would I get there if the dam water covered the stones? The lights changed, and the traffic surged forward, and it was just another ordinary day.